Throw Me to the Wolves

Throw Me to the Wolves

PATRICK McGUINNESS

BLOOMSBURY PUBLISHING

NEW YORK · LONDON · OXFORD · NEW DELHI · SYDNEY

BLOOMSBURY PUBLISHING
Bloomsbury Publishing Inc.
1385 Broadway, New York, NY 10018, USA

BLOOMSBURY, BLOOMSBURY PUBLISHING, and the Diana logo are
trademarks of Bloomsbury Publishing Plc

First published in 2019 in Great Britain by Jonathan Cape
First published in the United States 2019

Bloomsbury Publishing Plc does not have any control over, or responsibility for,
any third-party websites referred to or in this book. All internet addresses given in
this book were correct at the time of going to press. The author and publisher regret
any inconvenience caused if addresses have changed or sites have ceased to exist, but
can accept no responsibility for any such changes.

ISBN: HB: 978-1-62040-151-4; eBook: 978-1-62040-152-1

LIBRARY OF CONGRESS CATALOGING-IN-PUBLICATION DATA

Names: McGuinness, Patrick, author.
Title: Throw me to the wolves / Patrick McGuinness.
Description: New York : Bloomsbury Publishing, 2019.
Identifiers: LCCN 2018031888| ISBN 9781620401514 (hardback) |
ISBN 9781620401521 (e-book)
Subjects: LCSH: Murder—Investigation—Fiction. | GSAFD: Mystery fiction.
Classification: LCC PR6113.C483 T48 2019 | DDC 823/.92—dc23
LC record available at https://lccn.loc.gov/2018031888

A catalogue record for this book is available from the British Library

2   4   6   8   10   9   7   5   3   1

Typeset by Integra Software Services Pvt. Ltd., Pondicherry
Printed and bound in the U.S.A. by Berryville Graphics Inc., Berryville, Virginia

To find out more about our authors and books visit www.bloomsbury.com and sign
up for our newsletters.

Bloomsbury books may be purchased for business or promotional use. For
information on bulk purchases please contact Macmillan Corporate and Premium
Sales Department at specialmarkets@macmillan.com.

When I die, throw me to the wolves. I'm used to it.

Diogenes

A place where it's always now

Near the school is a bridge. To get to the playing fields on the other side of the estuary, the boys have to cross it. They do this three times a week, rain or shine. It has to be pretty wet for any match to be cancelled — even the crummiest remedial game. 'It's *corpore* fucking *sano* time,' says Mr McCloud, the heavy-smoking, whisky-perfumed form teacher who talks to the boys like mates from the pub and discusses historical figures as if he'd known them personally. He can tell you how their breath smells, what they have between their teeth; how they walk, what their fingernails look like. The boys like him, though he's tetchy and unpredictable, and when he's angry he's feral and looks like he'll bite. He's big and barrel-shaped, and wheezes like an old accordion when he bends over to tie his laces or pick up some chalk or a dropped cigarette. He remembers nothing, mixes up their names, turns up late and leaves early, but the boys think he tells good jokes. What they mean is that he tells dirty jokes. Some of the older boys go to his house at night to smoke and drink and watch films. When they come back they smell of adults.

They all have their reasons for going to the bridge: mostly it's to smoke the cigarettes and drink the vodka or gin they can buy from the corner shop; later it will be to meet girls or just for the view. One boy, now a successful entrepreneur, collects the pages of porn magazines from around the bridge, and from the caves and crags near the cliffs, that have been thrown out by passing cars or hedgerow masturbators. Unless he's very lucky, they're usually damp and dew-soggy, so he takes them back and dries them out on the school radiator so that he can sell them. There is a price list: the whole pages are expensive, and there are discounts for the shredded or lopped-off partials. They are available to rent, too.

We are not far from the port, from which the ships, whose foghorns you can hear when the wind points the right way, haul their tonnes of containers across the English Channel. This is a watery county, veined with tributaries, fringed with inlets and estuaries, the chalky coast harried by the waves, its rivers draining into the sea. It is a county of bridges and piers and viaducts, and it is hard to go anywhere for long without facing the fact of water. Sometimes, when the waters are high, the bridges seem to be combing the river rather than crossing it. McCloud took them to see the Medway viaducts once, where three lines of trains and traffic cross the river and where soon they'll build a tunnel to France that McCloud tells them will make the ferries obsolete.

The bridge joins the two halves of the city − one side genteel and residential and upper-crust, the other a spread of housing estates, industrial zones and low-end shopping complexes. There are B&Bs for travellers who arrive too late for their crossings, and pubs for those who arrive too early. 'Two cities separated by one bridge,' McCloud jokes each time they cross it: 'Got your passports, boys? Had your jabs? We're heading into the dark continent now ...'

The temptation to look down into the brown sludge of estuary, the glistering oyster grit and the silt, the little drain ditch of trickling water, thin as rain coursing down guttering, is hard to resist. In the sunshine the mud flexes and ripples. It doesn't need much light to look alive. And inviting – a cushion of shimmering brown silk. It's tempting to jump.

The schoolboy is fascinated by the smell that rises and catches on the wind. It's the smell of estuaries: on the one hand, drains; on the other, the open sea. They should clash, but here they seem to go well together, like sweet-and-sour cuisine: one is blockage and rot and stasis, the other escape and freedom and drift. He recites the rosary of port names – Zeebrugge, Ostend, Calais, Cherbourg, Dieppe, Rotterdam ...

And you can always jump. You can jump anytime you want. Mostly it's curiosity rather than suffering that makes you look down and find yourself wanting it, sending your mind up ahead to imagine what it's like to fall; to fall and fall and fall. The boy feels hypnotised by the view, by its completeness. Not many things feel so total as what he sees when he looks down here. It's not dying in itself that's attractive – he's nowhere near unhappy enough for that, though he likes to imagine precisely *how* unhappy he'd need to be: what sort of dosage, millilitre by millilitre of unhappiness climbing the notches of the desolation-syringe, degree by degree in the sorrow-thermometer ... No, not dying so much as its hypothetical nature. It's the idea of seeing yourself afterwards that draws you in, lifting off, peeling away from your body like a pen nib rising from the letters it leaves on the page, then looking down at your shell as you leave it, then at the people in the distance. Though really it's you in the distance; you *are* the distance; dead, you've become it.

He imagines death as one of those aerial shots in a war movie like the ones they show at school, where they have to leave some soldiers behind and rise in their helicopter, and the soldiers run but can't catch up and they shout and cry out and stretch out their hands for their comrades, fingers meet and grip and hold on and are prised apart; and the helicopter rises, shakily at first, and then steadies and pulls away, sticky and reluctant, and the soldiers get smaller and the enemy catch up or mow them down, and everyone becomes a dot and then everyone is gone; then it's all jungle and then all just sky.

And, well, there's also the advantage of just not having to drag this beast of a body around with you, no longer being shackled to the burning animal you are.

There is a legend of a Victorian woman who jumped from the bridge and lived, as the saying goes, *to tell the tale*, thanks to her big dress ballooning out into a crinoline parachute. She had been jilted, she was lovestruck. But if suicide has an opposite, it's what happened to her: she survived, went on to meet someone else, got married, had three children and lived deep into old age.

There's little possibility anyone would survive the fall today, the boy knows, since 1) the velocity at which you hit the water would kill you outright; 2) your heart would explode from fear long before, the way dormice burst inside when you pick them up; or 3) you'd hurtle so deep into the mud that you'd suffocate. It's the lady's image the boy has in mind when he and his friends peer down, or drop balls of paper, sweet wrappers, handkerchiefs or coins over the edge and try to time their descent.

A few feet up, water is hospitable. It opens up and lets you in. After about seventy it is like stone. It will break you as if you'd hit a quarry floor. They learned that in physics.

Another reason it's tempting to let the mind play with the idea of falling is that it's so banally possible: the parapet is only a little over four feet high. For most of the boys that means barely shoulder-level. One modest high-jump, using the wood of the handrail for leverage, and you'd be up and over, over and down, down and dead. Maybe then the fall would feel endless, though it would take just a few seconds. You could live a whole lifetime backwards in those seconds: back to birth, as the myth goes, the dying watching their lives rewind before them. You're interested in whether the same story told backwards is the same story at all.

Back then, back there in the then, back on the bridge, you think it'll take a few seconds and a whole lifetime to reach the estuary silt; the cool, shiny, hourglass-fine sand. Maybe you could change a few things too, second time around, who knows? Make corrections.

The boy sometimes takes his introspection, which, like the rest of him, needs exercise, for a walk there. It's probably the only part of him, even in that sporty school, that gets any genuine exercise. There's always someone else on the bridge, and though he thinks of it as a place of extreme loneliness, he realises, years later, that never once was he actually alone on it. There were always others, sometimes as many as half a dozen, all doing the

5

same thing: looking out and over and down. Once he saw someone writing the number for the Samaritans, whose notice is posted on the buttresses at each end of the bridge, on the back of his hand with a biro. For now, the boy leans over, dangling his arms, the handrail wedged in his armpits. His grandmother is a dressmaker, and she made him his school suit. The way the wind nips and tucks at his clothes like a tailor reminds him of being measured for his jacket and trousers. He's being measured for a suit of air, so he can be sleeved in the rush of falling.

Years later, he comes back to the bridge. The Samaritans number used to be local; now it's an 0845 number – like insurance companies, mobile phone operators, telesales. The parapet is the same height, but now it has been supplemented by a four-foot grille of wire that curves inwards at the top. To jump off now you'd need a ladder.

Going back in time is like climbing into an old photograph. He imagines it in sepia tone; remote as an old postcard. But it's a postcard of his life: the treacly air, the heavy school furniture, the gelatinous glaze of things seen through a syrup of time and tears. If he dived into the photograph now, or ran his fingers along its surface, it would be the texture of cream, not the hard floor of water below the bridge. He remembers the wooden desks with their – even then – long-disused inkwells, rims impregnated with black and blue spillages. Cocks carved with compass-points and fuckwords etched into the grain, past the varnish and into the pulpy meat of the wood. All that stuff looks a little prehistoric today, as far away and tribal as bison on cave walls. You can get the desks now on eBay – 'Complete with graffiti,' the sellers announce, by way of authenticating them.

6

For all the tonnes of iron and steel, the bridge looks delicate as lace, the cables taut as harp strings. Sometimes you can hear the wind pluck them and fancy you hear a song. It is the song of the air which is the sound of falling. The boy thinks he'd like to hear that song through to the end, that he'd like a long, long fall so he can hear it over and over and never hit the ground.

20 December

'My childhood?' He looks amused.

'I didn't have a childhood. I think of it more as a childhood-themed infancy. I mean, there were plenty of toys, but my relationship with them was more curatorial than anything else – I was more like a museum attendant than a child. I polished them and looked at them and put them away. I stacked and tidied them and laid them out. But did I actually *play* with them? I don't think so.'

He pauses, looks around the room as if assessing the colour-scheme: grey eggshell with a perspiration gloss. 'Also, I kept the boxes.'

Gary tries to cut him off, but he's already finished. Our timings are all wrong; it's all out of kilter.

Gary: 'We don't give a shit about your childhood, you sad clown, we want to know about that poor girl, how you killed her and where you dumped the body!'

The body or *her* body? And why the difference? Why do I keep asking myself these tiny questions, like the thin end of a doorstop: you start with grammar – *her* or *the* – and end up with a fat wedge of darkness. It's *the* body now. Wherever her *her* was, it's not there anymore.

'Gary – let him finish.'

'You did ask about my childhood, you know you did; it was *in* the question, if not strictly *the* question.'

We say nothing, so, in his own time, confidently and with a top note of mockery, he goes on:

'There's a picture of me looking at the underside of one of those rides you find outside supermarkets. In some seaside resort, the tautologically-named Gravesend probably. I don't suppose it matters where, even to me. I'd put the money in, kneel down, then watch the mechanics of it, the axles turning, the cogs biting ... The undercarriage I think it's called – funny word that, smacks of *Carry On* films ... I'd play with the idea of playing, but I don't think I ever played. Does that mean I toyed with the idea of toys? Perhaps.'

'*J-e-e-e-e-sus,*' Gary seethes through clenched teeth. Mr Wolphram looks up at the ceiling, breathes in, samples the closeness of the air, breathes out, starts again:

'I've never thought about it. Just because you're the people with the questions it doesn't mean I'm the one with the answers.'

The key to interrogations is leaving the suspect time, giving them an unfenced, shelterless acreage of silence to get nervous in. But he's doing it to us. Staring us out in turn: me, Gary, the confused officer guarding the door behind us. Then, when he's ready:

'Anyway, why do you ask?'

Why did I ask? Maybe because it was my childhood I wanted to know about. Because, though the man we were questioning does not know or cannot remember, he was there.

*

9

Mr Wolphram, cold sheen on skin so pale it was almost blue; the colour of a vein deep below the flesh. Marble. Or salt. Yes: the blueness of salt in a salt mine. Huge eyes, perhaps black (it's not that I can't see, it's bright in here, it's just that they won't give up the precise tinge of their darkness): steady, ironic. He hardly blinks. This isn't a game, but still, he's playing. If we give him too much slack, he'll run us in circles; if we close him in too tightly, he'll enjoy the constraint. As soon as there are rules, anything becomes a game.

He speaks in long, fluent, perfect sentences. Grammatically flawless, he talks from an inner thesaurus where everything is tinged with something else, every colour seeping into the next. It's like a posh paint catalogue: no black, no white, no red, no blue – just a sequence of in-betweens with double-barrelled names.

And that voice: when your nightmares come out as an audiobook, he'll be the narrator.

He has paint on his hands. I only notice this now, though I was the one who fingerprinted him. Later, when we send the samples for analysis, we'll know the name of the paint: Mole's Breath, a velvety brushed grey.

His every emotion is undercut, adjusted, infused by something else. By what? By something that isn't emotion. Does he know too much to feel? Is that what it is? Does he have no feelings, or does he know them so well that he no longer feels them? *Childhood-themed infancy* ... where does that sort of phrase come from? From learning the words for things before you know the things themselves, that's where.

But does it matter, in the end, what order you learn them in?

The room is stifling. Gary sweats, losing both temper and weight.

Does he recognise me? I'm not that different, and it wasn't so long ago.

Actually, it was, if you're measuring it in clocks-and-calendars time. But if you're measuring it in ... what? Inside-time? Heart-and-blood time? Lining-of-our-lives time? ... in that case it's yesterday. It's always yesterday there, in the lining of our lives.

He hasn't changed. He's got that briny sameness some teachers have, even decades later: onion skin, see-through almost, like wet cigarette paper. His hair is the same cinder-grey as it was thirty years ago; straight and shiny, fringed to just above his eyebrows and so fine that it expresses the contours of his skull. If he has aged, it is somewhere other than here, somewhere other than the face. The clothes are the same, too: maybe it's even the same suit, the same red tie on the same black shirt. His wrists rest on the edge of the table, and he seems to be rolling something very small between the thumb and forefinger of each hand.

There's some kind of counsellor or shrink in the room, professional and frowning bureaucratically. I'm not sure if she's watching him or watching us.

*

He used culture like a flick-knife. That's what I remember. One stroke of the blade was enough. You didn't feel the pain until you saw the blood. Even then you didn't feel the pain until you realised the blood was yours. He'd pick someone, anyone, slice them, and for the rest of the lesson they'd be like a wounded shark, sniffed out by predators

11

for miles around and hours to come. It was like that —
blood coming out like smoke in water.

His moods were fire behind ice.

I told them this later.

*

Reading the red-tops that morning, there was the usual
fare: a footballer's wife's breast implants explode on a
flight to Dubai; a mouthy celebrity auctions her silence
on Twitter; something reality-show-based, where iPhone-
and iPad-addicted teenagers go to live with some kind
of Amish in Derbyshire. Light stuff, tabloid-spume: no-
news news.

Upwind of all that are the self-styled 'qualities'. Gary
knows that there's no upwind anymore, that we're all
in the same rank draught. He's heckling an opinion
piece in *The Times* about what to do with your children
when your nanny goes back to Eastern Europe to see her
family. 'Another article by some horse-faced Sloane called
Camilla or Imogen about the cost of cleaners in Fulham
and rising school fees. What planet are these people on?'

'Planet Them?' I offer limply, just to be part of a
dialogue. It's going to be a long, sad, grinding day and we
need to keep it lubricated with good fellowship.

'It's all Planet Them, Prof ... As far as the eye can see
— Planet Them.'

There's a pause, then a silence, where Gary tries — tries
and fails — to line up something lapidary to finish with.

It's Christmas, and Christmas is a violent time. It's not
the violence of police thrillers or TV detectives. No Poirots
or Marples here. No need. It's the dun, blunt violence of
ordinariness. It isn't shiny and it isn't complicated — either

to fathom its motives or to find its culprits. No one's going to be calling in Columbo anytime soon. It's simply there, a seepage of everyday darkness that pools and fattens and brims, and then one day it overflows.

It's our underlife, that's all: and sometimes it just pushes over the edge and pulls us down with it. The thin blue line they call us. I think we're more like a meniscus: we gather the overspill for a moment, halt it as it swells and curves against the air; it trembles, stretches, crosses over, and then drops.

It's dropping now. It's dropped.

Two domestics, an arson, a couple of break-ins. A Pound Shop ramraid. Even the thieves pitch their fantasies low these days, their ambitions tailored to an austerity idea of loot. Black Friday riots in supermarkets. Flat-screen-hysteria, white-goods-stampedes. Technology bringing us back to animalhood by another route.

Against it all, under the police work, under the courts, the unseen plumbing of the system, is violence against women. Especially at Christmas. It's the pulse, the beat you hear like bass from some car or basement you'll never locate. Or that's gone or moved by the time you get there. Wife, daughter, girlfriend, the repeat beating, the 'one-off' that keeps happening, the twenty years of one-offs, the mind-hammering cruelty of the words; women with burned-out nerves and minds like blown circuits, scared, punch-softened until their flesh is tender as veal. Gary and I see it so much we think this is another one. It isn't.

When the call comes I'm putting a line through five boxes on the calendar. That's my holiday up ahead. As I close in on it, I always get nervous. All it takes is one case, one crime out of the ordinary, and it's gone – *deferred* they call it – to some shimmering horizon point in the future I'll never reach. I know already that I won't reach it now. If anyone can tell from the ringtone what a call is about, I can. This one tells me that everything will change.

No need for a siren, they said. We know what that means: the siren screams time, screams that there *is* time. But we are quick nonetheless, Gary and I. He drives. I look out at the shop fronts as they slide past, the expensive school on the hill, the old zoo they closed years ago but where I still think I catch the barking of the seals, the smell of their fish. Then the bridge towards the brownfield outskirts with their stalled cranes, the half-built credit-fuelled flats now credit-crunch-frozen. The designer shops that decline into Pound Shops. Then what Gary calls Brexit-land. 'Like New York,' he says, 'it's not just a place, it's a state of mind.' He laughs a dry, yellow little laugh, then sings 'Brexit Land my only home' to the tune of the Soft Cell song 'Bedsitter'. I don't know how he knows the song or when he heard it, because he'd have been a baby when it came out. Unlike me – I bought the single, though I had nothing to play it on. Even then I was late – when I bought it second-hand and it already had someone else's name on the sleeve, someone else's scratches on the vinyl.

You hear it now sometimes, on those reruns of *Top of the Pops* from the 1980s, or those variety shows with the presenters filleted out because they're disgraced or dead or in jail. 'The show with no presenters,' my niece calls it – she knows there was something there once, in between the songs, the acts; the glitz and the showbiz and the jokes. She just doesn't know what. But Marieke has an ear for what's gone. That's why she loves the zoo so much, the empty, haunted zoo. The animals ghost-calling behind the boarded-up enclosures. That's why she likes visiting Mrs Snow, too. All that goneness. 'Silence isn't silent,' she says, 'it's a hum: *listen* ...'

Then there's some greenery, before the commuter-belt unspools and we reach a place the satnav calls 'Unnamed road'. We know we're there, because there's an ambulance, a patrol car and two unmarked Fords. Everything is slack, unurgent. It all smacks of the *too late*. Someone I can't see is smoking and the smell comes in ragged little wafts across a surprisingly large distance. Plastic bags are twisted and thorn-snagged in the blackberry bushes. The blackberries have hung unpicked for months: first they're hard as buttons, then soft, and now they're the colour of spider thread, dried-out and shrunk and fat with mould. The kind of people who come here don't pick fruit.

We walk but we don't rush, because for now we're caught between the moment when what happened happened and the moment it becomes a fact. I can feel all those events massing there, just on the other side of the discovery we're about to make, and I want to spin this short walk out, hold it all off. It helps me think, I tell myself: *you can't live between tenses for long, make the most of it.*

Then this:

Two officers are taking a statement from a woman with a dog on a tightrope-taut leash. Its nose points down the lane; whatever it found, it wants another look, another go at it.

'Why's it always dog-walkers who find them?' asks Gary. 'It's such a fucking cliché.' I don't answer. 'At least it's not doggers.' He walks round the car and opens my door. It's not deferential, or to do with rank. It's just that I'm not wholly there. 'Doggers don't do mornings.' Gary urinates against the car before we head down. 'Don't want to contaminate the scene, do we?' he says. I can smell the coffee off his piss and it's not even breakfast time yet.

I know this road. I can't name it, but I know it.

We dispense with the statement for now. In good time, I think. In *due* time, I mean, because there'll be nothing *good* about time now: the only advantage of being too late is that you can choose the order you take things in. At least we have that. It's the consolation of the defeated. We'll get to her and her dog soon, then the press will. Most likely Lynne Forester will get to her before the others. *Mad Lynne*, Gary calls her. If it's who I think it is out there, who we fear it is, out there beyond the trees. There's no such thing as too late for Lynne.

Most finds like this are the same: dog off leash; dog bolts off on its own; one scent among the thousands reels it into the undergrowth; dog refuses to come back when called; owner finds dog nosing through ... what?

Let's see.

I hang back, but I know the way.

It's a damp, off-cold early dusk in late December, and the arc lights are on. They're visible up ahead, plus a luminous white tent and some white-clad figures. Camera-flashes, police ribbon. 'Santa's Grotto,' says Gary, and I know I should laugh, just to keep things rolling. Also, it's better than his usual jokes, so I smile and catch him looking sideways to check. Smiling is better – it makes him think I'm stifling a laugh. My forced-out smile looks to him like a laugh-held-back. I think it's enough to see us through the next few hours. The conviviality-tank replenished. We'll need it.

He's suspicious of me, a ponderous fast-stream university blow-in. I'm suspicious of him, a borderline-racist throwback from central casting: a fat, uncomplicated sexist who sweats processed chicken-water and smells of gravy. If he was a pub, they'd be marketing him to hipsters and tourists as *defiantly retro*, or possibly *vintage*, though definitely not *gastro-*. But to each other, we're both from central casting. It's just that he's from a seventies police show, the kind where they smoke and hit suspects, drink on the job, scorn paperwork and call women 'birds'. Gary likes all that stuff. It's his idiom. Learned behaviour they'd call it, and because he's younger than me he's only ever seen it on TV. I call it Gary's *learned self*, from the observation post of my own learned self.

'She's been more than killed,' someone says. 'She's more than dead.'

The corpse-side factuality, yes, but no banter. There's something about this one. I can tell from the flatness, the sadness-undertow. We all know.

Someone is bent over a body. I can only see the feet, but it *is* a she: one leg straight, the other up, kicked back and frozen in a delicate dance move. Charleston. Dead chorus girl, dredged from some thirties musical, a body from a river. *Never the same river twice*, I think, unsure why, and then I whisper it: *never the same river twice*. More and more I talk my thoughts as I think them. A decent lip-reader would know my mind.

The river, the real one, is not far. The floods have slowed, but the water stays fast and violent down here, and the rubbly riverbed makes it foam and spit. It sounds like motorway traffic. The M25 frothing at its banks.

'I'm not confirming anything yet, and I'm not using any names, but you can start now on the basis that it's her.'

I know this. I learned it at uni: it's hard to recognise someone when they're dead. In the early days of morgue photography, they displayed photographs of the latest corpses outside and people walked by as if they were window-shopping or going to the races. Some morgues let people in to see the bodies. Whole families went out in their Sunday best to browse the dead. It was like Tinder for corpses; swipe, swipe, hold, swipe, add to favourites, block, DM ... But many of the relatives couldn't recognise their loved ones as dead. It had nothing to do with the state of the body. It was just the goneness of life that made it look other than it was. How to explain it beyond that?

My first case – a hit-and-run – the father stood by the body and looked carefully. We'd asked him to come in and identify it. He shook his head and claimed it wasn't his son. We knew it was but had to go through the protocols of believing him, apologising, pretending we were going back to the list of missing persons we had culled him from in the first place. He rang back later and admitted it was him, said that admitting it was like flicking a switch, *his off-switch*. He couldn't do it. 'The button between making it real and keeping it unreal,' he said. That's where ghosts live: not in a place, not in spooky houses and graveyards. They live in the time it takes for the outside fact of their death to become an inside fact in us. This is why we free them, not just ourselves, by admitting they've gone.

But who knows what the dead will do once they're free? Where they will go?

No one says anything. One of the constables scribbles something in a notebook, but it's just to keep his hands occupied and his eyes away.

She's twisted strangely and garbed ... I write – *garbed?* I feel stupid using that word, scratch it out, replace it with – *attempts have been made to hide her in refuse sacks.* I scratch that out, too, and put in *binbags.* I don't know why

I go through this protocol of euphemism and officialese; it's just myself I'm talking to, myself I'm writing for.

Garbed? For God's sake ...

Later, I'll think that what I was doing was trying to lay her out on a bed of words, as softly as possible, because I already knew what would happen to her when the papers got hold of it. 'Like a broken doll in a binbag!' wrote Lynne Forester later. Mad Lynne hadn't seen her, hadn't even seen the photos at the time, but that's what she wrote for the whole country to read. She wasn't going to mess her readers around with words like *garbed.*

'I've been here before,' I tell them. Below me, to the side, Gary is already squatting, and I see his head jerk upwards. He has understood what I mean, though the others haven't. Gary is intuitive; he notices feelings and the changing tones of people's moods. This doesn't fit with his self-image, so we all conspire not to see it.

Still, I should have told him first.

'We've all been here before,' says the pathologist without looking up, without turning around. 'Each death different, each death the same.'

'No, I mean here. This place. I've been here before.'

Then the rest of them look up. I'll explain later.

*

It's strange how we think of haunting as a people-thing: something fundamentally sociable, however unnerving or scary. The haunters are still versions of us, they've just gone over to the other side. Ghosts are domesticated creatures, like dogs and cats, because we have invented them (maybe they think the same of us) to replicate our actions, which they repeat (repetition is important to the ghost-life: like pets and children they need routine) slowly but often with surprising exactness. They are spectral replays of our matches, won or lost, and we impute to them something of ourselves we do not like to see: an inability to move on, a hunger for return. We're the ones haunting them. All they want is permission to leave.

That's why you can't haunt somewhere you've never been, not properly at least, and though there have been ghosts who erred into other stories, other hauntings not their own, the effect there is comical, of actors stumbling into the wrong play.

As a child I found ghosts disappointing for these very reasons: how constructed they were, how made up they are of all they've left behind – how made up they were of *us*. It was our lack of ambition for ghosts that disappointed me; as if, with all we knew about the unknown, we couldn't imagine something better for them than repositories of our unfinished business. I'd have liked them to pull away a little more, to peel off from us, but no: they were hemmed in by their patterns, which were our patterns. A lost opportunity, I thought; for us in our imaginations and for them in their imagined reality.

This is because haunting is just another way of belonging. For some of us, it's the only way.

My ghosts are places. This is one of them: an intermediate scrubland, a satnav-anonymised interzone between some school playing fields and a brown river banked by mud and fringed with plastic bags, paint pots and bike wheels. The Kent Downs are a few miles away, an 'area of outstanding natural beauty', England at its greenest and cleanest. These places are their shitty cousins, their shadow aspect. Some defunct white goods still shine in the undergrowth, and just beyond them the river gargles what looks like a fridge door. Nearby and further up, hidden by the trees so serried that even leafless they block the view, is the bridge.

There's something about fly-tipping sites; their slow, sad, furtive accumulation of debris from our daily life. First, a piece of edge-land is inaugurated, modestly with just an old TV, or perhaps grandly with a six-foot fridge-freezer; and then, like iron filings to a magnet, the rest of the stuff arrives. People know, they're drawn to it; after dark, wrapped in shame, headlights off, they slide here in their cars and vans and dump their crap. It's a no-place – who cares? But by the end, it's like some sort of showroom, a Walmart of the jungle, a futuristic shopping centre where the future's been and gone. It doesn't decay, biodegrade, compost or erode. The earth refuses it all: the fridge gases, the battery acid, the MDF, the swingers' leatherette sofa and the stained mattress speared with rusting coils.

It's a no-place, yes. But it's no place to die; no place to be found dead in.

As for me, I live in the present; it's where I eat and drink, sleep and wake, draw my salary and take my niece to the park or to the shops. But my home is the past. Most people take day trips there – an hour or a minute's musing, an old photograph here, an old song or smell there, then it's back into life as we think we live it: forwards.

That's because most people are tourists of memory. I moved there, and whenever I visit the here and now I feel like an expat, as bemused by the old country's sameness as I am by all the changes that have happened while I've been away.

Big Pasts, Small Pasts

I don't know who it was who said the past is another country, but, studying the school photographs, the 1980s certainly look like another planet.

Gary has brought thirty years of Mr Wolphram's pictures and we're sifting them. He's not sure why yet and nor am I, but, as the saying goes (or doesn't, not yet anyway, since Gary just made it up), *Everything's evidence until it's not.* It's like the innocent until proved guilty rule, but in reverse – after all, he says, 'People have more rights than things, right? *Right?*'

'Right,' I answer with a lack of confidence he catches and, by now, probably shares: because Mr Wolphram has no rights. It's going to be open season on him: his sexuality, if he has one, his bachelorhood, his education – especially that. Even before he's been charged they've dredged up old pictures – class photographs, something from the premiere of a play he directed, his graduation photo (stark, backgroundless, him with a gown and scroll), him playing a guitar in his short-lived Oxford student band, Horspath Driftway, and even, God knows how, a couple of holiday snaps of him as a child. Thin cold legs and lumpy kneecaps that look like knots in rope.

Alone.

No toys.

No parents either, Gary points out. No brothers or sisters.

In the first picture, he's withdrawn, looking for somewhere to hide his eyes. It's classic childhood self-erasure: hoping that by seeing nothing he will not himself be seen. He's alone, averted not just in gaze but in body; averted in self. In the other, as if to compensate, he looks straight out at us. It's the same look you see in the consumptive sons of aristocrats in old pictures: that doomed, remote yearning that looks like arrogance and sometimes maybe is. Or in the deep foal-eyes of the Romanov children as the bullets wait for them, snug in the chambers of Bolshevik rifles. Somewhere down the telegram line, ticking away along the minutes that haven't yet come, waits the order to pose them for a family photograph, then gun them down and quicklime their dainty, soap-white corpses. That's the sort of face I mean: pale and papery as a moon dissolving in daylight.

'All that's missing is a sailor suit and a governess,' observes Gary.

We read photographs from left to right, like sentences; like words. But on either side of the frame it's time we see, not space. Before and after, flanking that paper monument to the dead *now*.

He's ... what? Nine? Ten? That would date the pictures to the late fifties. Black and white, of course, but that variety of black and white that suggests there was never any colour in the first place. *England in the fifties black and white* is a shade which deserves its own place on the colour chart of grey, somewhere between soiled-headrest-cover grey and the grey of a pigeon's underwing. 'When did they invent colour?' asked my niece one day. The adults laughed, but we knew what she was asking.

Children have no difficulty imagining mummies and cavemen and Incas; Cleopatra, Stephenson's Rocket, Stalin and Hitler, Gin Lane and the guillotine. No problem. Dinosaurs roam the dream-jungles of children's bedrooms everywhere, as ruminant and heavy-footed as ever they roamed their Jurassic filmset world. Dinosaurs are safe. They may be extinct, but they're thriving.

But try describing to a child the sound of a record scratching between tracks, the whistle of a steam kettle or the squeaking turn of a cassette-head in a car stereo. Have you tried that? The real gulf is between the now and the recent, the now and the just-gone; not between now and the distant, far-off past.

Marieke divides them between 'Big Past' and 'Small Past'. My niece knows it's the small past that's gone for good, that the big past can look after itself. The Big Past has museums and TV programmes to look after it. It has governments, schools, armies to fight its corner ... The small past has nothing. When she asks me the difference between the forgotten and the never-known the question is so basic I can't answer it. 'It's like that pop show with all the presenters missing,' she says.

Marieke tells me this: 'They look the same, though, don't they? Two nothings. Two missing things. Something that's gone looks the same as something that was never there.' It's true, I reply, but it's myself I'm explaining it to: *0* is a fact, but *1 minus 1 = 0*, well ... that's a story, it's the story of everything.

My childhood and hers? That's where the gulf is.

This is why she and I are making the archive, the archive of small pasts, lost sounds, of all those things that slide direct from the everyday into ... nowhere, into nothing. It is the things that were everywhere but are remembered nowhere that interest her, as they interest me. Sigrid tells me I'm passing it on to 'her girl'. Passing on what? I ask. *Passing on your* ... she hesitates, the word is too big for what she means, but perhaps what she means may grow to fit the word, perhaps it already has. So she puts it out there for me: *affliction*.

Marieke is my niece, my sister's child. *Marika* is how you say it. Little Marie it means. How that'll play out when she grows up I don't know, but in Dutch we keep the diminutive when we grow up. We wear it to the end. Somewhere, to someone, and maybe especially to ourselves, we are always the child we began as.

Marieke is twelve and already tall for her age – five and half feet. Her favourite activity is recording things. I started it, her mother keeps reminding me, by giving her a digital recorder the size of a lighter for her ninth birthday. From that day on she recorded everything: the sound of a toilet flush, the electronic bell on the bus when she pushed the button for the next stop, her teachers telling someone off. She spies on the sleeping world, archives the evidence. She actually calls it evidence. It's something else she caught off me, because she's fascinated by my job, more than I am by it, and she imagines one day putting the whole world on trial with the material she has gathered.

Since she exhausted the usual things – sirens, car horns, bird calls – her tastes have become more recherché. One day I found her recording the fog, leaving the machine out as it took over the garden. Fog makes no sound, I told her. *No, but it makes things have a different sound*, she insisted, *listen*: I heard nothing but the creep of another night happening, trees rustling in a small wind, some creature padding along the grass, faint cars and train sirens bending around the distance. Marieke tells me that's the sound of the fog, the muffling. I tell her no, and she becomes frustrated, puts down her Nutella sandwich — she spreads it to the very outer edges of the slice, right up to the lip of the crust, like a skilful plasterer at a wall — and looks it up online. Triumphantly she finds it on her favourite web-page, *The Everyday Scientist*:

Q: Does fog change sounds?
A: Great Question! — Yes it does. Fog consists of tiny particles of water suspended in the air. Sound comes in waves and vibrations, and the droplets of water in the air absorb some of the vibrations so the sound reaches you fainter or travels less far. Higher pitch sounds are even more affected by fog, which is why the foghorns of ships have a very low pitch — so they can travel further and be heard further away.

I cede to her again. Her curiosity is unassuageable but selective. She is closed to fashion and pop music, to peers and peer-pressure, to soft and hard toys, computer games and cartoons. Everything that is obviously intended for children she ignores. That includes teachers.

Marieke tries to record herself thinking, holding the machine up to her temple and thinking hard and loudly about all the things she likes. There are many things she likes, and she spends hours at this. She would hold the recorder to the mouth of a dying world if she thought she might catch its last breath on tape.

She gets into trouble sometimes. Teachers don't like it, and there are issues, as they put it, *around data protection.* There is a suggestion that she might be obsessive or autistic, or have one of those disorders they keep finding new acronyms for. Sigrid used to take her in for tests, and from time to time when Marieke was younger various specialists would come in and observe her playing at school or at home.

I just think she is curious: curious and with an uncommon ability to concentrate on what interests her and to leave everything else aside.

I have her twice a week in the evenings, often overnight, when my sister is out late with friends, or dipping her toes and more than her toes into the online 'dating pool'. When she's knee-deep, waist-deep, over her head in the pool, Marieke and I find things to record.

*

Back here, back in the now, there's no hiding, no looking away for Mr Wolphram. Not for him, and not for us. The press have done something to the pictures they've got hold of. They must already have got to his neighbours and ex-colleagues, paid them in cash or flattery. The pictures have been, as Gary puts it, 'weirdoed up'. It's hard to put your finger on exactly what the picture editors do, but he's startled and flashbulb-shocked and he sweats guilt.

But is that the same as being guilty?

'Man taken in for questioning in Zalie Dyer bin-bag murder: police question local teacher,' says the *Evening Post* online, 'Close to an arrest?' It's Lynne Forester's byline. Inset, Mr Wolphram, a close-up cropped from some concert in the eighties. Wide eyes, a look of shock and anger, the pallor of his flash-drained skin. He wears a hat, a black bow tie and a coat that, billowing a little in the wind, looks like a cloak. Later this will be one of the shots smeared across the front pages. 'Mr Drac' one of the tabloids will moniker him.

Ironic, really, since it's they who'll be feasting on his blood. But, yes, there is something of the prised-open coffin about the picture.

He doesn't know it yet but he already looks like what he is: prey.

Soon they'll find someone to lie about him, too. It's just a matter of days, maybe hours. I haven't read the papers, not the tabloids, and there are no print editions yet, but even in the qualities it's coming: the vilification and the smear, the innuendo and the rumour. It's like rising damp, dry rot, woodworm and any other fierce and exultant form of fibre-dissolving, fabric-eroding corruption you'd want to use as metaphor.

Gary didn't mind it when the media relations officer sent us the link to the *Evening Post*. He still doesn't — he thinks he's guilty and it'll smoke him out, but we're not there yet and Gary is uneasy. 'Just a spot of monstering,' he says. A *spot*. Like you take a spot of tea in your milk or do a spot of gardening when the sky clears. Now it's proliferating on news-sites, filling the search engines, starting its hypnotic, looping, tickertape scroll along the headline bars below the presenters and their TV sofas. … MAN TAKEN IN FOR QUESTIONING IN ZALIE CASE … … THOUGHT TO BE LOCAL TEACHER … £ SLUMPS AGAINST EURO … MAN TAKEN IN FOR QUESTIONING IN ZALIE CASE … … THOUGHT TO BE LOCAL TEACHER … FATBERG 'SIZE OF A FERRY' … MAN TAKEN IN FOR QUESTIONING

IN ZALIE CASE ... ... THOUGHT TO BE LOCAL TEACHER ...

But Gary worries, because however much his blood fizzes at the thought of what Mr Wolphram has done, Gary is not as sure as he wants to be. His blood *boils*, he says, pauses, looks for a word for the next notch above boiling, then settles for *literally*, which is always the next notch up.

Literally: think of blood rolling, hot in a smoking steak pan: that's what's happening inside Gary, along his arms and neck, under his skin; that's not liquid in his veins, it's skittering taut globes, red and hard as billiard balls whacked by an invisible cue. You can hear them smacketing off each other.

However much he hates Mr Wolphram and his kind (that's what happens when you become a suspect: you suddenly have a *kind*), he still thinks it's the police who should rip him apart and not the press or the vigilantes on the streets, already circling his home with their spray cans, half-bricks and baseball bats. Like all unfair people, Gary depends on the unfair advantage of no one else being unfair.

But even Gary is pulling back. He wants him caught and tried *fair and square*, and if it were up to him (*iffissuptome*) given a special one-off capital punishment – Gary-administered. But it's not coming together. No confession, for one thing, and then no evidence. The timings are wrong, too. No alibi either, but then what sort of an alibi can a man have when he lives by himself, watches almost no TV, makes two phone calls a week to an old aunt in Hastings (we have the records: 6.45 p.m. Thursdays and Sundays, always between seventeen and twenty-three minutes), and listens alone to opera box sets on a music system that costs a month's mortgage?

He also has videos and DVDs of Scandinavian films. *Not that kind, Gary, not that kind.* But for Gary that makes it worse not better, because 'a bit of porn'd make him more normal'.

Mr Wolphram could just have been an ordinary porn-pervert, but now he's a no-porn pervert, a cold-blooded, flesh-hating asexual.

If innocence can look this bad, who needs guilt?

We have his outgoings, too. The bank has been quick: classical records, DVDs of European cinema, books of poetry and top-end food from top-end supermarkets. The shopping habits of a well-heeled solitary: little; often; expensive; precise. Mobile? Smartphone? iPod? He empties his pockets, but his pockets are already empty, so he turns them out and they hang absurdly like socks from his waist, shedding a confetti of flaked tissue and seam-fluff.

'I don't own any of those.'

It's all set up: Mr Wolphram is going to be the nation's High-Culture Hermit-Ogre.

Meanwhile, on the outside – like the people we put away, we call the real word 'the outside' – it's all moving as if it were cut and dried; or, as Thicko has it, 'cut and pasted'.

Thicko is the station idiot, his stupidity so banal and so generic it doesn't warrant an individuating nickname, even from Gary, who doles out the nicknames from his desk the way Adam named the animals in Genesis. *And whatsoever Adam called every living creature, that was the name thereof.* Hence *Thicko: Does what it says on the tin*, says Gary (who has no nickname), invoking a famous DIY range whose genius lies in advertising the superfluity of advertising.

When Gary arrived the station chief was known as 'The Drone'. It wasn't so original, but when word got out he'd had a vasectomy, Gary knew it could be improved: now we have 'Unmanned Drone', adding a little Shakespearean double entendre to Gary's usual range of lowbrow smut. Usually it's just 'Unmanned'. Unmanned is there, slow and depressed but always watchful behind the great aquarium wall of his office. 'Like some kind of fucking deskfish,' Gary says. So 'Deskfish' sometimes wins out over Unmanned, or even, when Gary feels like a more classic cop-show joke, 'Ironside': 'on account of if he's got legs no one's seen them'.

Deskfish looks cleverer than he is by giving the air of someone who hoards thoughts and expresses them reluctantly. It fools his superiors but not those who work with him every day. It fooled me, too, for a few minutes. 'Inscrutable' I called him on my first day at work. 'There's nothing there to scrute,' Gary corrected.

Gary doesn't bother giving the lawyers and duty solicitors nicknames, that's how low they are on his ladder of life-forms. To him they're either 'this wanker' or 'that wanker'. My nickname is 'Prof', because of my *crim' and psych'* degree. Sometimes he calls me 'University Challenge', after the country's least glamorous quiz show. It has difficult questions and no prize money, which Gary says reminds him of his life. 'Fingers on buzzers,' he called out when I arrived. Each of us likes the other more than we let on. If I'm on top of things, he compliments me with 'Prof's got his finger on the buzzer today'. But it's been a few weeks since I heard that.

I leave them to it, Unmanned Drone, Thicko and the new guy, Small-Screen Dave, who behaves as if he's in a pilot show for a made-for-TV crime series that never got made. And Gary. While Mr Wolphram is overnighting at the station, Gary's going to broil at his desk until he can order a takeaway, which he'll eat in front of the computer, and then, at around midnight, he'll drive back to his flat, sleep badly, cut himself shaving, skip breakfast and shout at the radio. Central-casting stuff, behaviourally speaking.

Small-screen Gary, small-screen all of us.

Our lives are contracting to fit the telly. First the cameras pulled back and went wide-angled to fit more of life in; then, somehow, without noticing, we made our lives smaller so they'd go into the screen.

Is that what happened?

We know the story is making its way out there. It's starting small, no names yet, but it's pretty obvious: 'A man, thought to be a former teacher at a local school ...' Then the officialspeak: *Helping with inquiries, been taken in for questioning, connected to the victim.* So far no specifics, just the general leakage and seepage that means that tomorrow or (if we're lucky) the day after the station will be on every TV in the land. But his face is unmistakable, and though nothing has been alleged, they're already commenting on all the internet news-sites.

It's the descant of loathing: the loons, the cranks, the do-gooders and the coffee-break shrinks, the haters and baiters, the homophobes and beer-pump racists, all with their pseudonyms and *noms-de*-keyboard-*guerre*: WhitePride, Swordoftruth, Brexitron, Feminazi-hunter. Capital Lettrists and triplers of exclamation marks. Union Jacks in the Twitter handles. Lions and eagles.

'At least it's democratic,' I say, banally.

'Toilets are democratic,' says Gary, most of whose metaphors come from the production and management of waste. Since the fatberg, he can't stop talking about it.

It's not the machines that frighten me, as the saying goes, it's the people becoming avatars on the end of them – no longer quite human, like some new kind of centaur breed: half flesh and half ... touch-screen, Twitter-handle, gaming name. Two years ago we investigated the cyberbullying of children. When we caught the culprit it wasn't a spotty teenager or a maladjusted microwave-burger-eating fatso. It wasn't an unfriended, wanked-out geek with skin like basement-meat like you get in films. It was a good-looking, smart, forty-one-year-old man with a wife and two children at Chapelton College, a good job in insurance and a house up near the university. For an hour or two every night he pursued teenagers on Facebook, Twitter, Instagram, everywhere he could track them down. Not difficult – kids huddle in the internet-gunsights of the everyday psycho like antelope at a watering hole; aim your mouse, click, and pick them off.

Freshly clicked for you goes the motto of one supermarket's home delivery service. It could be the jingle of the web's child-hunters, too.

He mostly went for kids who lived near him. I think it was so he could enjoy the thrill that maybe he'd walk past them on his way to work, or brush against them on buses or in town at weekends. He told them to kill themselves, that their friends and families hated them. He directed them to suicide sites. He even checked in with them to ask what they were waiting for, *to go ahead, do it, do yourself and everyone else a favour* ... None did, not within the time frame that allowed us to connect word and action, his saying to their doing. Saying and doing: what's the cut-off point where the one can't any longer be said to cause the other? A year? Five? Ten? Is there a statute of limitation on words and their consequences?

When we went to question him he was cooking spaghetti bolognese and piggybacking his laughing eight-year-old as she whacked him with a wooden spoon. His thirteen-year-old was at her homework, his wife was drinking a glass of chilled white wine, holding the stem the way they do in adverts. Her hands and neck held the last of a half-term tropical tan, topped up by increments of health spa visits. The whole scene was like an advert: for family, success, lifestyle, for having children, for being well off, for being at the top of life's constantly shuffling deck and knowing you'd stay there whoever was dealing. That more often than not you'd be the one dealing. He took us to his study, logged on to his laptop, showed us everything and admitted it straight away. 'Just a bit of fun,' he said, 'how was I to know they'd take it seriously? It was role play.' His life was shiny. So what darkness in himself was he filling with this stuff?

He had been careful, too – nothing sexual. There was no – as they say now, that poor maligned word that used to mean something small and innocent, with its old-school menswear-shop ritualism – *grooming*. When Small-Screen got married to a woman twelve years older, Gary gave a best-man speech where he congratulated *The Bride and the Groomed*. But no 'grooming' here; just malice, amoral curiosity and casual evil. And we are lenient on malice, spite, hate ... because the law cannot touch what it cannot define. He got six months suspended, convincing the judge that he considered it a form of gaming. 'I'd never have done it in real life,' he said. *Real life.* It gets harder and harder to hear that phrase, to see the join between the real one and ... whatever else it becomes after a few hours with a console or a keyboard.

'I've seen two murders,' said Gary, 'drugs and drink — bashed-in heads and blackouts. I've found dead people no one remembered, rotting on sofas or behind avalanches of junk mail, their fingers nibbled by their cats. Scummy stuff, sad stuff, bits of filler between the celeb deaths and the flashy TV car chases. Dead people no one loved or even knew, some of them. But the only thing that's given me nightmares is a family man in his des res telling other people's kids to kill themselves.'

If anything is going to displace that in Gary's prime-time nightmare-schedule, it's the case we're on now. Not because it's gruesome — on the contrary, it's so savagely clean — but because of the places in the mind we'll have to go to before it's all over.

The Fatberg

The media are out sniffing for Mr Wolphram's ex-pupils and colleagues, for stories to make stories from. If he's innocent they'll just move on, jettison him by the information roadside to make his broken way back to whatever life they've left him. The *Evening Post* has something already, but we've managed to get them to hold off doing any more. At a cost. That cost is Lynne Forester. 'Interesting fact about Mad Lynne Forester,' Gary tells me, 'she's got a Twitter following of ninety thousand, that's forty per cent bigger than her paper's entire readership.'

The nationals are circling; they smell it, too, the wafts of news-decay on the air. They scent it like crows scenting roadkill.

Outside the station the rain is a light smirr that settles on your face in a saliva-thin layer, the air puffy with a gauze of fog that makes it look as if we're seeing everything through a damp mosquito net. The bets on a white Christmas are optimistic in proportion to their unlikeliness. We've all put a fiver on white. You have to.

There are vans and lights everywhere and for a moment I'm afraid the story is already out there. But the strobing lightbars are from council vehicles, their regulation caramel glow, not TV vans. They're excavating.

Out in front, between the main square and the police station, they're digging up the road and cleaning out the tons of fat that have solidified in the sewers and drains. It's the seepage of millions of fry-ups and Sunday roasts, all that pale carcass-slither oozing its way through the undercity. I watched it on the local news, where they'd mapped out the seweropolis, its avenues and streets. It was where all the waste we thought we were getting rid of was curdling and hardening up a few feet below. It's like we're looking at ourselves in a mirror of shit, says Gary, who gets it right without needing to refer to Freud or Jung or the Narcissus myth: 'Instead of kitchens and toilets and bedrooms, it's shit and fat, nappies, Durex and tampons. Everything we do up here finds a way to happen down there.'

Now they've opened up the ground, and under the thin rain the tarmac they've sawn through glistens on either side of a swelling, half-solid, half-malleable ooze, a rippled yellow-beige cream marbled with brown, and stuck like a porcupine with bottles, foil, papers, bits of plastic.

The fatberg, they call it, but, unlike icebergs, fatbergs don't calve. They grow and inflate and ball up and expand and are indifferent to global warming and temperature changes; to whether it's a white or a grey Christmas we're going to have.

Gary watched an interview with the chief engineer who told us that if we didn't unclog it soon we'd have our own shit coming back up to meet us before we'd even flushed it. 'Those weren't his exact words,' specifies Gary.

The fire brigade is power-hosing the fatberg into slabs, which are then scooped by JCB into skip-lorries or spaded on by men in masks. The job will take nine days. The hoses are drilling it into moveable blocks and it hulks there, veiny and seamed, rifted like ore being mined. Occasional suitcase-sized pieces fragment on the pavements, where they slide and skitter on their own foam like hot lard in a pan. There is a smell, but it's nothing like the stink of detritus and shat-out carrion you'd expect: it's sweet and quite faint, discreet enough to tempt you into taking in another inquisitive noseful. It's when the mind registers what it is, when the knowledge synchs with the sensation, that you want to retch and block every part of you that opens and lets the world in: eyes, nostrils, ears, mouth.

Among the fronds of selfie sticks, a young mother is being sick as she watches, splashing the liquorice-coloured tyres of an expensive pram. There's a Mexican wave of mobile phones flashing as people take photos. *#Fatberg. #FatbergSelfie.*

Reporters are ready for the local segment of the six o'clock news, when the voice from the centre of the country announces: 'It's time for *The News Where You Are.*' They're leading on the fatberg. Or, as they call it on social media, 'The 'berg'.

'Him in there,' says Gary not using his name − he doesn't like to, because naming someone is a way of making them happen as people, and Gary is afraid of that. If Mr Wolphram happens as a person Gary won't be able to do and say the things he wants to do and say to him − 'he's got at most twenty-four hours before the press get hold of it, before they skin him and yank out his bones, mince up his crappy little life and shame him for all those books and operas in that big shiny head.'

With all that's coming to him, it's almost for his sake that I hope he's guilty. Does that make sense? I think. I only *think* I think it, because I realise I've said it aloud.

Gary says it quietly: 'Yes. Yes it does.'

He moves to the window, scratching his neck with a biro. 'It's a funny old world when the only thing standing between you and a lynching is a supermarket-sized ball of shit and fat.'

*

Michael Wolphram is sixty-eight, and took early retirement ten years ago, when the school went mixed. *Correlation is not causation*, the law says, but that won't matter to the press. Or to us, if it comes to it.

To me he's the same, though I notice − I quickly calculate − that I must have known him when he was in his thirties. Younger than I am now. Doesn't this always happen with teachers? They seemed so old back then, so far ahead. Years later we feel we've passed them the way ocean liners pass each other as we watch from the shore: they come side by side, one disappears behind the other, is gone, then noses up ahead and breaks free.

Perhaps I've aged and he has not; perhaps I've passed him now; perhaps Time chooses who it's going happen to and how.

He has put on no weight, accrued no wrinkles, lost no hair. He dresses as snappily retired as he did when he worked. In the *weirdoed-up* pictures they've emphasised the almost unnatural youthfulness of his face. In most of them, he wears a hat – one of his trademark trilbies or fedoras – so it is easy to conjure up the image of a shifty spy, or a half-shaded, lamppost-leaning villain from an old B-movie, the face uplit by a struck match.

He's perfect freak material. And he reads books.

When we brought him in through the back of the station, the photographers were ready. Above all their shouting there was one, a voice in the scrum, clean and loud as a firecracker: 'Get a shot of that book bag!' I looked – yes – he had one of those free hessian book bags. 'I love books!' it declared, the *love* done as a big Valentine heart and the shop's name and address – an arcade in the old town – happily blazoned across it. The bookshop had to close. They got bricks through their windows, shit through their letterbox. I ♥ Books, *AKA* 'Monster's secret book obsession', as Lynne Forester had it.

In other words: the man loved reading.

In Mr Wolphram's flat the next morning, we have at best six hours before he hits the news. Before the news hits *him*. Let the fatberg slide down page: make way for the Monster.

Forensics have been and gone, and though they haven't confirmed it, I can tell they've found nothing. But it's not the right kind of nothing: it's neither an exonerating nothing nor an evidential one. It won't help us charge him and it won't help him get off. The white plastic suits have been in and out of the place all afternoon while neighbours take pictures on their phones. There are no journalists yet, but a few people must have sold their smartphone snaps to the *Evening Post* because they're already on the website.

Small-Screen Dave is going through the opera box sets, whistling if there's something there he recognises.

Gary is looking through boxes of photographs. We were pleased to find them; they looked promising: children, schoolboys in uniform and out, sports days, school plays and swimming pools. Gary relaxed; tucked in. He thought he'd found it. 'Found what?' I asked. 'I don't know,' said Gary, 'just *it*.'

But so far, no *it*. The photos are legitimate: one shoebox for his own childhood, eight photographs marinating in stale air. We'll get to those. First, the three other boxes: those long, scrolled school photos with their panorama of faces barely detailed enough to recognise, class photos, newspaper clippings, concert programmes. We've checked Mr Wolphram's computer, and it's clean, almost empty – *suspicious*, says Gary – but they've tested it. Nothing deleted and nothing downloaded other than concert and cinema information, holiday brochures, sheet music, school circulars. In other words, *not suspicious* at all. But Gary would be the first to tell you that not being suspicious is the new suspicious. There's no history of deleted histories either. His searches are specific – information about books and editions, classical music, writers ... – and his search terms are laboriously worded. It's as if he's writing longhand to a person rather than typing keywords into a machine. 'Where can I buy piano hammer felt in the South East area?'

Gary taps the computer screen: 'Does he reckon there's a little man in there typing the answers if you ask nicely?'

These searches of his, almost every one of them, correspond to items he used to buy in real shops until the shops closed down. Mr Wolphram's taste is for things that have taken sanctuary on the internet, endangered species whose high-street habitats have been destroyed: second-hand books, LPs and LP racks, styluses, tape-head-cleaning fluid, electric shaver leads, shaving bowls. Some of these have been given a new life by hipsters in retro shops, but he probably doesn't know they exist.

'A bit of an internet surfer, are we?' asked Gary.

Mr Wolphram doesn't hear the taunt, only the question it comes wrapped in. He thinks about it as if it were a genuine question, genuinely asked. Is he nonplussed by the surfing metaphor? Because he seems to consider it. Is this the first time he's heard it? Maybe. He seems less certain of himself today, frayed and uneasy.

'I wouldn't describe myself in that way, no. More of a deep-sea diver.' He says this a little proudly, glad to bat back the metaphor, to be back on the right side of words: on top of them, where he's used to being.

He blinks and tries to smile and for a moment even Gary sees he's trying to be helpful, that he's a naïve, unworldly pensioner who finally – after the archness and sarcasm of the first interview – starts to understand this isn't a game. It's his second day at the station. We haven't told him we're going to apply for more time to question him, but he knows. He keeps checking his watch. With all the crime shows on TV you'd expect him to have a better sense of the situation he's in.

'Someone to get back to?' asks Gary. There's no misunderstanding the tone now. It flexes menace and contempt.

Mr Wolphram looks down at the desk. Thinks about it. 'No, there's nobody.' He says it with surprise, as if he'd only just realised that he lived in a world where people have people to get back to. He checks his watch again, then pulls his cuff back over it like a schoolboy caught out willing the lesson to end. 'Nobody.'

That's why Gary is pleased to find the photographs, and why he calls them a 'stash'. If something is *a stash*, or *in a stash*, or *stashed*, it's bound to be wrong, contraband. It sounds bad. Gary tries not to show it, but he is intelligent. He thinks being clever is effete and maybe 'a bit gay'. At the very least *metrosexual*. He doesn't want to be mistaken for the kind of person who orders olives or wasabi peas in bars. He is also kind. But because kindness is not part of his self-image as a coarsened, cynical cop with no life beyond the job and a tabloid-swagger turn of phrase, we have an unspoken agreement to pretend he isn't. It isn't hard today, because he's especially ugly and insensitive. He's wearing yesterday's clothes and he smells angry. He's going for Mr Wolphram, sweating him, brutalising him – first with words and then with no words, with nothing but stares and silence. Gary has a way of doing this – I've seen it – and people start to wish he'd hit them just to break the ice: to break the ice with their face if necessary.

Now Gary's there in his house, happy and cross-legged, sifting the photos, holding them up, putting them back down. 'Deep-sea diver ...' he sneers, 'okay Jacques Cousteau, let's see what you've got below deck ...'

Gary is onto something. He *thinks* he's onto something. Child + bare flesh + photograph = *something*. He clenches his jaw and sucks in the air; it sounds like a radiator being bled. The gaps between his front teeth are overgrown with tartar the colour of kettle-bottom limescale. Occasionally he dislodges a piece with his pen top, crumbles it on the desk, then flicks it off into that office void where hairs and skin flakes and bogies finish up and begin their journey into dust.

'Ever wonder where it all goes, Prof?' he asks me, and it's not a big metaphysical question, it's a very precise one: 'All the skin and hair and nail parings, cuticle-skin, nose-food? All the offcuts, all that sediment?'

Gary is obsessed with, as he puts it, *where it all goes*. But with him it's not a question about the soul or the spirit or mortality. It's very specifically about waste, litter, the outgrown and the cast-off and the used-up. 'We drink last week's piss and drain water after it's made its way through the system, and we'll drink it thousands of times over before we're forty. We go on eating dead stuff, shitting it out for machines to clean, until all of a sudden everything's clogged up and we've got a bloody great fatberg under our feet.' He pauses. 'So the answer to where it all goes is: it doesn't — it all stays.'

The fatberg has become Gary's way of seeing the world. He spends his time when not working looking it up on the internet, looking for other fatbergs: he has found them in Mexico, in Texas, in Slovenia, in China and India. Cousins of our own fatberg, they squat on the news-sites of their nations and provoke the same mesmerised disgust. The one in Texas is oddly lozenge-shaped, like a U-boat made of dirty lard. The one in Mexico has crept up and lifted manholes like a dandy tipping his hat to a lady. But they're family and there's a fatberg family resemblance. The contents are probably a little different, depending on diet, infrastructure or climate, but it's the same principle: the infinite story of our waste.

There's even a portrait of the fatberg pinned to the cork board by Gary's desk, in the place where you stick photos of your husband or wife, or the pictures your kids did in school.

For Gary it's a memento mori, like the skull on the desk in the corner of some Renaissance painting: *Eram quod es; eris quod sum — As you are, so once was I; as I am now, so you shall be.* Fatberg-slime, flushed meat, cemetery-landfill.

Then, typically, comes Gary's theory of civilisation: 'Since the first man took his first shit, we've been running from it. We were all nomads 'til we invented sewers; for thousands of years we kept moving just to get away from our own excrement, and then Bingo! someone invents a sewage system and we stay put, build houses, art galleries ... universities for people like you. Toy shops and police stations. Waitrose. Bloomingdale's. We're still shitting in the river, mind, just not actually squatting over the edge. That's not me telling you that, Prof, that's the Discovery Channel.'

Right now Gary is quiet and completely absorbed in the photos. He's sorting them into two groups: children and adults. Clothes, fewer clothes, but no *no-clothes*.

I pick up a batch of pictures — a *stash*. They're neatly stacked, a rubber band holding them together like playing cards, with Post-it notes marking each year. Gary has got through 1979–84 and found nothing. Nonetheless, he's taken a few out and put them aside. I can see what he's after: it's the pictures of boys in sports kit, or in muddy shorts; one where two of them are taking off their football shirts; another of the swimming team. The swimming team photo looks, from a distance, like a line of cuts in a butcher's window: five chops for a tenner. Their goosebumpy chicken-drumstick skin shows how cold it is back there, back then: back in the days when they made us swim in open-air pools in January.

I know what Gary wants, and it's what we all want: a chance to make the Knight's Move from kiddie-pic-hoarder to woman-killer. It's two steps forward, then one to the side. That's the way we solve crimes – or at least the ones that aren't basic, off-the-peg crimes. Anything more complicated than what Gary calls the *fixed price menu* – husband kills wife, accountant defrauds own company, teacher sleeps with schoolgirl – and it's the Knight's Move.

These pictures are innocent enough in their context, they're only a fraction of a whole meticulous photographic record of his time at Chapelton College. Wolphram edited the school magazine, so his box files are full of photos and brochures, cuttings and page proofs from pre-digital days when pages had to be set by hand. There's a manual on desktop publishing on his bookshelf, a run of twenty years of *The Chapeltonian*, and various newsletters for Old Chapeltonians across the world.

Gary knows that the pictures need to be abstracted from their context. That way they can shine with the darkness of their innuendo.

'You okay there, Gary? You're going to get cramps squatting like that. Want me to take some off you?'

'Knock yourself out, Prof,' he says. 'I can't put my finger on it, but I know there's something not right here, all these files and boxes and index cards and all these fucking Mozart papers with their squiggles ...'

'Musical scores, Gary, sheet music—'

'Banjos on the wall—'

'Lutes ...'

'Old cinema posters, DVDs and videos, foreign films, Fred Astaire and Ginger Rogers musicals ... This is more your world than mine, I can tell you.'

*How right you are, Gary — how accidentally,
unknowingly right you are.*

But you'll know soon. Because I promise I'll tell you first.

I take 1983–7 and carry them to the desk. To get there
I must step over piles of paper — corrected essays, poetry
handouts, lesson plans and a file marked 'Teaching
Review'. There's a stack of photocopied 'Feedback Forms'
from pupils, and a letter from the headmaster about the
school's 'Reviewed Mission Statement'. They're at least a
decade old, yellowing at the edges. I wonder how a man
who can't answer a question about his own childhood
without wondering if he played with his toys or curated
them copes in a world where 'quality' is used as an
adjective, and where teachers are called 'knowledge-
brokers'.

The flat is large and expensive and takes up the ground
floor of a Georgian mansion on Parktown, the poshest
crescent in the poshest part of the city. The whole street
is listed. It's the kind of street where they dial 999 if you
use a non-heritage colour on your porch. Or, as Gary puts
it, 'The kind of neighbourhood where guys are called
Cecil.'

Why are we here, Gary and I, snouting through
Wolphram's flat while the neighbours peer out of their
windows and take pictures of us?

Wolphram is one of Zalie's neighbours. We don't know
if they liked each other or even knew each other much
beyond a good morning or a pleasantry called out over
a fence, but we know he helped her bring her shopping
in a few times, and we know he gave her a lift to the
ferry terminal last summer: he was driving to France, she
was meeting her boyfriend off the boat. Tim. He lives
in Saint-Omer and came to see her two or three times

a month, either by ferry or by Eurostar. He hasn't left France for two weeks so we ruled him out immediately.

We also know, from Zalie's text messages, that she and Wolphram had last spoken the day before she disappeared. We know she thinks he's *a bit odd*, that he *doesn't do chit-chat*, because she messaged Tim about how awkward it was to talk to him, that she couldn't decide whether he was shy or arrogant.

We will find traces of Wolphram in her flat, and traces of her in his car. But that will mean nothing. Not unless it's blood, some skin or a more than usual number of hairs. A tooth.

We're here because of the way he answered our questions, because of the way he spoke about her as if she might be dead before even we knew she was. The tenses threw him. For a man in control of words, it was odd that he couldn't decide whether he *knew* her or *knows* her; whether she *lives* or *lived* down the road. If she *had* or *has* a boyfriend.

Death's tenses are important: it's one of the ways the shrinks and forensic speech scientists catch the inconsistencies in the murderer's stories – how they might accidentally use the past or overemphatically use the present; how they are relieved when the body is found because they don't any longer need to watch their tenses, because they can finally talk about their victim in the past – which is where they put them.

Mr Wolphram must have been clearing out his papers, because there's a green recycling bag beside them, already half full. We'll check that, too. Like hesitating between tenses and hovering on the line between *was* and *is*, the urge to clean, to clear out, to bag up and purge is also a guilt reflex.

They've taken DNA from her place, now it's his turn. With her it was hairbrushes, sheets and pillowcases, lipstick, a doormat, dirty washing-up and a laundry basket; even the foot scraper by the bath with its shavings of hard-skin parmesan. The nail clippings on the toilet cistern she never got around to flushing down. At some point, in some lab in Swindon, on an industrial estate patrolled by private security vans, they'll sort it and repeople her last days with the DNA of others. Traces of who she saw and knew and maybe touched will come up on a computer screen in sequences of 0s and 1s, strands of colour-coded atoms twisting like bunting.

Until then it's just me and Gary and Small-Screen, poking around inside the shell of her life in white plastic onesies.

I've asked Small-Screen to find out where Wolphram's money comes from, because by any standards the man is rich. His salary is good but nowhere near this good. Even if he got in early with property, which he did, the flat would be expensive to keep up on: high ceilings, complicated coving, dado rails. It's carpeted neutrally wall to wall with an oatmeal-coloured pile, the same in every room. His bedroom contains a double bed with one bedside table, and a wardrobe with four suits, three pairs of drainpipe trousers, three jackets and four identical red ties. A red silk scarf hangs off a peg inside the wardrobe. A trilby and three fedoras stand in a row, each on its own stand. The 'stands' in Wolphram's case being vintage wooden milliner's heads, just detailed enough – eyes in bas-relief, the crest of a nose, the tapering of a chin – to scare Gary with their almost-faces as he draws the curtains and reveals them lined up along the dressing table. There's a dress suit, a dress shirt and a bow tie, still

49

in its dry-cleaner's polythene shroud. I check the receipt to see when it was last cleaned, and it was two days ago. Three days after Zalie went missing, one day before we found her. Do people commit murder in black tie? Only in Dorothy L. Sayers novels. But, still, I make a note to check what was on that night in any of the theatres and concert halls between here and Brighton.

There's one room with nothing in it; not empty so much as never filled: nothing on the walls, no dents in the carpet weave where chairs or tables or lamps have printed themselves in. Not even the ghost of furniture, not even a picture hook or the dust marking the frame of a frame. He has been trying out paints on a small patch of wall, just under the windowsill, and the tester pots are lined up neatly on the floor, separated from the carpet by an old copy of the *Times Literary Supplement*. There's a kitchen with one of everything out on the drying rack, and second of everything in a drawer. No one to get back to.

The kitchen has a bookshelf with cookbooks ordered according to country rather than title or author. I take one out, and it's Moroccan cooking. It has a few spatters on the pages, some recipes bookmarked and cramped handwriting that isn't his. Maybe there was someone to get back to once? Maybe there is someone to get back to occasionally?

Later I will realise how it bothered me that he had only one bedside table, on the right, and how it jarred. Most people have two, even if they're single. Don't they? Is it for symmetry? It must be, though solitude is asymmetrical. Because solitude is asymmetrical.

His life happens in a study-living-room where he keeps his books, his records, his three guitars — two acoustic, one electric — a lute, his television and his VHS video machine. There are several eclectic shelves of sheet music: *The David Bowie Songbook, The Kinks for Guitar*, Salvation Army band music, English madrigals and Welsh harp music, Thomas Tallis. Wagner spine by spine with The Who. The music collection takes up a whole wall, the books the remaining three. There are even bookshelves over the door and around the doorframe, and a stepladder so he can reach the books that touch the ceiling. There is an antique chaise longue beside which, as in a film or a painting, a book has been languidly dropped, and a large metal-framed armchair, its black leather worn smooth and shaped to the body of a man who reads a lot and who lives alone and more than alone. It's overhung by an arching floor lamp with a chrome shade that gives a perfectly angled, cleanly bordered cone of white light. A three-piece hi-fi — turntable, double cassette deck, amplifier — at least twenty years old, is connected to waist-high speakers aimed at the chair like cannon. The last record listened to, still on the turntable and with the sleeve leaning against the armchair, is *The Kinks are the Village Green Preservation Society*. I notice a shallow, barely perceptible furrow in the carpet where the DVD player and television stand is regularly pulled on its coasters to face the armchair.

There isn't much in this flat, but what's there is the best of what there is: bought once and bought for a lifetime. But unlike the rich he lives among, there is little decoration, and the luxuries are for the ear, the eye and the mind, not for the body.

The bathroom is spotlessly clean and has the perfect whiteness of an igloo in a children's book. Forensics have removed the toilet and the bath, and have taken the base off the shower cubicle. They have bagged up a clotted dredging of hairs, and some sludgy coagulates of soap and grit and everyday life-sheddings. As Gary and I look in on it all, I expect him to come up with some fatberg-related wisdom about the clean surfaces of our bathrooms and the dirt in the grouting of our tiles, but instead he surveys it, nods and heads back to the hunt.

All Wolphram's photographs are in boxes and files; there are none on his shelves or walls, except for one on the dining table. It stands there, solitary as the last grave in a razed churchyard. Two young women in wide-brimmed straw hats, taken in what must be the forties, are posing beside some topiary in front of an Elizabethan tower. I know it's Sissinghurst, because all of us – even Gary – have been to Sissinghurst, that staple of school day trips and drives with elderly relatives. In the photograph it's sunny, and the women are happy. It's an uncomplicated, bright little image and for that reason alone I don't expect to find it here. It's full of warmth, too. I lift it, bag it, and give to Small-Screen – 'Find out who they are, can you?'

'We know who they are, sir, it's in his profile,' protests Small-Screen, who wants a more telegenic task, a whole more telegenic life. 'It's his aunts, and the one who's still alive is in Hastings, and we already know *that*, too.'

'Find out again, Dave. Then come and tell me again.'

Unlike Gary, I know what I'm looking for. Now, with him on the other side of the room and Small-Screen resentfully doing proper, and thus properly pointless, police work, I am as close to alone as I can be at a possible crime scene. I unsnap the elastic and spread the pictures out. There must be about two dozen of them. There are still a few black and whites, trespassers from a different era, but it's the colour photographs that look unnatural. Nineteen-seventies colours are washed out and bloodless. There are Polaroids, too, with their fat white frames, taken at parties or on sports days, fading as they emerged, as if they'd undergone a preliminary dose of Time even as they slid out wet and sleek in their skins of ink. You'd hold them by the edge and wave them so they dried faster, and sometimes they'd take the print of your thumb. By the early 1980s the colours are different; they're too primary and brash. They shout.

Everyone looks lost and otherworldly, even without that patina of extra-terrestrialism all adolescents have.

What am I looking for? Who?

There they are: Ander and Danny, together as they always were, at the start anyway. I see the others, too, whose names I remember but who are, one or two excepted, as irrelevant as extras in a battle scene from a costume drama.

I lay them aside while I riffle through the other photographs.

There was something of that pain and thwartedness in the teachers, too. I see it now, in the pictures, but, back then, like all adolescents, I was trapped in myself, the centre of my burning world. I saw nothing else, felt nothing else. I couldn't see it but it was everywhere in the angrysad eyes. There were so many things we couldn't see then, which we now see so clearly that we forget that not seeing it was part of it; that there was no way you could see it because, if you did see it, it meant you were on the outside of it, on the outside of yourself.

I will have to tell them soon. Time is running out. I can feel its vacuum-pack effect as it tightens around me.

Danny and Ander

They arrive on the same day: 1 October 1983. Everyone else arrives that day, too, but Danny and Ander somehow arrive together. Did they know each other before? That's how they feel and that's how the others see it. The teachers, too, who seem not to notice these things but do — who notice them all the more because they know what they mean, what they will come to mean, in time, as the bodies warp into adolescence and the minds push out and overrun. From the start, Ander and Danny are placed together in class and put side by side in the dormitory. Danny is Newcastle-Irish and has the name to prove it: Daniel Patrick McAlinden. But Daniel Patrick McAlinden says he isn't Irish, and he should know.

Ander is ... well, he'll explain later. He needs to line up the words in advance, find the right ones, then put them in order.

Danny is the son of an Irish dad and an English mother. That's what he calls them: *mother and dad.* *Dad* works in what's left of the shipyards, in the dry docks of Wallsend where his own father settled when he moved from Belfast for the jobs. *Mother* works in

Fenwick's, in the café where she used to serve food but now sits at the cash register, or does when she's well enough, because she's ill or she's ailing, and it's not quite clear what she has. That, or no one has told Danny in *so many words*. But Danny may not know exactly and Danny certainly won't say, because saying it makes it into *a thing*. The reason everyone knows everything about Danny immediately is that he tells them all of it in one go. He sounds different, yes, so there's more to explain. He has a scholarship, so falls exactly into that zone – intellectually superior, socially inferior – that makes the English upper-middle class uneasy.

He has a Newcastle accent, but everyone mistakes it for Irish because of his name. He isn't Irish himself, he says, because he was born in Newcastle and his mother is English. *Plus*, he tells them, *plus*... he's never been to Ireland. And, anyway, if he did it would be to Northern Ireland, because that's where *his people* are from. But people hear what they want to hear – if your name is Irish, as Irish as Danny McAlinden, then you'll speak like an Irishman because that's how you're heard. *Stands to reason*, says Mr McCloud, who should know better but doesn't: McCloud has a Scottish name but the voice of an English aristocrat from a radio drama. It is a confected accent, but he never drops it because he's had it so long that there's nothing left underneath it. Behind that expressive mask ... all he has left is an expressionless mask. Danny puts his biography out there so everyone knows. He tells Ander that he hopes that if he says it once, and all in one go, he won't have to repeat it over and over for the rest of his time at school. *Plus*, he says, a biography is just facts. It's not an actual life.

Ander is Dutch but with an English surname he has inherited but never properly inhabited: Alexander Widdowson — 'a great sixteenth-century name, proper English, that is,' says Mr McCloud. He seems to be proud on Ander's behalf. Ander's mother is from Holland, his father English. Up until now he has lived in Ghent, but with his father's new job halfway across the world he has arrived here. Ander's English is rusty without ever having shone, piecemeal without having been whole.

McCloud jokes that the boys who come from overseas — McCloud always points towards the Channel when he wants to suggest something far away — are *flotsam and jetsam.* Ander doesn't know the phrase, but he only ever hears the two words together, so he assumes they mean more or less the same thing. He looks it up in the dictionary: *flotsam — debris from a ship that has been wrecked or had an accident; jetsam — debris that has been deliberately thrown overboard by the crew to lighten the ship's load.* They might look the same but they're so different, thinks Ander, that they shouldn't be soldered together into an idiom like this. Does McCloud know the difference? McCloud seems so funny, so natural, so kind. He sounds so affectionate when he says it. He sometimes puts his arm around you, too, to make you feel better about it, about having been washed ashore to where he combs the beaches. Ander doesn't know if he's *flotsam* or if he's *jetsam*. He'll have to ask his parents, since they are the crew. Or are they the ship?

'Why Ander?' asks Danny, 'why not Alex? or Sandy? Like all the other Alexanders in history ...'

'Because Ander in Dutch means *other, the other one* ... when my baby sister started to speak, that's what she called me: Ander. People said it was funny and it got stuck.'

'Stuck' says Danny, '*it stuck* is fine – you don't need to say *got stuck* ...' He looks Ander over, trying to discern the source of his clumsiness with words. Is he foreign or is he just slow? *Either is fine*, thinks Danny, *but we all like to know where we stand with new people.*

'So that's how you started out?' asks Danny. 'As someone else?'

'Why not? It's a bit how I feel,' replies Ander. He's joking – well, not joking exactly, because he doesn't mind feeling that way, and, besides, he assumes everyone feels like that at that age – but the look Danny gives him gives no hint of a binding experience suddenly shared. At least Danny is reassured: *he's not slow, just foreign*, he's thinking.

Ander knows that look – he gets it every time he speaks English, though usually he doesn't know which they'd prefer: the foreigner or the dimwit. It's difficult to tell with the English. But in general, he thinks, they prefer you stupid. Especially if you really *are* foreign.

He's had many chances to choose between *foreign* and *stupid* and each time he's chosen *foreign*. Sometimes, that's exactly what makes him stupid. The stupid person is dealing in the same currency at least, they just have less of it than everyone else; the foreigner ... well, the foreigner is always at the bureau de change, always getting skimmed at both ends of the transaction: he means more than he can say, and by the time it's all been converted he's said less than he meant.

There's a silence where Danny says nothing and Ander fills the gap by repeating himself: 'It's a bit how I feel most of the time.' This time he tries to sound offhand and jokey.

'Not me,' says Danny, with certainty. Then, just after he says it, he frowns and rolls his tongue behind his lower lip. *Thinkily*, as Ander describes it to himself in that strange intermediate language he has developed inside his own head as a transition between his mother tongue and the public English he needs to learn. Ander feels like he's being dubbed, badly, as he speaks.

Danny is at least considering the possibility that he might *sometimes* feel like someone else.

'I'm joking …' Ander repeats, though he wasn't.

Those are their introductions. After that, it's intuitive, or at least unspoken. Neither asks the other who they are or where they come from or what they feel themselves to be.

Danny and Ander gravitate towards other ill-fitted people: Gwil Isaac, the Welsh farmer's son, and like Danny a scholar whose parents pay no fees; Neil Hall, gentle, gothic, interested in androgynous pop stars, make-up, paisley shirts, and slightly ashamed to be the son of a very rich lawyer; Richard Nicholson, the school intellectual who wears spectacles with plain glass because it makes him look like some poet he keeps mentioning who fought in the Spanish Civil War. Joining them when he remembers that he has friends is David Sweeting, an academic prodigy, but so quiet that you can't tell if he's just shy or if he thinks that anything that isn't happening inside his head isn't really happening at all. They like him, but they are not sure that he believes they exist.

Both Ander and Danny are bad at sport, but in different ways; in their own ways. Ander is just bad: he can't run fast, can't catch things, kick things or hit them with a bat or racket. There's a place for him, though, because, as they say, sport is *inclusive*, sport is *for everyone*. For *inclusive* read *compulsory*. It's that kind of school, the *mens sana in corpore sano* kind. His place is at the bottom of the ladder, *corpore sano*-wise. He's always the last to get picked for any team, after the puffy diabetic kid, George Cobbleson, the rake-thin club-footed boy Rupert Flynch, and even after Tristan with the 'special suitcase' that contains some sort of medical kit no one understands, and which Tristan himself can't properly explain the workings of. 'It's got dials on,' he says helplessly, opening it to reveal something that looks like a wireless radio from a war film with liver-coloured tubes. Tristan has a jaw like the broken bumper of a car, which is why he lisps. The front of his mouth is just out of reach of his tongue and his mouth is always full of saliva.

He is hurt, he gives off hurtness: the hurt leaks from him, he walks through puddles of the stuff, it pools at his feet whenever he stands still. But no one hurts him, they just navigate around him without touching or talking to him; he has his own airspace and nobody strays into it. It's the airspace you make around you when you're in pain.

Tristan gets left alone, even by the bullies. No bully wants to feel tautological.

There's Leighton Vaughan, a burly South Walian rugby player who hates Gwil because Gwil speaks Welsh. Vaughan is the tame Welshman; domesticated. His father is a town councillor from Newport, and Leighton is beloved of the sports masters because his dad sends them tickets to rugby matches at Cardiff Arms Park. Sometimes, when you catch him thinking, or moving his mind around in a grudging pastiche of thought, you see the melancholy that certain people have when they realise they are trapped in their own clichés but can't quite see a way out.

Vaughan spends most of his time with Hugh Lewis, who has the eyes of a boy planning a school shooting. Around them, they have gathered a posse of boys who resemble them and know them for their own kind.

There are cruel words, most of them only half understood or not at all: 'mong', 'spastic', 'abortion' ... Ander and Danny don't use them, and no one uses the words on them. They're more like background music to them, a song they catch snatches of as they move through the day: breakfast, class, break, class, lunch, class, class, class, sport ...

Then come the evenings, where time dilates and there's nowhere to hide.

But at the moment they don't notice. They're too busy just keeping hold of the changes happening inside them, in their bodies and their minds, wondering if it's still themselves inside that head, on the end of that hand, if that skin really belongs to them or if it's been replaced by a shirt made of flames.

They're thirteen, going on fourteen. Ander remembers that Greek myth, the one about the shirt that killed Hercules, the Shirt of Nessus, and that's how he feels he's wearing his own skin, wearing it to flaming rags. He thinks he sometimes smells it burning, and when he licks his arm and smells it, the way he does after swimming, to sniff the chlorine, he fancies he scents fire.

*

'Whoa!' Gary calls out from the other side of the room. 'Kinky.'

I turn, and find him holding a black cloth, some kind of velvet hood or bag with a drawstring at the bottom.

"What d'you think that's for?' Gary asks.

'Dunno,' I say, and it's true, up to a point. 'What's in it?'

'Nothing, Prof, nothing at all. Fluff. Maybe a bit of hair ...' he turns it inside out and things that are too small to have names fall from it: 'It was just there, folded up at the back of a drawer in his desk.'

'Forensics?' I ask.

'*Frenzics*,' confirms Gary.

*

Every Sunday night, for those boys who board and don't get to go home and see their families, there is letter writing. They sit in the cold assembly hall, overseen by a resentful teacher whose turn of duty has come on the weekend rota, and write on the regulation paper using the regulation blue ink and fountain pen.

What the boys express in their letters must be regulation, too, because when they finish them, add their kisses or hugs or their sad little 'best wishes' (*best wishes?* Ander thinks later, years later, 'I was sending *best wishes* to my parents, the people who made me, whose flesh and bone I am, as if they were semi-strangers from the bank or the local council?'), they must leave the envelope open. If they really want to push the boat of their feelings out, they're allowed to write 'fondly yours'. Or as McCloud quips when he's on duty: '*fondlingly* yours'.

Later that night, every week of term, the letters are read by the deputy headmaster, Dr Monk.

'The Doc' is the only teacher in the school with a PhD, and he makes sure everyone knows it. If you forget and call him *Mr* Monk, you are given one of the Doc's speciality punishments. You are 'given' them, but really it's the Doc who gifts them to himself through you. The 'curly-wurly' is a favourite, in which he grips a cluster of your hair from the base of your neck or just above your ear between thumb and forefinger, and pulls it slowly, first in tiny circles, and then, tightly, in widening circles, the way you'd wave a sparkler in slow motion at a bonfire. He pulls higher and higher, raising his arm gently, so you have to get off your chair, then stand up, then stand on the tips of your toes to stay ahead of the pain. When you can rise no higher, he just pulls and turns and pulls and curls until your hair comes off in his fingers.

The boys learn very quickly that the pain is worse the less hair there is — a fistful of hair hurts less than a precisely chosen, small patch in the places where the taut skin of the skull begins to loosen into the skin of the face — places where nerves start to crowd together. It is a raging, burning, meat-seared-in-a-pan pain, and the more you show your agony the likelier he is to stop: like all sadists, he likes the illusion of being merciful. If you keep shtum and don't cry out, he keeps going until you do. Danny and Ander are pretty good at holding on; it is like that, *holding on*, a little rodeo of pain where you just cry out in your head and say *fuckit* and suck the air in and hold on as long as you can. But at some point they give in, as do Neil Hall and Rich Nicholson, they let the pain buck them though they all try out defiance for as long as they can. Defiance is always a good look, but you need to know when to stop before you over-defy and start to break. The only one to hold on until the Doc got tired and had to stop, or began to look stupid and no longer in control, was Gwil, the Welsh boy. But it cost him quite a lot of the hair around his ears and the top of his neck, where the skin is raw and puckered and pinpricks of blood clot the follicles.

The punishment involves very little touching, too — the Doc is particular about that. Most of the teachers wallop the boys in messy, imprecise ways: a clip round the ear as they pass, a kick in the arse, forgetful brutality dispensed in flashes and with a randomness that is even sometimes reassuring because it suggests it isn't *you* personally they want, just the fact of your body. Not the Doc: the Doc is scholarly in his approach to physical punishment. He is precise and attends to detail. The pain he inflicts has footnotes. The snap of the torturer's glove is as pleasurable to a certain kind of person as the pain it presages, and the Doc is that kind of person. He even makes notes in a little book on his desk. The pages have three columns: date and name of boy, misdemeanour and type of punishment.

Gwil says the Doc reads it at night and touches himself. 'Don't rule it out,' says Danny.

At letter-writing time, if what the boys write home is not, as the Doc puts it, *mature, grown-up* and *showing you and the school in the best light*, then they're in trouble. Often Ander has his letters returned for rewriting. One of the Doc's pleasures is to take someone's letter and read it out in a childish voice, or in a theatrically tearful tone. It is one way of making sure no one says too much, puts too much of themselves onto the page. Shame their bodies, yes, but be sure to shame their souls, too. Or what they think their souls are. Ander thinks his soul is a mixture of him and what he'd like to be, *plus* (*plus* as Danny says) whatever he'd like to do, which is be an adult so he can get out of here. Plus all his thoughts, not just the complete thoughts but the hazy ones he never finishes thinking, and also the ones he's slightly ashamed of, the ones he pushes to the side. The Doc looks at you as if he sees those thoughts, too, he looks as if he's drilling into the boys, into the crude oil of what they are, the thick, unmixed, unfiltered stuff inside.

To begin with, Ander was too sad even to finish a letter. He missed his parents, and told them so. He tried to tell them in Dutch, too, his language, his mother's tongue and also — but not for long now — his mother tongue.

The Doc returned the letter and told him to do it again — in English.

The day his parents dropped Ander off at school: they pulled up in the car and left the engine on, as if to signal the briefness of the goodbye, the need to curtail it, to have a reason not to stand there watching as he put his arm over his eyes, hid his tears in the crook of his elbow, like someone trying to block out the sun. *Those pillows*, he thought that night, when he got to his bed in the dormitory with the saggy mattress and the metal frame with chipped paint and the springs rusty from generations of bedwetting ... *those pillows*: do they still hold all the tears that have been cried into them? He puts his own ear to his pillow, the way he once put his ear to shells to hear the ocean, and he hears the tears of others, and cries his own, his little tributary that feeds into the sea.

Ander wondered what he was doing here, speaking English laboriously and eating brown food in a scratchy uniform with boys who didn't wash properly and teachers who checked that they were wearing pants with what seemed to him, even then, to be a kind of zeal disproportionate to the enquiry. He didn't have the word *zeal* then, or *disproportionate*, or even *enquiry*, but as he grew older, as he learned the words in English, he went back over the moments when he had no words and slotted the words in: into the gaps, the blank bits where the feeling or the sensation was there but the word hadn't been.

The words are all in place now, but mainly because it's too late, because they came after he needed them, like the fire brigade arriving to a smouldering rubble. The words are too much in place, even. Because now he often throws out the word and then waits for the feeling to pearl around it. Which he is sure is the wrong way around.

Later, when he looks back over his childhood, he will think it was like a crossword: the gaps for the letters that would spell out the feeling he had, the sensation that passed through his body or across it; or that stayed in his body and wouldn't leave. For a while at school he had no words because he was already too far from the old language and not yet close enough to the new one. *Tussen twee oevers*, he would say to himself in Dutch, and then in English: *between two shores*.

Small things tug at him: the Dutch on the lorries as they head to the docks; the names of the ports, *Ostend, Zeebrugge, Den Haag*. What would happen if he hid in a lorry? Under one? One day, when he sees a Folkestone-bound HGV parked in the lay-by near the wasteland under the bridge, the driver sleeping in the snug little bed-length cabin draped with an *FC Bruges* flag, he crawls underneath it to see if there's anywhere to lie down, anything to grip to. He wedges himself in between the bumper and the undercarriage; squeezes between the spare wheel and the floor of the lorry, held up by the straps that rock a little as he settles in. Then the engine starts and he scrambles down, rolls out and watches it go.

Unmoored, he thought. *Unmoored.* Though he spent a lot of time unmoored before he learned the word *unmoored.*

What order do the words come in, he keeps thinking: before or after the thing, the feeling? Does the feeling change suddenly because it has a name? Yes, he thinks, the name contains it, or gives it a border so it doesn't spill and splash around into another feeling. Homesick, for instance: *Heimwee.* Home-*ache* in Dutch, Home-*pain.* Home-*woe.* It's better than *sick.*

He aches. He has home-ache.

He wonders when they'll build that tunnel under the sea that McCloud keeps talking about. McCloud says the trains will go underwater, that you'll be able to drive to Europe without getting out of your car.

Back there in the *then*, he said what he felt, what he meant, didn't use words to distance his feelings from the mouth he spoke them with, or from the places where he felt them. So his words were returned to him for rewriting. The same happens to Gwil, who writes home in Welsh and whose letters the Doc rips up and bins. 'Do it again in English – you're not with the sheep now.' But Gwil is steely and refuses to give in. It's a perpetual standoff: Gwil sits there with pen and paper before him; each time writes home and each time has his letters torn up. Gwil thrives on defiance. Eventually, he changes his method and writes nothing: hands over a blank sheet, though he always writes his parents' address on the envelope. He might be a martyr, but he isn't a fool: he has a phone card, which he uses to phone home, and which he lends other boys when they need it.

The Doc hates Gwil, and he is suspicious of Ander, of Richard Nicholson, Neil Hall and anyone else who doesn't arrive preconditioned to conform. But it's Danny he goes after. Why? asks Ander early on, in the first term. 'Because of the Irish thing,' replies Gwil. Ander nods. Though he has no idea what Gwil means, he doesn't want to look like he's not in the know.

But Ander pieces it together from graffiti and shreds of news overheard on the radio or seen on TV. The graffiti on the bridge, the graffiti at the bus stop, the graffiti on the toilet walls, the graffiti on Park Street, the High Street and near the bus station. He learns quite a lot of English that way, too.

Hang the Birmingham 6.

Starve Irish Scum.

And *Internment Now!*, which he has to look up and thinks it describes something not so different from being in Chapelton.

'Anything to do with the graffiti?' he asked once.

'What graffiti?' replied Danny with a jolt. But Danny knew, he just didn't want to know, didn't see why it had to do with him.

Ander and Gwil took Danny to the bridge and showed him:

Starve Irish Scum.

Gwil says: 'There's some on the bus stop on the green, too.'

Danny looks at it. 'Maybe it's that,' he says, trying to sound noncommittal.

*

It's still there on the side of the buttress: *Starve Irish Scum.* The council tried to get rid of it but only managed to etch it deeper in. The stencil of Bobby Sands with a target on his forehead was easier to clean. That went sometime in the nineties. But *Starve Irish Scum* is now so much part of the stone it's like letters in a stick of seaside rock. You could chip away at the bridge and it would still be there when the buttress was the width of a tooth.

*

The Doc dislikes scholarship boys because he is afraid of what they know of the world outside school — farms or housing estates or big cities — and of what they might have learned there that makes them less malleable to the likes of him.

'Let's see what Fenians write home, shall we?' he says, and snatches Danny's letter from the table.

In a mock Irish accent, as bad as it is exaggerated, he reads out Danny's innocuous letter contemptuously, inviting the others to laugh. Many do. He makes the obligatory joke about hunger strikers, asking Danny whether his parents have eaten this week, this month, this quarter. Danny starts to dread any meal with potatoes, because the teachers and some of the boys, the ones who've read a bit, who know their *current affairs*, make jokes and point at him.

The Doc reminds the boys that the bridge in town, the bridge they cross every day, was twice attacked by Irish terrorists: 'Once in 1939 when we were about to go to war against fascism, and once again last year when our troops were fighting in the Falklands. I hope you remember that whenever you cross the bridge, Mr McAlinden.'

So Danny learns the hard way not to say too much, not to cry onto the paper with his ink. Ander and the others learn by example.

For Ander, English becomes the subterfuge-tongue, a place with words where he can hide, where no one knows him, where he is in disguise.

Danny's mother is ill, in ways they don't understand because they aren't really told, but they're sure she won't get better. A few of the boys make jokes about *calling off the hunger strike.* The Doc laughs. A teacher's laugh is worth ten pupils', so the joke catches on. Hunger, hunger strike, solid food, nil by mouth, force-feeding. Danny takes it all. He never hits out. He's like a surface which absorbs light but doesn't reflect it.

A child with a sick parent, a terminally ill mother or father, always looks like he is carrying something heavy but invisible. So Danny is already guarded with most people. His mother's illness is always there, like a late-afternoon shadow over their games and their talk. Danny's letters must allude to the illness but not to its terminal nature. That is the English way.

Doc Monk is short, sanctimonious and has the soul of a school prefect. Or of someone who wanted to be a school prefect but never made it. People like him teach in schools so they can reach, a second time around, the heights of power they were too scorned and marginal to reach the first time. They teach so they can take revenge, so they can keep on perfecting their mis-hit childhoods when they're adults. These schools are strewn with such people. Everyone recognises them: as teenagers they were the last to be befriended, the last to buy booze and get invited to gigs, the last to get fucked.

So now they're back, haunting their lives while thinking they're reliving them: the grievances of children moving through the world in adult bodies.

Monk has a special bond with the headmaster, Mr Goodship, who he aspires to be in this life, and with the prefects, who he aspired to be in a previous one. Monk enforces discipline by proxy, and, as deputy head, he is the one who metes it out, using the phalanx of prefects as his instruments. Sometimes the punishment is official – like a hundred lines, detention, toilet cleaning – and sometimes it's a little more *under-the-counter*.

Chapelton College is a mini-state, and, like all such schools, is based on the colonial model: a pyramid of percolating authority, where the top consists of an oblivious headmaster buffered from reality by a small group of deputies holding the levers of power. Below them are the normal teachers, uninterested in discipline and who just want to do their jobs, or get away with not doing them. The next layer is a rigid internal hierarchy of boys, starting with prefects who in turn command using a stratum known as 'powers' or sub-prefects – a crew of yes-men-in-waiting, physically imposing intellectual cowards, and pocket-sadists on the climb. Below them: everyone else.

Monk's special gift is 'turning' troublemakers. He has found that ex-rebels make the best enforcers, and he prides himself in being able to sniff out the conformist inside all of them. In exchange for the small privileges he gives them – advance warning of which pubs will be patrolled so they can avoid them, finding them a place to smoke, paying them in booze or cash, taking them out in his sports car – they take care of discipline for him. He picks the beefy and the stupid, the vicious and the cunning, the stunted, the thwarted and the pathological. But he always picks the right ones. He can read them.

Ander's English is misshapen, ungrammatical; a jumble-sale language. But he learns fast, takes on the accent so quickly that within a year he's a natural. But when he speaks English he still feels like he's trying on a dead relative's clothes. It has the smell of charity shops, the feel of folded things.

Ander cannot remain himself for too long in a place like this, not on the surface at least. So the surface must change; he must paint a new self onto the glass so he can go on living behind it. He thinks of the stained glass in the cathedral in Ghent, a few streets away from the school he was at before: dull and dark on the outside, but aflame on the inside, from where it's really meant to be seen. Glass was never transparent for him, so it is no great feat to come here and imagine it opaque.

He takes on the mimic-pronunciation he hears around him, or on the radio, which some teachers still call the *wireless*. This helps him, too: he can imitate anyone after just a few seconds of hearing them speak. He knows immediately how useful that will be. The boys like that and find it funny. The teachers don't. There is something unnerving about being imitated, having your own voice returned to you, caricatured but unmistakeable; it is mockery by ricochet.

Doc Monk's adenoidal voice crackles and changes pitch when he's angry or excited, which is mostly. The boys compete to imitate him, because his voice is so exotically, complicatedly absurd. But only Ander gets it right.

To start with, there are problems, because Ander begins his sentences like an English boy, but the words don't come, the gaps begin, the holes in the language he has not yet learned to fill. It is his and not his.

For the first weeks Ander and Danny think they pass unnoticed. *Under the radar* is the phrase Ander learns. Danny teaches it to him. Ander thinks it's also like another phrase he heard, in a war film: *no sudden movements*. Stay low, stay down. But Danny being Danny simply *is* a sudden movement: he's confident, suave, articulate.

They know about the boy who was dangled over the bridge once after games. He was already alone – thin, sad, underfriended. They never saw this, but they heard about it: one day as everyone walked across the bridge back from football, some of the fifth-formers waited for him and launched him over the parapet, holding him by the ankles, still in his sports kit, and let the air batter him as he flailed in the weightlessness. One detail stands from the endless tellings of the story: how he shat himself, but because he was upside down the shit sprayed out and ran down his back, his neck, his terrified face. His hair. He was heavier than they thought so it needed four of them to hold him. They thought they'd lose him. When they pulled him back he was covered in shit and piss and lay crying and vomiting on the walkway.

He was gone the next day. A car waited for him outside the school gates while his wordless father, an Old Chapeltonian himself, came to take him home, probably to send him somewhere similar after a few days.

Danny and Ander and the rest of them know the signs of bullying as they gather on the horizon. *A storm brewing*, goes the cliché, but really it's more like an orchestra tuning up: a note here, a note there, an off-note, then two instruments in synch; then the rest joining, spreading; then a pause, you think it's over but it's not over, because they're just drawing breath, everyone draws breath, then it starts, properly starts: slow or fast, whether it builds or unbuilds, it's there now, always, there's no way out except *out* ...

... is how Ander remembers it.

If only he could have that time again, take a different turning. Take no turning at all – that would have been enough.

All this is for later. In his mind he keeps making incursions into what's up ahead, the life he might have when he's left here, and into what's just behind him – the life he had before his father's job changed, before the family moved halfway across the world. Anything to get out of the present, to take some time out from the now. Yet he knows that's wrong, that you can't mix up the tenses like that. They can't touch, or it all short-circuits.

Ander is tall and uncoordinated and not in charge of his body. Danny is different: he's lean and easeful and looks like he should be dancing or miming, not ankle-deep in mud with his socks rolled down to the lip of his trainers. He's still bad at sport, but in that way that suggests he's good at something else, not like Ander, who's good at nothing that involves, or mainly involves, having limbs.

No one uses the word, because it feels a little sexual, arousing, and some of them don't know it, and even if they did there'd be no occasion on which to use it, but Ander knows it. Ander uses it, but only in his head, he won't speak it out: Danny is *graceful*. He has a face like a girl. Hair black and shiny as the paint on the railings of the bridge and skin that's the colour of cream. There are no girls in this school, not until a few years later, so any resemblance the boys find *with persons*, as the saying goes, *living or dead*, is accidental and, biologically speaking, approximate. But Ander knows what they mean; he feels it, too. If the others mock Danny it's in that fearful, hands-off way that betrays how much they want to touch him. And they do want to. Danny knows that — there's a lot he knows. It's like he's had another childhood before this one, one he half remembers and whose moves he's always half repeating.

In class they compete, but not on each other's terrain. Ander is better with numbers, Danny with words.

Behind the school is the 'Medway City Zoo', though these days zoo is putting it strongly. It's more like a sparse menagerie, a ramshackle library of animals. Built in the 1930s to entertain wealthy locals and day-trippers from London, it now staggers towards closure, one animal at a time, as the city spreads around it. No new animals have arrived since 1981, and those that remain are not replaced when they expire. The zoo squats, with its art deco dome, its modernist reptile house and hushed aviaries, on prime building land. Developers eye it like an old relative whose death will make them rich. Quietly, the animals seem to know it, too. 'Death Row', Mr McCloud calls it. The gift shop sells faded postcards of the zoo in its roaring heyday, end-of-range souvenirs of its famous buildings, and sweets you have to blow the dust off before eating. The old lady who runs the shop has cataracts so some of the boys steal defiantly before her eyes, knowing she can see what they're doing but not who they are.

The back of Chapelton College looks out onto the monkey house, the penguin enclosure and the concrete hillocks where a thin, nicotine-yellow polar bear pads in figures of eight behind the moat that separates him from the public. Most of the big animals are single now, unpaired, mateless. Just out of sight, behind the high barbed-wire wall, are the seals, and when it's cold, which it is that first October term, the smell of fish guts haunts the air long after feeding time. Sometimes it's enough to make you sick, and the boys hold their noses as they pass. You'd think the cold would kill the stink but it's the opposite – it sharpens it, makes it jagged. In the summer they don't yet know, the smell will be more copious but softer.

*

'I wonder what his lessons were like,' says Gary. 'Imagine looking into those big staring eyes ...'

I don't wonder and I don't imagine it so I don't reply.

'I can't see him managing in my school – not with some of the kids we had. We were taught English as if it was a foreign language. It certainly felt that way with some of the poetry we read.'

He picks up a book and leafs through it. 'I remember this from school – the way teachers would stick little bookmarks in so they could find their page year after year, until the book just fell open by itself.'

What book is that? I ask Gary in my head.

'Listen to this': he clears his throat, puts his hand on his chest in his poetry-declamation-posture, and reads:

It seems to him there are a thousand bars;
and behind the bars, no world ...

'Sounds like one of those all-inclusive holidays for young people, you know, Club 18–30 ... a thousand bars, behind the bars no world ...'

'It's about a zoo, Gary,' I tell him bad-temperedly.

'I know Prof, I know … just trying to cheer you up a bit.' He puts the book down and tries to be serious: 'You know, we should probably get onto some of his pupils and colleagues. I mean, just for background info … before the papers get there and before they've been fed too much stuff about him. Build up a picture of him before it gets totally distorted.'

*

Halfway through their second term, they study a poem about a caged panther with a new teacher. He seems to come from another world, somewhere to the side of this one. He hangs up his coat, and they notice how he takes out a handkerchief and wipes off the chalk before placing his hat carefully on the desk. They notice the way he styles his hair, and they can't decide whether he's hopelessly out of date or cresting the wave of some new retro fashion. He has sideburns and hair that is older than he is; flat and straight and the colour of mercury, it comes down to just above his eyebrows. He is lean, angular, exotic, but no one mocks him, even in this world, where teachers have only two ways of dressing: cheaply badly or expensively badly. It's not that he lacks mockable traits – on the contrary, there's plenty there, from the hair to the hat and the drainpipe-trousered suit with the red tie, the tie-pin and the sharp-toed shoes – it's just that as soon as he speaks, all the boys' mutinous courage drains away.

The teacher asks the class what the poem is *about*. He asks in a certain tone of voice which Ander thinks of as the 'poetry discussion voice': heavy and serious but at the same time slippery and indirect. It's not about a panther, he tells himself. 'First law of thermo-poetics', Danny tells him later, when they've left the classroom, 'it's not *about* what it's about.' He decides he might actually get to *like* this stuff.

The teacher reads it aloud first. Important, he says, to hear it, to read it out. He emphasises the *out* and makes a gesture of throwing something towards them. The man is lean, thin-framed, long-fingered. When he speaks nothing prepares you for that deep baritone of his, like the bottom of an expensive whisky barrel or the bowl of a pipe. It clears a space for itself in the middle of any noise. Even the low-level rioters at the back of the class stop punching each other, farting and squirting ink cartridges at each other's collars.

The classroom smells of cheap floor polish, overapplied deodorant and badly wiped arse. Bottle that and you'd have a whole country's 1980s in the form of a spray. Minus the smell of girls. The new teacher has opened all the windows despite the wind gusting outside. The boys can smell the zoo, hear the animals. When they look across at the monkey house, where the monkeys jump, fight, lope around and wank, it is more like a mirror than they think.

The new teacher is a one-off. He has taken over from the regular one, Mr Trundley, who makes them write notes in silence from his overhead projector, onto whose plastic sheets he has photocopied extracts from books. His lessons are assault courses of tedium. 'Hypnos', McCloud calls him, after the Greek god of sleep, because even the other teachers endure him with heavy eyelids. They've never heard the new teacher speak, but they've seen him around the school. He only teaches the older boys, and you never see him refereeing sports matches or taking the boys out for drizzly runs. He doesn't jog around, wheezing, in a wretched track suit blowing whistles at the remedials, where Ander and Danny can be found every Monday, Wednesday and Friday afternoons, playing whatever sport is in season, and doing it so badly that it's only by the shape and size of the ball you can tell what it is they're meant to be playing. He doesn't make stupid jokes like McCloud and try to be chummy with you, or attempt to look cool with football references or pop music trivia. You never see him slinking in corners, or shuffling around, or on the street, or looking lost and dorkish in shops, badly disguised as a civilian. He's either there, imperiously, visibly, centre-of-the-situation *there*, or he's gone. Ander thinks he too is *graceful*, because he never loses his temper or trips up, drops things or says the wrong word. The last thing especially. He has a way of speaking – it's like a book. But a book you'd actually *read*, says Danny.

He dresses ... it's hard to describe because it's so unlike his colleagues; let's say he dresses with a kind of tightness and consistency that probably counts as style – among teachers anyway. He's not like the others with chalky old jackets, frayed ties and shoes that give *extra support*, or *extra comfort*, that squeak down corridors like unoiled hinges. Nor is he like the Oxbridge brigade with their brogues and blakeys and their college ties, their spiel about the boat race and 'the other place', who are fake even when they're real, who don't realise that the reason they *are* fake is that they're real.

He listens to Wagner and watches films that have subtitles and last four hours. Ander and Danny find that out later, when they're invited to his after-school culture club. Even the term 'Culture Club' would sound dickish if it wasn't him running it. They've heard that he plays

The Who and Bob Dylan records to the sixth form, that he plays Bowie songs on his guitar or the school piano and discusses the lyrics as if they were poems. If you go to his house, they say, he'll make you listen to Nick Drake and then William Byrd and compare the chords. He hums when he plays, so it feels intimate, like you're inside his head, behind his voice.

Ander eavesdrops and gathers all these titbits of information. He eavesdrops on teachers, on sixth-formers, on conversations in buses or in shops. The native hears, but the foreigner overhears.

But for all that Wolphram is not cool and he doesn't want to be. He is stern, and he doesn't do pleasantries or waste words on what is evident: the weather, the food, the school sports results. He looks fragile and dislocated everywhere except his own classroom. His fastidiousness is absurd: his spotlessness, his expensive, out-of-place clothes – as McCloud puts it – 'like someone who walked out on a band just before they made it big'. So that became a rumour, too: that he was poised for stardom and then lost out, that his bandmates are all millionaires and he's stuck here teaching English and music.

He never leans back in his chair or forward onto the table, and some days he teaches class after class standing up. He has a way of being, of walking and sitting, where he seems to be trying to touch the world with as little of himself as possible.

He gets left alone even in that cruel little world of school where you find what someone's trying to hide then rip into it because that hiding place is where they've put all they've got left of themselves. You take what they care about and hold it hostage. But not Wolphram, despite his daft suits and his hats, his foreign films and his records. Maybe the definition of being cool is that no one gets you for the bits of you that aren't cool, thinks Ander. So how would Ander describe it? Mr Wolphram sort of ... *hovers* above the everyday stuff, the assemblies and classes and milk-farts, the shouts and the dirty tracksuits, the bog-door graffiti and the smell of stale wanks ... just high enough for it not to touch him.

Basically, Ander thinks, everything Mr Wolphram does, everything he says, is like it's in italics. *He* is in italics.

Ander doesn't know what's meant by *respect*. The closest he's come to defining it is being a little afraid of someone while having no specific reason to be. Perhaps that's all respect is anyway, he thinks, or at this school at least: a fear of someone who just hasn't (yet) given you cause to fear them. But maybe respect is the right word for this teacher, since he's not the kind of teacher you exactly like, but at the same time you wouldn't want to disappoint him either. You don't want to give him a reason to think less of you. Ander is getting to grips with the lingo of the school, he likes deciphering it, and Danny and he spend their afternoons laughing at it. *Leadership qualities*, for instance, they've worked that one out: it means *bully*, the sort of boy the teachers give responsibility to so they can abuse it and exert the low-level oppression they call 'discipline'. The new teacher isn't like that. His authority comes from his words, yes, but also from patience.

He doesn't fear the silence.

Like now:

Mr Wolphram reads the poem about the panther:

It seems to him there are a thousand bars;

and behind the bars, no world.
As he paces in cramped circles, over and over,
the movement of his powerful soft strides
is like a ritual dance around a centre
in which a mighty will stands paralysed.

Ander thinks that the man's voice frees the poem. It's ironic, really, he thinks, since the poem is about the opposite of freedom. Then he lets a long pause stretch out over the room. Someone tries to speak and he raises his hand to stop them. 'Let it settle,' he says.

Silence – and there's something endless about it though it's only a few seconds long. It's not one of the usual varieties, either: embarrassed or agonised or apathetic or insolent.

If it were just about a panther in a cage, says Danny, who is the first to speak, we wouldn't be here discussing it. Ander comes in over him and says *but it needs to be* about a panther in a cage before it can be about anything else. It needs to work as a poem about a caged animal first; after that it has to be about something else or else it's not really a poem. He's surprised to hear himself, and to begin with he's not even sure it's him speaking.

'It's like the opposite of speaking normally,' he goes on, and it sounds limp and clumsy; and anyway, he thinks, as the words clatter from his mouth, why would you want to do that?

The teacher looks interested by this. The glaze of indifference burns off his eyes because he starts to look at them properly. He blinks slowly. It's the down-tug of the float on a fishing line, very slight, but enough for someone who knows to know: a tremor of interest, the knowledge that there's something down there.

'Go on,' he says. It's encouragement. This, too, is new to them.

Ander says it's like that polar bear out there in his enclosure, who maybe remembers the white acres of his cubhood, but also that it's like people, who have *desires* (he feels strange using that word, it excites him to speak it, and he enjoys having a place in which he can use it, even if it is just a poetry discussion) but whose world shrinks until they forget the bars and think their cage is all there is. Ander doesn't quite use those words, not back then, but he remembers it as if he was saying those exact words.

Eventually the bars don't even need to be there, he goes on, it's like when you take the bucket off the sandcastle and the sandcastle stays up. That last bit, about the sandcastle, he doesn't know where it came from, but it's something he remembers from the fag ends of the summers in Ostend, the sand already wet, like it doesn't even need the sea anymore. Like the sand under the bridge, too. He thinks he'll like poetry − that way of advancing with words without actually going forward. He likes the way things can be explained always by what they're *like* not just what they uniquely but boringly *are*.

Everyone is quiet. The teacher nods, smiles.

'You suppose our bear was born in the wild? Or that the panther was? Perhaps the bars are all it knows.'

'Maybe it's ... I don't know ...' says Ander, 'maybe it's not actual memory but just something he feels, like an instinct?'

'Maybe. And what sort of cages do you think he means? What sort of bars?'

'Classroom!' someone shouts out. Everyone laughs.

'The classroom. All right, that's certainly one kind of cage, yes. And not just for the pupils,' replies Mr Wolphram, looking to see if anyone gets his modest joke.

'Jobs,' says another, 'Nine-to-five.'

'Oh, absolutely.' It is Mr Wolphram's first smile.

'Getting married,' offers Jonny Kebab, the class Casanova, who claims to have fingered his friend's sister. Jonny Lansdale got his nickname by being skewered by a javelin one sports day. Everyone remembers it because of his dad, who ran onto the field as if to tend to his injury, but instead slapped him for getting in the way of the athletes.

The smile goes. Mr Wolphram looks at Ander as if to say *You started this, now finish it*: 'An instinct for what?'

Ander wants to get it right, supposing there is a way of getting this sort of thing right.

'Your body, the things it wants but you don't know about ... the things it does that you don't want it to ...'

'Or that you do?' answers the teacher.

No one speaks. The teacher leaves Ander's comment and his own hanging in the air and explains the poem. Ander was right, it isn't about a panther. The panther in the cage is ... a word he hears for the first time, and wonders why he went so long without knowing it – fourteen years is a long time when you don't have the right word – a *metaphor*.

'This is a poem about captivity,' he goes on, 'about what holds us captive. Nowadays we would say that the panther suffers from zoochosis, the kind of abnormal behaviour you get in animals – like that polar bear – that are imprisoned in unnatural environments without enough space for their bodies and enough habitat for their senses to stay exercised. But maybe we don't need to be animals in a zoo to suffer from zoochosis?'

When the lesson ends and the bell rings, it's as if an alarm has gone off everywhere. There's a shocked pause, not the usual flap of books and papers being packed up and chairs grinding as boys bolt from the room. No one moves until Mr Wolphram has closed the book and thanked them.

They've never been thanked before, and they don't know what they've been thanked for, but they all leave slowly, lingeringly, half wanting more, but not knowing what sort of more there might be.

When Mr Wolphram leaves the room, Danny says to Ander, 'That was weird.' Ander doesn't know if Danny meant anything specifically or the whole unforeseeable hour.

The next day, it's double English. Mr Trundley is back with his dead eyes, his bad shoes and his transparencies. The panther is forgotten, but nobody has forgotten the bars.

Tributes

There they are, Ander and Danny, in Mr Wolphram's box of photographs, sometimes together, sometimes diluted by others, the bit-part players – everyone is someone else's background – but never alone.

'You're creeping up on me, Gary, I can sense it ...' I've fanned the photographs out, and, as Gary approaches with his puffy breathing and the wet, blistery squeak of his oversize shoes, I slide them back into a deck before he reaches me.

'You found anything?' he starts. 'If I didn't know you better I'd say you were lingering over those a little too long, Prof ... lingering over of a shoebox full of kid-snaps ...' He leans over me before I can put them away. 'Look at those two. A right pair of Little Lord Fauntleroys. Bet the one on the left had to watch himself in the showers ...'

'Just making sure, Gary – you said it yourself – if there's anything to find here, it'll be in those boxes.'

He looks at me suspiciously, reluctant to go ahead of me in case I swipe something. He's right to. He's still eyeing the photographs and I'm still holding them.

'See anything you like?'

Ho ho, Gary.

He puts out his hand for the pictures. He is still truffling for the child-porn he imagines he'll find if he looks hard enough. The pictures I'm holding don't have what he wants, but I don't want him to see them so I try to keep them facing my chest, casually enough not to look like I'm hiding them.

'Tomorrow, Gary, tomorrow — I think there's nothing here for us, but tomorrow there might be … tomorrow I'll let you finish up the lot and you can make up your own mind.'

Gary takes a step back and holds up a DVD from Mr Wolphram's collection: 'Catherine Deneuve,' he says, brandishing Buñuel's *Belle de jour*, 'now there's an interesting case: totally gorgeous woman, but I could never finish a wank to her.'

'Thanks, Gary, that's a fresh, nuanced take, and puts her in a very special category. Perhaps you can give a talk at the European film club at the uni or something?'

He laughs but doesn't move. He stays there watching me. He has seen something, he just doesn't know what it is. That's what people don't notice about Gary: he's always thinking, always watching. You can turn him low, but you can't switch him off.

'You going to put those pics back before we lock up, Prof? Or are you intending to *work on them at home?*' He leers knowingly — ironic, because *know* is precisely what he doesn't.

I'll let him unknow a little longer.

I put the photos back, close the box. We leave the room together. I'd have liked some more time with them, but it's okay. They won't go anywhere, even if the stories they tell are always changing, alive and yeasting up in the darkness.

The corridor is filled with light. There's a big, flagrant sunset outside; it fills the half-circle panel of glass above the front door and sprays flames across the ceiling and the tops of the walls.

I have my hand on the door. Gary is talking. At me, to me, around me, over me: 'The thing about working cases with posh people is you learn new words. That window thing …' he follows my gaze up to where the light is coming in, 'it's actually called a fanlight, I looked it up. The bit between it and the top of the door is called a transom. Did you know that? Do you live in a house with a fanlight and transom, Prof? Fanlight and Transom … sounds like a detective duo, doesn't it? Which of us is which? I think you're more of a Fanlight to be honest. I'm definitely Transom.'

I start to give him a lofty appeasement-smile, but there's no time because as Gary turns the latch and I pull open the door there's a ripple of silver flashes. Then a dozen more, cameras all the way down the drive. Noise, shouting, questions: who, where, what, how … her name, his; our names, ranks.

We shield our faces, blink away the flashbulb burn-holes in our vision: six journalists and a handful of photographers. It's not many, nothing compared with what's ahead, but the surprise of it knocks us back against the door we've shut behind us and which is now bolt-locked. We are the last out and I can't remember if we have the keys.

My reaction is to turn and go back in, but Gary tells me no: 'Forward, Prof – we walk down and out and get into the car. We got nothing to give them anyway. You know the drill from the telly. Just please don't say *No Comment.*'

He nudges me on by the base of my spine, down the stone steps, down the gravel path, and through the double iron gates we forgot to close behind us. The journalists part and let us through. Why they aren't following us, I don't know, but when I look back they're rooted in their silhouettes, and in the fierce red of the sun they look like puppets thrown onto a fire. On the other side of the street, five neighbours are on tiptoe, craning their necks to see. One day human beings will look like giraffes from generations of peering over crowds to ogle accidents and celebrities, says Gary. They too are completely still, and look switched off for the day. Gary opens the passenger door for me and, as I turn back towards the house to lever myself, arse-first, into the seat, I notice a bunch of flowers leaned up against the gatepost next door. It's held together at the bottom by wrinkled silver foil and looks assembled from two petrol station bouquets. I recognise the supermarket livery. It's Zalie's first bouquet.

It wasn't there when we arrived. I know because I was looking. I'm always looking for them. You can map the city, any city, any town, any village and anything in-between – from edgeland to new-build estate, motorway hard shoulder to caravan park – with the bouquets and the soft toys and the plastic-covered messages. And the bridge. Wherever there's a bridge there are tributes. It's hard to be in this job for long without making your own map of the sorrows. Bus stops, railway stations, car parks and pubs, football terraces, street corners and the lost overgrown alleys where the nettles reach your waist and the dogs go alone to shit and find each other's smells.

Tributes, they're called. *Shrines*. When did they start? Or did they always exist? I can't remember. I don't think so.

I'm not saying death knew its place; I'm saying death had its place. Okay, so we organised things around it, you can't not, but we had it zoned, as urban planners say. We divided our territories; it was part of the long truce our ancestors made with it. When I was young it was graveyards and cemeteries and crematoria: you had your grave, your headstone, your alcove for the ashes, and you left what you needed to leave there: your last words, their last words, the big unsaids and the small; your flowers or your card, your stone, your bread, some toys, your teddy. *Their* teddy. A candle. There's nothing brighter than a single candle.

There was always the celeb-grave-truffling, but that, too, was contained: the bottles of booze by Oscar Wilde's tomb, the cigarettes and joints by Jim Morrison's. (The desperate graffiti: 'Jim, you were my only friend!'. 'Oscar, you set us free!') Maybe that's where it started, all this ... what? ... Display? This business of death and mourning as public property, like the Olympics or royalty.

Once upon a time, we had death localised; we'd put it in places we designed for it, in the earth or in memorial gardens. There's the morgue, the funeral parlour, the hearse, the coffin, the urn: all there so we could clear death up and get on, wipe our daily places clean of it, so we could do the school run or go to the supermarket, the betting shop, and not have to pass the stabbing spot and think *death happened here, death came here, look around can you still see the hole where someone was, then wasn't?*; so we could eat in the dining room where the father of four choked and fell face-first into his Sunday roast; so we can still use the garden where the toddler drowned in the pond reaching for the frogspawn that felt like jelly. So we can buy the house where the husband beat his wife, in the red-brick cul-de-sac show home that looks like everywhere else but isn't; that secretly leaks dread and mute violence. That's why we have those places: so we can claim back our places long enough to finish living in them.

We knew that we were renting the space from death. Death was the landlord who came in with the master key sometimes when we were out, for maintenance or to check the inventory, but basically left us to it until the contract was up. Now we've handed it all over. Death is all soft power. Look at the way it quietly moves in on us; and look at the way we let it, with our monuments and plaques and floral tributes, the teddies and Smurfs and Paddington Bears. We're becoming its colony. It's love-bombing us, and we're making it cuddly and writing cards to it, saying *take our streets, our homes, you've taken our people, take the rest, come live with us.* Death has a new PR company to help it with branding: the PR company used to be called religion. Now it's more like showbiz.

Some of these bouquets, these *tributes*, are discreet. They sit at the edges of the event, in nobody's way, a handful of flowers, sometimes picked from a garden or from what's left of a greenfield site. I like those. (*Like* isn't the right word.) They register the small touch, the hit of the mortal, but they understand, too, that we need tact and distance, that we can't keep claiming what isn't ours.

But some of these tributes are shouty and brash and barge into the middle of it all with big-lettered messages and expensive child-size soft toys. They traipse over strangers' grief in tuxedoes and sequins and they drink people's tears through a drip called the news.

'You still with us, Prof?'

Empathy, sympathy, whichever one I mean (anyway: does the one exclude the other? Is it a zero-sum game? The one feeling *with*, the other feeling *as*, it's not possible – is it? – for a feeling to be in two places at once?): how do you know when you've gone past the point where you're allowed to feel for or with someone else, accompany them some of the way before they pull out of sight into the place in their grief where they must go alone? To the point beyond sharing?

It must be possible to have a protocol for those fields of toys and flickering tea lights that sprout at the scene of the latest outrage, the newest sorrow, tomorrow's celeb death when grief becomes a free-for-all, a big party with a pain-piñata made of newspaper-mâché. You'd have a code of conduct, a Grief Ombudsman. The Grief Ombudsman would say: 'There's nothing more dazzling than a single lamp burning at a window.'

Now it's a field of battery-operated tea lights like you get in restaurants and pubs.

Whenever Gary is driving, to zone out his chat or his complaints about traffic, I reach for a theory and examine it. Here's one of mine:

It's a ripple-theory of public and private grief: an event is a stone dropped in water, and the people it affects are ripples. So far so obvious. The closer to the drop the harder the ripple: first you have the hard, tight circles, but as it reaches out you get to the wavy, intermittent rolls at the edges of the movement, it's no longer movement; it's just twitching at the edge, a slackening ripple of a ripple, barely a ridge in the creaming water. By then you've reached the victim's neighbours' neighbours, the newsagent, the primary school classmate.

They all want to be part of it, to take their place in the black sun of the story.

Which ripple am I, whose wave?

The stone has been dropped, but I am several rings out. I estimate six, if the first ring is lovers, parents and children, the next siblings, the one after takes in best friends, close friends, cousins and in-laws, the fifth ordinary friends and work colleagues you socialise with, the sixth ...

'That shithead on the telly.'

I don't know who Gary's talking about, and nor does his choice of descriptor narrow it down. But he brings me back into the here and now, that foreign country I was born in, before I can ride the thought to its end.

'You off on one?' he asks.

The sixth ring. That's where I am. I've counted.

The bouquet at Zalie's gate: two days later it's still there, but by then it's one of hundreds in a terracotta army of candles and toys. Some of them are sophisticated, like garden-centre displays with plaster animals and wind chimes. There's even a solar-powered plastic water feature designed to look like weathered stone. How long before it can be cleared away? What makes a 'decent' interval *decent*?

It used to be the time it took the soul to reach the place it would spend eternity in. Now it depends on when the binmen come, or when the council decides it's a fire hazard or blocks the pavement.

But there is this odd thing that distinguishes this particular bouquet: the fresh flowers sit alongside their predecessors on the turn, starting to wilt, the heads drooping and the petals crisping at the edges. The visibly dead bouquet with the for-now-invisibly dead one, I've never seen that before – usually the old one is taken away and binned. That's the form, the language of these things. Here it's different. It seems that something important is being said that I can't quite get to.

'Where now?' asks Gary once he's seen that I've returned from the place in my head he calls my home.

He is squeezed into the driver's seat and hulks there, making the car feel tiny. Gary is overweight the way a certain kind of Englishman is. The skin is drum-taut over the fat; there's no sag or flab like with Americans, the punctured sausage look, doughy bits overhanging collars or leaking out of sleeves, tumbling out over waistbands and swallowing belt buckles. His stomach and arms are hard, and his skin is tight, as if it hadn't been informed that he was fat. If you pushed your finger along it, it would squeak like a balloon inflated to just before bursting. He's quick on his bulk, thinks fast, moves fast. He's made of heft and instinct. And when his instinct fails him, which is not often, his heft never lets him down.

'Could you drop me at Mrs Snow's?'

Gary doesn't like my visits to Mrs Snow, but he's stopped complaining. 'A two-crank fantasy', he calls it. It's easier to remember than the technical term, *folie à deux*, he says. 'Well, two cranks and a ghost.'

'Shall I wait outside?' he asks.

I tell him no, it's late, it's almost dark, he should get home.

'Ah yes, *home*,' he says, fingertipping quotation marks around the word.

To get to Mrs Snow's, we have to skirt the outside perimeter of the zoo, half a mile of pale plaster like

93

cracked icing with bricks showing through, topped by barbed wire that straggles along for a while and then gives up. The city degentrifies as we go. The delis become corner shops, the shops selling designer lighting or bespoke wallpaper give way to betting shops and 'amusement' arcades. Litter twitches in porches. But the houses are tidy.

The zoo has been shut for eighteen years. When the last polar bear died in 1993, all that was left were a giant tortoise, a few seals, a rhino with melancholia and parrots that kept escaping their tattered aviary to harass the residents of the old people's home – the Three Ports Senior Lifestyle Community – next door to the school. By then the zoo had been rebranded a 'sanctuary' – a way of depressing expectations while simultaneously banking the pathos. Even the staff were on their way out, and by the time it shut its big iron gates for the last time, the average age of those who worked there was fifty-four. It closed down the year I joined the force. I remember the articles in the newspaper, its always-imminent demolition. The photographs of the tortoise and the rhino being sent for rehoming in London.

Built to resemble a space-age city, its clean edges and white concrete are now grey and flaking. The mosaic tiles that decorated its avenues have been stolen or pointlessly smashed. By the end, the animals were kicking chunks out of the walls that held them in. Kids threw stones at the glass panels of the dome at the centre of the zoo's main square. Its low Tecton buildings are covered in mould and damp. The thin spiralling ramps in the penguin enclosure that once looked delicate as slivers of peel are crumbling. Skateboarders use them, tag them with gang names and slogans. But there is a splendour about it, an optimism. It looks like a housing estate for people who don't yet exist.

In the 1980s and 1990s the zoo's airy design provided no protection from the urban foxes that started to move into the city, and which now run free in the parks and edgelands. They killed what they found, usually penguins, puffins and flamingos. The gulls and the rats, the badgers and the crows found their way in, drawn by the free food and the smell, and unbothered by the ragged exotics with which they had to compete.

Predators inside, predators outside: the Lansdale-led Medway Regeneration Company watched it throughout the eighties, kept offering money for the site, boasted of building two hundred flats in the heart of the city. But the owners held fast to their fraying asset. Maybe they loved the animals – that's what we told ourselves when we were children – but they were probably holding on for the very best price. They held on until it never came.

The Lansdales lost big in the 1992 crash. Their most valuable possession was their name, so they sold it, along with their big shop and their classy outlets in Hastings and Tenterden, but kept enough shares to stay rich. Lansdale's remained on the shop fronts, the bags and the uniforms. After the Lansdales, it was the multinationals, the asset-strippers, the loss-adjusters, the debt-buyers and the liquidators who went after the zoo. That's when the whole country learned that you could be fucked paternalistically, by someone you knew and could occasionally catch sight of, and who lived close enough to insult and spit at and piss through the letterbox of, and you could be fucked anonymously, remotely, algorithmically by a calculator and some graphs on the other side of the world.

But what saved the empty zoo was its Grade I listing. No one saw it coming: while the developers argued and the accountants pushed their numbers around, the whole complex was declared a site of unique architectural value. 'An iconic part of the South East's built heritage,' said Historic England. It is untouchable, but also unusable, and stays there like the remnants of a lost civilisation; or sometimes, in the right light, the foundations of a civilisation to come.

'A hipster paradise,' says Gary, and he's right. It's a big attraction for the urbanists of neglected places. There's rarely a month when it isn't being used for photoshoots or filming. Usually sci-fi and *noir* movies. Once they filmed a *Doctor Who* episode where the protagonists end up on a planet that is 2050 as imagined by the year 1936. Even the future dates, and the way we imagine the future dates us. Nothing ages you, anchors you to your here and now, more perfectly than your idea of what the future will look like. The zoo reminds us of that; it is the past's idea of the future.

The gates are open today. There's a Christmas market there all month, craft stalls and street food caravans. Gary slows down. 'You ever go when it had animals in it rather than scented candles?'

'Yes, a few times. Often, actually.'

'What was it like?'

Vera

Mrs Snow is waiting, as she always is, though not for me.

Her tea is strong and she never puts enough milk in it. Her kettle boils and calls from its hob; an urgent, uneven yodelling, and she lets it fill the house before she sees to it, waits until the sound has visited every room, drilled into every corner of dead air.

She passes me the cup, sits down and says nothing. We are building the silence to speak onto. Partly that's why I come here, to take silence at its source, to hear her clock tick distendedly. It seems to be adding time to the world, not counting it down. When Marieke is with me, she always records that first, the way a sound engineer takes the room's hum. 'There's no such thing as silence,' she says, 'listen: ...'

But I hear nothing.

'Welcome back,' Vera Snow tells me. 'It's been ... what? ... three weeks?'

'Three weeks,' I confirm. Mrs Snow likes the basics reiterated: weather, politics, state-of-the-nation details such as bus-route cuts, tabloid front pages, neighbours' rows. 'No Marieke today?' she asks. 'Activity Club,' I reply.

'She hates it, and they won't let her record anything, so she has to play. Pretend to. But what can you do? She admitted last time that she quite enjoyed it, so that's a step in the right direction.'

Mrs Snow doesn't have the internet, and the local paper hasn't been delivered yet, so I'm surprised when she says:

'You think he did it?'

'I'm starting to hope so, yes.'

'And Gary?' she asks. She has met Gary: 'Not the sort of Gary that's short for Gareth,' she observed. 'What does he think?'

'Same I reckon.'

She says nothing, pours a third cup of tea and sets it beside the usual armchair, the one with the doily-fringed square of lace over the headrest. Like they used to have on trains, with rail company logos, and which caught Brylcreem smears, dandruff, scalp-grime.

'We're not sure,' she says, 'are we?' She nods at the chair; shakes her head. 'Not sure at all.'

The reason I don't ask who the 'we' are is that Mrs Snow's husband is dead, and has been for almost a year. Looking at it from the outside, which I no longer can, she's in denial. Looking at it from the inside, where I have begun to find myself, she's fighting a battle with death, and isn't necessarily losing.

I am part of Vera's charade now. I've started feeling Victor's presence. Today, his armchair seems a little, well, warmer. More *sat on. Imprinted. Lived in.* The bookmark in the novel he was reading seems to have advanced a dozen or so pages since I last visited. He was always a slow reader so that isn't bad going, especially for a dead man. Today I even imagine I can smell him

– alive I mean: smell him alive, though I never knew him alive.

Her neighbour claims that he heard them talking, not just Vera herself but Victor: his voice, his kind, careful voice as it trails off.

'Must have dreamed it,' said the neighbour uncertainly, 'or the radio.'

'Must have, yes.'

'Happened a couple of times since, mind,' he looks to me for confirmation or denial and I can't give either.

One person can be mad. Two can share the same madness. But three? There's no *folie à trois*, is there? One is a one-off; two is a coincidence; three is a pattern. Three stands for everything that comes after.

Victor's budgie, Joey, has taken the loss badly: he has moulted, stopped chirping, and shed all his feathers except on his head. Gary says he looks like a testicle wearing Aztec headdress. He moves slowly, scratches around on the bottom of his cage, climbs laboriously with his beak along the bars. They used to leave the cage open so he could flap around the house. He even has a perch on the mantelpiece, but since Victor went he hasn't been out.

From the start, Vera Snow knew that her husband's death need not present any insuperable obstacle to their life together. There was grief, of course, and plenty of it, because she loved him; they had been married forty-eight years and still laughed at each other's jokes. Especially the old jokes – especially the bad ones. 'Because it's important,' he'd say. 'Because it's important,' she'd agree, 'because you feel closer to someone over a bad joke, because you each have to bring something to it.'

So there was nothing good about his death, and as he hadn't been ill there wasn't even any stoical relief to be had in his suffering coming to an end. No, she thought: you can't spin this one: it's bad.

As she told friends: 'One minute he was there, the next ... well, he was still there actually, but dead.'

She remembered the ambulance. No siren, of course. She remembered the lameness of her greeting as the medics came in, her apology for bothering them, her embarrassed explanation: 'I think he's dead, I've checked, but I thought you'd be able to give me a second opinion.' *Second opinion?* What is this? An estimate for a loft conversion? she snapped at herself. You ridiculous woman! A quote for a new bathroom? The way she behaved as if she was taking some faulty goods back to a shop, or had called in a plumber. Dripping tap; U-bend blockage.

No: she didn't need a 'second opinion'. Besides, death *is* the second opinion.

Above all, she thought, death is *embarrassing*. The fact of it is one thing: it's absolute and has a cleanness to it that was attractive to a certain kind of mind. Hers, for one − she had always been tidy, liked facts, and realised that facts were hard and clean because the life they were facts about wasn't. So from the point of view of tidiness she couldn't really fault death. But the rest of it is untidy: the body, the papers, storage of corpse, booking of funeral, clearing of house, closing of bank accounts. The odd socks, the half-finished book, the half-empty bedside blisterpack of Warfarin. The half-done crossword. Untidy and embarrassing.

The moment, as she heard the paramedics talking when they thought she wasn't listening, he went from being *him* to *the body*. As if in all this cleanness the *him* had suddenly slunk off on the sly, the part of him that said 'me' and 'I' and 'we'. The bit of her that said 'you' to him went, too. Death took his personal pronouns away.

She remembered all that, and decided she wanted no part in any of it. 'This ...' she stopped and thought; she wasn't very good at finding the right words, 'this ... *charade.*' That's it. *Charade.*

'I'm not having it.'

The first thing to do was get allies, and they could be found in unlikely places. They could be found, she thought, in the very places that seemed to be conspiring against you.

Daily life, for example: does the news stop coming on at 1 p.m. because your husband has died? Does the number 31 suddenly stop running, does the janitor (do they still have *janitors*? she asks herself as she speaks the sentence in her head) padlock the school gates and do the shops shut for an hour, a day, a week?

Though she did, she admitted, wonder whether it would be on the news, the local segment, the news where she was: 'Victor Snow, aged 84, died unexpectedly this morning at his home.' *Now the news where you are*, it would start, and maybe it would come quite late on, after the unsafe playground in Strood but before the retirement of the ninety-year-old lollipop lady in Hythe.

But the fact was that nothing cared about Victor. No *thing*, and only a few people. The first job therefore was to co-opt (that's the word she used, not then, but she found it later, when things started to need explaining, to neighbours, to the police, to social workers) the world's complete indifference and to make it work for her – for the two of them.

So now, in Vera's house, the clock still ticks, his favourite radio programmes still go out, the detective series he records because it's after their bedtime and watches the next day after tea is on tonight, as always. They're still on VHS video cassettes and their telly is one of those 1980s models you only see in skips nowadays. 'A few dozen of those and you could build a sea wall,' Victor would joke. Along with Mr Wolphram's, that makes two VHS recorders I've seen lately; more than I've seen in twenty-five years. The video player's little computerised hook was embedded in next week, a line Victor cast into the days to come, the days he'd never see and where he would not be, except in the form of these little digital crampons, fishing lines thrown downriver into a life without him: Tuesday 10 p.m.; Wednesday 9; the late film. Let them stay there, thought Vera, let them reel the future in.

Let the milkman continue to deliver their two pints, their six eggs. Let the dogs bark, let the phones ring, let the freight trains run to the no-place where they go.

Let all that happen, let things go on as always. *As always* she keeps saying to herself: *as always*.

I met Vera eleven months ago. Eleven months and eight days, if I'm precise. Maybe the eight days are important; maybe they aren't. But something has happened in the weeks since I last came here. She is less of a shocked widow and more of a worried wife.

I look at her there, with her tea and her open packet of biscuits, the boring ones Victor liked because they were good enough to eat but not good enough to eat all of, the packet with the clothes peg she uses to seal it afterwards and keep the biscuits crisp, and I see someone who is just waiting for her husband to come back.

Okay so she's waiting for her husband to come back from the dead, but she manages to do it with such ordinariness, such a sense of the quotidian, that I expect him to walk in right now, apologising, saying he got held up. He used to like walking around the zoo, looking in sometimes if it was open. That's it — he must have lost track of the time.

Vera didn't — to start with — have the air of someone swimming against death's black tide. She was an old lady who looked a bit like the Queen: powdered and jowly, kind-eyed and hardwired for duty. The sort who dead-headed roses, listened to *Gardeners' Question Time*, and left the TV on when she wasn't watching it — 'for company'. She has the kind of face you'd find on the banknote of some universal currency.

Something about Vera's situation appealed to me — the resistance, and the futility of the resistance — so we are now regular visitors, Marieke and I. The house was cold and empty. It feels fuller now, bodied out and warmer. Each time we come, the air feels brighter, more inhabited.

Lynne Forester

Mr Wolphram has deteriorated since yesterday.

'He's having a bit of DNS,' says Gary. DNS is Gary's abbreviation for Dark Night of the Soul. It's what we wanted, but still, I am surprised. Wolphram hasn't seen the press yet, nor had access to a computer or a phone, but he senses it all gathering around him and he is changed. He stutters a 'Good morning', gets up, sits down, gets up again; begins a sentence – 'Could you please tell me how long ...? ... how much ...? ... when you'll ...? when I can ...?'

Anyway, it's all the same question in the end, and we all ask it eventually: *why me?*

He is grimacing in front of what he must know – from the films and TV shows, surely he watches them? – is a two-way mirror. On the other side, we can see both him and the man going mad inside him.

He has developed a twitch; shakes his head every few seconds. He's already protesting, denying, fending off imaginary accusations. As for real accusations, they're starting up, too.

Sleepless, he has bitten his fingernails and chewed his cuticles. His food is untouched, though he has drunk the water and the tea they've left him. The fatberg drilling has kept him awake, he says. If he has no complaints about how we've treated him, that's because he doesn't dare complain: he knows that Gary is about to arrive for what he calls 'Round Two – the round without a ref'. I know Gary would never physically harm him, but Mr Wolphram doesn't, and this is how Gary wants it. He has also left the *Evening Post* there for Mr Wolphram to read, and is now watching for a reaction behind the glass.

Wolphram doesn't move, except to sparrow-jerk his head sideways and chew his nails. His lips move. He practises his answers, tries out the questions. He's dividing up, splitting off from himself: he asks a question, tries to reply, asks it again. He looks crazed. They've taken away his hat, his tie and his reading glasses and his eyes are wide open and staring. But there's nothing to see except sweaty walls and a mirror, old tea and chipped Formica, so they skim around with nothing to fix on.

One shot of him in the papers with those horror-film eyes and those pale, long-fingered hands in their black shirtsleeves, and the whole country will march here for the lynching. I can see them already, walking with torches and laying siege to us until we give him up. It's like a Western, like life stripped down to a Western – a crowd, some hate, and a rope.

He hasn't asked for a lawyer, and this is because he still hopes he'll be released. Released where? Into what? There's no back. It's like catching an animal, torching its habitat, then letting it go into the wasted nothing that's left. Whether innocent or guilty, it's all just a scorched aftermath for him now. You can tell that just by the graffiti on the walls around his house, the death threats in the comment sections below the newspaper articles.

Lynne Forester has been clever. She got in ahead of all the nationals. She has the angles and the contacts. She's persuading his neighbours to talk about how 'weird' he was, how they 'always thought there was something off about him', how he 'looked at you strangely'.

The way he looked at you − it was like he was trying to see through your clothes ...

He never looked at you when he spoke ... eyes always avoiding you ...

Long fingers ... that's what I remember ... suspiciously dirty fingernails ...

He was very smart and neat, long nails always suspiciously clean and manicured ...

Always at his window, watching ...

'We called him The Wolf' − Tomorrow: ex-pupils come forward ...

Lynne will be selling versions of the story to the tabloids − in pieces, of course, to spin it out, the way the zookeeper feeds the tigers and the bears: in morsels, kilos of meat cut into strips and slung in pieces to be caught in the maw.

We've had to give Lynne a 'soft launch'. It's where we promise to make one journalist our conduit for news, in exchange for them keeping the write-ups as close to our version as possible. They chose Mad Lynne because she's local, ruthless and close. She'd have got there anyway. So we try to keep her on our side, though really there's only one side she's on.

We've been told to work with her, and Deskfish has scheduled a visit. In fact, he's the one who shows her in: first to his office where they speak and he nods and laughs anxiously at her jokes, and then into ours, where she sits at our conference table.

I've never met Lynne. Gary has, and he hates her with the kind of cautious admiration we reserve for people who do bad things well.

Firstly, I'm surprised by her — she isn't the lowbrow purveyor of clichés she appears to be on the page. She speaks like someone who sees through what they do, who you will never wrongfoot, hurt or offend because whatever you say to them, whatever you say about them, they've said it to and about themselves long before you got there. Nor is she a slick media woman in a power-dress suit. She has spiky black hair, styled gothically; she wears white foundation and thick eyeliner that deepens her eyes, and her mouth is lipsticked in the shade of heavy red you find in stately home dining rooms. She looks like an eighties punk singer, feral but delicate. She's all in black except for a cobalt mohair pullover, which, when she takes off her coat, gives her body a blue gas-flame shimmer.

She must be a couple of years older than me. Like Gary she's local, has the accent, but more varnished than his. In the time it takes me to parse it Lynne has come in, been shown across the room, and sat down in front of us. Gary has greeted her with some profanities and she hasn't even noticed them, they are as bland to her now as *how do you do?*

'I know what you think of me,' she says. But she's looking at Gary, because I don't know what I think of Mad Lynne Forester. But already I know this: one thing she isn't is *mad*.

'How do you do it, Lynne?' says Gary disgustedly. He points at the pile of headlines, some hers, some modelled on hers. He lifts the *Evening Post* and holds it away from him like a shitty nappy or a slice of fatberg. 'You make it look so easy ...'

'Get me a cup of tea or coffee – don't care which, can't tell the difference any more – and I'll let you in on some of my trade secrets.'

Gary returns with tea and more disgust. But he is interested.

'This is how it works:

'You need information? You just ask. Usually you get it. People just want to be part of the story. You're giving them a chance. The bystander. The distant cousin. The neighbour five doors down. The childhood friend who never suspected a thing … But for the right amount of cash … well, they can bloody well start suspecting retrospectively, can't they? They're always ready to talk. Oh – *hang on* … you need *more* than information? Innuendo? Something they don't know and don't think but you need them to say they do so you can print it? Ah well, that's a bit different. Not *that* different, though.

'Are you sitting comfortably?' she asks, mimicking the storyteller in a children's bedtime programme, 'Then I'll begin:

'First, take them to one of those caffs full of air-kissing milf and cappuccino-sipping yummy mummies, you know the type, *mwa mwa*, babyccino for the kids and some *biscotti*. Remember National Milk Bars? Loved them. All closed now. Now we've got national milf bars, smoothies and power shakes and soft-play areas and floor-jigsaws. The dads think they're in a Tony Parsons novel, the mums think they're the kind of women dads in Tony Parsons novels fantasise about.

'A wine bar's good, too, a gastropub, a craft beer place. Anywhere middle class basically. Somewhere with artisan breads, beers and beards. Main thing is to make them feel classy, because they're about to go low, to scrape the bottom of all that's decent. So you surround them with nice things – *aspirational* things. You got to make them feel like classy people, like it's *you* forcing the money onto *them*. Expensive lunch. Hotels with chocolate on the pillows. Make them feel they're important, that they're starring in the film of themselves. If they want to get a bit *conflicted*, a bit *tortured*, let them: don't cut them off too soon and flash the cash, because feeling a bit bad about what they're doing is a way they tell themselves they're good people. So take it slow. It's like fishing. Don't yank. Go with their movement and then take it over yourself.'

'Here it comes,' says Gary, 'there's always a fishing metaphor ...'

Lynne ignores him: 'It's the middle classes who're the worst. The proles aren't as greedy as you think.'

'Don't patronise me, Lynne. I'll always despise what you do, but depending on what you're going to say I might just – *just* – find it interesting.'

'No pressure then ... okay, I take them there. I'd size up the place, 'cos I know they're the type to like a bit of retro, so long as they knew it was retro and not just old. Sounds better, doesn't it, nicer label? It's all in the words. Listen: *There's an old café on the corner, let's go there.* And: *There's this really great retro coffee bar, let's pop in there.* Cappuccino or milky coffee?

'First you let them pretend they're not doing it for the money. They need that, it loosens them up. We all fool ourselves anyway, but sometimes we need a bit of extra help. You know, as the man said, *Let us deceive ourselves together.* That's Jacques Lacan by the way ... Anyway, they're already wealthy, they're doing fine. Then you go for it, because, well, you know: having money is just another way of wanting it.'

'Deep ...' says Gary sourly. But this is the kind of thing he says. He recognises it as his own Garified idiom, and he doesn't like it coming from someone else.

'Five minutes, you give them — then you take out the cheque book and whack it on the counter.' She slaps her hand on the table. 'They jump, like they've been shot. *Exclusive*, you say, and offer them a price. No one uses chequebooks these days, but I do because it's a great prop: they see it hit the table and watch you fill it out by hand. Bank transfers don't feel real, and pure cash looks dirty. Chequebook? A bit archaic, old-school, sure, but it's just right.'

She pauses. Looks at us. We say what she wants us to say: 'Go on.'

'Then sit back and watch them computing the cash, seeing the zeros filling out their bank statements — funny thing with zeros: the more nothings there are, the more cash there is — and they're off. For some it's a holiday, for others it's a conservatory, an extension, some school fees or a nudge closer to early retirement ... I've seen them all, gone through the whole gamut: from the life-changing amount of money to the merely weekend-improving. But they've all got one thing in common.'

'What's that?' asks Gary too quickly. He's fascinated. She has him on her hook.

'You're not going to like it ...' she says teasingly, tilting her head to the side, 'I find these people not because they're evil or weak or stupid or plain greedy — doesn't matter if they're rich or poor or in-between ... I find them because they're *there*. Because they're everywhere.'

Gary is silent. Furious, too. And depressed. Lynne is speaking a language he thought he'd invented.

She goes on:

'But listen: there's one mental operation they make, though, and it's this: they get angry with the person they're about to shaft and lie about and fuck over – angry because that person's putting them in that position, they're the ones forcing them to shaft them, fuck them over and lie. *Disgusting*, they think. The anger flashes in their eyes: *How dare that bastard/bitch put me – me! – their friend, in the position of betraying them?* Then away they go. Spilling it out.

'It's always the same. I just wait and let them go through the objections, ticking them off in their heads like a kid with OCD checking all the switches before going to bed. Then ...' she shapes her fingers into a gun, a starting pistol, '*Bang!* They're off. Hard to stop them after that. It's like the money is compensation to them, compensation for being turned into liars ... the chequebook bandage over their wounded pride.'

'You don't give a shit about people's lives.'

'They start with the truth, and I play along, pretending that's what I want and they're pretending that's all they want to tell me ... Then we move into the kind of speculation based on truth that's a step in the right direction (*I never actually heard him/her say that but ...*) and then the outright lie. Because when you're taking money, truth and lies aren't opposites, they're just points on a continuum ... as far or as close to each other as you want to make them.'

'That's a fucking atrocious philosophy.'

'It's not a philosophy, Gary,' replies Lynne with seminar-room triumphalism, 'because philosophy is just stuff you have theories about but can't prove. This is stuff you can prove so totally you don't even need the theory. What's the point in trying to prove it?'

She gets up to leave. But first, she reaches into her bag. She pulls out this afternoon's edition of the *Evening Post*.

First, she has published a picture of Mr Wolphram, befuddled and answering the question – badly – that got him into this mess. He stood outside his house and said he'd seen her and a friend leave. But he's lying or he's confused. This is where it all started.

Lynne has put the video on the *Post*'s website. It's already on YouTube. Three thousand views since last night. Her article also contains four stills from the film, chosen for drama and menace. Wolphram in front of the cameras with his book bag, giving a word-perfect but chronologically incoherent comment on his neighbour's disappearance. Practised liar or just a practised speaker getting something wrong?

His face seems to explode a little behind the eyes each time a camera flash catches it, like a horror-film house in the obligatory lightning storm.

A detail from the main image has a picture to itself, inset underneath, the way art catalogues scope in on particular squares of the canvas: thin white hands and long nails (guitarist's nails, but who cares? From now on they're pervert-fingers), all the more visibly sinister for the shortness of the jacket sleeves and the way he defensively touches the brim of his hat. The thin wrists. Fat black hairs on the backs of the hands. He has the damp, grey flesh of fish in a freezer. The eyes of an eel. They've photoshopped out the street, the houses, anything that might give him context and normality, and replaced it with a black silhouette of the school buildings so he looks like a ghoul in a cheap horror film.

He's been Boris Karloffed, says Gary.

He says he saw Zalie leave the house with two friends the night before last, but this is impossible since she's been missing four days now and dead for only a little less than that. He can't make the chronologies meet, the before and the after; the two broken bits of time don't match.

And yet, I don't think he is lying. Lying is to push a large thing through a small hole in the language, and he's not doing that. It is more that he's caught up in the momentum of his misremembering. If he goes back on what he told us, we will ask him why he told us things that were untrue; if he goes forward with the untruths they will unspool and entangle him and we will catch him out. He can only try to stay still, but no one can stay still in a police station. Not with Gary standing over them, the press turning up the volume of their innuendo, and Deskfish/Ironside/Unmanned being hassled by his superiors for a result before New Year. Ideally before Christmas. The man with a gun to my head has a gun to his head, and so on in an endless recession of barrels at temples. The country − *the nation* as the BBC now calls it at every opportunity − needs a resolution before the presents hit the floor under the Christmas tree, before the choir of Westminster Abbey clear their throats, before the Queen's Christmas message.

'He could be mistaken,' I tell Gary, 'it's stressful up there in front of the cameras.'

'He could also be lying,' says Gary. 'How many times have we seen it? UTP, remember? We learned that in college, Prof. Classic UTP. Man, poor distraught man, appeals for missing wife last seen heading to airport or station. Public appeal, TV face, flowers outside and *B-i-i-i-i-g* Sympathy. Hankies. Community pulls together to offer support. Oh, but hang on, what's all this? Husband's killed her. Weeping, broken, *my-life-will-never-be-the-same* husband. Yeah, that one. The very same. The one who *helps in the searches* and *made an emotional appeal to the public* ... She never left, never took that plane to Alicante. She never went off to Sussex to get *a bit of time to herself.* Never went on that City Break to recharge her batteries. She's Under The Patio.'

Gary is right. All the statistics say so. *UTP: Usually The Partner.* Gary's version, *Under The Patio,* is essentially the same, but it's been Garified, and what it's lost in academic precision it's gained in immediacy. That's what Garification does.

'He's not the husband, though, is he? He's not anyone's partner either, let alone hers.'

'He's the neighbour, Prof. It's his patio. *Figuratively* speaking. We know he went in — he told us. We know he's lying about when he last saw her. They were never more than a few metres away from each other. He could hear her toilet flushing, he could hear when she went in and out. Maybe that's not all he heard ...'

I look down at the desk and fiddle with an old lanyard left over from a training day the Drone sent us on in April: *Workplace Synergies.*

'Look, Prof,' says Gary: 'in films and thrillers, when a guy wakes up in the morning and there's a dead woman covered in blood beside him, it means he didn't kill her. In real life when a guy wakes up and there's a dead woman covered in blood beside him it means he killed her.'

Gary is right. The whole detective-thriller-police-procedural genre, with its twists-in-the-tales and courtroom exonerations ... that's just a place in the culture where we've put the world's missing complexity.

So we clocked Mr Wolphram, as did the shrinks and the speech analysts and the body-language specialists, and we brought him in.

Mr Wolphram said he knew her 'a little', that he helped her put the bins out, gave her lifts. Then he says, defensively, puzzlingly, that he has never had any trouble with her, though 'we weren't friends; no, one couldn't say that'. He simply means they didn't know each other, but he puts it in such a way as to suggest that they got on badly. Motive? Maybe it is, but why did they get on badly? What's the motive for the motive?

He has nothing more to say but, nervously, he keeps adding until it becomes a confusion of detail, an impasto of unnecessary information. 'All trees and no wood,' says Gary as we replay the tapes later. But the police shrinks agree there's something there. The liar always over-answers.

'He might be guilty of something,' I say, 'just not this.' They ignore me.

One thing at a time: this thing, now.

I am not even sure he is the same person we interviewed yesterday: session one, he was helpful, yes, but contorted, indirect and – how can I say it? – twisty in his answers; always replying at an angle – not lying as such, more parallel answering. Politicians can get away with it – they do it all the time, deny things they were never accused of to stop us looking where we should – but not suspects. Session two: he was sly and almost mocking us with the childhood and personal life stuff; mocking our own obviousness, like we were all small-screen Daves and *he* was analysing *us*;

session three ... well, let's see:

Everything is different now. Lynne has written: 'Mr Wolphram, 68, a retired English and music teacher at top private school Chapelton College, described seeing Zalie Dyer for perhaps the last time ...' A little later, it's 'Zalie's eccentric neighbour, the bachelor Mr Wolphram ... has a taste for expensive suits and formal attire ...' Then, in a separate online 'update' from twenty-six minutes ago: '68-year-old Mr Wolphram chose early retirement when the former all-boys college went mixed, and has lived opposite his old school, in a Georgian mansion close to the iconic City Zoo, for thirty-four years.'

Gary: 'You've got to admire Mad Lynne. It's a full house in Perv-News Bingo: girls, boys, an eccentric bachelor, a mansion ... all that plus animals!'

'No animals, Gary – there haven't been any animals there for years.'

Lynne keeps updating the page, freshening it up, making sure she gets the details in that will help single him out.

Join the dots.

Actually, don't bother – you don't need to: these are self-joining dots. Watch them stretch out until they touch and make a line. Until they make a story. Until they make a noose. Everyone knows it's him, and now the press are starting to tire of the fatberg, they're going to hunt him down.

We're about to go in for the third interview. 'This is basically prejudicial,' I tell Gary, gesturing at the open newspaper. 'She's more or less identifying him before we've even charged anyone. People are going to get the wrong end of the stick.'

'Prof,' says Gary in the tone he would use to explain something to his children, if he had any, 'Prof – this stick only has one end.'

In we go.

Mr Wolphram jumps up from the bolted-down desk-and-chair combo when we come in. He looks at me, then at Gary, then back at me, full in the eye;

finally he sees it;

says in a new voice: 'I know you.' He is standing up now, and seems taller, calmer.

Danny and Ander

School is different now. To start with, the newness of it all made every day sharp, jagged. People, places, feelings: all of it was fresh and distinct. Even if it hurt, that was okay, in its way — it took its place in how you felt alive. And you were learning, too. Waking and even sleeping were eventful: the boys who cried out in nightmares or wet their beds then woke when their sheets got cold to the smell of sticky piss and fear, the sound of birds in the early morning, the bottleclink of the milk float at 5 a.m. The sobbing that you heard and that felt far away, a few beds along, in the next dormitory. You listened out and tuned in, wondered who it was, felt sorry for them, then realised it was your face cowled with tears and you'd have to pity yourself as you lay there being a child ...

After three terms, daily life has run through its repertoire.

They've changed classes and moved up a year. At fourteen, they're in the fourth form. Their form tutor, Mr Moreton, is erratic and sweats alcohol. He's decent enough when sober, and fair, though more through apathy than any special commitment to justice. But they'll take that, because it's when he's drunk that he starts to pay attention. To them. His nickname is not subtle and not original – Morbender – and nor are his methods: he gropes you and puts his arm around you, and when he decides to punish you he hits you hard but lingeringly on the arse. He puts you over his lap where you can feel his erection pushing into your stomach. It's muffled but definitely there, and depending on his level of arousal it's either like a finger jabbing you in the ribs or like a stone you can feel through the sole of your shoe; like those small bumps at pedestrian crossings so the blind can sense them on the pavement. Though his trousers are pressed and look clean – he is ex-army – his groin smells of bins. The children normalise all this because, well, part of being at the bottom of the heap is having someone else define your normal for you.

Ander has worked out that the big struggle here is not about defining extremes, but about defining the normal, the everyday, and trying make it liveable. It doesn't come to him as some big revelation, and for a lot of the time, to start with, he doesn't even know he's discovering it. But later, looking back, which is what Ander chooses to do early on – long before he's old enough to have much to look back at – he sees it.

Morbender has the face of a badly painted toy soldier, the hues a little too rich and exaggerated, and overlapping onto areas they're not supposed to be. Add the alcohol-blush on the cheeks and the crumbly looking nose with its violet cracks, and you have someone who looks a lot like a dirty puppet. There's always something that resembles damp breadcrumbs in the creases where the different pieces of his face meet: between jaw and earlobe, nostril and upper lip, eyelid and brow. It's a yellowish putty at the joins of his features, as if they've been mortared together with cheese. Sometimes when he takes off his specs and rubs his eyes to wake himself up you can see the stuff stick to his knuckles. There's a white paste at the corners of his mouth and when he pushes out his tongue to lick it back in Ander feels sick. Can he actually say – can any of them? – that Morbender has crossed the line? Even if they knew where the line was, that there *was* a line, could they say anything? After all, no one is hurt, no one bleeds. Some even forget, or push it into the parts of themselves they call forgetting.

It's ironic that one of the things Ander most remembers about school is the phrase 'forget it'. He has heard it in so many ways: affectionate and helpful (put it away, leave it behind, cast it aside and choose what goes into your story), careless or fatalistic (drop it, we've all had it, just move on), harsh (you're nobody, only somebodies remember, only someone who's *someone* has the right to memory).

First, everyone told him to forget; then he started telling himself.

Maybe that's why, even decades later, he feels like he has been condemned to remembering, like a child-Faust who cut a deal years ago to make the present bearable: in exchange for spending your childhood imagining a better future, the time will come when you have to hand that future over to your past and go back to live there. That was the pact.

Ander remembers all the forgetting he's done, tries to recall what he was like before he came here. What it was like when he was younger and wasn't yet English. He used to remember it as a film, where the actions and events were continuous with each other, linked up and lived.

But that's gone. He now remembers it as photographs, all broken up, and it's hard to tell what order they come in or what happened in the spaces between them. He remembers in stills and frames now. He remembers in shards. He remembers in pieces, but even the pieces wouldn't any longer fit. It's all broken but now he isn't sure it was ever whole.

He has become English. That's how he writes home: he no longer needs to formulate it all in Dutch and then translate like he did just a few months ago. Now it all comes ... *naturally* (he's not sure that's the word he wants; oh, it's the right word all right, it's just that he doesn't *want* it) in English first. The only time he uses Dutch now is to scribble a few words at the end of his letters home for his sister, who is four years younger.

When they speak on the phone Sigrid tells him how she can't wait to come to boarding school in England. He tells them how great it is, how happy he is, what *characters* the teachers are. It's what parents want to hear, so that is what he says. His voice in the phone is always so loud and round, theirs always so faint, it's like they're draining away. The little perforations in the Bakelite shell of the receiver over the earpiece look like a plughole. The click as their phone goes down sounds wet, like someone swallowing, like Morbender's mouth when it opens and his lips unstick. Goodbye, he says, *Vaarwel*, and that's it for another month.

The thread that holds him to them is thinning all the time. It isn't just adolescence and distance. That's just what parents tell themselves. When he goes home — *heim* as it used to be — he's like an automatic child, a machine-boy, doing and saying all the things he used to do and say. The automatic child eats all the same food and watches all the same shows as the other one, so no one can tell that Ander has been replaced. Anyway, after what happens in school they probably wouldn't want him back.

Even his eyes, if anyone bothered to look there, have a painted-on quality. If the eyes are windows into the soul, as he has read, then his are bricked-up windows with windows painted onto them.

*

'I know you,' Mr Wolphram says again. There's something about the way he stands. He looks big, leans forward, puts both hands on the desk so only the fingertips touch the table top, and stares me out until I blink and look away. Gary is at my shoulder, and in my peripheral vision there hulks the big pink blur of his face.

'Do you?' I ask. As repartee, it's not top-of-the-range, but I'm still avoiding Gary's look, and if I don't ask my questions others will ask me theirs.

'I haven't yet recalled your name, but, yes — yes I do.' He seems to be growing as he speaks — it's like someone is pumping air into him. 'I can place you, and I can more or less date you. French? Dutch? German? Mid-eighties.'

Gary interjects: 'We're not discussing fucking vintages ...' then, to me: 'Can we have a minute outside, please?'

Mr Wolphram says, softly: 'But there were always two of you, weren't there?'

I am about to answer. My mouth is already open.

'Prof! Outside!' Gary yanks me by the elbow and drags me out.

Mr Wolphram adds, watching me go: 'Well, not always. Not at the end.'

'What the fuck?' asks Gary when we're outside, and it's a good question, maybe the best yet. Nonetheless, I'd rather not be answering it.

I'd have liked to get just a little further, one more trip to his flat, a few more pieces of evidence (evidence of what?), a little more momentum.

But I have run out of time, so I tell him all there is, that Ander was me, that Ander still is me, though when I talk about me then I think of me as him. I tell myself to myself as *he* not *I*. I change pronouns when I change periods inside myself.

'I was there, Gary, at that school. He taught me. I knew him from age thirteen or so 'til I left.' Gary is shaking his head. 'It's nearly thirty years ago,' I add. I do the sums – I haven't until now, despite all the thinking and past-foraging I've done, actually calculated the time that has elapsed since I last sat in a classroom with Mr Wolphram. I subtract eighteen from forty-seven. 'Twenty-nine years since I left.'

'And when were you going to tell me? Or maybe you weren't?'

'I was, Gary, I just didn't want to cloud things up. It was years ago, and if I was one of the thousands of kids he's taught, so what? It doesn't make any difference to what's happening now.'

'It's all fucking cloudy, Prof: *you're* cloudy. You talk to yourself, mumble bits of poetry at your desk, stare out the window at fatbergs and spend your evenings with an old kook who's convinced her dead husband is coming back. The only thing you do that might be normal and healthy is spend time with your niece, and you spoil that by playing her old kettle whistles and vacuum cleaner noises.'

He turns around, looking for something to kick, and chooses the skirting board, leaving a smear of rubbery police-shoe sole-grease. He's done it before, because there's a row of scuff marks all down the corridor.

'All true, Gary, all true. I didn't want to say anything because it was irrelevant—'

'It's not irrelevant, Prof, you know that – if you're connected to him you needed to say straight away. Instead you sat there with your vague detective face, listening to him talk about toys he didn't play with while you listened like some fucking ...' Gary stops, he's got it: 'like some fucking schoolboy.'

'It's how he talked in class, Gary, it was exactly like that: precise, word-perfect – sentences full of commas but always grammatical. He never lost his thread. He'd lay the sentence up ahead like rails and then run the words down the tracks like long exotic trains.'

Gary puts the back of his hand against his forehead and fake-swoons.

'Oh, the fucking poetry of it ... Great, so he's a master of the English language and the normal rules don't apply? He's a suspect, Prof. Murder. You know? That thing where someone gets someone else and makes them die? It's generally frowned upon, even when poets do it. And who knows what else is in there in that flat? You've been in there fiddling about, moving stuff around. And you deliberately kept back your own connection. What if what we found is ruled inadmissible because of you?'

'It's not a connection, Gary, is it? He taught me thirty years ago – that's basically a lifetime. I haven't seen him since; he hasn't seen me. He didn't recognise me, even. Until now. I'm perfectly capable of separating that from the investigation.'

This last bit is not true, but it is what one is supposed to say. I've seen it on TV.

'He recognised you just now,' says Gary. 'That's a bit odd, isn't it? I mean, he's seen you for hours, sat in the same room being asked questions, and he only recognises you now.' Gary looks at me and tilts his head, trying to see what has happened to my face, my manner, my bearing.

'That's the way it works, Gary. Recognition's not always a flash, it's more of a slow dawning—'

'I don't give a shit about your theory of recognition, Prof. Fact is, when you were in his flat, I thought you were investigating a crime. Actually, you were having a little nostalgic trip back to your schooldays. All that's missing is your stupid little uniform ...'

'Depends what you mean by nostalgic, Gary, but, yes. I'd been down that street, across that gravel, up those stairs and in that flat before, and that was me in those photographs.'

'Jesus. You'd probably been in that fucking bedroom, too, knowing what happens in those schools.'

'No, Gary, there wasn't any of that stuff with him. Not even a suggestion of it. And, anyway, when any of *that stuff* happened, it wasn't their bedrooms they used.'

There's a pause. Gary changes tack.

'You know how I feel sometimes, Prof?'

'No, Gary, I don't.'

'I feel like the whole country is vomiting back the seventies and eighties and we're the ones cleaning it up. It splatters at our feet, day in day out, and it's us wiping it up.'

'You've been following too much fatberg news ...'

'No! No, stay with me on this, Poetry Boy: the whole country sat there for twenty years, gobbling it all down, and it tasted good: the music, the showbiz, the politics ...

tasted great, sounded cool, looked fantastic. Punk, Mods, Glam, New Romantics ... boys with make-up, girls with crew cuts, *Top of the Pops, Swap Shop, Blue Peter*... okay, so there was a bit of naughty stuff, but what d'you expect? It's all uncharted territory, we're all groping our way round ...'

Gary looks puzzled when I laugh at the *groping* because for once he doesn't intend the pun. The punner unpunned. Then he gets it.

'Yeah, okay, *ha ha*, Prof. What I'm saying is this: then it turns out your teachers were paedos, your DJs and presenters and football coaches were predators, your social workers were vultures, schools and hospitals were pervert safaris, your child protection services pimped out their charges, your police weren't any better and your politicians either doing it themselves or turning blind eyes to it.'

I don't correct him. Exaggeration is a language like any other, and Gary is fluent in it. Also, he isn't finished:

'Now that it's all coming back up, rancid and nasty and burning our throats as we retch it out, we're all pretending we didn't know about it. And now look at us, Prof – you and me: we're doing a fucking colonoscopy of the whole country, we're the tiny little camera burrowing through the shit trying to see what's still caught in there, clogging up the system ...'

Gary is no literary man, it's true, but he knows where to find his metaphors. 'Why don't you start a poetry workshop for coppers, Gary? I'll see you there.'

Gary stomps off to have a word with Unmanned, or Ironside, or Deskfish ... whatever he's calling him today. He'll be asking him whether it's okay for me to stay on the case, to remain involved with the investigation. I can see them both behind the glass with their jerky, exaggerated film gestures. Finger-jabbing, phone-slamming, bin-kicking.

Mr Wolphram looks calm. Serene, even. Maybe recognising me has given him something to orientate himself by. He even looks strong. He still hasn't picked up the newspapers Gary left there. He knows he's meant to, so he doesn't.

We called him The Wolf ... says one of the 'ex-pupils' Lynne Forester has dredged up. I think back. Is that true? I don't recall anyone calling him that. But now they are. *The Wolf of Chapelton.* Just look at the verbs Mad Lynne has lined up: he *prowls*, he *stares*, he *snarls*. Silver hair like fur in the moonlight. They are saying he is *vain, unnaturally neat and tidy, strangely formal, expensively dressed, obsessively groomed.* They're calling his flat *The Lair* and publishing pictures of it against darkening skies. What can you expect with a name like Wolphram? We should have seen it coming. Now, suddenly, little oddments of rumours and stories attach to him, get snagged in his reputation until they become his reputation.

The Wolf: they've turned him into a predator, a sexual scavenger with night-flashing eyes.

No one ever called him *The Wolf.*

We let Wolphram stew, sweat, broil, simmer, caramelise in the interview room with the tabloids and the *Evening Post* while we all decide what to do.

*

Sigrid is still at work, so I fetch Marieke from the 'Activity Club' she goes to in the mornings. She loves the police station, loves the glass walls, the endless screens, the litter of papers and the corridors of interview rooms. Usually, she sits and reads by the front desk, where we have left board games with missing pieces and toys with missing limbs or wheels. There's a Christmas tree with empty boxes wrapped as presents.

'What would you like to do?' I ask her. She is surprised to see me, because I wasn't supposed to fetch her today.

'Why are you here?'

'I'm not needed in work today. Maybe not tomorrow either,' I reply.

'What have you done?' What's the point in hiding things from her?

'I forgot to tell my chief that I knew the man we've caught who might have killed someone. I knew him a long time ago, when I was a child – he was my teacher – and they think it'll stop me doing my job properly.'

'It's because you still know him,' she says.

'Where shall we go?' I ask her.

'Mrs Snow's,' she replies, excitedly. As we drive, she asks, as she always does: 'You remember how we met her?'

Even though Marieke was there, she likes hearing the story. She loves the telling, and then she loves the retelling. She loves the sameness, and then she loves the variation on the sameness.

'How could I forget?'

As we drive, I tell her, and she chips in with details or corrects me when I exaggerate or misremember. I exaggerate and misremember deliberately because she likes it.

We met Vera shopping for basics.

We were passing a supermarket, Marieke and I, when I saw two police officers running – beat bobbies from my station whom I didn't know or couldn't remember. They overtook us and swerved inside.

We followed them in. I assumed the classic shoplifting scenario. I was expecting a ragged tracksuited waif pinned against a wall by a couple of guards or some local have-a-go-heroes, a sad haul of cans in his pockets. They nick the cheap stuff. It's only in films that thieves aim high, that they're allowed to dream. Still, you never know how these things pan out, where they finish up: you chase one shoplifter down the street, catch him, and he'll hand back what he stole with a sigh, or sometimes even a laugh; you chase another and he'll turn and stab you in the face. Some of them bite, because their mouth is all they have left to defend themselves: their spit, their germs, the threat of their saliva: hepatitis, TB, HIV. When you're sick or desperate or racked with disease or drugs, your mouth is your last weapon. I keep an eye on the hands, yes, but it's the mouth I watch.

There was a commotion at the tills. People were shouting, a few angry men, tabloid-faced and scarlet with headlines about migrants or scroungers or benefit cheats – randy for offence and glad to find it here, at the end of a supermarket conveyor belt, in the shape of an old lady unable to pay for her shopping.

'If you got no cash, don't go to the shops!'

'Ever heard of a food bank, you crazy old cow?'

'Should be in a home, you demented old biddy!'

Vera sat on a chair, her hands resting on the tartan shopper trolley she had brought with her. She was trying to be impassive, but you could tell she was toughing it out. She was all the tougher for not being immune to the abuse, as she sat there trembling and biting her lip, but not giving in to the tears or the urge to run away.

Each insult made Vera blink. Stacked up before her was her modest shopping. Bread, tea, some tins of meat, a short-sell reduced-price cut of roasting beef, and a few vegetables. A bottle of the supermarket's own-brand sherry and − a nod to luxury − a plump, top-of-the-range fruit cake. People hate the poor buying luxuries. If they're not eating out of bins and watching the wallpaper instead of TV, they're the underserving, ungrateful poor. So: no cake.

'What exactly is the problem?' asked the WPC, stooping to speak loudly and slowly, her mouth aimed at Vera's ear via an imagined ear trumpet.

Vera answered so everyone could hear: 'I can't pay for my shopping.'

'You've come to a shop but you can't pay for it?' asks the WPC.

'No − she can't bloody pay for them!' shouts someone from the back of the queue, 'and we're all waiting for her to bugger off so we can get on with our shopping.'

'She does this every week,' explains the girl at the till in the sari. She is kind but embarrassed, because this has happened on her shift. Again. 'Every time she comes we all dread being the ones at the till. She always takes out her purse and shows us it's empty and puts it down here. Like now.' She lifts up Vera's purse and opens it up. There's a bus pass and a library card but nothing else, not even small change, in its gusset. 'It's like an act,' she adds, 'but she isn't acting − she really doesn't have the money.'

'We've given her loads of chances but she keeps doing it,' the store manager appeals, 'this is the first time we've called the police ... it's just getting too much. Customers are complaining − look around − it wastes massive amounts of time ... and in the end *someone* gets charged for it. Customers, that's who.'

The WPC puts her hand on Vera's shoulder, as if she might make a run for it. The police constables are sweating embarrassment. It's hardly a high-octane action callout. But it is a *situation*.

'Why on earth do you go to a shop when you can't pay for what you're taking?' asks the WPC. It is the question we're all asking, because this old lady is no thief, no renegade, no shoplifting miscreant. Vera doesn't answer immediately, but instead looks around her. When she feels people are listening she replies:

'I just don't have the money. I'm a widow and I'm on a state pension. I've used it all to pay for the central heating and the rent and there isn't enough left in my account to buy food ...'

'Surely there are places you can get assistance ...' the WPC tells her.

She means food banks and charities, but doesn't want to say the words *food banks* and *charities*. Everyone is listening now. The shop is quiet. This is like street theatre, and for a moment I think maybe that's just what it is, that someone is recording it for TV or some psychological experiment ... Some people saw the police and started to film it on their phones, but they've stopped bothering now that there's no violence in prospect.

'There are places, yes, but I'm afraid that isn't the point, is it?'

'Oh yeah? Then what is the point?' asks someone at the back − a young man behind me, loudly enough to be heard across the shop. If this were a TV show, he'd be in on it, because he has fed Vera her big line.

She rises on tiptoe and speaks to the crowd: 'The point is that if people like me don't keep going to the shops, people like you will forget that we exist.'

Everyone is silent. The WPC has let go of Vera's shoulder.

'That's why I'm here — to remind you that we exist even if we don't have money to buy things. We are not going to stay indoors or in shelters and soup kitchens and get forgotten. We're not going to hide so you don't have to see us.'

Now Vera falters, because she hasn't planned to say anything beyond this, but she has called such attention to her that people expect more.

But the faltering makes her words even more effective. The new rhetoric is to have no rhetoric, to run dry of words in exactly the place you are expected to soar away with them.

Vera sits down. She has finished.

I may be old, poor and alone, she means, *and my wants may have been winnowed until they are aligned with the most basic of my needs, but I won't disappear between the cracks, hide in my house or go to food banks just so you don't have to look at me. There are thousands of us, hundreds of thousands, and we're not rats and we're not going underground.*

Marieke recorded it all, but likes to hear it again. That way, the story breathes differently around its facts. I told the constables I'd deal with Vera, take her home, sort out any legal comeback from her supermarket sweep.

Now look at us: in her house sharing tea and biscuits with her, Joey the budgie and Victor's ghost. It was a coincidence that I happened to be walking past that supermarket at that time and on that day. I say *coincidence*, but coincidence is just a word we give to the contraction of the world around us, the tightening circles of its happenings.

I met Vera because — plainly — I was meant to.

As I made small talk with Vera that first day, Marieke wandered through the rooms recording, trying to see if Victor was there. She hoped to catch one or two of his breaths maybe, a few oddments of words he'd left behind. She concluded that he was 'mostly in the living room'. Vera agreed.

Now I'm a regular visitor, and Marieke often joins me, though Sigrid disapproves and Gary says it's crazy. But why not? Marieke likes biscuits and she likes hauntings.

So here we are now, the three of us, and something that is no longer quite an absence.

Marieke has disappeared upstairs to take a few soundings from the rooms to see if Victor has 'spread out'. She tells Vera that she can hear 'the back of his voice'. Vera is pleased. 'Me, too,' she says.

But today she wants to help me with the case.

'This sounds rather cynical of me, Inspector, I hope you don't mind,' she begins falteringly, 'but if your schoolteacher turns out to be the sort of man who does things to young boys like they're implying, then the chances are he's not the sort of man who does things to grown women.' She looks across to her husband's armchair for assent, and she must get it because she goes on, more confidently now, 'but what do I know? Anyone can do anything in the right circumstances – isn't that what they teach you at police college or whatever it's called?'

'I didn't need police college to teach me that, Mrs Snow, but, yes, I know what you mean.'

She is right, mostly: sexual behaviour is usually about specialism, but violence is the great all-rounder. But I didn't come here to discuss Wolphram and Zalie with her, so I shift the topic: 'Is there anything I can do for you while I'm here?' I have taken to doing odd jobs like unclogging the conservatory guttering and changing fuses – the sort of thing Victor used to do and which he can do again once he's … what? Recovered? A little less dead?

I've stopped trying to challenge her reality; it's easier to give in, and where necessary to share it with her. Anyway, I can't pretend I'm not fascinated by it.

'Thank you, you're very kind. But we're fine, aren't we?' She looks across at the armchair, then smiles at me.

We finish our tea in silence. Mr Snow's tea stays there untouched, cooling on the side table by the Tru-Flame wall-mounted fire. Beside it is his last crossword. The last biro line in the top left row of boxes is longer than I remember it and maybe − or maybe I'm willing myself to see it − is beginning to resemble the start of a word, the spine of a letter: L? P? Capital E? The rest of the crossword, the section with the clues, has been cut off. There are words starting to show, not yet legible but feeling their way through from the other side of the paper. It is like cloudy water in which you can make out shapes under the surface, but can't tell whether it's the shapes clouding the water with their turbulence, or the turbulence making you think there are shapes.

As for the words that are there, I try to read them for meaning but can't. We always think the other side has something big to say, though there's no reason to. It's not up to the dead to be meaningful. If anything, it must be a relief for them not to have to be. Still, I scrutinise the letters, and find them bland and impermeable as the lino on Vera's kitchen floor: 'Ticket', 'Bristle', 'Des-Res'.

She is willing him back, prising open the tiniest crack in the darkness to let him through.

I think he's returning, little by little.

Or that he's dead, that she's gone mad, and that I've joined her there.

European Cinema

One afternoon Mr Wolphram decides to spend the double English class on a film. It's a long Scandinavian film about a brother and a sister whose father dies and whose mother marries a grim-faced, authoritarian clergyman. That's about all the boys understand, and there are subtitles which put them off even more. To start with. Mr Wolphram tells them, chillingly, that it lasts for five hours ('three hundred and twelve minutes' is how he puts it), and he slides the first cassette into the video player he has wheeled in, half-hearse, half-cinema, from the staff common room.

The boys at the back are whistling and smacking each other around the head. They can't decide whether no work and ninety minutes in the dark, ninety minutes of farting and squirting and bas-reliefing dicks into the desks, is better than having a class where there's at least a break, and the lights are on, and you know where you stand: in the midst of a familiar boredom. They're easily bored, but more to the point they never expect to be interested. The best they can hope for when they get up in the morning and go to school is a change of boredom, a selection of different varieties of the stuff: science-boredom, test-tube-boredom, word-boredom, numbers-boredom, Jesus-boredom, toga-and-senate-boredom, Kings-and Queens-boredom. That's the curriculum, so a film, a Scando film, too, where there might be tits and some humping, is promising.

The film, to begin with, is not. Even without knowing it lasts five hours, you can feel it giving off the five-hour-film vibe. Every moment is doubled, tripled, seen from every angle. It is as if an expanding Time-foam had been injected into every join of the camerawork, the story, the action, the words. It is a poor start to Mr Wolphram's European cinema afternoon, and no one knows why he chose it. The boys are fighting in the back, a few go out to the toilet and stay for too long; a couple of them might cram in a wank. Some of them giggle and laugh and throw stuff around. Mr Wolphram has gone out. He probably can't face watching a film he loves mocked. But, then, why did he show it? Even Ander and Danny, who feel that they and boys like them have a responsibility to appreciate it and set an example, find it hard.

There are good students among them: Dave Sweeting at the front, who does everything well but indistinguishably, without preference. There's Neil Hall, a kind of semi-Goth who pierced his own ear with a compass using a deodorant anaesthetic, so that for three months now his ear has had a crust of burgundy-coloured blood crystals green-streaked with pus around the septic hole. Gwil Isaac, who likes film and has film posters all over the small part of wall that is his in the dormitory. Rich Nicholson, the class poet. Even they are restless. 'So far, just one arse – a bloke's – and no tits,' someone says from the back. There is a scene, some way in, where a man farts out three candles through his elaborate underwear, those slightly stained, grey-washed long johns they wear in films and in cold countries from the past.

Then, quietly, like a takeover, a slow, rippling coup, they stop talking, start watching, frown to catch the subtitles, even try to hear the language without them. Ander and Danny notice it first: they're paying attention, but so is everyone else. The film's slowness is punctuated by something else, something hard and dark, sharp pieces of joy and sharp pieces of misery. The helplessness of the children when their father dies, stuck in the cold God-filled yet empty world their stepfather makes around himself, is something desperate and compelling. What really catches Ander about the film is the echoes: the place is so big, the floors wooden, the walls reverberating. The world has been arranged to make you feel tiny. Like here, Ander thinks, like all around me. The echoes in the film are like the echoes in the school, too. They make you feel abandoned, and yet watched; listened to; unable to move without dislodging both your own noise and its echoey ghost.

Mr Wolphram comes in at the end of the double session and presses 'Pause'. The tape whirrs to a held stop. He tells them that anyone who wishes to can come in the next afternoon, Saturday, and watch the rest – that he'll be here and put it on for them.

Saturdays are precious. It's free time, going-into-town time, buying-booze-from-the-newsagents-far-from-school time. The idea that anyone would willingly give up their afternoon in the city to come and watch this Scandinavian time-glacier melt across a screen for another three and a half hours is crazy. And in a classroom, too. 'Yeah, right – see you there,' says Jonny Kebab uneasily. No one endorses his comment; they just leave lingeringly, stickily, hovering by the video machine, by Mr Wolphram who stands there watching them, nodding them out one by one. 'Yeah, right!' Jonny repeats, looking for assent and not getting it.

And yet, the next day, there they are: not just Ander and Danny, Neil, Rich and Sweeting, a few of the others from the middle rows, but a good number of the boys who only yesterday had been farting and laughing and dismissing the whole thing as a long, tedious joke. They file in, quietly, a little ashamed at being, for once, studious and engaged. Some have brought sweets or crisps. Even Jonny Kebab is there, with a pint of sherry disguised in an orange juice carton. He has plastic cups with him, too, so he can sell his booze like a cinema usher. Mr Wolphram comes in and if he is surprised to see so many of them he doesn't show it. Out of a class of eighteen, thirteen are there, for a Scandinavian film with subtitles that they don't even have to watch, that has nothing to do with their English classes, let alone any exams, and that will swallow their Saturday afternoon.

But they have come, and now they stay. Ander sees it getting dark outside, the afternoon ebbing, but he doesn't care. None of them care. They're engrossed, they half understand, they're drawn to the cold ice of rebellion in the boy, who is scolded and beaten and locked up but stays defiant and sweats revolt. He sees through the adults, sees through their God, sees through the palace of cold glass the adults have built inside themselves to honour Him.

When Ander hears the boy, Alexander Ekdahl, say, 'If there's a God he's a shit and piss god and I'd like to kick him in the arse', he feels weak with excitement. Light.

It's like he's evaporating.

A Broken *Herat*

The forensic reports come back and tell us everything we knew, only more of it. It's facts, but not facts that will help us: she had been in Mr Wolphram's car, he has been in her hallway. She *had*, he *has*. It's hair, mostly, the odd print; no skin, no blood, no signs of violence or sex. Her hair and some scalp grease on the wall of her hallway consistent with her being pushed up against it. There are other traces in both places, other people, but we don't know whose. We've catalogued them while we wait for matches. Gary wants to test everyone on the street, but Deskfish says *why bother?* We have our man, don't we?

She was hit once, very hard, in the throat, and again at the temple where presumably she turned away. Then she was strangled. So far as we can tell, the strangling took place in one action, one consistent pressure, uninterrupted by her fighting back or the murderer's own hesitation. Most stranglings have the reprise marks, where the killer loses his grip (always *his* – despite the new seminar on gender-neutral language in report writing), and starts again somewhere different, a little higher or lower up, invisible to him but clear to pathologists, who can see the fatal pressure line and then one or two above or below it.

You learn a lot about time by studying bruising. Bruising is a study in time, in how the flesh remembers.

There's not much you can tell from Zalie's results, except that the murderer was strong, and that, however hard she fought back, his grip didn't fluctuate and he didn't hesitate or change position. It wasn't quick either. Also, the pressure has been applied downwards, not upwards or level; this means he was taller than her.

Mr Wolphram is taller, but is he tall enough? We have measured his hands, too. He asked why, but he knew why.

We've been told to concentrate on Mr Wolphram, so there's no urgency about the neighbours. We'll get to them eventually, but Deskfish has ordered us to focus on Mr Wolphram as *prime* suspect and on any possible witnesses to corroborate. The door-to-dooring has thinned out, and the CCTV footage that's coming in is mostly useless. Later, we will have the family and her boyfriend in for a televised appeal. There will also be a police reconstruction of Zalie's last known movements – her walk back from the pub, via the supermarket, and back to her flat. I hope I am taken off the case for long enough to miss those, but no longer. They will replay her last hours: the walk across the bridge to the Harcourt Arms where she had two drinks with her friends, her walk back, her stop in the supermarket to buy the 'Dine in for Two Meal' she never opened and which sat in the bag she left on the dining table, and is now being checked for prints in the lab.

They've found a WPC from a neighbouring force who matches her in size and build, and they've been out to buy the nearest clothes they could find to what she wore that night: grey bobble hat with a fake-fur pompom, green knee-length coat, jeans and white trainers.

Her computer records are in. They are more interesting than Mr Wolphram's. They show three searches for 'Stalking' and one for 'Peeping Tom'. She spent only a few minutes on each site, and she didn't click very widely around them: one is the police site which gives generic information about online safety, caller ID and blocking, and a local women's safety group; the other is the national helpline website. The last search was on 29 November, three weeks before she died. It looks like what we call a 'curiosity search' rather than a 'help search'. Still, I'll follow it up. The CCTV at both ends of the bridge and briefly outside the supermarket are all we have. We see her walking fast, unfollowed, over the bridge and then back, in and out of the shop. Apart from that, it's all just the residences, neighbourhood watch stickers, the high-end cars and the off-street parking of well-heeled suburbia.

I have taken the walk myself, remade her steps, as if the streets, the pavements, the air itself, might contain traces of what happened. When we 'retrace', as the saying goes, her steps, we think we may rewind them, too, and find the moment when, by a different turn, a different street, a different December darkness, she might still be here, doing what she should have been doing: phoning her parents, readying herself for her boyfriend's return, getting the Christmas food in. Setting up her 'Out of Office' email. On Castle Street, halfway between the bridge and her flat, there is some new graffiti. It's opposite the shop where she bought her last uneaten, unopened meal, and the CCTV is clear on that at least: she walks past number 44, with its tall stone wall and long garden leading to a three-storey Georgian house, two 4×4s parked on the gravel. As she walks those ten or so recorded yards, the wall is bare. But by the next morning, so the CCTV tells us, it has been graffiti'd with huge letters: **SALLY YOU BROKE MY HERAT**. We don't know exactly when – the CCTV goes off between midnight and 6 a.m. – but at 11 p.m. it is not there, and by 6 a.m. it is.

'Must have been in a right state,' says Gary, 'so upset he can't even spell. Bet he didn't go to your school, Prof.'

'Grief is like that, Gary,' I tell him, 'it makes a jumble of our words right there where we feel them.'

'No shit, Prof—' he replies sarcastically, 'I'm just a yob who's a stranger to emotions.'

Later we will have to visit number 44 Castle Street and speak to Sally, breaker of *herat*s, because if her jilted boyfriend was in the area spray-canning his muddled grief, he may have seen something.

I drive back to the house where Zalie lived, this time to look outside and not in.

Danny and Ander

Because they're in the top set for English they have Mr
Wolphram on his home territory. Some teachers, the
senior ones, don't change classrooms. Their classrooms
are their HQ, as personal as their bedrooms — maybe
more personal in the case of people like Morbender and
the Doc. They put up their own decorations and posters
and the rooms have their own auras. Mr Wolphram
has cinema posters: *Quadrophenia, Blow-Up, Last Year
in Marienbad* and that one Ander can't remember the
name of where death plays chess with a knight. There
are poster-poems and portraits of writers, and posters
from art exhibitions in foreign galleries and concerts.
There's a framed poster advertising The Who playing at
Knebworth. It's signed, but so approximately there's no
way of telling who by.

There's a painting, by Caravaggio, of the beheading of
John the Baptist. Ander keeps looking at it, at the limbs of
both beheader and beheaded in the balmy spotlight of the
picture's centre, as the darkness in the background slowly
gives up its detail: the distempered wall and the barred
window where two prisoners watch the scene. Another

thing he notices: the dying man has his left arm pushed up at an angle, the elbow pointing up; the man killing has his right arm up at the same angle, the elbow held in the same way. There is blood on the flagstones, but less than you'd think, and the executioner's arm is tensed to hold down the Baptist's head, which is already severed. Or is he picking it up, now that the job is done? Wolphram told them that, when the painting was restored, Caravaggio's signature was found written in the blood. They can't see that from the poster, but it's exciting to think that even a four-hundred-year-old painting is still alive enough to change. The sword lies on the ground, its tip catching some of the painting's sparse light. It's silver, while the rest of the light – on the skin, the faces, the dish which a bending woman holds out for the head – is all variations of gold. What is the detail Ander most thinks about? It is the horrified woman looking on, holding her head with both hands, as if it might fall, or to check, thinks Ander, that it's still attached, still where it should be and not on the floor or in a golden bowl. Ander has read somewhere that the head is heavy, much heavier than you'd expect, given that it's mostly mush and a bit of bone to give it shape, to hold it all in. The skull is really just a dreamcatcher made of bone.

Why's it heavy? He knows the head is heavy from all the time he spends looking over the balustrade of the bridge. The pull of it. It's ridiculous, he knows, and totally unscientific, but he thinks it's just because it's where everything we call ourselves happens and where most of it stays. Everything has its own weight, its own heft, thinks Ander, and the head is the heaviest because it's where we keep everything, and everything must weigh something.

Mr Wolphram's room is like the inside of someone's head. Not just *someone*, but a particular person. Ander imagines that the inside of Wolphram's head is like this classroom: stuff stored in draws and cabinets, messy in some parts, tidy in others, some things getting used all the time, others packed away and forgotten about but always there – quietly and always still there. And just because there's stuff in the bin, that doesn't mean it isn't there.

Mr Wolphram is the only teacher whose shelves contain books that aren't on the syllabus, and he lends them to boys if they sign them out of his little blue ledger. Ander hasn't borrowed any yet and is disappointed not to have been asked if he wants one. He's seen a few he likes the look of, the titles at any rate. *Vile Bodies* is one, what's not to like there? *Troubles* is another. He has his eye on *Corruption and Other Stories*, too. But he hasn't dug for the courage to ask for them. The thought that there might be some sex, just a little, even if it is wrapped up in long words, aerates his mind and arouses his body. *Mens sana* and all that, but in reverse – that's what he hopes. Danny has already borrowed three books, because Danny asks and, anyway, Danny is good at English, the best of any of them, and has a confidence the others don't.

A few of the teachers are kind, in a distracted, erratic way. One or two are focused and professional, but they are the ones who don't stay on beyond school hours. They have lives of their own, children and wives or husbands, and homes that are not flats or bedsits in the school grounds. Chapelton's only two women teachers, Mrs Pizzi in Art and Mrs Mason in French, are treated like exotics by the boys, and like a different species by most of the male teachers. Ander notices the hormonal fizz they cause, not just among the adolescents but among their grown-up colleagues. The miasma of frustrated sex, innuendo and masturbatory sulking follows them around like a theme tune in a film. They have their arses looked at and sighed about, their cleavages investigated, their eyes avoided or held too long. The men raise their eyebrows conspiratorially at the boys when the women leave the room and make comments about their clothes and shoes. Sometimes they ask the boys outright what they think of their legs or tits, or what they might be like in bed, whether they *got any* last night. When the women are there they snigger at the universal in-joke of being male. The boys pick it all up, learn it all, until that mix of sexual threat and sexual fear fills up the classrooms where Mrs Pizzi and Mrs Mason have to teach. They must be tough, thinks Ander. He's glad they're tough, because he likes them and doesn't want them to be unhappy or humiliated. But then he thinks: why should they? Why *should* they be tough all the time?

Ander has a head start in French, so Mrs Mason likes him, and he can paint and draw, so Mrs Pizzi spends more time on his efforts – a still-life of a pineapple, a watercolour of a sunset he's never seen but thinks should definitely exist – than on other people's. Mrs Pizzi is a potter, and Ander enjoys the lessons when she shows them how to mould the clay and turn it on the wheel. He loves the way the clay can be anything you like until it dries, until it's fired. Then it stays and won't be bent or twisted, only broken. It reminds him of the estuary clay he gazes at from the bridge and wants to scoop up with his hands and sculpt.

But Mrs Mason and Mrs Pizzi are semi-detached from the school, and as they aren't form teachers they have no spaces which are theirs. Before the end of the day, they go off and pick up their own kids from school, and Ander notices neither of them sends her children here, to Chapelton. He's glad for them, being able to leave like that, but when he sees them with their children he's a little jealous. Mrs Mason's son, about whom she speaks but only in French, as part of the class not from personal confiding, is fifteen and in the local comprehensive, where he has a girlfriend and is getting ready for his O-levels. Ander would trade places with him, even with the O-levels. He'd sit through the exams just to have Mrs Mason to come back to in the afternoon. Since he can't imagine sex with her, he has so little to go on and his anatomical knowledge is piecemeal – he knows all the bits but can't place them together in ways that make sense – he imagines instead what her house must be like. That already feels too intimate, too intrusive. He's a burglar with his mind but he just wants to look. Maybe to touch if he can. He thinks he's the only one to do this, to piece the world together from scraps of knowledge, overheard things, fragments of the glimpsed, a body that doesn't obey the mind and a mind that doesn't want the body to obey it anyway.

One day, after French, when no one is looking, he runs his mouth around the rim of the cup she drank her tea from; another time, he put his cheek to the seat of her chair, still warm from her. He doesn't know if it is scraps of motherhood he's after or scraps of sex.

One or two of the teachers are in more pain than the boys. More shy, more delicate, certainly more sensitive, a few of them last just a term or two and then disappear. Some are gone in one go, like Mr Willis, the pudgy, sad, gentle and extravagantly bald geography teacher: 'One big Nagasaki of the head', Danny called it. Ron Willis turned up one day with no shoes or shirt and smashed up the classroom, put his hand through the window and twisted it until the skin of his arm opened like an envelope, then cried at his desk until an ambulance stretchered him away.

Other teachers seem to wear away at the edges: they start to stoop, their voices get quieter, they let the insults go, the late work, the no-shows; they miss classes, the supply teacher comes in more often than they do, and then suddenly their names on the noticeboard or mentioned in assembly are the most solid things about them.

They like the young English teacher Mr Lawnder, but he is too delicate for teaching. He is gentle and distracted, his voice is soft and he hesitates, takes time to think before he answers their questions. Most of them have never seen that before and take it as weakness. Lawnder gives off a faint woundedness. He has a way of looking at the ground when what he loves isn't appreciated that ignites your pity and makes you want to take him somewhere safe. He is freshly out of university and he seems always absorbed in his imaginary life, the life beside this one where he is an acclaimed poet among sensitive readers. He lasted two terms, but they were good terms, and some of the boys, Ander and Danny among them, miss him still. He was less strict that Mr Wolphram, and there was more scope for wandering off the syllabus. But Mr Wolphram liked him, and the two teachers got on well and shared the group harmoniously. Sometimes they arranged trips to the cinema for Mr Wolphram's Culture Club, or a visit to the National Gallery in London. You saw them chatting in the corridor sometimes, laughing at some learnèd jokes or literary puns, or enthusing about books and recommending things to each other. Mr Wolphram once called Mr Lawnder *free range*, like he was a chicken or a pig or something, in front of the class, and Mr Lawnder beamed because he knew it was a compliment. But he didn't have Mr Wolphram's steel, Wolphram's ability to be in the school but not, somehow, *of* it. The poems he read affected him – he blushed or went pale as he read, shook and sometimes wiped tears from the sides of his eyes. He wasn't like Wolphram, who was so forensic it was like he was operating on the poem; with Lawnder it was as if the poem was part of him. He flinched when you said something stupid or thuggish. Wolphram just ignored you, let your stupidity hang in the air and accuse you.

Lawnder takes the boys on tours of the zoo. He knows the architecture by heart, all the materials, the specifications, the time the various buildings took to erect. He is so innocent he actually uses *erect* and looks puzzled when the teenagers snigger. He loves the zoo, is always taking photographs of it. He thinks the animals spoil it by shitting everywhere and leaving bones and feathers and moultings lying around. 'Probably thinks people spoil houses by living in them too,' says McCloud, and he's probably right. Lawnder hates to see the wheelbarrows full of dung and the art deco bins overflowing with crisp packets and soggy wrappers and chip-paper.

Mr Lawnder involved the boys in discussions and asked them their opinions and let them speak. Most boys didn't like this because they thought *his job* was to *tell them stuff, not ask them.* So Mr Lawnder's classes are often rowdy and mutinous, and there are rumours of complaints about him for lacking discipline, or any of those words Ander has learned to suspect and fear: *authority, leadership, respect. Shit words*, he thinks, in English, because now he has started to think in English, it's easier, he doesn't have to translate himself as he speaks, *bastards' words*. He's the one who's been translated now.

One day Mr Lawnder was visited by Doc Monk and hauled out of the classroom for *a chat* because the class had become unruly and could be heard two corridors away, in the headmaster's office. The Doc took over the rest of the double lesson: eighty minutes of dictation from a coursebook with covers the colour of gravy.

Lawnder didn't last. His real passion was gardening. One day the summer term arrived and he didn't. They still see him sometimes working in the city parks, where he rolls cigarettes and rakes dreamily among the flowerbeds. Ander tried to talk to him once, in the public gardens by the bridge. Mr Lawnder was cleaning graffiti off the buttress wall, where it had seeped into the porous stone. *Starve Irish Scum.* Someone seems to refresh it every month or so: each time it's a more vibrant colour, a louder red, a deadlier black. Lawnder didn't recognise him. Ander tried to jog his memory with a few episodes from school life, talked about one of the books Mr Lawnder taught them, but it was like trying to remind someone of a dream they'd long ago forgotten.

Mr Lawnder, Mr Willis: both of them breaking, but differently: one exploding, scattering pieces of himself all over his life, the other imploding so quietly, remaining so firm of outline that you only knew it when you got up close and saw the empty-house eyes, the vacated premises he had become. Two ways to go, thought Ander for years afterwards — thinks Ander still — now that he's seen dozens of people go one of those two ways: the centripetal or the centrifugal breakdown.

Parktown Again

I look at Zalie's flat, a basement bay window in the front, and a bedroom at the back with a window onto the garden. These are the only places from which she could be watched, as the bathroom window is painted shut and frosted with a pattern of ferns. The sash windows of her living room are 'sited', as estate agents say, facing west, so on a low dark winter afternoon, if there is sun, it comes in gravel-scrapingly low, splashes the room and blinds you as you stand there looking out. But then it goes almost as quickly, and you're in the dark again even as the people upstairs are still watching it sprawl across their walls. To peer into Zalie's you'd have to come in off the street, crossing the front garden for about twenty yards, in full view of the neighbours. At the back, you'd have to sidle through an open wooden door, past bins and bicycles and onto a lawn. You'd also be walking over a crunchy gravel path. Easily heard, even with the windows winter-shut because they aren't double-glazed. They're big, too, thin sheets of glass in wooden sash frames and probably listed. We've taken samples of the gravel: it's called Cotswold Shingle (Small-Screen had it tested) and there are pieces all over the flats, in the grips of shoes and the carpets of cars.

There are no other ways of Peeping-Tomming her without a telescope or binoculars, but they're out of the question because there are two playing fields opposite the building, and the houses on the other side of them are too far away. Unless the distance, the strange, muffled, approximate nature of the peeping was what you liked; unless the graininess was not a barrier to the pleasure but on the contrary part of what got you going. I'll check it out, mindful of Gary's motto: 'It takes all kinds, especially with perverts.' The peeper is one species, the stalker is another, and the killer is another still. But they are species who regularly interbreed.

Zalie mostly looked at the first pages of the help-sites. She rarely clicked on the sub-pages or the links. Maybe a thought occurred to her, and she checked it out. Maybe she was curious, or doing it for someone else. Maybe she thought she was being watched, then just changed her mind. Maybe she *was* being watched, suspected it, then thought better of her suspicions. She wouldn't be the first to talk herself out of knowing what she knew.

There was — there is, there ongoingly *is* — an internet dating profile created eighteen months ago. It is dormant — no updates, chats, and even when she was on the site she didn't reply to any contacts. She must have given up, or found someone and let it drop. She looks at messages but doesn't answer them. That tallies, more or less, with when she met her boyfriend, Tim. We'll ask him. Does he know she was on a dating site for a while? Is it how they met? No, and anyway it's irrelevant, as I discover as soon as I've asked the question: she had no contact with anyone on the site, and must have thought better of it, or not liked what she saw. Her profile is skeletal; she's a vegetarian, likes jazz, reading, watching sport and travelling. *Drinks*: cider and white wine, G and T and cocktails, 'sometimes on the same night!!!' On screen she's a consensual character; her identity modular.

There's a profile photo which underplays her attractiveness, as if she didn't want it to be the main draw. Not that it stopped them. Her face is still there, fresh and happy, on the site: *ZD, 31, South East*. I'm interested that she doesn't actually say where, or name the city she lives in. She could be anywhere from the edge of London where the Tube trains start to the tip of the wet sand of Hastings; from Brighton to Margate or Southend. That suggests that she's unsure about internet dating, about being too easily located. *Likes*: box sets, sport, modern art, gardening. Music: Manic Street Preachers, Super Furry Animals, seventies disco. There is a chance to say a few words about yourself, a catchphrase or a strapline. Hers is 'You never know until you try – and I try!'

She has a hundred and eighty-three unanswered messages, and another two hundred-and-something unopened ones. I'll ask Small-Screen to go through them, spot anything odd or threatening. I want a list of everyone who has browsed her, who touched her information with their mouse or skimmed it with their eyes. He'll hate that. He wants a car chase and I've got him snorkelling through paperwork. But there are no dating dialogues. No one knew her, no, but her profile had been viewed over a thousand times, cyber-fondled, screen-groped, eyed up and trackpad-fingered, put on lists and bookmarked and favourited. There are hundreds of come-ons and messages, most of which she hasn't even opened. But Gary says that's normal. Women have hundreds of visits to their profiles, men a handful. Sometimes none. The most recent looks at her profile were last night: 'Bruce from Middlesbrough' and 'Medway Man'. There's a bloke describing himself as 'Husky, dusky and musky', which Gary says sounds like Snow White's three sex-offender dwarves.

There isn't much here about her, but there's enough for the men out there to get on with. The lonely mind can dream a whole life from skeletal information and a couple of photos. That is how the stalker works, too, because the stalker is a storyteller, a dramatist, a lover of detail, an amateur shrink, a detective, a plotter, a maker of plots and a violator of lives.

She's dead, but she lives here still: the messages ping in, the adverts are based on her search history and they throb in the top right of the screen, algorithmically produced and tailored to look tailored. There's a voucher for a tenner off a wine club purchase. There's an email from her phone provider about her direct debit payments. If you can buy something, you're still alive; if the money is still being syringed into utility bills, cable TV bundles, wi-fi, you're still with us.

You're not dead until your phone contract says so.

The undeletability of it all causes me the kind of fretful sadness that I can only explain by saying that I miss the finality of it all. Not that I ever knew finality. Finality would be a start. The world never had an OFF button, no, but you could at least turn it down sometimes. I am also worried that Lynne Forester will track down Zalie's screen-life and make something of it: dating profiles, shopping, tweets, Instagrams. Because Lynne, too, is a stalker, and she and the tabloids will play up the dating site element, the sniff of sexual availability, the imputation of a secret life. They've already found bikini shots of Zalie, holiday snaps of her with a drink, or dancing with a guy in Lanzarote. They put out a call for previous boyfriends to get in touch. 'Had a relationship with Zalie Dyer? Are you a friend from school or uni? We'd like to hear from you.' You can phone a special number. *In confidence.*

Going after Wolphram is one thing. Going after Zalie is another. It's chasing the dead into their darkness.

Vera hasn't even visited Victor's grave, let alone put flowers there. As for ordering a headstone, 'certainly not'. I asked her why. She replied that placing flowers was 'giving in', that they would 'load it down'. I didn't know what she meant. I do now. Ghosts are light, see-through creatures; we think they are made of memory and that they happen in our heads. So, in the world of things, the one outside of our heads, they need to be weighed down so they don't float away. Wreaths and flowers are their gravestone-ballast. They stop the dead from getting on with our lives.

What must Zalie's family be going through – already caught in the brutality of this, the fat messy fact of her murder, and then dealing with the virtual reality of it all, too, the spreading, fanned-out self that replicates on screens and databases? Maybe things were better when people only had one photograph of someone they loved on their wall or bedside table, a few letters or a handful of snaps in an album.

Zalie is all information and trace; she is something spilled and still spilling. Her online self is still there, still receiving info about bargains, potential lovers, profile matches and road-closure information. Two energy companies are competing for her heating, and the local MP has sent her his end-of-year newsletter. Her tweets bask in the ether. Occasionally, someone retweets one of her comments and fresh strangers rub against her, take her traces into their own worlds like saliva or hair, or the lipstick-rim on a pub glass that goes from drink to drink, kiss by kiss, mouth to mouth. Mouse to mouse.

Victor Snow had it simpler – at most, he would have had a bank account closed and a newspaper cancelled. The second milk bottle. A hearing aid thrown out. And, further down the line, a quiet ripple in someone else's life, he would be an address book entry deleted in a handful of homes. Address books beside phones – remember those? They even call them 'landlines' now, as if they were trees, sprung from the soil of suburban hallways. Who still has landlines, with those pigtail-coils of flex that used to catch in the fingers and loop itself into knots? Mr Wolphram does. Vera does. Victor did. I do. Gary? Maybe. But not Zalie. She was already mobile. Her flat had no landline. The cord was long cut. She probably didn't remember a time when phones were attached to anything, though they still come down to earth to feed at a charger for an hour or two, to refuel like planes before flying off again. For Zalie, it was all tweets and emails and passwords and PIN numbers. Not *was* – *is*: they're all still pulsing behind screens and along cables, bits of her, the phantom of her information-self roaming the algorithmic fields, searching for a mate, for a bargain, for news; for news of herself as the news spreads that she's dead.

Her Twitter account is still there, and hundreds of people have already DM'd her to tell her how sorry they are that she's dead. On her Facebook page, the condolences are mounting up. They're addressed to her, as if she were checking her social media on the other side. Is that what they think she's doing? *Write to me*, her icon winks, *text me, message me, Instagram me: where you are, I once was, where I am, there you will be.*

Have we checked Zalie's answerphone? I cannot any longer keep it in my head — what we've done, what we haven't, precautions taken, untaken. For all I know her voice is still embalmed there, receiving messages, receiving those phone calls people make when they know their friend has died but want to hear the line dead, too. There are people who do that — some who can't quite believe it and others who want to hear what not being there sounds like, who want to know if being dead makes a different kind of silence. Marieke has probably thought of that.

The desk sergeant has shown Vera into the room. I am surprised to see her. She looks about her, sits down at my desk which is fenced off by partitions, and finally tells me what she came to say.

It's not like her to leave her house. The thought occurs that things can't be going well with Victor, but, then again, since he's dead, we would be starting from a low base.

'How are things at home, Vera?'

'Cold,' she says, and looks like she's about to cry, 'cold and lonely. I haven't had *that feeling* for a few days now.'

That feeling, in Vera's parlance, is the feeling of Victor being nearby, there or on the verge of being there. You can't *be* until there's a place for you to do your being in. That's the first law of haunting: it's less about who than where. So she keeps the place warm and cosy. She is reserving his place, but he is late to his haunting.

'It's like he's changed his mind, Alexander, like he won't put in the effort anymore.'

I put the empty cup to my mouth so I don't have to look her in the eye. When I'm at her house, I almost believe the fiction of his presence; but outside it, it just feels like the ordinary, desolate madness of grief. She says: 'It's all gone ...' she looks down, 'it's all gone ...' she can't find the word, then finds it: '*slack*.'

Behind me, Gary is at the window. 'You'll have to put the *seance* on hold, Prof – I'm baffled, I'm completely dumbstruck,' he says, 'but they're keeping you on. Orders from Deskfish himself.'

*

The *Evening Post* afternoon edition carries a front page, with three pages of story. THE WEIRD MR WOLPHRAM is the headline. PUPILS COME FORWARD.

'Mad Lynne's excelled herself,' says Gary, dropping the paper on my desk. 'Three fucking pages of the stuff. She's worked fast – how she got them to come up with the goods I don't know.'

She has a by-line in the *Daily Mail*, as well as the *Evening Post*. Lynne is their person on the ground, their local guide, and her piece for them is a brief gallop through similar unsolved murders in the city over the last twenty years. 'Will police reopen cold cases in light of new evidence?' she asks, and details the cases, each time emphasising the distance between Mr Wolphram's street and the place where the bodies were found, or the victim was last seen. Lynne evokes crimes all over Kent and Sussex, on the peripheries of London, in Sevenoaks,

Tunbridge Wells, Ebbsfleet. She zeroes in on one in particular. *Unsolved sexual assaults in the early 2000s around Ashford Eurostar terminal near the Channel Tunnel opening in Cheriton led police to speculate that the perpetrator might be a cross-Channel commuter. Wolphram was a frequent visitor to Europe* ... writes Lynne: *Time to reopen the case?*

I remember the case, because I was one of the officers by whom those crimes were unsolved.

'What goods?' I ask. 'What goods has she *come up* with?' Gary doesn't answer, just nods at the paper and stuffs his hands into his pockets, waiting for me to take it in. *Pupils come forward*: she's clever. It's all in the words: 'come forward' suggests ... what? Fear, hidden outrage, shame, suffering-held-back, trauma and now the freedom to speak. It's part of the *lingo* now − now that we are, as Gary says, *puking up the decades.*

Come forward with what?

'He taught me for five years, Gary. There's nothing to come forward about, not that sort of stuff anyway.'

'Remember the fatberg, Prof, there's always something down there. Maybe you've just ... what ... repressed it?' He says it with a fat Gary-smirk.

The front page has a photograph of Mr Wolphram with his book bag, the white cuff of his sleeve against the black sleeve of his suit as he tries to pull his hat over his eyes. This is now his signature-image: a cadaverous, manicured *noir* villain snarling among the flashbulbs.

The television and internet are replaying the short film of Wolphram from which the image is taken, when he was still just a neighbour among neighbours, one of many vox pops, albeit the most distinctive. Other neighbours were interviewed, too: the young couple in the top flat, Ben Phelps and Chloe whose surname I can't remember, two dog-walking ladies from nearby streets, the couple three houses away, him a solicitor, her a manager at the pharmacy. Lynne has spoken to them all. Whether excited, gleeful, afraid or depressed, they are all in their different ways making the most of the situation. But not Wolphram – and he makes the mistake of talking a little too long, a little too word-perfectly, and a little *rehearsed*.

Towards the end of the segment, Mr Goodship walks into the frame with his terrier. I do the maths: three or four terriers ago he was headmaster and I was a child in his domain. He looks sour and jowly, with that lonely-retirement fastidiousness you see among people who can't live, in time or place, too far from where they worked. There's a subtle wind, so Goodship's combover occasionally lifts off its hinge of lacquer like the lid of a pedal bin. His double chin, once so full and bloated, sags like a bib made of tripe over his check shirt and woollen tie. The extent of his authority is now the length of a dog lead. He passes Mr Wolphram as he speaks, but keeps his head down as he goes. He must be in his eighties.

My contempt for him is like a fire I left on in a room I know I'll come back to. It doesn't matter whether it's in half an hour or in half a century, because, when it comes to him and people like him, I have my contempt on thermostat.

In the background, in front of Mr Wolphram's flat, is his car, now with forensics. It is like all of his belongings: expensive, old, looked after. A 1978 Jaguar which Gary tells me is a classic and maintained so well that, apart from the mileage, it may as well be new. Last used, we know, the day after Zalie disappeared. There are traces of

Zalie in the passenger seat, a few hairs on the headrest, prints on the door and dashboard, but nowhere else. Translated into investigationese, this means: not in the boot.

As I predicted, the fatberg is in the sidebar of the front page, looking squeezed in an indistinct and slightly elongated photo. 'Fatberg – Page 4.'

Gary: 'Yesterday's ooze.' He has tried out every available pun, but this has to be the last one in stock.

The first three pages are essentially a one-man show by Mr Wolphram. I scan the images first, try to track the tale they tell the eyes before the words do their work. Page 2 has a school photograph, a close-up of him in a gown and academic hood. He is younger and wears narrower glasses, and his hair is darker. There's no date, but I know the date, or at any rate the year and the season. The larger shot it's taken from, a panorama of the whole school, is against a blue sky on a cricket field, 'College Green', opposite the school chapel and the library.

I can date the picture because I am there, my blanked-out face, three rows from the front, aged fourteen, in my blazer and tie, standing between Danny and Jonny Kebab. I remember myself blanked out back then – blanked and blanking – so it is no great challenge to adjust to being represented thus. The teachers' faces are all distinct, or as distinct as they can be in a three-decades-old predigital photograph. The Doc, Mr Barnett, Trundley, McCloud, Goodship and Morbender. Mr Willis before he cracked up and Mr Lawnder before he faded away, along with Mrs Pizzi and Mrs Mason. And the rest, whose names I can probably recall but can't be bothered dredging for.

'Recognise anyone?' asks Gary, and it's almost caring, almost gentle.

I point out my shoulders with the biro I'm holding.

'There,' I say. I was behind Morbender, in the first row of pupils behind the staff. Always better to be behind Morbender than in front. There was dandruff the size of breakfast cereal on the shoulders of his gown. I could smell his trousers.

Lynne Forester has certainly lined them up: two ex-teachers, four ex-pupils, the school headmaster, some neighbours, and a man who used to work in the recently defunct music shop I remember at the top of Jackdaw Lane. Wolphram was a regular there, a good customer, and I can't imagine what the man who sold him styluses and guitar plectrums and CDs has to say. She has more in store, I know, because she needs to ration it all, keep on with the sneak previews, the tasters and the titillations. Lynne and her like can make anything happen if they want to, back there in the past. You can retrace a dead girl's footsteps, but you can't change the turning she took. No, but you can take a man's past and coat him in guilt.

I try to replicate how we read newspapers; how the newspaper reads itself inside us:

I look at the photos first, then I leaf through the pages with that half-alert eye which makes us flick to the end of the paper – tabloid or broadsheet, it makes no difference – taking in a few images and headlines, a few adjectives, the eye-to-brain shorthand of the newsprint-browser, until I get to the letters and horoscope and sports pages, where I stop and turn back. I have a small word-hoard already, a shiny catch from the eye's first, slack, dragnet: *dandy, aesthete, strange, creepy, sexual, death, obsessed, boys, homosexual, temper, inappropriate.* Then *Emily*

Dickinson, gay poet Thom Gunn, suicide, Sylvia Plath. It is like the cream at the top of the milk in the old glass bottles, something distilling itself upwards, a thick fat foretaste of what lies below. The words wink at each other across the columns. They are in on it, too. Then a diaspora of other words, more innocent, but infected now by the purpose they're put to: *alone, loner, distant, intellectual, always overdressed, formal,* and then, laughably but I'm not laughing, *books, foreign films, poetry, death.*

Gary's coffee is there. He has made it himself and not used the machine. It tastes no better, but this small act of consideration suggests he has bad news.

'They're charging him.'

The Doc

As deputy head, Doc Monk also teaches other subjects, and, just when they've abandoned Latin in the hope of avoiding him forever, he returns in the guise of a history teacher. He keeps his trembling Jack Russell in a basket by his desk, and every now and then the dog takes a turn around the room, its crusty arsehole displaying icicles of fur-trapped turds. *Stalagshites*, Danny calls them. Doc Monk covers his walls with posters of Caesars and emperors, maps, battle scenes and monuments. What he teaches is obedience and manly incuriosity, and if the school has an ethos, it is that. It is how empires got built. History is kings and queens and beheadings and wars.

When Danny asked him, 'Was there any other history going on?', the Doc replied, 'Such as?'

'I don't know,' said Danny, who is by now confident and sophisticated but unnervingly innocent at the same time: 'in factories or farms; in shops and in people's houses.'

The Doc takes off his spectacles, rubs his eyes, puts them back on and stares at Danny. He is performing the *patient teacher explaining to stupid pupil* script. He has all the scripts filed away in his head, which is a library of malice: 'History is about events and the men who make them. If you want to be a social worker you can do that in your own time.'

'Does history only happen to certain people?' asks Danny, pushing it.

The Doc looks at him sideways — Danny is at the front of the class. The Doc tends to stand right up against the first row of desks, while the boys lean as far back as their chairs will let them — they look like flowers bending in a gale — and though he can't quite catch the irony, he knows there's something a little serrated along the comment's edge.

'I'm talking about History capital *H*. No one's interested in factories and farms and debating whether women cooking and cleaning counts as *history* ... that's sociology and we don't do that in *this* school.'

'Who decides what history is then, Dr Monk?'

The Doc doesn't like where this is going. He doesn't like, either, the barely perceptible weight of sarcasm on the *doctor*.

'I wouldn't blame your classmates if they put you in your place from time to time,' the Doc replies, looking specifically at Hugh Lewis and Leighton Vaughan at the back, who are alert for any encouragement to violence. 'And, anyway, since you're interested in history, perhaps we can discuss the murderous history of your terrorist compatriots. Perhaps you yourself are one of them, some sort of sleeper — after all, that's how they work, isn't it? Sprinkle a few Fenians in our towns and cities, leave them to blend in, make friends, get jobs, start families, and then BANG' he smacks the table with his palm. Everyone jumps, Danny most of all: 'Suddenly there's a dozen dead and injured, blood all over the walls and people's remains are being spooned up by paramedics. SPOONED UP!' he shouts. 'That's *your* history. Shall we study that?'

Danny is suddenly shot down; first his face drains to pale and then it burns red, an agony of blushes. Being an adolescent is like that: you feel strong, funny, subversive, you swagger and go out too far on the ledge of yourself and then you fall.

'Maybe *you're* one of them?' says the Doc quietly.

The laughter stops. There's a pause, while people compute the change in tone. It's as if the air has been replaced. Then, snarling comes in where the laughter was. Things have moved from ordinary bullying, common-or-garden humiliation, standard-issue power-play, to something else. It is like a break in the weather where the storm has prised open the sky and counts the seconds before it hits.

'I'm not Irish,' says Danny defensively. *Defensively against what?* he thinks, gathering himself and adding, 'Not that it would be a problem if I was. If I was I'd be proud.'

'*Proud*, are we?' says the Doc quietly, his eyes on the class rather than Danny. 'Well, you're certainly better fed than many of your countrymen. I think we have a *sympathiser* here; maybe even our very own *sleeper*.'

Vaughan walks brazenly to the front and smacks Danny across the back of the head — the muffled knock of knuckle on skull. You know it's got to hurt, and when Danny looks up with his eyes stinging with pain and tears pearling, he finds the back-row bastards laughing. Vaughan rubs his knuckles proudly and returns to his seat. The Doc appears to be consulting his ledger and he pretends not to notice.

Danny has been getting cocky for a while. He's cleverer than anyone else. He answers back, has a way of exposing other people's stupidities that embarrasses them all the more because he doesn't mean to. There's something dangerous about unintentional offence – the way it provokes people even more than pushing mockery or contempt into their faces. He is also elegant and self-contained, and Ander notices – they all notice – how he seems to grow more proportionately than they do. He doesn't have the El Greco gangliness of other adolescents. He gets taller, fills out in just the right ways; he's not clumsy, doesn't get the rash of spots over his forehead or sweat so hard he steams in the frost. He wears better clothes, too. Actually, no: clothes just look better on him. Not that he looks bad unclothed either, as they all notice on the way in and out of the shower, or when they're changing for the various sports they're crap at.

So, yes: Danny has it coming. *Had* it coming.

'I've got something lined up for you,' says the Doc with a sunniness they've never seen before. 'Come and join me here at the front.' He waits. 'There's nothing to be afraid of.' If the Doc were the type to reassure, then it would be reassuring. But Ander knows immediately that things are looking bad.

'Me?' asks Danny, wrongfooted by the Doc's constant change of tone. The Doc is smiling, and it seems to hurt his face because his eyes waver and bulge with the strain of it. There's a lot of tooth in that smile, thinks Ander. A lot of bite.

'Yes, you, Danny McAlinden, we're going to put some of your ideas into practice. Come and join me up here.'

Danny is suspicious, but there's still enough trust in him, or, rather – not quite the same thing – enough *wanting* to trust, for him to get up and walk the three or four steps to the front of the class where Doc Monk beckons him.

'Sit down,' asks the Doc gently, putting his hands on Danny's shoulders – though Danny is taller – and pushing him down into the seat.

Danny sits.

What is now about to happen Ander has never stopped replaying in his head.

The reason we return to things isn't that they've happened, but that somewhere inside ourselves we think they can still be made to happen differently. If only we can find the right seam, the ridge in the roll of Sellotape which the finger runs over and over trying to feel, so we can pick it with our nail and lift it and unspool it all.

The Doc is small and weak, but the energy of his sadism gives him enough sinewy strength to drag Danny, still in his seat, sideways and up to the middle of the front of the room. When the Doc gets angry or excited he starts very faintly to smell. It's not pungent or nauseating, like Morbender's smell of intimacy and decay – it's more like he's fermenting, bubbling up slowly. He then tells Danny to stand and takes the chair and pulls it to the front, so the back of the chair is against Danny's waist. Automatically – it must be the accused in all of us, the defendant inside – Danny places his hands on the back of the chair like someone awaiting sentencing. It is strange how easy it is, how learned the behaviour: put someone in front of others, make them stand alone before a crowd, and they start to behave like they're on trial. The Doc knows this. The rest of them are about to learn it.

'One of the foundations of modern society is the rule of law, along with the right to a fair trial,' he begins. Danny looks at him hopefully, and later the boys will think that was Danny's undoing, trusting the Doc and smiling, because that was the signal to everyone else: the signal that everything goes now, that it's open season on Danny, that he was ready and waiting for his own dismantling.

Doc Monk: 'Think of this as an exercise in democracy: a chance for everyone in the class to come up and explain the charges against you or speak in your defence should they so wish. We will later take a vote on whether you are guilty or innocent of each of the charges individually. Since we don't have a jury, your peers will be the jury. I will be the judge, just to keep things ticking along. You will of course have the chance to defend yourself ...'

'I don't ... understand ...' says Danny, panicking. There's a crackling of excitement at the back of the class – approved bullying, and in a theatrical context like this, it's an unexpected thrill. The courtroom idea is especially delicious, because it adds an air of ritual and unreality to the base brutality to come. It's like sharing a high.

Not everyone sees where this is going, but Ander is beginning to, as is Neil Hall a few rows behind. He can hear Neil gasping *fucking hell*. Danny, because he's in the middle of it, hasn't grasped it yet.

'A trial, Mr McAlinden, a trial. You seem so interested in all those communist heroes of yours, your Trotsky, your Lenin, your International Brigades ... closer to home your Irish Republican Army and your striking miners in their little Moscow ... this is a chance for you to help us relive one of their favourite pastimes: the Show Trial.'

Danny tries to leave, but Doc Monk stands in his way: 'Come now, what are you afraid of? This is part of the lesson – think of it as historical re-enactment, it's all about bringing history closer to us ...'

Danny could just get up and push him away — he is a head and a pair of shoulders taller than Monk, it wouldn't be hard — but power doesn't work like that, and nor does submission. Even before it begins, Danny is shedding his aura of intelligent calm, his physical composure, his elegance and authority. All the things the others envy him, he is about to lose in public. The worst of it is that even those who like him might secretly enjoy it, just because he needs to *be brought down*, brought closer to them in their fragility and anxiety. They'll even like him more because of the humiliation and the pain they'll watch him endure.

Danny tries to speak but the words have deserted him, and every now and then the Doc mocks his accent when he tries to raise his voice. The Doc, meanwhile, is gathering the decor for the courtroom vibe — Bible for witnesses to swear on, black gown for the judge, an old pipe for a gavel. Ander wonders if he's done this before — the props are so close to hand.

'These historical re-enactments are all the rage these days: you know those medievalists in their chain mail with their swords and shields, those battle-recreations they sometimes have near the bridge … well, let this be our own little version of that …' he laughs.

'Perhaps we need a couple of courtroom security staff to keep the defendant in place?' he says, summoning Lewis and Vaughan from the back. Burly, thick, vicious and obedient, they come to the front and stand on either side of Danny.

Even Doc Monk's dog has woken up.

Squeeze the Day

I notice Gary says *they're charging him*. Not *we*. It's a
Deskfish decision, because while Mr Wolphram has been
sitting in that cell, fidgeting in that interview room,
the secondary sweating has been done behind me, by
Deskfish in his executive aquarium with the trophies and
the certificates left over from his predecessor, who died in
the saddle and whose family never claimed them back.
Deskfish uses them now, and figures, correctly, that no
one checks the name on certificates and trophies, only
the achievements they testify to. 'Police Communicator
of the year: Regional Winner, Derbyshire' is Gary's
favourite.

It was based on this certificate that Gary invented
the game 'Niche Accolades', in which competitors are
tasked with inventing superlatives for activities with
diminutive catchment areas and restrictively specific
eligibility conditions. 'Best-performing Moldovan bank',
'Miss Frodsham', 'Yorkshire philanthropist of the year' ...

'*They* haven't got enough to charge him,' I tell Gary,
keeping to his choice of pronoun.

'They've got enough circumstantial stuff, Prof: her in his car, her in his flat, him in her flat ... him getting times and dates wrong, telling lies or looking like it. The car was used on the day after she died, maybe with her in it. She's worried about stalkers, she's looking up help sites. He's incapable of giving straight answers, he's got no alibi—'

'People who live alone don't tend to have alibis, Gary, you and I of all people should know that.'

'*Touché*, Prof, but, come on, let's face it ...' Gary's voice tapers off because he wants me to say it for him:

So I do: 'He's *not exactly normal*, Gary, is that what you mean?'

'Ah, Prof — you beat me to it.'

We say nothing. I stir my coffee, tap the spoon against the chipped rim of the cup. It says 'Best Dad in Norfolk' on it, and it too belonged to Deskfish's predecessor. It is the specificity that gives the title its lustre: less is more.

'Look,' Gary goes on, 'they need a result, Deskfish needs something to tell people. Okay, he's a spineless desk-humper surrounded by a dead man's certificates [Gary pronounces it *stiffikuts*], but he's also the one they go to first: the public, the newspapers, the TV reporters, the top brass worried about PR, the shopkeepers spooked about Christmas footfall ... They're all at him, Prof, phoning, tweeting, emailing, texting ... I feel for him, Prof. A bit.'

'And he's just given in — the whole point of getting a *result* is that it's the *right* result, not some morsel to keep the outside world happy ...'

'It's about running out of time. Look, we've got this great big turd hanging by a tiny thread over our heads, thin as a baby's hair, Prof, just waiting to fall on all of us, you, me, Deskfish, everyone—'

'It's a sword, Gary, the sword of Damocles—'

'It's a turd now, Prof — where d'you think you are? *Lord of the Rings*? The point is to get out from under it before the thread snaps.'

'But now we have to spend our time proving he did it rather than investigating who might *actually* have done it. That's two very different things.'

'Let's hope they're the same then, shall we?' Gary shrugs. 'Look, the balance of probability is that it was him — you know how it goes: husband/boyfriend, relative or neighbour. Boyfriend's across the Channel, relatives were up in Newcastle, neighbour ... well, neighbour is weird, tells lies, is obsessively clean and tidy, and has traces of her in his flat and car. Face the facts, Prof: what are we supposed to think?'

'It's not facts, though, is it? Facts is what we don't have. You don't believe any more than I do that it's right to charge him. Even if he is guilty there's nothing to hang it on. We've barely finished house-to-house, we haven't had all the computer checks in, we haven't spoken to witnesses properly yet and we haven't even recreated her last movements. There might be a dozen people out there whose memories are about to be dislodged.'

Gary looks down at the desk, picks up a pen and stirs his coffee with it. 'It's all about *time*, isn't it? We're running out of time so they charged him. Get your head around that and work with it.'

'Running out of time in relation to what? Lynne Forester's articles or solving the actual crime? Anyway, he didn't even consult us, did he?'

'He didn't have to, Prof. It's his call. He's the one who deals with the front-of-house stuff, the PR and the explaining, so he's the one feeling the heat. Anyway, look at it this way: we need to charge him to keep him in, and we need to keep him in so we can charge him. And when he's seen the papers he'll be grateful, 'cos if he gets out they'll string him up. Everyone's a winner!'

Gary takes the remote control and flicks on the twenty-four-hour news: it's Mr Wolphram's flat thronged with reporters and photographers. A permanent crowd of neighbours, well-heeled in expensive coats, and a few men and women in tracksuits and football tops who have come by bus to check out the 'scene'. Soon there'll be SCUM PAEDO MONSTER HANG HIM in spray paint across the walls, but as long as the police are there it's just shouting. A guard of three constables stands awkwardly in front of the gates. It's live-streaming news, and the darkening sky I can see from this office window is the same darkening sky that lowers itself, half a mile away to the west, onto Mr Wolphram's house, drapes itself over the iron gates and settles onto the gravel. All the floors are now black-windowed; even the talkative couple in the top flat must have left to escape the attention.

To start with they were thrilled to be so close to it all. (What were they called? Ben and Claire? Chloe? – that's it: Chloe and Ben.) You could see it in their eyes. They'd seen stuff like this on the telly, but now ... *well, now it's right here, isn't it?* They were garrulous, and for all I know texting or tweeting or Instagramming pictures of us as we went in and out of the building in our white forensic onesies. She even said, as they all do at some point; as, maybe, we all do when atrocity skims us: 'It's amazing to think that could have been me out there in the fields in binbags.' The boyfriend puts the statutory *arm of reassurance* around her shoulder, the hand coming in to stroke the top of her breast a little below the collarbone. She takes the hand, looks at us, and shivers with what she thinks is palpable distress (she probably has the phrase *palpable distress* in her head as she does it) but which we recognise as the thrill of the safe. They asked a few questions, pretending to care. They tried out various frowns of sincerity, but really they just wanted details to dine out on or to pin down their *could-have-been-me* scenarios. He wanted to know about forensic stuff, she asked if we know whether Zalie was killed here, in this house, or somewhere else. His peculiar attention to detail – amateur sleuth questions, but precise and oddly interested in the science of it – was different from her prurient excitement.

'Everyone's a detective now,' said Gary when we left.

Anyway, it looks like they're gone now. They probably found all the attention too much.

So I watch the live-streaming of the darkening house. It's unexpectedly soothing. The clouds I see from the office will pass over theirs in two, perhaps three minutes. All this is happening in real time – Mr Wolphram downstairs, the solicitor on his way in his executive saloon with the suit jacket on the hook at the back window, the police at the front of Mr Wolphram's house, me sipping my coffee, Gary sticking pins in the map on the wall, Deskfish on the phone: we are watching it all and we are part of it all, too. Even the neighbours are part of it, to whom nothing happened but who have tasted the limelight and for whom something is from now on always happening. It's all happening in real time (what other time is there?), in twenty-four-hour news.

All that *now* and yet we're somehow always too late.

The truth is out; so are the lies. Both look the same.

Our parents and grandparents had to buy the morning papers to find out what had happened in the night. If there was more they wanted to know, they might follow a story by listening to headlines on the hour. Their idea of riding the foam on the wave of the *now* was buying the *Evening Post* afternoon edition when they came back from work and reading it on trains or buses. They knew that things kept happening when the news wasn't on: people died or got killed, wars started, trains crashed, hotels got bombed and rebuilt, football teams won or lost. They weren't stupid or uninformed, and I am not sure they understood less about how the happening happens than we do now, choking on the live-streaming present. Gary says that living in a live-streamed present changes how we live it.

When I was at school, I'd set my watch according to the shopping centre clock in Port Vale Road. I knew I'd be losing time, that my own little watch would slow down, that I'd forget to wind it up or the batteries would die out, so I went to the clock every now and then and, as they saying went, I'd *set it by* the big clock, which was itself *set by* a bigger clock, and so on all the way to some great clock, the clock of all clocks. Where was that, I wondered? The moon? The sun? I would walk away from the fake *olde worlde* clock by Wimpy and Woolworths, long-dead shops with names that are still alive, my watch tightly set and newly in time with the time. It was like I had a full tank of it. But already, before I'd taken the first three steps, I knew it would be leaking accuracy, slowing down, that I was carrying sand or water in my hands, an estuary between my fingers, and that the only real story my watch was going to tell me was that. The only time it really told was less time, lost time, and then no time.

Mr Wolphram told me once, after a lesson: 'You are obviously a glass-half-empty sort of boy, because another way of interpreting the sad fact of Time's one-way ratchet is that you should cram as much as possible into it: *carpe diem*, seize the day.'

Which for months after I misquoted as *squeeze the day*. It probably amounted to the same thing. Like the other big adult word I misheard in the early days, when English came to me in mondegreens, a thread of potent mishearings: Returnity. *For eternity* they said. *For returnity* was what I heard.

Glass-half-empty stayed with me, because it was the only time Mr Wolphram ever used a cliché, and he warned us about those.

'You off on one, Prof?' Gary interjects. My coffee is now gulpably cold so I swallow it in one and slam the mug down on the table, hard enough to look decisive, but not so hard that it breaks.

'Are you a glass-half-full or a glass-half-empty man, Gary?'

'I need to know what's *in* the glass before I can answer that question. That's crucial contextual information, that is ...'

'Exactly, Gary, and it's the one piece of information that's never given when people ask ...' I get up decisively and sling on my coat. Gary looks startled. 'Let's check where the couple at the top have gone, shall we? Chloe and Ben. I've got a feeling they've been bought by a paper and moved to some tabloid safe house to be vivisected for their story, then paid off.'

'There was me thinking you were on one of your internal safaris. But, actually, it's all been whirring away in there, hasn't it? All that *horlogerie* in your brain tick-tocking ... I'll go and check.'

'Then we're off to talk to the bloke with the broken *herat*, find out what if anything he saw, and after that we're back here to talk to Mr Wolphram. By then he'll have seen his solicitor.'

'I like it,' says Gary. 'That's a Prof with a plan.'

'Then I want to see the statements of everyone on the street, every neighbour, delivery man, courier, leafleter, binman, peeper and curtain-twitcher, neighbourhood-watch busybody ... plus whatever Small-Screen's found checking the dating profiles.'

Gary makes a call. Someone puts him on hold.

I thought Chloe and Ben had gone to escape the attention. I should have suspected it was a better, more remunerative, kind of attention they were after:

'Yep, you were right: they've gone. Left last night. I called Ben on the number he left us and there's a voice message saying to direct all enquiries to Lynne Forester at the *Evening Post*. They'll be in some posh hotel or a safe flat somewhere while she milks them for information.'

The charged man is back in the interview room. Unshaved now for nearly two days, his stubble rises almost to the cheekbones, creeps down to the collar of his shirt. He looks like an intellectual Mexican bandit in a spaghetti western, or the kind of prisoner who in films helps other inmates write letters to their sweethearts. His skin is shiny, greased with sweat, and his pores are big and open. His nails are bitten down and raw on their delicate long fingers. He has no strings to pluck, no pages to turn, so he is lost, wordless and tuneless in the glare.

All he has is a watch, and he turns the strap around his wrist, adjusting the volume inside his head. He seems to be meditating. Every now and then he closes his eyes slowly, languorously, and opens them again – perhaps he expects to open them on something different and is giving the world a chance to rearrange itself while he isn't looking. Sometimes he rocks back and forth very gently over the table, where two cups of untouched tea have cooled down in their thin, ribbed plastic cups.

I'm going to recommend suicide watch. He seems to be trying to exit his body. He is so slight, so pale and frightened; so thin that he might leave his flesh the way you'd leave a house one final time: shutting the door behind you and dropping the key back through the letterbox.

'Looks like the last lobster in one of those posh restaurants before the chef pulls him out of the tank and boils him,' observes Gary with affection. 'I'll have a bottle of Chablis and the schoolmaster Thermidor, please ...'

He has been interviewed three times overnight. They waited until Gary and I were off duty. Deskfish and Small-Screen have done it themselves, but the transcripts show they got nothing out of him: 11.30 p.m., 1.45 a.m., 3.30 a.m. Each time for an hour.

It is like dialogue from the Theatre of the Absurd, with the sluggish menace of a Pinter play:

Deskfish: 'You haven't been charged with anything, so you can speak freely.'

'Free or not, I have nothing to say that I haven't already said, often several times, albeit in several different ways.'

Mr Wolphram may be exhausted, but he is still in charge of the words — even those of others, because Deskfish commits one of the basic errors of police interviewing: asking questions that aren't questions:

'That's the problem,' says Deskfish. 'You keep on saying the same things, but we'd like to hear something different, wouldn't we, Sergeant Binns?' I realise I've never even known Small-Screen's surname; he isn't the sort of person to whom a surname would add much.

'That's right, sir, something different's what we need.' He is trying to inject some *bad cop* into his voice. 'And you'd be helping yourself, too.'

'I rather think I'd be helping myself by saying as little as possible, don't you? And that is certainly what my solicitor will advise me to do when I ask for one. Which I have not, you will have noticed, because I am cooperating as a witness. If I am something other than a witness, you will tell me, won't you?'

Deskfish sighs a police-drama-interrogator sigh: 'When was the last time you spoke to Zalie?'

'Probably on 18 or 19 December. In the morning.'

'What did you talk about?'

'I can't recall. The usual pleasantries, neighbourly things – bins, recycling, the day's usually depressing news. She was an easy person to get on with, and doubtless if we had known each other better we should have been friends.'

'What time in the morning?'

'Half past ten. Twenty-five to eleven. I went to buy the newspaper at about ten and returned half an hour or so later. She was taking her bicycle out of the shed.'

'Half-past ten/twenty-five to eleven is specific, isn't it?' Small-Screen cuts in. This isn't Good Cop/Bad Cop, it's Thick Cop/Thicker Cop.

'All times are specific, Officer, it's people who are not.'

There's a long pause, in which I can imagine Deskfish and Small-Screen looking at each other in panic, faces poached in sweat, then the tape is switched off. We still call it 'the tape', but it's a digital recorder, and it's so sensitive we can hear Mr Wolphram breathing in through his nostrils the way I remember at school when a lesson ended: the head rising, the chest inflating, the books closed.

'Wow,' says Gary, who is listening over my shoulder, 'class dismissed or what?'

'You see what I mean?' I ask. 'He isn't exactly one of those teachers who scares people, but somehow you never wanted to mess with him.'

'If I could do things like that with words I wouldn't need to hit people.' Gary has never hit anyone, but he likes to summon the ghost of violence whenever things get complicated. Violence is his idea of a tie-break in an argument.

Mr Wolphram may be broken and alone, sitting in that room, in that cell, confused and fidgeting, but when he's confronted by people, he is strong again. There are reserves in him. Of what, I don't know, but if he doesn't collapse and confess it's either because he's innocent or because he has the will to hold out and to keep holding.

Next session: Deskfish and Small-Screen sound more tired than he does. They're now trying the amateur shrink line and asking him about his early life. We've been there already – it's where we started, and look where it got us.

Mr Wolphram: 'I'm never sure why people look at childhoods for answers, it must be a relic of the days when we expected people to cohere the way stories do.'

Small-Screen (getting a bit above his pay grade): 'Stick with the facts please, sir, leave the theories to us.'

'It's precisely your theories I'm afraid of, officer, but if it's facts you want . . .' He takes a breath and begins: 'I was mostly brought up alone. My parents died – separately, which is how they lived – when I was small: my mother when I was six, my father when I was ten. They had the sort of marriage that made divorce unnecessary. When she died I was sent to live with two aunts in Hastings. My father was a military man, strict but with no real rationale for being so – I was certainly no rebel – and wanted a man for a child rather than a child. You know when people say of someone: *he was the father I never had*? Well, in my case that was my actual father: I never actually had him. And that was all right with me, frankly.' He sighs, bored: 'Look, I have discussed this, or a version of it, with your colleagues: the large angry one and the one who looks like he isn't listening. At least with them there was some semblance of give and take. Need I go on?'

Silence.

'Very well. My aunts were Salvation Army. The military, in a way. I was an atheist as far back as I can recall but I loved them and they loved me. It was very simple really. One of them is still alive and I treasure her. But you know this, and maybe you have spoken to her.' Pause. 'Have you?'

Deskfish and Small-Screen say nothing, because they don't know the answer. They are totally unbriefed, amateurish and unprepared. (No: we have not spoken to her. We will.) They haven't even looked at the transcripts Gary and I left for them. You don't need to be a connoisseur of silences to realise that they're gormless and lost and have no idea what they're doing. Mr Wolphram can tell, because he can sniff it out. It's not so different from school, sensing who has and hasn't done the reading, who has and hasn't done the homework. Deskfish and Small-Screen are just back-row bluffers.

'Shall I carry on?' he asks. He is interrogating them. When once again they say nothing, he carries on:

'I saw the point in everything my aunts did, even if I didn't believe in their supernatural reasons for doing it. The church, the band, the hymns, the feeding of the poor, the hatred of poverty, of misery ... I saw the point in that and I admired it. They were people who did things out of kindness and out of care for others, not because of God. If God didn't exist, or were to suffer an unexpected accident, they would have done it all anyway. I see it as a mark of their selflessness that they used Him as a pretext for what they did: anything not to claim the glory for themselves. What can I say? They were kind people, and kindness is hard to sustain. Unlike love, which is glamorous and depends on stimulation, kindness is all about consistency, about going the distance, even when you run out of breath or your heart's no longer in it.'

Gary is interested now. He's not mocking him, laughing at him or calling him gay, perverted or a child molester. He switches off the machine. 'Laurel and Hardy are out of their fucking depth, Prof. He needs a wordsmith like me in there, running rings around him – with the back of my hand ...'

'Switch it back on please, Gary':

'My aunts were religious people, but they weren't strict or especially devout. There was a great deal of laughter in that house, and they let me do what I wanted, say what

I wanted, read what I liked. You could call them God-fearing, but I've never liked that phrase: either God exists or he doesn't — there seems to be a lot to fear either way, doesn't there?'

End of interview.

In the car, as we head to Castle Street, Gary asks: 'Don't you think we should meet his aunt?'

'Why's that, Gary? If we've got our man, I mean ...'

'Belt and braces, Prof. She might have some nice background story on him, and the papers are going to get there anyway. I can imagine her already: nice warm fire, tea, maybe some cake — home-baked by a neighbour called Olive — surrounded by photos of him in his shorts, bucket and spade, sticks of seaside rock ...'

He's right. They'll have tracked her down and laid siege to her. I can't imagine she'll take their money, but she might believe their lies: *we'll protect you from the other papers who are out to shred his reputation, we can give your side of the story, doesn't he need someone to stick up for him*, etc. If not already, then soon. Everything is happening fast now and the worst is about to happen: charge sheet, lawyer, primetime news, headlines and editorials, old friends lying for cash, colleagues cutting him loose, official statements from the school ...

There's no one in when we get to Castle Street. The owners have been told not to remove the graffiti, so it blazes there in its fuzzy aerosol, across the rich people's wall. I hope they're furious and embarrassed. Gary gets out of the car, says he's off to stretch his legs. There's an old butcher's nearby. I remember it from school. It just about survived the supermarkets and the out-of-town shopping centres. But now that the old stuff has come around again, the vinyl, the scotch eggs, the craft brews and the beards, they're suddenly doing good business. Just no longer to their old clientele. The old clientele can't afford it; and, anyway, they've moved. They've *been* moved.

Gary likes it there, because it's where his parents shopped, back when people like them lived in this bit of town. He's gone to buy a pie or a sausage roll, the old traditional stuff he remembers from before the council housing dried up and the sushi and the chai lattes arrived.

He comes back, pork pie in each hand, complaining about the price. 'Symbol of gentrification, Prof.' He takes a bite so large that all that remains is a collapsing rim of crust between his thumb and forefinger. Chewing, he goes on in the manner of a TV history programme presenter:

'Look on any pub menu: the nearer the food comes from, the more expensive it is.' Gary has a theory about everything, and at mealtimes it's usually the theory of global capital that gets aired: 'First they kill off everything local, close the butcher's and baker's, the pub with the beer that tastes of eggs, and then, when it's all gone, some twit with a beard and a check shirt called Max moves in and starts selling it again. At three times the price. To people like you. People like me are in the supermarkets buying stuff from the other side of the world 'cos that's all we can afford.'

There's a piece of pie crust in the crotch of his trousers, and when he has finished chewing he picks it up and pops it into his mouth. 'As the man said, everything comes round twice: first time as life, second time as lifestyle.'

Then he opens the paper and reads one of the headlines.

'Here's one of his ex-pupils, Prof – could have been in your day,' says Gary: 'Jonathan Lansdale, 1980s – is he anything to do with the shop? Does the name ring a bell?'

'Jonny Kebab,' I tell him, 'what's he got to say?'

'Take a guess, Prof …'

'I don't want to guess – just read it please. All of it, don't give me a Garified precis, I want the exact words.'

'You want the headline, too? Here's my time-saving precis: *Barmy Bookfucker Behind Bars*. Does that give you the gist?'

'Gary – I want the whole lot: headline, caption, paragraph by paragraph. By-line as well. We've got the time.'

Gary clears his throat, takes a swig of his orange sports drink and opens the paper across the steering wheel.

THE WEIRD MR WOLPHRAM
Lynne Forester, chief reporter.
Prime Suspect in binbag murder of Zalie
Dyer, Mr Wolphram, was a book-loving, dapper loner.
Asked boys about puberty. Page 3. Strange Eyes.
Page 6. Strange Hair. Page 7. Strange Clothes.
Page 8. Strange Hats. Page 8. Strange. Page 10.
Eccentric Loner – Colleagues remember 'The
Oddball Poetry Man'. Page 4. 'Obsessed with
David Bowie'. Page 5.
Watched black and white films. Served alcohol
to boys. Page 5.

'Here you go: a fatberg made of words.' Gary starts reading aloud:

One of Mr Wolphram's former pupils, businessman and entrepreneur Jonathan Lansdale, remembers the reclusive teacher as an eccentric with a short fuse. 'He was creepy,' said Mr Lansdale, 48, 'we were all afraid of him because he could be violent. He showed us strange films and asked if we were sexually active.'

Gary: 'Did he?'

'No ... *Entrepreneur* for Jonny Kebab is ironic. The only business he started at school was picking up sodden porn magazines from the Downs, drying them on the radiator, and selling them from his "office", which was the toilets by the Geography department. I still remember his price list. Keep going, Gary.'

'Is that a No, or is it a "I don't know but he never asked *me* that"? You sure he just wasn't interested in *you*? Things have got so screwed up that not being abused is the new being abused – is that right?'

'It's a No. To both questions.'

'If you say so, Prof:

Mr Wolphram was known for his love of poetry, and made us read poems about sex and death. He took boys to his flat after school hours to listen to opera and recordings of poets reading. He had original David Bowie records, played us Pink Floyd, Velvet Underground ... quite adult music by groups that took drugs. We listened to Velvet Underground's 'Heroin'.

That true, Prof?'

'Yes, that bit is. But he didn't *take boys to his flat*, he *invited* them, and many came.'

'See what they've done there – *after school hours* is a nice touch: makes it sound dodgy, like it's something a bit secret and naughty. *Adult music* ... Poems about sex and death, eh, Prof? I'm no expert, but aren't all poems about sex and death, when it comes down to it?'

'Keep going, Gary — we can do the lit. crit. later.'

One ex-pupil, who asked to remain anonymous – I bet he doesn't want to be anonymous when he's cashing the fucking cheque they gave him! – **recalls: 'We'd go to his flat. It was always quite dark. He was obviously rich, and had state-of-the art technology – hi-fi, TV, video recorder … Huge speakers. He'd open a bottle of wine and make us drink before starting the film.**

'See what they've done there, Prof: *always quite dark, make us drink?*

We weren't allowed to drink, it was against school rules, but we didn't dare say no. If he felt we weren't paying attention in class, he'd throw books at us and shout. Everyone was afraid of him.

'Did he ever shout?'

'No. Yes. Once. Only once.'

'You afraid of him, Prof?'

I take my eyes off the blurry middle distance and turn to Gary. I'm glad he has asked, because it helps me put into words something I was never quite sure of.

'I was … not afraid, no. And he had good wine and he never offered more than a glass. I've said: I liked him; we all did. I thought we all did anyway. But maybe I just wanted to be liked by him, and that looked like the same thing for a while. I didn't want to disappoint him, I was maybe afraid of that, scared of disappointing him by not *getting* something he said, or something he made us read, or not liking stuff he thought was good. He *wanted* us to like things, it was important to him. But was I afraid? No. Ashamed sometimes maybe – of being slow, or not understanding certain words, not feeling the right things in front of a picture, or some music ... that kind of thing.'

'There's a lot to be said for shame, Prof. There isn't enough of it these days. Too much shaming but not enough shame ...' Gary is watching a woman and her daughter walking towards the house. They have shopping and carry large clothes-boutique bags. 'You think that's them?'

'Who?'

'Sally and her mum. *Hello* ...' he taps his head, 'the reason we're here.'

Ah yes. They unfasten the catch of the metal gate, close it behind them and walk to the front door. We give them time to put their bags down and flick on the kettle.

The doorbell is an electronic version of Big Ben, a big brassy chime, and from its echo we can already tell it's a large hallway. Rich people take ages to answer their doors because they have further to come, and because, somewhere in their embedded class memory, there's a servant doing it for them.

The girl who answers is about eighteen. She looks alert but distracted. She is in the middle of texting, a flurry of thumbs. She opens the door, looks at us, shouts, 'Muuuuuum ...', turns around, and leaves us standing there.

'Maybe we're meant to use the tradesmen's entrance,' snarls Gary, walking in as noisily as possible. He hasn't wiped his feet — that's deliberate — and has dragged a sooty line of kerbside drain water onto the marble tiles. 'You coming in or what, Prof?' He's getting wound up already. 'Or you going to leave your visiting card on a fucking plate while you wait below stairs with the housekeeper?'

When Mrs Latimer arrives, we tell her it is her daughter we wanted to speak to. She is friendly and unexpectedly polite. Gary is thrown by this. She asks him to sit down, offers him tea, tells him not to worry about the puddle of water in the hallway, and asks how she can help.

Gary is sullen, even angrier now that she has confounded his expectations by being considerate and pleasant. He looks around, hoping to fault the decor, and finds that its only real fault is that he can't afford it.

'The graffiti on your wall …' I begin.

'Yes, you told us to leave it there. I'd very much like it gone, as I think you can imagine.'

'We need to know who wrote it.'

'I don't want him to get into trouble. It's just a bit of graffiti, and all it takes is a tin of paint stripper and a wire brush to get it off.'

'It's not that, Mrs Latimer, it's nothing to do with getting him into trouble. It's to do with another case – the possibility that the graffiti was painted during a time-window that interests us in connection with something else, and that whoever painted it saw something that could help us.'

Mrs Latimer is not stupid. She works it out. For the second time today I am taken aback by her warmth and decency: she does not get excited, gloat, thrill or pry. Instead she just helps.

'I think I know what you're saying, and of course I'll do what I can. His name is Jack, Jack Glass. He's nice, we all liked him, but Sally moved on when she started at university – how many relationships back home survive freshers' week? He took it badly, he's a bit … dramatic. I don't know his exact address but it's somewhere in St Leonard's.'

'Could you ask Sally to give us his address and number?' asks Gary.

'I could,' she answers, 'but the problem there is that she'll tweet about it, text it, put it on Instagram and milk it for all it's worth ... because it makes her part of the story. It's what they do. If she finds out it's connected to what I think it is, then I think your work – and our lives – would get a great deal more difficult.'

She shows us to the door. 'Let me know when I can get the wire brush and the white spirit out,' she smiles, and sees us off.

'I hate it when people like her turn out to be okay,' grumbles Gary as he squeeze-folds himself into the driving seat. 'People should choose their clichés and stick to them. Like me: overweight, mid-ranking white copper. People look at me and say to each other: *See that guy over there? There's a sixty per cent chance he's called Gary*. Saves everyone time and mental adjustment.'

Jack Glass is an unhappy-looking seventeen-year-old with thin stubble and a tattoo on his forearm that's still covered in plastic. An anchor through a heart, he explains, though it looks more like a joint of vacuum-packed meat that's gone off in its bag.

'Just had it done,' he says. 'Cost a bomb, hurt like fuck, and when I get back I've been dumped.'

'That's sort of what we wanted to talk about,' says Gary. 'The graffiti on the Latimers' walls ...'

'Yeah, I'm sorry – I was just so pissed off ... I felt ... I felt sad, that's all, and angry – so angry I couldn't even fucking spell and look like even more of a dick. I'll clean it off. I told them I done it, I said sorry, I said I'd clean it, but Mrs Latimer ... she said to leave it.' Like Gary, he speaks with the local accent, and I can imagine Sally and her friends, with their estuary English mixed with received pronunciation and MTV Euro-American hip, laughing at him. Those curled *r*s, the round vowels ... they'd have enjoyed mocking that. I remember that all the time I was at school, I only ever heard that accent among the kitchen staff or cleaners, on the buses in town or in the shops. At Chapelton we were encouraged to mock it whenever we heard it.

But at least back then it was everywhere. Now, it is receding. You can find it holed up in the parts of town the media doesn't care about but the police know too well, or among old people in retirement homes or Bingo halls. It's rare to find someone as young as Jack speaking such a pristine version of it. Even Gary, who doesn't care what people think, has planed his down to fit in with the rest of us, our commuter-belt English, the Milton Keynes in our mouths.

'We're not here about your spelling, Jack,' says Gary. I notice he turns up his accent for Jack: *we're from the same place, you and I* is what it says. Has Gary done it deliberately, to edge something out of Jack, or has he done it subconsciously? 'We're here because there was a crime committed nearby, maybe at roughly the same time you were painting, and we want to know exactly when you did it and if you saw anyone or anything. Okay?'

Jack looks at him suspiciously. I don't want him to work it out. If he suspects why we're asking, Lynne Forester's going to have another story, and Jack might make enough cash to recoup both his tattoo money and the cost of removing it.

'I shouldn't really be telling you this,' says Gary, and I am about to stop him when he says, 'but a burglary was committed a few doors away – a serious break-in – sometime between eleven and six a.m. the next day, and we're looking for anyone who might have seen anything suspicious – even if, in your case, it was someone else doing something suspicious ...'

Gary is good: 'As you know, the police are busy with a very serious matter, stuff that's out of our league, but that doesn't mean the ordinary grunt-work suddenly stops. The everyday business still needs doing: burglaries, assaults, stolen cars ... the boring bits no one notices.' Gary gives a little snort of off-handedness. 'So we'd like you to tell us when you got there, how long you stayed, and when you left. And what you saw. So PC Plod here and his commanding officer', Gary gestures to me mock-deferentially, 'can get back to the station and fill in some forms. Just like you don't see on telly. Take it slowly. Don't leave anything out. There's some banker missing a few grands' worth of hi-fi, flat-screen TVs and Jack Vettriano paintings, and we're the ones getting the hassle.'

Jack looks disappointed. He scratches his raw inked-and-needled skin.

'Okay ... I cycled over at around half past ten, got there round quarter to eleven ... sat on the bench opposite and banged out a few texts asking Sally to come out and talk to me. I just wanted to talk. I WhatsApped her, so I could see she'd read the messages and wasn't answering. That made it worse. I didn't threaten or anything, just said how fucking sad I was, what a bellend I felt for having a tattoo that meant we had an unbreakable bond, and that she'd dumped me the same day. I sent her a picture of it. I'd saved up for weeks ... chose it from the catalogue ... looked up what it symbolised and everything ...'

'It's a nice tattoo, it'll still look good when this is over and you've forgotten all about her.' Gary smiles: 'At least you didn't have her name inked in …' If the angry Gary is discomfiting, the gentle, caring one is properly unnerving.

But only to me, it turns out, because it works on Jack, who looks at him gratefully. 'You reckon?'

'And when you've learned to spell.'

Jack nods, laughs. Gary has him exactly where we want him.

'I waited about an hour. Bought some fags from the corner shop across the green. A couple of tinnies. They were about to close. I didn't see anyone, just the guy at the counter. I sat there and drank the first tin, had a couple of smokes. Maybe a spliff, actually, if I'm honest …'

'A spliff or two never hurt anyone,' says Gary steadily, 'keep going.'

'I heard the rattle of the shutters as the shop locked up. A few cars. None of them parking up or going into the houses, just driving by on their way somewhere else.'

'That's good, Jack, all good. Anyone slowing down by the houses?'

'No, I'd have noticed that – 'cos I was watching out for a chance to, you know, make my move … so I'm sure no one stopped or slowed.' Jack is pleased with that answer because it's clear. All witnesses get a buzz from giving one definite answer in the swamp of hypotheticals. Even the innocent need a clean truth to hide behind.

Gary puts on a look of disappointment. He is certainly better practised at that than smiling. 'What sort of time are we talking about?'

'I dunno, maybe half past eleven.'

'Any people?'

Jack thinks about it. Chews the inside of his lip.

'A few people coming off from the bridge, a few people going across it. Dribs and drabs, though. Around midnight there's a group of blokes, a bit pissed, on their way back from the pub. A girl, but I can't really see as she's got a woolly hat on, with a shopping bag. She's on the phone but I can't hear what she's saying. She's not talking loudly but she's got that thing about her voice when you can tell someone's talking and smiling at the same time. I noticed that. All low and warm. Whispery. It was nice.'

Gary gives nothing away, but I can feel it: something important there, behind what Jack thinks is just a detail.

'I remember thinking *lucky guy on the end of the line.* Then two or three blokes. Sports tops, maybe trackies, jeans, laughing, joking, couple of them lighting up as they went – was it them?'

Jack doesn't know it but he has identified Zalie on her last walk home. She was on the phone to her boyfriend in Saint-Omer at 11.18, for eleven minutes. She had a shopping bag. Gary needs to circle around the information he wants without letting on that this is what he's after. He doesn't even look at me, afraid to show how, now, amid the decoy information he has elicited, the real information is within reach.

'Describe them – anything you spotted.'

'Tall, one with a hoodie, one with a sort of tracksuit top, all walking a bit unsteady, I just thought they were back from the pub – Harcourt Arms stays open 'til midnight – chatting, having a laugh. It's their beer and burger night, too, so it gets full.' He sniffs, looks down. 'We were going to go, me and Sally, they don't ask for ID and she looks a lot older plus she's pretty and that gets anyone in ... You reckon it was them?' he asks again.

'It may have been them, yes,' says Gary. 'What about the woman? Did you get a look at her?'

Jack frowns. 'Why you asking about her?'

Gary, quickly: 'She might be able to give us a better description ... if we can get hold of her. Did she overtake them, or did they overtake her?'

Jack thinks about it. 'She was walking faster than them, they kept stopping to light up or roll fags, so ... yeah, I guess she did. I s'pose she might have got a look at them as she passed.'

'Where did she go?'

'She turned off before they did – down Elms Road, I think, or the next one, Hythe Street. Round where the posh school is. Heading that way. She was walking downhill, towards the playing fields. They definitely went on right to the end of the street, and past where I could see them.'

'Then what?'

'When they'd all gone I got my spray can out and walked over to Sally's. Did a quick double-check, and that was it. Said what I had to say. Took a long time to spray – much longer than I thought, the stone's really crumbly ... absorbed the paint so fast I had to keep going over it. I kept looking around, then I threw the can over the wall and biked off. That's why I spelled it wrong. I was so stressed I couldn't think. The only thing I saw was a fox sniffing around the bins by the bench. If it was those blokes then they must've doubled back when I'd gone.'

'Thanks, Jack – we might ask you to come in and do a photofit – anything you remember – of the men you saw. Don't worry if you can't remember now, people's memories improve when they've got the images in front of them. We never really know what we know, do we? what we've taken in ... Write down your mobile number here, please ...'

Back in the car I congratulate Gary.

'Thanks, Prof ... He's a decent kid. Local school, left at sixteen, going out with a girl from the posh ladies' college who's dumped him in her first term at uni. Like me, but without the girlfriend ... Poor sod with his broken *herat* ...' Gary has told me nothing about his upbringing, his love life, his schooldays. All I know is that they didn't involve red wine, Georgian houses and Swedish films. Not Swedish arthouse films anyway.

'I'm not sure how useful any of it was, Prof — all that scenario established was that she was there around half past eleven and headed home. But we knew that anyway.'

'Not really — there's different ways of knowing the same thing, and this is one of them: we've established she wasn't followed — *probably* — and that whatever happened to her happened somewhere between the Latimers' house and hers. That's clear now. We've narrowed down the *when* and the *where*. We're talking about a window of about twelve minutes and a distance of less than five hundred yards.'

'That just leaves the *why* and the fucking *who*,' says Gary sourly, 'and I don't really give a shit about the *why*.'

'I thought we had the *who* ...'

'I said *probably*, Prof, *probably*, and to be absolutely honest with you, I'm not feeling very *probable* about it.'

'You've changed your tune, Gary. This is what you wanted, isn't it?'

'I don't know any more, Prof. I mean, look — let's step back a bit, not that *you* need to step back — it's all you ever do: Zalie was almost six foot, played hockey and tennis. He's ... what? Six-one, six-two *max*, thin as a rake and all he plays is the guitar and the medieval banjo—'

'Lute.'

'Whatever ... I mean: how's he a) going to strangle her without her screaming or fighting back, and b) going to sling her over his shoulder or drag her out, bundle her into his car, drive her across the bridge, down that wet soggy muddy path, dump her and then come back. All without leaving mud, dogshit, bits of crap on his clothes or in his car or in his hallway. Not to mention scratches or bruises on him? Remember that, too, Prof: he's been swabbed, examined, poked about. Clothes checked, washing-machine drum analysed, toilet lifted off and drains checked. Nothing.'

'I don't know, Gary – maybe you could have asked those questions before.'

'That's a low blow, Prof ... You're the one leading the investigation. You're the organ grinder ... I'm just the monkey. If you hadn't spent so much of your time dreaming about your schooldays and trying to find pictures of yourself in shorts, you might have actually taken the lead. You know – used your brain for something other than dreaming.'

'You seemed pretty certain he was guilty, Gary—'

'I was, yes, because I go with what's obvious 'til it stops being obvious. That's what people like me do. That's our job – in homes and offices across the land, in films and novels, that's what we're here for. But you ... you're officer class, you are, Prof ... it's people like you who tell us plebs what to do. In World War One you'd be sending me over to check for snipers, then if I survived I'd be bringing tea and newspapers to your bunk and calling you *Sir*. You're the one with the school blazer and the dictionary up your arse and the college degree ...'

He's right. I shouldn't have let myself be carried off by Gary's rush to box things up: teacher to weirdo to pervert to murderer in three moves. Gary was being Gary. I was being ... indecisive, unprofessional, weak and unfocused. Blurred inside. I was being me.

I phone Mrs Latimer to tell her we've spoken to Jack, and that she can scrub off his graffiti. We won't need to talk to her or Sally again.

'Thank God for that,' she says, loudly over the radio news. She turns the volume down: 'At least you've got your man now.'

*

The announcement comes just in time for the hour-long *news and comment* on Radio 4. In traffic jams, on trains, in pubs and at tea-time dining tables across the country, they learn that we've arrested Mr Wolphram and charged him with murder and with perverting the course of justice. *Perverting the corpse of justice* is how Gary puts it.

It's no longer 'a spot of monstering'. This is the shredding of his life, the murder of all he is.

They've had forty-eight hours to work up their stories, assemble their 'witnesses', their 'friends-and-colleagues-came-forwards', their 'asked-not-to-be-nameds', their 'pupils-break-their-silences' and their 'neighbours-always-suspecteds'. What Gary read to me earlier from the *Evening Post* was just the vapour off the sewage of their 'news' compared with what's happening now. I see Lynne has syndicated much of her information, and is named as a co-reporter in the *Daily Mail*. She'll be getting paid serious bonus money from her usual paper, plus one-off fees for every piece she writes for the nationals, all the syndicated articles she sells. Every paper and TV channel has someone camped outside his flat, outside the station, around the school. They're stopping random people, current teachers, sniffing out the pupils. In the Fleet Street offices they're combing through electoral registers and databases for addresses and phone numbers, racing each other to find ex-pupils, ex-colleagues ... anyone who can give them a story. The foreign press is here, their correspondents translating third-hand headlines and pumping out the factoids.

'Got to keep telling ourselves he's guilty,' says Gary, 'or we'll go under.'

'When you have to keep telling yourself something, it means you don't believe it, Gary. It's like whistling in a haunted house to show you're not scared. It's because you're scared.'

Gary looks miserable. Even the tight fatness of his face has gone slack, and the skin seems to hang suddenly, liposucted by disappointment and self-doubt.

Deskfish is about to make a statement on the police station steps, we hear on the car radio. Neither of us can face heading back to work straight away. Gary doesn't need to tell me, but I know: he thinks Mr Wolphram is not our man. That realisation has been settling on Gary so slowly that I hadn't seen it until it was there.

I have parked a few streets from the station to avoid the crowds of reporters and rubbernecking gawpers. Gary has turned the radio up, and Deskfish is talking: 'We have this afternoon charged a sixty-eight-year-old neighbour in connection with the murder of Zalie Dyer.

We can confirm that he was a teacher at a local school and lived on the same street. We would like to thank the public for their patience and all those who have come forward with information. Most of all we would like to thank Zalie's parents for their bravery in this tragic time ...'

It's a cold, dry, clear-skied evening. The fatberg remains there, the workmen are still at it, miners at a blubber coalface. But there are no spectators. It looks like an abandoned Leviathan made of lard, yesterday's attraction being packed up into trucks as the circus leaves town. The selfie sticks and camera flashes have moved on. They're outside the station now, front and back, and Gary and I have to pick our way through.

Inside, it's a chaos of ringing phones and pinging screens. Deskfish is talking on both of his landlines – one on speaker and the other receiver to ear. 'Same shit, different phones,' says Gary, barging past Thicko and Small-Screen, who are standing proudly at their desks, enjoying the attention. In their heads, they are in a mini-series and they're congratulating each other just as the credits start to roll and the theme tune kicks in. The incident room's three TV monitors are tuned to different stations – one radio; one twenty-four-hour news, where different photographs of Mr Wolphram and Zalie come on, spliced with on-scene reporting from the street, the school, outside the zoo; and another showing the last ten minutes of *Pointless* before the six o'clock news. A quiz show that involves getting the fewest points possible, the banter and the jackpot are puny but somehow reassuring: despite the killing, the violence, the famines and the wars, on magnolia sofas all over the country, middlebrow life goes on.

The Headmaster

Doc Monk has moved up in the world, or in his version of it: he's the headmaster of Chapelton College, and here he now stands, with the school looking like a film set behind him: the sports fields and the cricket pavilion, the Victorian gothic library with its flying buttresses, the dining hall and the quad, the statues of generals and brigadiers. The kinds of people Gary thinks of when he imagines people like me sending people like him to war. It is a postcard-perfect view, an advert for the English upper classes: imposing enough to intimidate, but not so remote that it can't be reassuringly purchased. The roofs are finialed at each end, and topped with cockscomb ridging, so that, silhouetted against a deep blue sky, the buildings look cut out of black cardboard. Their windows glow Christmas-card red and gold.

There is even musical accompaniment – if you listen carefully you can hear the choir singing in the chapel, whose huge rose window glitters from inside, burns like a brazier behind its leaded glass. It's not a concert, because the organ keeps reprising the notes and the choir keeps starting again mid-hymn, but a rehearsal for the

Christmas carol service tomorrow. Always full of visiting dignitaries, the occasional minor royal, it's one of the big days in the school calendar. This year it's being recorded live for Classic FM, so the school must find Zalie's murder ill-timed as well as embarrassing.

The Doc isn't taller, but he has cleverly stage-managed his appearance so that he speaks from the top step of the parapet. From here the reporters must film him from below, where they cluster on the grass of the playing fields. He has learned from the statues behind him: everyone looks bigger and better on a plinth. He has on his Old Chapeltonian tie, and somewhere along the decades he has swapped the three-piece tweed suits of an old-world Oxbridge intellectual for the navy pinstripe of modern management. Today's school might keep a few teachers dressed as teachers around the place for folkloric purposes, but this is the uniform that reassures the money men and the education boards.

The place used to be dead between terms or at weekends, peopled only by those students whose parents lived too far away for them to return home and by the bachelor teachers coming in for their free meals. Now it's a year-round buzz of seminars, office awaydays and conferences. There is even some confetti mashed into the quadrangle's flagstones where someone was recently married. Who the hell would get married in their old school, Gary wants to know.

Gary is now looking at the Doc: 'That's a lot of chins for one face,' he says, and Gary knows better than most of us how many chins a face can accommodate. 'Was he around in your day?' he nudges me with his elbow.

'Oh yes,' I whisper, 'I'll tell you all about the Doc later.' But for now, our eyes are on the TV.

The murder is the first item on the national news: 'There have been rapid developments in the investigation into the murder of Zalie Dyer. Following the arrest of Michael Wolphram earlier today, we've been informed that the school's headmaster, Dr Martin Monk, is about to make a statement on behalf of Chapelton College. We're going live to our East of England correspondent, Ellie Nash ...'

Ellie Nash – I recognise the name from a string of answerphone messages we never answered – is not what you would expect from a regional reporter catching a twenty-four-carat national news story. She has big, US-TV-News-anchor hair, and wears black trousers, a bright red jacket with shoulder pads and a chunky necklace made of heavy squares of jade. She has the air of someone reporting live from the 1980s, some faraway place down the decades where everything is raucous and overlit, and where everyone looks microwaved.

Slightly apart from the crowd, she speaks into the microphone more loudly and more breathlessly than she needs to, but this is part of the vibe she's after – the sense of a world where things are happening faster than they can be told:

'I'll be reporting live from Chapelton College, the prestigious school now in the limelight for all the wrong reasons,' she begins: 'Its alumni number politicians, actors, foreign presidents and prime ministers. These playing fields have been trodden by military heroes, elite sportsmen and Olympic champions in the course of the school's two hundred years of history. But now it's the centre of attention for very different reasons, because this is where Mr Wolphram worked, the man today charged with the murder of Zalie Dyer. Dr Monk, the current headmaster, was a colleague of Mr Wolphram's, and worked with him until he retired when the school began accepting female pupils ...'

'What's that you said about correlation and causation, Prof?'

There's no time to answer because Doc Monk begins:

'Chapelton College deeply regrets the death of Zalie Dyer, and extends its sympathies to her family and loved ones. On behalf of the board of governors I would like to make clear that Mr Wolphram retired over a decade ago and has had nothing to do with the school since. No current pupils were taught by him, and very few of the teachers remember him.'

'Did you and Mr Wolphram work together? Can you tell us about him?' It's Ellie Nash's voice, though we can't see her.

The Doc looks unsure. With a slight tilt of the head he turns to someone to the left of the screen, away from the crest of microphones in front of him. The cameras pull back a little, drawing the first row of journalists into the frame, and several worried looking Chapelton College governors. He's looking for help from a man in a suit much like his, who has the air of a lawyer or a PR professional, and the self-conscious grooming of a man who makes a living from damage-limitation. Definitely the kind of person who, in Gary's nomenclature, would be *This Wanker* or *That*. 'Lanyard-swinging corporate twonks', he calls them. The wanker gives a tight little nod that means *Go ahead but if you don't stick to the script you're on your own*, and then, in freeze-dried English, the Doc begins:

'We worked together, yes, for a number of years. I had very little to do with him. He was always a bit of a loner, very private and very particular and precise in everything he did ... many of the teachers, like me, kept our distance from him ...'

'They're cutting him loose,' Gary whispers, 'the fuckers are cutting him loose ...'

'Can you blame them? They can't say he was always a weirdo or they'll be done for letting him go on working, but they can't say they never noticed anything because it'll make them look like they were failing in their duty of so-called care ...'

'Plus they've got all those parents paying ten thousand a year – they don't want to frighten them off ...' says Gary, underestimating Chapelton's school fees with an innocence I find endearing: 'Hear that? It's the sound of chequebooks snapping shut.' He thinks for a moment, then remarks with jaded triumph: 'Funny isn't it – it doesn't matter how upper crust they are ... how rich or powerful ... when things get difficult they all tell the same story: *it's got nothing to do with us, Guv* ... like some chav in a trackie who's just got caught with a wrap or a stolen iPad ... Suddenly no one knew him, no one liked him, it was all a long time ago and the past is another country ...'

As Gary speaks, the Doc proves him right: 'Mr Wolphram was here long before most of the staff now teaching. He was always rather aloof and – I repeat – had very little to do with the day-to-day running of the school, he wasn't involved in the sporting activities of the school, and he wasn't ever on the duty rotas of the boarding houses. The only parts of school life he was involved in – apart from teaching – were the musical and theatrical aspects ...'

'What about you personally? You're an old boy of the school, you were a pupil here and then came back to teach after university ...' It's Ellie again, and she's done her homework. She knows the Doc was here as a pupil, and came back. She has compared the dates and knows that he and Mr Wolphram overlapped by over twenty years.

'Me personally?' The Doc takes a deep breath: 'I *personally* found him inscrutable, distant and arrogant, but he also had a temper, and several of us were concerned even back in those days when there were no proper channels for these things to be ...' he stops for a moment, 'discussed ...'

'Why did nobody raise their concerns? Why didn't you?' asks Ellie. The Doc has walked – no, not walked: danced – into her trap. It's not a sophisticated trap, but clever people are always so alert to the complicated catch that they miss the simpleton's ambush. The dogshit in the burning bag, the brick behind the football ... Not that Ellie is a simpleton – on the contrary, she's clever, and certainly clever enough to know how easy it is to catch clever people out.

'Because ...' The Doc searches for the PR man, but he has pulled away and is texting furtively behind two photographers, 'because many of these things only become clear much later on and you must remember that Mr Wolphram may not have been much liked, or played a large role in school life, but there was never any specific allegation about him while he was employed by Chapelton College. If there had been, the school would of course have acted.' The Doc sweats and his neck looks red and swollen in its tight collar. 'Our procedures are watertight and have been in place for years – we have an excellent record of pupil welfare and we work hard to ensure we maintain it.'

'The man with the wooden tongue,' says Gary.

Ellie isn't going to let go: 'Given what we know, now that several ex-pupils have come forward with claims about Mr Wolphram's ... *unusual and suspicious* conduct as a teacher, how can the school justify employing him for so long – regardless of today's revelations and the police charges against him for the murder of Zalie Dyer?'

There's an excited, assenting buzz among the other reporters, so much so that they don't even ask their own questions – just let Ellie draw him out. 'If pupils are coming forward with these concerns now, and with reports of the rumours that were circulating about him in their time at school, surely it was the school's duty to be aware of these matters at the right time and to have people in place to whom pupils could speak in confidence ...'

The Doc is out on his own now, and the school governors behind him, besuited barrister types and accountants with number-cruncher eyes, shuffle towards the edges of the picture. What they want to see is a rendition of Pontius Pilate, an institutional handwashing after which justice of whatever kind – legal, natural, or mob – can take its course somewhere far away from the playing fields and bank accounts of Chapelton College.

The Doc wobbles: 'All I can do is repeat that the school would never have stood for any improper conduct and would of course have acted at once on any allegations. The school invites the police to be in touch regarding any specifics we can help with, but Chapelton College and the governors received no complaints back then, and have not received any complaints recently of a historic nature. We continue to be a happy, thriving and high-performing school and I'd like to reiterate that Mr

Wolphram was always a marginal figure on the staff, that he is not somebody Chapelton remembers with any sort of affection, and that he has had nothing to do with us for a long time ...'

There's a clamour at the front for more detail, but the Doc cuts it short and raises his hand:

'Thank you, that's all I have to say ... Once again, we extend our sympathies to the family of Zalie Dyer at this difficult time. Good evening and thank you.'

The camera cuts to Ellie for the closing package. Her eyes are lit, fired like the rose window behind her. Journalistically, she has been blooded; she has the taste for it, for all of it: the hunt, the quarry, the kill, and now the delay that gives the kill its gratification:

'That's all for now from Chapelton College, but to many viewers, and certainly to the police and judiciary, this terrible murder has also shone a spotlight on a period in recent history – *very* recent history – when things seemed to happen differently: in broadcasting, in the media, in radio and TV, in schools and hospitals and politics, society tolerated behaviour that today would be unacceptable and even illegal. There will surely be calls, after the Zalie Dyer case has been closed, for a full investigation of the culture of abuse and bullying in our schools, and especially perhaps in our so-called elite schools. It was not so long ago after all. After the revelations about Jimmy Savile and others, and the opening of historical abuse cases around the country, is it time for a full inquiry into what happened in the schools that produced so many generations of the British Establishment?'

'I like her,' says Gary. 'I'd swap her for Thicko or Small-Screen ... we'd be solving crimes all over the city, sweating witnesses ... plus she'd wrap Deskfish around her little finger.'

'I just don't buy it – I'm not ruling out that he killed someone – anyone can kill someone – but this stuff? Boys, puberty, sexual suggestions, touching them? No – either these pupils are lying – Jonny Kebab, for instance – or they're confusing memories of different teachers. That's possible, isn't it? Anyway,' I change the subject, 'why d'you like her and not Lynne Forester? They're not that different, are they?'

Gary thinks about it. 'I dunno, Prof, I guess I think she's after the bigger picture and she goes about it with more class; Mad Lynne just wants dirt to sell ...'

The news has moved on to freezing temperatures in London, floods in Yorkshire, and the death of a quiz show host. The fatberg has gone now. Unless they find a body in it, the fatberg has had its fifteen minutes of fame.

'Thirty-whatever years teaching there and that's what you get,' Gary says: 'Cut loose in front of millions of people ... It's carte blanche to just go ahead and say any old shit.'

Gary takes out his phone and swipes the touch screen to open Twitter. 'Look!' he says. It's everywhere: hashtag Chapelton, hashtag Wolphram, hashtag Zalie, hashtag Justice, hashtag Monster, hashtag historic abuse, hashtag endless hashtags ... He scrolls down the reams of comments and links, breathes in, shakes his head, closes his eyes, exhales dejectedly.

'What do you see, Gary?'

'What d'you think I see, Prof? It's Twitter! I see a sordid hysterical zoo, that's what I see, and now his old school's sold him out it's even worse ...'

'They were always going to do that, Gary — loyalty is exactly what the school can't be seen to give. You can understand them, can't you? Almost, I mean. And, anyway, you won't get loyalty from Dr Monk. He always hated Mr Wolphram. The poison dwarf we called him. Not very original but you can see why. I'm sure you'd have come up with something better, Gary, with your gift for a good nickname, but we were kids and it fitted.'

'Yeah, well, I'll cut you some slack, Prof — looks like the classic sadist to me, if rather on the small side; pert little man; portable — you know, the travel version, fits in your overhead locker …'

'Let me tell you about Doc Monk, Gary …'

The Trial

The Doc orders Danny to stand.

'The accused is Daniel Patrick McAlinden, an Irish Catholic teenager *from* ... oh yes: Newcastle.' The Doc lingers over the *from* and inserts quotation marks around it with his fingers, tweezering it out of the sentence so it can be mocked. 'A Republican sleeper who was welcomed into an English community and who is here with us at Chapelton College through the generosity of our benefactors. While the rest of you pay, Mr McAlinden is here *because* you pay. There's always someone paying, isn't there? And today Mr McAlinden will pay us all back a little of what he owes.'

He laughs but nobody follows him. The Doc's jokes are usually abstruse and self-involved anyway – the boys who want to laugh don't know it's a joke, the ones who know it's a joke don't find it funny. That's what a lot of the Doc's classes are like. Today, he senses that he doesn't have the crowd with him, and this failure to connect makes him all the more vengeful. Even in front of everyone, winged and grounded and humiliated, Danny can still make the Doc look stupid.

'First witness,' Doc Monk calls out. He has put on his black university gown, from the Oxford college he refers to at least once every lesson. Danny, Ander, Gwil and Neil Hall play a game called Dickhead Bingo, where they cross out each word, each misty-eyed evocation, as the Doc mentions them: The Oxford Union, Punting, First Class Honours, The High, Balliol, My Old Tutor with whom I'm still in touch ...

Doc knows about Dickhead Bingo, too, since he confiscated Neil Hall's home-made Bingo Card one day. He has to go easy on Neil, because Neil's dad is a famous lawyer and old boy of the school.

There's never less hate and resentment and brutality in the world – it just sometimes seems that way through a trick of distribution. What this means at Chapelton College, here and now, is that there's just more to take out on Danny and Ander, on Gwil and a few others. So today, Danny is being tried for all of them.

'I'll take the role of judge,' the Doc tells Danny, 'just to ensure balance and fairness ...'

He looks out at the class: there are not many hands up, not yet, because most of the boys are too shy to be the first into the spotlight. They'll wait and see how this pans out, and take their turn when it's safe.

Lansdale is first, porn-vendor, entrepreneur-in-training, the latest in a long line of Lansdales at Chapelton College. His father and his grandfather and great-grandfather before him have owned Lansdale's, one of the few independent department stores left in the country. Their shop is almost as old as the school, and one of their lines is the Chapelton uniform and sports kits. Everyone has to pass through Lansdale's at some time or other. Because the school is split into different houses, and each house has its own tie and blazer badge, and each rung on the school's hierarchy – house power, school prefect, head boy and deputy head boy – has its own tie and blazer badge, too, the clothing alone keeps the ground floor of Landsale's abuzz with fittings. Some boys are so rich they have them tailor-made – you see them with their distracted mothers or their nannies outside the fitting rooms as the Lansdale's staff fuss over them. Some boys have parents who wince at the cost of the blazers with their heavy badges, embossed with house or school or sports club crests, thick as the oil paint in a Van Gogh sunflower. Ander's grandmother worked from photos of the school uniform to make his: for a month before leaving for school, he stood in her workroom as she measured him for a suit, two pairs of trousers and a blazer. To the blazer she stitched the heavy badge, and now, if anyone notices that Ander's clothes aren't from Lansdale's or any of the school's other 'approved' suppliers, they only notice because of the lining inside his jackets, which is rich and shimmering and pulses like a computer screen when he takes them off. Lansdale's jackets and blazers look classy but they're cheap on the inside. Danny McAlinden and Gwil Isaac had their uniforms paid for by their scholarships. 'The clothes you're wearing,' the Doc tells them, 'were bought by us.'

The boys go to Lansdale's on Saturday afternoons. They like the perfume and make-up department because they can ogle the salesgirls and dream of the sex behind those bored eyes.

The boys, like the teachers, are in thrall to that great adolescent haunting that you think will pass but never really does; that instead just follows the curve of your ageing: the thought of all the sex being had elsewhere by others. But most of the boys don't have the balls to look at the women face-on, and the women are used to being ogled, so the boys slink past them or pretend to be looking for gifts for their mothers or sisters. They invent processions of sisters so they can keep coming back. Ander loves the smell of the women – not the fresh perfume that blazes out of the vaporiser, but the weathered, mellow, skin-warmed scent that's a few hours old, that has been lived in by a body and compressed behind clothes, mingled with sweat or cigarette smoke, and that turns him on because it's so complex and individual. He'd lick the little gulf between the base of their necks and their collarbones because in his mind that's where people's smell is kept.

Doc: 'The accusation please, Mr Lansdale.'

Lansdale: 'He's arrogant … thinks he knows every-thing.' Lansdale has strutted his way to the front and puffed out his chest to speak. Only now, he realises he has nothing else to say and stands there dumb, rigid with embarrassment. He looks to the Doc to help him out.

'Can you be more precise, Mr Lansdale? The court understands the accusation and doubtless sympathises, but requires some hard specifics – particulars – to process the information.'

Lansdale thinks it over. Lewis puts up his hand, calls out, 'Sir – please … I've …'

The Doc cuts him off: 'You'll get your chance, Lewis, everyone in the courtroom will have their say …' He turns again to Lansdale: 'Continue.'

They say that, with betrayal, it's beginning that's the hard bit. After that, it slides along nicely on its own – after you start, you become a function of it, rather than vice versa.

That's certainly how Lansdale makes it look:

'He sits there, thinks he knows more than the teachers, answers the questions with irrelevant stuff. It's just arrogant. *He's* arrogant, he puts us all down, laughs at us behind out backs. Thinks he knows more than the teachers ...'

The Doc likes this. 'These are certainly serious accusations,' he says gravely, 'and they're of course hurtful and damaging to the school community, to the maintenance of respect and therefore to the delivery of sound teaching. It's the ungratefulness, too, that irks, isn't it? ...' He puts his head back, takes a breath, inhales a noseful of the air like a sommelier at a fine wine. His eyes are half closed. He's happy. This is the peak of what he is and all he will ever be: a man who has reduced the world to the size of the classroom that he rules, and to the duration of the lesson where he is master. He's trembling with contentment. It is as if he is being massaged from the inside – he might even be purring, though no one except Danny is close enough to hear. The Doc is exactly where he wants to be. He's powerful, he's in charge, and he has released a force that, for all its destructiveness, will remain his to control.

'Go on,' says the Doc in a tone of judicial dispassion copied from television. In the film of himself that plays in the Sunday matinee of his mind, he is a just but firm righter of wrongs. Solomon, maybe, or Rumpole of the Bailey. That, at any rate, is the metaphor Mr Wolphram will use later, when he apologises for the Doc's actions and says sorry for arriving too late.

There's a cheer from the back, from the backrow bastards, as Mr Lawnder called them before he cracked up and left. In the film they're all in, which has spread from the Doc's mind to the class mind, they've got a taste for blood. But they're in the right because the Doc says so. Danny is their quarry, and anything goes.

'He laughs at you behind your back, sir. Says you're ...'

'What, Lansdale, what? What does he say I am?'

'He says you're short, sir ...' Lansdale realises he needs to do better than this, because he has picked out one of the claims that is undeniably, undebatably true. He needs to recover or the prosecution is in trouble: 'that you've got small-man syndrome, you're ignorant ... a snob, says you're always going on about Balliol and Oxford and all the famous politicians you used to know from your pathetic − *his* word, Sir, *pathetic* − debating society at the Oxford Union who are now MPs and ministers and rich bankers and who can't even remember you, while you're ...'

Lansdale dries up − he hasn't taken enough breath to get the whole sentence out so he stalls on the words and breathes in another lungful. Also, he's afraid because he is getting to the bone, the marrow, of what makes the Doc the Doc.

'While I'm what, Lansdale? While I'm what exactly?' For a moment it's hard to tell who exactly is on trial: Danny or Jonny Kebab.

'While you're here, Sir, while you're here in your classroom teaching Latin verbs to bored children and checking the contents of ...' he looks around for help and there is no help, 'of boys' pants … *his* words, Sir, not mine, that's what *he* says.'

Jonny Kebab looks tragic up there – he looks like he's the accused, and he squirms and sweats like a paid witness breaking down in a courtroom drama. He's a scared, dishonest boy, but he's not, or not mainly, evil; not deliberately interested in causing harm to others. He's just in it for himself, and he does what is expected of him by whoever holds the power or the purse. It's not complicated. And, anyway, thinks Ander, after studying history for a couple of terms, who any longer thinks human beings are complicated? Certainly not us. Not me. Maybe Jonny Kebab is even sorry that he's got Danny into this trouble, because Jonny doesn't really do bullying, he just does self-preservation. If it hurts him to help you, he won't. If it doesn't, he will. Morally, he is the bubble in the centre of the spirit level. He is complete neutrality. Until he's under threat, or feels afraid, or is up in front of everyone and needs to find someone to take his place on the scaffold. People make armies and religions and economies out of the likes of Jonny Kebab.

He also knows that Danny won't hold it against him, that Danny is clever enough to know that Jonny has no choice, and kind enough not to look for reasons – beyond the Doc's malice – for what is about to happen. Jonny is … as he'll say later to anyone who'll listen … *as much of a victim in all this as McAlinden* … Even in betrayal Jonny is an entrepreneur, finds ways of rebranding his cowardice as victimhood and finding new markets for it.

Doc Monk walks up to Lansdale, and begins, as he puts it, the 'cross-examination'.

'These are all serious accusations, and the defendant will have the chance later on to respond to them. But there are other charges, more serious still, and these constitute the reason we are all here.'

Nobody knows where this is going. They knew it would be bad, of course it would, but they didn't know the turn it would take.

The Doc begins: 'Mr Lansdale, did you, at any point following the terrorist murder in Brighton last October, just a few miles from where we're sitting today, hear McAlinden expressing sympathy for the bombers?'

Jonny thought it was over but it's not. He wasn't ready for this. This is different. It's now not just a joke that got out of hand, the kind of thing you can look back on and say *went too far*, sprinkle a bit of regret over and then move on. This is a different agenda, and it comes from a place in the world that lies outside the school walls, a place where people get killed and maimed and blown up.

When Ander thinks about it later he likens it in his mind to a child finding that his toy gun has suddenly been turned into a real one.

'What do you mean, Sir?' Jonny asks helplessly. His grasp on current affairs is no firmer than on past ones. You can see him computing, in his messy mind, the fragments of news that reached him through radio headlines or overheard conversations. He tries to sort the political stuff from the football results, from the showbiz gossip and the various natural disasters in unpronounceable places across the globe. He remembers the school assembly and the minute's silence and he thinks he's got it. The Bombing. Yes. The IRA. Brighton. October. November maybe. The hotel, the injured stretchered out. The fury in the headlines. The graffiti on the bus stop by the bridge: IRISH OUT. INTERMENT [sic] NOW. The graffiti outside his dad's department store one morning:

HANG IRISH SCUM. They'd had to scrub that off before the shoppers arrived.

But none of that helps him because Danny hasn't said anything. He'd report Danny straight away *if* there was anything to report. O God, yes. Some people find it hard to lie because they're honest. Jonny Kebab finds it hard to lie because he doesn't have the imagination to stray beyond the truth.

'I'm not sure, Sir,' he says, 'we haven't really spoken about it.'

'I mean did you hear the accused comment on his sympathy for the atrocities committed by the Irish Republican Army?'

Lansdale has never heard anything of the sort. Anyway, if Danny ever *had* said anything like that, he wouldn't have said it to Jonny Kebab. What Danny *did* say was something else, but that doesn't matter in a show trial. And Jonny can't even really remember it, let alone work out what it meant.

What Danny said was, 'What do they expect? It's a war.' And he said that to Ander and Neil and a couple of others over lunch. He'd thought nothing of it – didn't even know who the *they* referred to.

'Like what, Sir?' says Jonny Kebab. What he means is *feed me the line and I'll say yes and then you can let me go back and fade into the crowd. I can't invent a lie, but if you build me a stepladder of untruths and hold my hand as I go, I'll climb it as high as you need me to climb.*

'It's obvious, Mr Lansdale: did you hear him say anything about how they had it coming, that it served them right? Comments that revealed support for the bombing? There are other witnesses, so your testimony is not strictly necessary, but of course it would help clarify the question.'

Jonny thinks it over. The Doc has done two things to push Jonny across the line: first he has told him what to say, and second he has said that there are others who will do the same. That way, Jonny is reassured that whatever happens happens regardless of him – being helpless and irrelevant is a huge relief to Lansdale.

'He said *they deserved it.*' Jonny is relieved to be of help. He looks at Danny, who shakes his head but doesn't protest. 'I heard him.'

'Can you remember the context and the specific date of the conversation?' asks the Doc.

Jonny Kebab hasn't had time to manufacture either the context or date of anything. He is a liar without a script. He looks lost. How can one be specific about a day and time for when something didn't happen?

'Just after it happened.' He blurts out. 'The day after the bombing. When it was on the news. He said it after assembly. Then he said—'

The Doc cuts him off before the lie becomes too obviously implausible. 'Thank you, that's enough. Were there any witnesses to what you heard?'

'I'm not sure. It was after assembly so there were lots of people around.'

'I heard it, too,' says Vaughan, always ready to help the Doc.

'And me,' shouts Hugh Lewis, who goes where Vaughan goes.

There's excitement at the back as the sadists and bullies start to call out and jeer. Then come the followers and the plodders, the herd sensing the direction of movement. Their chairs screech on the floor as they adjust their positions for a better view, or for more of the Doc's attention. The hands go up chaotically, like rifles in a *Dad's Army* parade. They heard it all, yes, that's what he said, and he repeated it later, said *they had it coming, good for them* ... 'He supports the IRA, Sir,' someone calls out. 'His dad's a terrorist!' 'Kneecap him!'

Then: 'SHOULD BE FUCKING SHOT!' someone snarls, but Ander can't make out who it was. Strange, because he knows all of their voices from having listened to their accents in order to learn his own. That snarl doesn't correspond to anyone in the class. Anyone in the entire school. It's from somewhere else altogether. He looks them over: Lewis, Vaughan, Dumbo Daniels, Midgley, Paul, Tristan, Cobbleson, Roger Bowden and a few others at the back or on the margins of the class. But none of them have the voice he's just heard.

Ander thinks that maybe all the hate in those words – the real, adult hate, the kind that makes people kill and torture each other, burn down people's houses while they sleep – required a different voice, a voice other than a child's, though it was a child it must have come from. He thinks maybe something possessed one of the boys and took his mouth for itself. Full-throated, burning blood-hate – it flashed there for a moment and then went. But not away. It never went away.

Or he thinks that he invented it, that it was all in his head.

Ander never heard it again at school, but he's heard it since, seen it at work, on streets after pubs close, in houses where men beat women, and at EDL rallies and football matches. He's almost familiar with it now; he can recognise it. It's the sound of hatred looking for an object to fix itself to. Roving hate. It all comes through the police station and goes out one of two ways: into the jails or back on the streets, back into homes and bedrooms and kitchens. Back behind closed doors and drawn curtains. He hears it a lot now, and though the people it comes from differ, it's the same hate he heard back then, back there. Back when he was a child.

Ander must be the only one to have caught it that day, because none of the others show any sign of having heard it. If they had it would have stopped the room. Even the Doc would have called it all off. He wonders if Danny heard it.

'They're lying,' says Danny struggling to stay calm, 'that isn't what I said.' His face burns, his neck especially, pocked with bright red marks like countries on a map.

The Doc: 'There are several witnesses, all of them credible, and all of them agreeing not just on the general gist of your remark but on the details of the words you used.'

'They're lying,' repeats Danny. 'What I said was different.'

'Be quiet: you'll have plenty of time to defend yourself as the trial progresses,' the Doc snaps. Danny still scares him. 'You can call some of your friends as defence witnesses as soon as the case for the prosecution is made.'

For the next twenty minutes, the Doc calls his witnesses. They say the same things, following the Doc's simple script: IRA sympathies, support for the Birmingham Six, the Guildford Four. Not just about the Brighton bombing anymore, but enlarging into a more general sympathy for Irish terror in all its forms, all the way back to the beginning. McAlinden hates us. His people hate us. And here we are giving them jobs and scholarships. Lewis, Vaughan, Carter and some of the others come up with a few sound bites about McAlinden's 'history' of IRA support. 'He's got form,' says one. Then they add a series of satellite charges – 'He's gay', 'effeminate', 'he's one of those queers, Sir', 'poof', 'intellectual' . . .

They're throwing it all in now, everything they hate and fear and envy about him.

How Danny sits through it Ander and the others will never understand. He trembles and bites his lip. He looks at the class and shakes his head, looks at his friends as if they are onshore and he's on a boat being carried out to sea. But he doesn't cry.

'What have you to say in your defence?' the Doc asks Danny.

'I said it was a war.'

'According to these witnesses you said it served us right, that we *had it coming*. Do you deny that?'

'I said *What do you expect? It's a war*. Those were my exact words. Nothing else. I didn't say anything else on the subject. I didn't say anything about anyone *deserving* it. No one answered me, so there wasn't anything else said after that. Ander I think it was just changed the subject.'

Ander gets up and says, 'Yes – that's all we heard, that's all he said, then we talked about something else.'

Neil Hall gets up and says, loudly and calmly, looking at the Doc: 'That's right. I was there. I heard. And, anyway, this isn't right. This whole show . . . it's gone too far, Sir.'

Gwil: 'Get a grip, Dr Monk, this is out of control!'

Dave Sweeting: 'Stop, Sir, please – it's all wrong.'

The Doc ignores them and addresses Danny: 'So you were indeed expressing support for the Irish Republican Army and their atrocities?' He says it in the tone that prosecutors in legal dramas have when they have someone cornered, when they have taken their words and ransacked them for meanings the accused never intended. 'Let me remind you of the facts: five people were killed on 12 October last year, and dozens wounded, and scores of innocent people have died in previous bombings — not just soldiers and elected politicians but ordinary people going about their daily lives in cities all across England. This is, in effect, what you support.'

Danny is starting to behave as if he really were on trial. He acts like a careful witness measuring his words. Ander thinks it's a mistake to appear to accept a situation that is as absurd as it is sinister. *Just go!* he thinks, *Get up and leave!* he shouts inside his head, hoping that somehow Danny will hear him from inside his.

Danny knows the Doc wants to trap him. Maybe Danny thinks he can write his own script to set against the Doc's? He speaks slowly, commandingly but not so loud that it's hard to sustain his pitch over several sentences, and enunciates every word: 'I said that the IRA thinks of it as a war and the British state does, too. You just don't admit it's a war. You call it *terror*. But if one side thinks it's a war that's enough — it's a war. To them the British government is the enemy.'

'*The Enemy?* Really? *Whose* enemy?' asks the Doc leeringly, 'You mean *your* enemy?'

'I didn't say that. I don't mean that.' Danny looks like he is about to say something, but doesn't.

'You are telling us that the *enemy* — as you put it — is the British. *Your* enemy, is that right? Your words, not mine. Are *we* your enemies, Mr McAlinden?'

Danny is silent.

'Let the court note the defendant's refusal to answer. What,' asks the Doc, pausing for effect and starting again,

'*What* is warlike about blowing people up in train stations, putting bombs under cars or killing people – civilians – in pubs in London and Birmingham? That isn't war, it's terrorism.' There's a cheer from the back. 'The Irish Republicans are no *army* – to call them that is an insult to armies the world over ...' There's a slight froth at the corners of Monk's mouth when he's excited, and it acts as a lubricant to the toy-debating-chamber eloquence he learned in Oxford. It is less sticky than Morbender's, more aerated, and if you look closely you can see tiny bubbles of saliva fizz and burst as his lips move. He wipes his mouth quickly and sets his jaw at a Churchillian jut, the way he used to do at Oxford after landing a *bon mot* on his opponent.

'Dr Monk,' says Danny shakily, trying to hold his own against the rising chorus of jeers, 'all armies kill civilians, whatever they tell you ... however advanced they are.' A scrunched-up ball of paper coated in ink hits his face as he speaks, then falls onto the front of his shirt. He has a blue splatter on his cheek and a smear down his neck and collar. The Doc turns around and walks to his filing cabinet, and while he has his back to them Vaughan walks up to Danny and spits into his eyes: 'Clean it off with that.'

By the time the Doc has returned to face them, Vaughan is back in his seat, asmirk and with his arms crossed: a proud worker surveying a job well done.

The Doc has something black in his hand, something velvety that shines like some animal's rich pelt. It's sleek and ripples like mink. No one can make out what it is. Perhaps Danny can, as he's closest, but he has other things to worry about right now.

'You are saying, are you, Mr McAlinden, that there is equivalence between the bandits of the Provisional

IRA and the British Army? And are you saying that Republican terror is justified and that you support it?'

Danny looks lost. He doesn't answer. He blinks. Quickly at first and then slowly and at longer intervals, hoping to open his eyes on something different, something other than this.

'I don't know why you're asking me,' says Danny, 'what's any of it got to do with me?'

'Answer the question, Mr McAlinden: are you justifying the actions of the Irish Republican Army? Are you supporting those actions as alleged by your fellow pupils? And do you wish to dispute the evidence put before the court? This is your last chance before we proceed to sentencing!' The Doc is almost shouting now.

'I said it was a war. That's all I said and it's all I meant. It's not an equal war and they aren't equal armies, but they're armies and they're at war. You're seen as an occupying army. Their army doesn't have tanks and planes and uniforms. But they've got guns and they've got bombs. Your army shoots people in the streets and gives weapons to death squads who kill people in their homes. It's a war, whatever name you give it. *That* is what people there say. I never thought it before, I always tried to stay away from it, it's got nothing to do with me because I'm here and I'm English ... but when I see you doing this to me I understand why they think the way they do.'

Nobody speaks. Nobody moves or breathes. No one knows where that came from. Danny has never said anything like it before, not like that. Danny himself, even as he speaks, looks half amazed to hear the words come out of his mouth. It comes from a place inside him that no one, maybe Danny included, ever knew existed.

'Well, well,' says the Doc, '*your* army, you say? *Your* newspapers? I think the court has heard enough. *Occupying? Right?* I think we have enough to make up our minds.'

Danny has given the Doc what he wanted. True, Danny didn't break down – there'll be time for that soon enough, thinks the Doc – but he gave him plenty. It was as good as a confession. No – actually, it was better than a confession, because a confession places the onus on the judge to be lenient. A confession works in the accused's favour by displaying honesty and contrition. This was defiance, and, though it has surprised the Doc as much as anyone else, it has also given him something even better than what he wanted.

No leniency called for here.

The Doc reaches for the black velvet cloth on his desk and lifts it up.

It is a hood, or a bag, with a little drawstring around the base where it can be closed to keep the light out, or the darkness in.

Ander gets up and leaves the room.

He runs down the corridor. As the sun streams in through the high windows he sees the skids of thick polish that the janitor has forgotten to work into the parquet flooring. The downstairs toilets are open and he sees the cubicle doors, all of them ajar, smells the permanent odour of a sewage-lagoon. The urinals jammed with chewing gum and cigarette butts macerating in piss. The toilets where there's always one obstinate stool lodged at the bottom of the bowl, rusting in flushwater like a submarine corroding on the seabed. He wants to go to the headmaster's office and tell him to come and stop it. But at the man's door he realises he won't stop it, because the head is the Doc's protector, and the Doc is the head's representative on earth, or at least this bit of it, and he turns back. In that great corridor, gravy-brown floor and walls the colour of dirty custard, he wobbles and hesitates, then runs in the opposite direction, back whence he came and up the stairs to English.

He listens at Mr Wolphram's door – the low rumble of words, a laugh, the kind you only hear when the joke is literary, a little cognoscenti-chuckle – then he knocks. The talking stops but there is no reply. He knocks again, harder.

The slow, deep-voiced 'Come in'. He stands there before a class of sixth-formers. They're doing a poem. Obviously. Mr Wolphram is standing up and has the book open in his hand, the spine balanced on his palm, the covers resting on his spread fingers and thumb. Ander notices again that Mr Wolphram has the handspan of a concert pianist. He holds the book almost at arm's length as he reads, and high up, as if he is about to release it into flight ...

The sixth-formers look older and cooler. They're relaxed, too. And interested, engaged in what he's saying. Mr Wolphram doesn't insist on them wearing their jackets or ties in class, so some of them have unbuttoned their shirts and hung their ties on their chairs. A few have tucked their ties inside their shirts, between the top button and the second in the manner of the day's pop singers. The head hates it, which adds the tang of defiance to the prestige of fashion. Wolphram doesn't care about stuff like non-regulation cardigans, thin ties and Bowie-haircuts. When he showed the fifth-formers *Quadrophenia* they spent the rest of the term trying to look like Mods, tapering their trousers, wearing the thin ends of their school ties forward, swapping their crappy school moccasins for sharp lace-ups with pointed toes.

They're all looking at Ander.

'Well?' asks Mr Wolphram. His eyes are wide open, eyebrows so high they've almost disappeared behind the fringe.

'I'm sorry to interrupt. There's something happening in Dr Monk's room and I ... it's not right and we need help.'

'What sort of thing?' asks Mr Wolphram. But Ander gets the feeling Mr Wolphram knows, or suspects, or has been here before.

'It's a trial,' says Ander helplessly.

Mr Wolphram snaps the book shut and turns to the class. 'Carry on without me—'

He motions Ander to leave the room with him, slowly shutting the door behind. Suddenly, he is quick, taking the corridor and then the stairs at a strangely athletic pace. It's not running, more of a fast hovering walk that Ander has trouble keeping up with. Ander starts to try to explain things to him but he's breathless and realises Mr Wolphram isn't really listening. Anyway, how do you explain putting a child on trial in a classroom with his teacher as judge?

As they approach the Doc's room, they hear the crack of what sounds like a bullet. It tears the air in half and then echoes along the corridor. Then silence.

When they reach the Doc's room, they see Danny in a chair, the black hood over his head, Vaughan and Lewis holding him by the shoulders. He's shaking so hard that even as they press him down, their hands shake with him. In front of the class a small circle of backrow bastards stands like a police cordon, pushing Neil Hall and Gwil and Rich Nicholson back. Gwil has his hand at one of their throats but the scene is still as a painting.

Jonny Kebab and several of the others are in their seats looking down, waiting for things to finish. They are people of the crowd, the great grey average. They are what's left when you've done your sums of good and evil. They know it and they are okay with it. They won't pull the trigger or put the noose around your head, but neither will they give you the keys to your cell or hide you in their cellar. The school produces them, too; produces mostly them, in fact. They are its human plasticine. As Wolphram told them once: 'While you may not have the talent to succeed, you can take comfort from the fact that your mediocrity will stop you from failing.'

Now Mr Wolphram's arrival breaks the illusion. They were having a good time but now it's no longer a game and here they are, stuck on the wrong side of the rules.

The Doc still has his hand on the huge *Oxford Latin Dictionary*, a clothbound blue slab the size of a child, that he slammed down on the desk to mimic the sound of the bullet to the head in his kangaroo court.

They're too late for the mock-execution.

What happens next Ander will remember for the rest of his life, and, unlike many important events in a life, it won't accrue extra detail with every telling (who would he tell anyway?) or fade away like a photograph left in sunlight. It stays clean-edged and bright; complete and squared-off in its frame of retrospect:

Mr Wolphram roars. It's a great, deep, rolling cry of fury. Maybe also pain. Ander can't quite tell because the fury comes in over and around it, but, yes, maybe some pain, too. Ander is attuned to that Möbius strip of anger and sorrow, fury and pain. Wolphram's roar seems to suck the air out of the room, out of everyone in the room. The Doc jumps; they all jump. In a moment Wolphram has taken the hood off Danny and brought him back up to his feet. It's now that Ander sees what they hadn't seen before: Danny's hands are tied behind his back with his own tie; tightly, it's true, though it's more for symbolism than for physical restraint. It's an extra humiliation, and for the Doc it's another detail to get off to. Mr Wolphram tries to unbind Danny's wrists but the tie is so tightly knotted that he needs to drag it over his hands and knuckles to get it off, rippling his skin and leaving his wrists white where the blood flow has been cut off.

Vaughan and Lewis have already gone, the crowd control at the front has disappeared, Rich Nicholson and Gwil and Neil Hall have sat back down. Only the Doc is still in place. The dictionary holds him up, gives him ballast.

Mr Wolphram takes Danny by the elbow and leads him out of the room. To the Doc, he says slowly, enunciating every syllable: 'You are a poisonous child hiding inside a man: a vicious, evil little coward.'

The Doc cannot lose face in front of his class, but he looks stupid in his gown and the boys have already sensed that the room's balance of power has changed.

He opens his mouth to speak and his voice trembles and breaks: '*I* will deal with discipline in *my* classroom as I see fit. I don't come barging into your class and tell you what to do. You have no—'

But Mr Wolphram has gone, taking Danny with him. The Doc keeps going anyway. He has to keep face, say his piece, make his stand:

'—right to question my judgement. This is *my* classroom and these are *my* rules.' He bangs his hand on the desk and looks around, but no one meets his eye. People are starting to leave though the lesson is not over – Ander and Neil, Nicholson, Gwil Isaac are all going. The Doc doesn't challenge them. Even Lansdale and the class cattle are moving off.

Also, the black velvet hood is gone.

They find out later that Mr Wolphram has taken Danny to the headmaster, who will do nothing. At first, he assures them both that the episode (that's what he calls it, an *episode*) will be 'looked into'. Then he adds that depressing rider we all remember from school, when one person is being bullied and the other is bullying them, and the teacher arrives and wants to hear 'both sides of the story', that he wants to 'hear Dr Monk's version of events before he *rushes* to judgement'.

A Hand down the Nation's Pants

Gary hasn't interrupted me, and has listened silently, sometimes wincing at details like the tied hands, the spit on the face — strange how we focus on things like that, how details are the rivets that keep our feelings close to their causes. He looks thoughtful, bites his lip, weighs up what to say. Nothing less than what Wolphram used to call *le mot juste* will do.

'What a cunt.'

There are different ways of getting to the truth, but if there's a shortcut, Gary likes to take it.

'So natty old Mr Wolphram came to save the day?'

'He saved one day, Gary, but there were others, there are always other days when you're in a place like that. But eventually it got better, yes. Mostly. Though I don't know if that was just getting older and less of the bad stuff came our way. Maybe it was still going on at the back of our lives. Or whether there was *progress* ... Not that McAlinden was there to see it ...'

'The Irish kid left?'

'He wasn't Irish, Gary. Christ, that's the whole point, but, yeah, okay – him,' I reply. 'He left. That's another story. Actually, it's probably the same story, but there's a sort of interval between the acts. All I know is that day Mr Wolphram took Danny back to his room to clean up his inky face, then took him to the headmaster to tell him the whole story.'

'What happened next?'

'He said *leave it with me* and it really was left. The Doc stayed, tamed a little, seething with hate for all of us, Wolphram especially, but he had to watch himself. He'd gone too far, got caught, broke the rule of keeping his stuff out of public view. So it was a bit different, yes – the Doc laid off us and we were all moved to another class after Christmas. They pretended that was a normal rearrangement. They shuffled the cards, they didn't change the deck. We got a different teacher and he was okay. It was a change.'

'Ah yes, the old private school motto: a change of hand on your arse is as good as a rest,' says Gary.

'Maybe there was a bit of that. Lots of the teachers were violent, a few groped us or touched us – one liked to put his fingers in your mouth – and some were just moody and kicked or slapped us then forgot about it. That all continued as normal. One or two would take us back to their flats for a few drinks and smokes, but we quite liked that – we watched horror films, a bit of porn, and when I was there nothing sexual happened. Though obviously now I realise they were getting off on us being turned on. But there was nothing *penetrative*, I mean; just the odd caress, the occasional boner pressed into your back like a hostage-taker's pistol, a touch of the leg on the way up from reaching for a dropped pencil. We heard stuff, but never knew the boys involved or the teacher had moved on, or the boy had left. It always seemed to happen one child away from where you were ... people moved school, boys *and* masters, they didn't start lawsuits or go to the press or the police. We heard the phrase *fresh start* a lot ...'

'So you watched *Top of the Pops* to take your mind off things, you envied the kids on *Jim'll Fix It*, you wanted to be pressing the buzzers on all those quiz shows and gyrating in front of DJs... but it was all happening there, too, wasn't it, Prof? British Light Entertainment had a hand down the nation's pants.'

'We didn't know anything else, Gary. The ten years − is it ten?' I make a quick calculation, I've been doing that a lot recently: 'Okay, nine − between you and me make all the difference. The atmosphere was heavy with suppressed paedophilia − *largely* suppressed, but there were moments when it *bypassed the mechanisms of control* as they said in the psychology course. But most of it stayed just this side of action. We breathed its fumes, you could say, but the element itself was buried quite far down.'

'The poet strikes again ...'

'The other teachers disliked the Doc because he was priggish and self-righteous and his needs were ... more about power than sex. He even got married when we were in the sixth form. Maybe that changed him, maybe it was a sign of his having changed. I don't know. People said he'd got better − you know, just as nasty and backbiting and status-obsessed, but not actually out-and-out persecuting kids. What he liked was his little rituals and role play and performance. So, while no one rushed to defend him, he wasn't exactly ostracised.' I think about the Doc being married. 'If he's got kids they're probably not far off your age, Gary.'

'Now you really are scaring me, Prof.'

'We started to hear things – that he'd done it before, that he was fond of these weird little games where people played roles, games which sometimes strayed a bit outside what was decent or normal. But really he got off on *not* touching you.'

'He got off on raping your mind, more like,' says Gary. 'What about Mr Wolphram? Did that stuff break the ice with him or what? Did he suddenly start high-fiving you in corridors and asking how it was hanging?'

'Hardly. He had borders.'

'That's not what I'm hearing in the *Daily Mail*, Prof, or the *Sun* – they've just had a readers' poll on banning single men from teaching ...'

'That stuff about him asking boys about sex or puberty? ... totally made up. Cash for lies. Maybe not even cash – attention is enough for some of those fuckers. That was why his outburst that day was so utterly, amazingly, shocking. Because he didn't express much at all. That stuff you read about his "short fuse" is total bollocks. He'd sometimes say something cutting and you'd baste with shame, but that was more because he was disappointed in you and you were disappointed in yourself – not because he was cruel ...'

'Hate to say this, Prof, but he sounds pretty decent.'

'He was. There was no spillage with him, no spillage of emotion or anger or frustration. Or sexual inclination. No small talk. We were still kids, he was an adult. You never saw in his eyes that flare of misfiring desire you saw in some of the others, the ones you *knew* liked children, or who'd been forced, over the years, to settle for them.

You'd be wiping their gaze off your mouth, your neck, the space in your shirt where you'd forgotten to button up and your belly showed. Some of them were always looking for the gaps between buttons or shirt-tails and trousers and they'd give you what we called *sticky looks*. You'd stretch in class sometimes and as you brought your arms up you'd feel your shirt pulling upwards and the gap of stomach opening as the shirt rose. You'd look at the front of the class and the teacher would be looking at exactly the spot – like they'd heard it, the cotton riding up the flesh and the skin stretching, getting taut. Even the teachers who didn't primarily like children but just weren't getting it through the normal – so to speak – *channels* did that from time to time. Not him. Never. No one's behaviour was further from the sexual than Mr Wolphram's.'

'This is the point in the story, Prof, in films, where I say: *Go on...*'

'Wolphram had nothing to do with the boarding part of the school or with discipline or any of that. A lot of teachers just taught, nothing more. He was one of them. Generally avoided eating in the school dining hall. Our worlds were different. Kids don't imagine teachers with lives, so we didn't know if he went home and switched off, went cruising in bars or if he met his friends in restaurants, listened to records, went to the theatre and had holidays, drank good wine and drove a nice car.'

'The latter, by the looks of it,' says Gary. 'More's the fucking pity really because we still don't have what we need to make a case against him. The more we find out the more – not normal exactly, hardly that – but the more joined up his life seems: he likes being alone, but he's got friends. Big deal. Call the cops! They say he's a loner but actually he knows a lot of people and has loads of interests and hobbies. There's a lot of fucking normality hiding under that weird exterior. It's meant to be the other way around.'

'What d'you mean *joined up*, Gary?'

'I mean exactly that – the different bits join together. Mad people, psychos and murderers and abusers and whatever ... they're not joined up, there's holes, fucking great chasms the size of the English Channel between the different parts of their lives. The different bits of their minds. Like that guy who told kids to kill themselves on the internet: there's just a big black hole between the way he kisses his own children goodnight and the shit he tells the other ones to do. You can't explain it except by saying there's a fucking great hole there. The hole doesn't bother him because he's made of it, made of holes, made up of the darkness. Normal people can do abnormal stuff, but it's always somehow connected, you can see the join, the slope that leads up or down or the place in their heads which makes them do bad things. Your Mr Wolphram is like that: he's not exactly an ordinary guy, but inside his life it all fits, each bit leads into the other. Like ours.' He looks at me. 'Well, like mine.'

Gary is right – in his Garified way he has explained it. And as it becomes clearer that Wolphram is probably innocent, so, in the press and media, in the police and among politicians, it becomes clearer that he's guilty.

We're responsible for that, Gary and I, and though it might have happened anyway, it would have happened later, and so it would have happened differently.

'That's news to me, Gary – you couldn't wait to get him strung up. You took one look at his flat, his stuff, his "gay little sheet music", and you were ready to put him in clink … You thought the black hood was some kind of auto-erotic toy.'

'And I was right, Prof – just not his.'

'All I mean is that you just went hurtling to conclusions—'

'That's not me, Prof, that's my conditioning. That's my education. That's the class system. That's what makes this country great. That's why we put bulldogs and lions and Churchill and Union Jacks on our Twitter handles …' Gary is taking the piss. Fair enough. I deserve it.

'So where are they now?' he asks: 'Lansdale and the Welsh guy and the geeky one, all the teachers – what happened to them?'

'That headmaster's still alive. Goodship – I saw him the other day. In the news footage – he's the old guy with the dog who slows down and looks but doesn't quite stop. I thought he was dead. He certainly looked like he had Death on a try-before-you-buy basis when I saw him at the post office last Christmas. He had that look some old people have when they think they recognise you but aren't sure – their eyes plead with you, asking you to tell them if they remember you, asking your memory to do the job of theirs because theirs has all gone soggy, their basement's flooded. He once hit me over the ear with a book for saying *kilometres* instead of miles. I'd been at school for precisely four days.'

'Early Brexit hero – there's probably a statue of him in Dover.'

'He had this odd thing: he collected old Mars bars, used to bring them in in glass cases with little labels and dates. The oldest one from the 1920s. Just Mars bars. "I'm not interested in any other confectionery," he told us. I don't know about McCloud – he used to accuse us of "flirting" with him, threatened us with "love and detention", liked all that innuendo and checked us as we showered to make sure we reached, as he put it 'every nook and cranny' – but he was already in his forties back then and didn't look hardwired for longevity. The Doc is there, Dr Monk, as you saw. Monk must be early sixties, enjoying the velvet coffin of the Headmaster's House and the Top Table dinners. Free school cufflinks and ties. A few of them are still there probably, the ones who were young in my day. I realise now I was taught by people who were only five or ten years older than I was then ... As for the other boys, well, Danny left, I stayed, along with a few of the others – like Gwil who's now a TV producer in Wales, does those detective thrillers set in Snowdonia, improbably violent and ritualistic murder stories—'

'Love it,' says Gary, 'I watch it with subtitles on cable TV. I listen to the Welsh and I look at the English underneath. It's great. *The Hunt* it's called.'

'That's the one.' How many has he seen, I wonder.

'Four of the first nine episodes involved people coming back as adults to get their revenge on former teachers or care-home workers ... One of the victims was the school chaplain, the other was the ...' Gary slaps his thigh in recognition, 'the fucking Latin teacher! Oh yes, that's too good, that is. Now I know where he got the ideas from. Dark as hell.'

'I must watch them,' I tell Gary, though I've seen them all, and I've known for years where the ideas came from. I remember Gwil, one night over his pint, promising us he'd make sure it all came out. It did. He has. But as fiction. Maybe that's better than nothing. 'Then there was Neil Hall who gave up on being a New Romantic and went to law school ... I looked him up once and he was a partner in some big London firm, Rich Nicholson went to Oxford, did okay, wrote for a bit, now a publisher, Dave Sweeting's a professor – a real one, Gary – of physics at Imperial College or UCL ... But we all lost touch years ago. Twenty, twenty-five. For a while we met once or twice a year in the Folkestone Grand Hotel – not Danny – but Gwil and Rich and Neil and a few others who came after Danny left and were okay, but that fizzled out.'

'Well, I still see my mates from school,' says Gary: 'Three of them are called Dave: there's Dave, Boring Dave and The Other Dave, there's me, the only Gary, surprisingly given what you'd call the C1 social class nature of the friend-group; and Jonny, Lisa, Sarah, Hannah and Holly ... yeah, Prof, we had girls in our school and they weren't an alien species and we didn't have exotic names and weird punishments designed by grown men to wank to when they got home. We weren't taught by men who thought Childline was a home delivery service. No one made us take our clothes off and sit in cold baths while teacher took photos. Then again, none of us went off to be MPs, bankers, Chair of the National Trust, newspaper columnists or BBC directors, so maybe it's us who missed out. We meet in the Cornmarket Vaults at Happy Hour and talk about normal stuff. When we talk about putting hoods over boys' heads, dangling kids off bridges and checking to see if they've washed between their buttocks, it's because we've seen it on TV.'

Gary drinks the dregs of his bad coffee and wipes his mouth. 'Now that I think of it, one of the episodes in your friend's detective series is about three blokes who capture their ex-teacher, stick a bag over his head and put him on trial for all the shit he did to them when they were kids ...'

'Do they kill him?' I ask.

'No spoilers, Prof.'

I laugh for the first time in days. (They do, yes. It is grisly, drawn-out and gratifying. I've seen it twice.)

'I don't want you to think it was all like that. The younger you were the worse it was, but it got better. There were a few good things, good moments. And in places like that the good things mean more than they actually are, because it takes the edge off the shit. We had some normality. Eventually. Girlfriends, bad half-sex on benches, fingering up by the bridge, pubs, cigarettes, buying drug wraps that turned out to be shoe polish in tinfoil and being too scared to go and complain ... I *think* we were normal. I got a girlfriend, I was happy as I could be in that world. We could travel, go to the coast, go to Brighton, Canterbury, London. Eventually, I left. Well, I stayed, but in a different way.'

'Sure, Prof, staying is the new leaving, haven't you heard?'

'I changed, too – my name I mean: I'd started out as Ander but by the time I was sixteen I was English, like I'd had a transfusion. Of words, of language, a whole new childhood. When I was around fifteen people started calling me Alex and Alexander and that stuck. By the time I left school I had a different name and spoke a different language from when I'd started. Wolphram was a good man and a good teacher. I owe him my English. He told me the dictionary would be my best friend.'

'I can't say I've noticed much competition for that accolade ...' says Gary. 'In my school your Doc Monk would have got walloped before he even got started. And I mean walloped by the teachers—'

'I think about that all the time, Gary: what would have happened if someone had just gone up to him and smacked him in the face, if we'd all just got up and walked out ... but you don't do that, or you didn't then, it was like there was software in our heads that made things that seem obvious now completely unthinkable – literally unthinkable, I mean: you really didn't *think* them ...'

'Yeah, I know, Prof – I've heard versions of that. Maybe without the poetry, but I've heard it ...'

Gary spent two years investigating abuse in a care home in Oxford. He learned a lot in Oxford, he says, all of it bad. Gary was on the Iffley House case, and even the name, *Iffley House*, sounds like a posh prep school. But it wasn't: it was a home for vulnerable teenagers who were pimped out by the people paid to look after them. Part of the investigation involved Gary staying in a guesthouse, undercover, and biting his tongue while he heard kids being plied with booze and pills and turnstile-fucked in the rooms around him. He still wakes up to the sounds he heard at night in the Meadow Lane Bed and Breakfast. So I don't have much to teach him about that side of things.

'And people pay for this shit? They actually look back on it and say *those were the days*? It's like wanting old dentistry methods back, or fucking leeches and lobotomies ...'

'Back then we accepted all kinds of stuff which – if we'd thought about it – was absurd and damaging and probably abusive ...'

'Daringly innovative use of the word *probably* there, Prof.'

'Well, afterwards, when you've left and got some distance from it and you've realised the world wasn't made like this and other people live differently, you think: *this was my life – for three years, five years, ten ... this was the world I lived in and these were the rules I lived by and this was the normality ...* But you only think that later, when you're free, and maybe some of them aren't ever free. Some of *us*.'

'Hard to tell with you, Prof. If you're free or not, I mean. If you're one of the *them*.'

'Hard for me to tell, too – some days I'll feel completely separate from it all – seeing the school as I drive by or recognising the odd ex-teacher in a shop, the kids in their uniforms crocodile-filing down the road ... doesn't have any effect on me. It's like I was never there. Other days I feel like I'm watching myself from outside, like there's a faded photo or film of someone doing all these things, going to school, sitting in class, getting touched, smelling the breath, watching the bullying, tasting the tears, feeling the pain, wiping off the spit ... and I feel sorry for the poor kid and I shake my head – I actually *shake my head*, Gary, at what they went through and I'm sad on their behalf ...'

I realise that my voice keeps cutting out as I speak, that something has been dislodged in me. It's only faint, but Gary can tell, too.

'It's okay, Prof, I don't need to hear any more, I've got the gist—'

' ... and then I look closer and think *he looks familiar* ... and I look more carefully, and watch the way he turns inwards, closes up, talks a little sometimes, but only to himself, and I realise it's me, and I'm looking into a mirror and all those things I was examining from the outside are on the inside, and I'm so broken I'm actually looking at myself from outside myself, that I've been split off inside, that I can only approach what happened to me side-on, like you creep up on animals so they don't run away or attack you ... tiptoeing around inside my own head in case I wake up the inhabitants. Does that explain it?'

'Not to me, Prof, not really, but that's part of the point, isn't it? One generation looks at another and thinks: How did that happen, how did they let it?'

'Well, that's what it was like back then, back in the eighties ... for all I know it was even worse before, in the seventies and sixties and fifties ... and these boys, many of them, had parents who'd been through the same thing, some of them, like Lansdale, in the same school, same house, among the same furniture, writing on the same bog walls, albeit a couple of coats of paint later. Often the same teachers. Imagine that! You can't go crying to your parents because they're the ones who put you there—'

'Yeah, well, that's why this country is the way it is. If you want to know how they work, *those people*, what makes them tick up there in their houses of parliament, their banks and country houses, their judges' benches and their newspaper soapboxes ... my theory is that under all that finery they're still wearing a pair of little school shorts ...'

Gary chucks his cup into the bin. 'What about Jonny Kebab – I'd like to pay him a visit.'

'On what pretext?'

'Curious, Prof, just curious. Though to tell the truth I'm mostly curious about how many teeth I can knock out of his mouth ...'

'Well – it was in the papers a few years back, maybe even an article by Mad Lynne, come to think of it – Lansdale's got bought up but kept its name as part of the deal. Jonny K sends his two boys to the school, so he must have liked it, if only in retrospect. These days he tries his hand at various little businesses, sits around opening restaurants in the latest up-and-coming area—'

'Yeah, and closing them soon after … I've read about him – a posh hipster with a wanker's drawl. Carpetbagging gentrifying tosser. But deep down he's still selling shredded jazz mags. Now I realise why so many of the upper classes are so kinky, why those MPs and judges and hedge-fund managers always get caught with rent boys or in massage parlours or strangling themselves with suspenders with oranges in their mouths … It's because when they were kids their first exposure to sex was torn-up pornos, bits of elbow or foot, or half an arse on a scrap of wet paper. Generations of upper-class men turned into fetishists by people like Lansdale and the schoolboy wankonomy …'

I start to laugh and then realise that, actually, it isn't such an implausible explanation at all. You take sexual shame and sexual frustration, you top it up with wealth, hierarchy, and mental and physical violence, then serve it in a large glass called entitlement, and you get … well: you get what we have.

Danny

When Danny's mother dies, it is a surprise. We are surprised by what we expected, because if there's one thing worse than being unprepared for the death of someone you love, it's being prepared. You hate yourself for it: getting ready for them to die while they're still living. They're still fighting, but you've already signed your treaty, up ahead, with the illness that will take them. You watch them: they sit up in bed, ruck up the pillows and lean forward, try to walk to the shops or to the living room. Sometimes they have a *good day*, or pull a sudden burst of appetite from their wasted body, their caved-in belly. One day they're even well enough to come and visit, though they shakily grip the rim of the car door as they climb out, their hands are all chalky knuckle and joint, their muscles just tendon-gristle. They tire fast, but they're here and they're battling on. You're not. They are so thin that when you help them back into the car it is like folding a deckchair. Meanwhile, what have you been doing? You've been having talks with the enemy behind their backs, that's what.

You've been preparing.

Those weren't the exact words Danny used – we didn't have *exact* words then, because unless you were Mr Wolphram the words came fuzzy and too late – but I am pretty sure it's how he felt. Danny had been ready for some months. But he was not ready for how it made him feel to be ready.

His mother's illness had many false dawns – a medication or a treatment that extended this or managed that – and many false sunsets too: a fall, a sudden dip, a death rattle that wasn't, a final decline that became the next swerving pull-back from the brink. These last weeks, however, she has been in a palliative ether, the kind designed to smooth the passage from life to death, so the chasm that separates them becomes no more than a ridge, a speed bump between worlds.

Danny's last words to her were spoken into the receiver of the public phone in the school corridor on Tuesday. There was a queue behind him, other boys waiting, grumbling, telling him to hurry up as he fed his coins into the slot. They were 2p coins back then, and they'd weigh in the boys' pockets as they headed for the phone, and we'd stack them up and watch them dwindle as we spoke. It wasn't a phone booth, just a receiver hung on a wall, so we developed an odd, semi-private, semi-public way of speaking to our parents or family, knowing we were being listened to. It was another way, along with the letters, of making familiar relationships formal. What could you say to your parents in a corridor with boys watching, listening, waiting, laughing, telling you to hurry up? Sometimes the phone queue was so long they were at your elbow as you held the receiver. You couldn't cry in public, and they had made it so you couldn't cry in private.

It is the Doc who tells Danny. He calls him into the classroom and makes him stand on the other side of the desk with the Latin primers and the bound slab of doctoral thesis he leaves there for people to see. He doesn't ask him to sit down. Why would he? With news like this you're afraid that if you ask someone to sit down they'll never get up. Besides, Danny is *ready*, he's been *ready for some time*, the Doc informs him. 'This won't be a surprise to you,' he begins. But it is. Danny holds the front of the desk as the Doc speaks. He steadies himself. It is the same desk at which he stood just a few weeks back, at his 'trial'. The Doc is trying to show sensitivity, and Danny can tell. But he won't stop hating him.

He is ready and not ready. He feels like he will fall, faint, blank out in the face of the fact of it. He feels that all that readiness won't help now — now that what he was ready for has happened. There'd have been plenty of time to be ready when it was too late; now he suddenly hates himself for spending that time when she was alive preparing for something he couldn't ever prepare for, for wasting what little time she had left by habituating himself to a future that would come whether he was ready for it or not. It's not the past that haunts us, it's the future, he thinks. He is desolate and angry and silent.

In Doc terms it's probably a sympathetic interview. It must be, because Danny is 'let off' the rest of the day's classes. It's a Friday. This coming weekend he'll be allowed to go home and stay until the funeral. A notice goes up on the school board, telling us that Danny has lost his mother. It is signed by the headmaster. Sympathies are *extended* as if they were deadlines, which is what they are for people like him. And whatever can be extended can also be retracted.

Mr Wolphram's class that day is muted, because, though not everyone likes Danny, this is as close as they want to come to bereavement. It is as if everything they discuss has changed scale: the doll's house of literature, with its doll's-house people with their doll's-house furniture and feelings, has suddenly become a real place you walk into and find yourself lost and small and alone. The books don't work anymore, full of paper people leading lives of ink. The word *death* has stopped being a few letters in a poem or a story. Now it is a hole in the page you fall into and never come out of.

Mr Wolphram knows this. He speaks softly, but still his voice has no problem carrying. He goes off-syllabus today, gives them a humorous short story to read by Damon Runyon, makes them each read a paragraph and try their hand at a hip American accent. Ander is by himself in the front row beside Danny's empty seat, because the others have pulled back, afraid of grief's contamination. Ander carries the spores.

He does not see Danny again that day. He looks for him in the usual places – out by the cricket fields, near the school theatre, up on the Downs and along the bridge, which he crosses several times.

Danny is not there. Nor is he in his bed in the dormitory. Ander sees him once more, a week later. He has come to get his trunk and clear his locker. It is Mr Wolphram who takes him to the station, and Ander's last view of Danny is in the front seat of the car, the same car Mr Wolphram owns today and which is now at the auto-forensics laboratory. Danny looks at him and looks away, then looks back and half waves, half brushes it all away: their two small years of friendship, and it is something like a childhood that he wipes from behind the window.

A Letter to the Newspaper

'That Irish kid – what was his surname again?' Gary interrupts.

'McAlinden. Danny. Daniel.'

'Well, he's obviously taking an interest. Come and look.'

Gary leaves me his seat and points to the computer screen. It's the lead letter in the *Guardian*.

Dear Editor,

I was lucky enough to have been a pupil of Michael Wolphram's at Chapelton College in the 1980s, and I remember him as an excellent and generous-minded teacher who gave his time unstintingly to pupils who were interested in ideas. I knew him well at school and stayed in touch with him afterwards.

This doesn't put me in a position to know or give an opinion whether or not he killed Zalie Dyer (I have the quaint notion that maybe the police and courts can help with that), but it does mean I know the claims made about him both in the tabloids and in the 'quality' papers are outright lies, and that he has been tried by the media for looking, sounding and being different. In today's Britain, this seems to disqualify one from being innocent until proved guilty. It also seriously prejudices the Dyer family's hopes of seeing a fair trial.

But it's not just the redtops and the gossip mags who have shown their viciousness. The posh curtain-twitching neighbours who queued up to get on TV to berate his 'strangeness' and 'oddity', the school's spineless headmaster whose first response was to claim that no one at the school knew or remembered him, the anonymous but scandal-randy 'Old Chapeltonians' who lied about him for a quick tabloid buck ... all of them remind us that when it comes to persecuting people who are different, British society can overcome the class divide and really get stuck into a common cause.

Yours,
Daniel McAlinden
Newcastle

I read the letter and wish I'd written it.

'Bet you wish you'd written that, Prof.'

*

The drive to Hastings takes us along the motorway, which is a white-van cloggage of junctions and business parks, of skip-lorries layered with bathtubs and doors, of catering vans, taxicabs and airport-bound people-carriers. I am at the wheel, and Gary is staring fiercely at the dashboard. I drive too slowly for him, but Gary gets road rage just looking at pictures of roads. The *word* 'road' makes him angry. It is one of his *triggers*, as we're learning to call them.

Sometimes we see birds of prey — kites, maybe, or hawks, it's not as if Gary or I can tell the difference — scrutinising the tarmac for squashed mammals from their speed-camera perches.

'Why are we doing this again?' he enquires through clenched teeth, enviously side-eyeing the traffic going in the opposite direction, which, like all traffic going where we aren't, is moving faster and more smoothly than us.

'Because we want to, because it's our day off, and because we've been told not to.'

He seems satisfied with that. This was his idea anyway.

We smell the sea before we see it. The Salvation Army Hall is close to the beach where the fishermen's nets and tackle are strewn messily around their huts, interspersed with boats that have been dragged up and which now loll on their sides in the wind. There's plastic everywhere — plastic drums, twine, binbags, balls of fishing line blown like tumbleweed along the shingle — and a stink of fish guts and fish heads. Gulls caw and swoop down for offal, or hang in clouds just above our heads, looking, Gary says, *for a nice shiny police car to shit across.*

When we arrive the volunteers are unbagging donated clothes from bin liners and setting a long trestle table for the Christmas lunches they'll be serving up until New Year. The notice by the door, chalked onto a sandwich board, invites the homeless, the friendless, the poor and the abandoned to eat with them. A couple of sullen-looking reporters are staking it out in the cold; another is peering at the entrance from behind the flipped-open lid of a pizza carton. Whatever they've come for, they haven't got it.

It hasn't stopped the stories. 'Exclusive: Zalie Accused's Aunt Is Soup Kitchen Major', ran the *Daily Mail*, which has now led with a 'Comment' piece about why single men should not be allowed to teach in schools. Another paper has a Readers' Poll: Gays and Children? Should they mix? No – Phone 0845808080; Yes – Phone 0845818181.

The papers have a dilemma: they can go down the 'dead mother' route, with the 'brought up by women, loner, pervert and woman killer', and combine that with overtones of 'religious cult' to produce, for the nation, the classic *Psycho* vibe. Or they can take a different approach, less flashy and harder to laminate into a headline, but more troubling, and certainly likelier to insinuate itself into the culture: 'Christmas Murderer was *much-loved* boy, claims auntie': then *respectable Christian upbringing, bible class, charity work, we gave him everything* and ending: *we made a monster.*

Everyone is *speaking up, coming forward, breaking their silence.*

There's a man selling the *Hastings Herald*, whose front-page headline – 'Murder Accused Was Hastings Grammar Pupil. Classmates Speak Out' – is pinned to the front of the kiosk.

Inside, there is the smell of polish and detergent. Leaning up against the wall, a dozen or so cases for brass instruments. A sousaphone has been unpacked and takes up a whole corner. Its case, huge and rounded and black, looks like a shadow that has uncoupled itself and is now trying to sneak away from the body that cast it.

Gary is respectful and a little awed. For no reason other than instinct, because the place is noisy and clanging with pots and pans, he whispers.

Evelyn Price recognises us immediately. She is not in uniform, and still has her coat and scarf on, though the place is suffused with the thick chugging heat of a dozen fan heaters. She is at the back of the room, holding one of those large institutional teapots with an extra handle on the front. The band she is serving tea to is in uniform. Old men and women and a few adolescents are eating and chatting, their coin buckets and charity boxes by their plates. We take off our coats. Gary is already glazed with sweat.

'I remember the Sally Army from when I was younger,' he says, 'the brass bands and the kids at the front rattling the boxes for change. *Small* change, 'cos that's all they ever seemed to get, and it's all *we* ever had. They had stickers, too, on those little rolls like miniature bog paper. Shield-shaped badges you stuck on and that fell off after about two hours. I always wondered what the children felt like, seeing their mates wandering past with their cigs and their tinnies, outside shopping centres and stations, while they were stuck there looking like toy soldiers having the piss taken out of them.'

'Maybe it didn't bother them,' I reply, though I'm not convinced. 'Most of these people are Salvation Army families, they were kids and now they're parents and grandparents. Lots of them leave probably, but it doesn't mean they're embarrassed or think it's weird.'

'I dunno, Prof, I'm just making conversation, but it'd be a sick world if we laughed at people for looking after those who've got nothing. 'Specially at Christmas. I quite liked some of their songs, about how they were going to kick poverty's ass ... Anyway, let's get Mother Teresa out of the way and go home.'

'Mother Teresa' is a nimble, bright-eyed eighty-six-year-old. She is quick on her feet and even quicker of mind. She puts down her teapot and takes us to a back room, a sort of office with papers and calendars and piles of Styrofoam cups and plastic plates in cellophane.

There is a large banner above the desk: Salvation Army Hastings Corps. Framed pages of the Army newspaper, *War Cry*, are unevenly nailed to the walls, as if put up by people of different heights at exactly the same time. There's a flag with the motto *Blood and Fire* splayed out square above the door. Evelyn doesn't exude blood or fire, but she is warm, intransigent and tough.

'That woman is nails,' Gary says admiringly in the car home, 'nails wrapped in cotton wool.'

But first:

She offers us tea, which we accept. Always accept the hot drink, and always drink it slowly – it magics up a pool of time from a few shallow minutes. It's also harder for people to tell you to leave if you're still eating or drinking something they've given you.

Gary cups his tea with both hands. Evelyn Price lets us begin. She has the same calm manner as her nephew, but none of his chill. I am not looking at the face of an octogenarian, because the eyes are soft and blue, the features barely wrinkled. I would put her age at mid-sixties, not much older to look at than Wolphram himself, though I know she's nearly twenty years older. She extends a box of fancy cakes with bright yellow and pink icing. They are factory-made, shop-bought and mass-produced. So much for Gary's fantasy of Olive's home-baking. The tea burns our tongues, and already has a cracked, hard-water lid of scud settling over it. The office is unheated, so the tea steams, and Gary and I put our coats straight back on, feeling the sweat go cold on our skin.

'You're here to talk about my nephew,' she begins, and it's not a question. 'But since you've charged him and I haven't been allowed to see him, I'm not sure what you expect me to say. I've dealt with the reporters, telephoning at all times of the day and night, and they haven't got anything out of me. Some of them have even started leaving ... the only one I spoke to is the one in the car, the large one who looks like he's always hungry.' She looks at Gary, realises that she has described him, too, and looks a little embarrassed. 'He asked me if I wanted to put "my side" of the story. That's what he called it: *the story*. He had a chequebook and a pad of receipts.'

'How much did he offer?' asks Gary.

'We didn't reach that point,' she replies firmly.

I begin:

'Though we are involved with the case, I should tell you that we are not the ones who decided to charge him—'

She looks at me, and then at Gary, and there is no sign of any of the reactions we expected: anger, surprise, fear, wariness, distress.

'So why are you here?'

'We'll be honest – we aren't sure. They have charged him, yes, but that doesn't mean our investigation is over, because there are a lot of things to clear up.'

'Can you tell us anything about him that might help?' asks Gary.

'Help who?'

'All of us – the police, Zalie's family, maybe him?'

'I can't imagine what I could say. I haven't seen him for some months – we see each other four or five times a year and he was due here for Christmas, which won't happen. When we speak on the telephone he's exactly the same. And so am I.'

'What sort of things did you talk about?' asks Gary.

She looks surprised. 'What do people talk to elderly relatives about? The weather, house prices, television?

Immigration? The things you tell yourselves we worry about.'

'Tell us about what he was like,' I ask.

She leans back in her chair and takes off her coat. 'My nephew was a gentle and unusual boy ... who became a gentle and unusual man. He's not as he appears in those photographs for one thing – he isn't arrogant or cold – and none of the things the papers say about him are true. None. But I can't see how you'd expect me to say anything different, can you? He's just ... not like other people.' She thinks it over. Adds: '*Most* other people. Because a lot of people are not like other people.'

'Can you tell us why you're so absolutely certain that he's incapable of doing what they say he did?' Gary keeps on with the *they*.

She sips her tea and thinks it over.

'How much has he told you about his life?'

'Not a great deal, just that he was brought up by you and your sister, here in Hastings, and that he was happy. He seems happy still. Apart from all this,' I add, stupidly. *Apart from being arrested for murder, being disowned by his colleagues and neighbours and having the whole country salivating to string him up. Yes, apart from that it's all good.* 'Maybe not surrounded by like-minded people and overwhelmed with what they call *peer-group friendships*, but happy, and that he obviously loves you both very much. And felt loved by you.'

Evelyn looks down and smiles. It makes her happy to hear this – though she knows it completely and doesn't need to be told.

'He was always reading, always thinking. He had a tape recorder, an old cassette player, and saved up to buy music from the record shop. It's gone now. The shop – not the tape recorder. He keeps everything. Some of it is still in his room. He still sleeps there when he comes. It was never really a child's room, so it's not like he's going back in time, to his childhood or anything. He joined one of those music clubs, where they reel you in with a special deal, then send you things you didn't want and make you pay for them. Unless you returned them within two weeks. That's how they made their money – they banked on you forgetting or not being bothered. But he never got caught out: if he didn't like something he'd take it back to the post office, perfectly wrapped, and return it. I remember seeing how excited he was when he got a new tape, but however much he was in a hurry to hear it, he'd unwrap it really carefully. One day – he was about sixteen – he ordered three performances of the same piece of music. We asked him why. He said so he could compare them and choose which one to keep. We couldn't hear the difference, but he could. He can tell which orchestra is playing a piece, and when. And who's conducting and where and when it's being performed. Imagine that.'

'He didn't get any of that from you?' I ask.

'No. Not really. And not from his parents. It seemed to be there already. It's hard to know, isn't it, whether people are shaped by their upbringings or whether they can invent themselves from scratch?'

'I suppose the truth is that it's half and half,' I say.

'Maybe, but who wants a truth that sounds like it comes from a cookbook?' Gary snaps at me. 'Did he learn to play music with you?' He asks his question so softly that he needs to repeat it before she hears.

'Yes,' she has no idea either how any of this is relevant, and she's right, because it isn't. It's just that Gary wants to know, because wanting to know things like this is a sign that he doesn't think Wolphram is guilty. 'His mother wasn't an Army girl. The family was never Army. Not like most of the people here,' she gestures at the open door and beyond it into the hall, 'a lot of them have been for generations. We're new really. One generation. I joined in the late forties, and then Ida – my sister – came in about two years later. When Michael was a boy, when his mother died, we took him out with us and he asked if he could learn the trumpet. It was a bit late really – ten or eleven – but he took to it straight off. Less than a year and he was as good as any of them. Better. Then he wanted to play the guitar, didn't like the music we played, found it all, I don't know, a little basic. But also he didn't much like playing with others, the whole band bit. I bought him a guitar. It took him six months to get good enough to start doing the exams. My sister said that it wasn't like he was learning to play, but rather that he was remembering it from a past life. That's not the sort of thing we say in the Salvation Army, stuff about past lives, and I remember her being embarrassed about it and changing the subject. He was skilled all right, but, make no mistake, he worked at it so hard it was as if nothing else existed. Hours and hours of it, he could go for half a day without even looking up from his guitar or his books.'

'Can't have been easy,' says Gary, trying to reach something, some sense of trauma or unhappiness or hidden suffering.

'Not easy, maybe, but it wasn't the way you think. He had friends, he laughed at jokes and made them, too. I used to watch him chuckling while he was reading and ask him what was so funny, and he'd tell me what it was and I didn't find it funny. He found people who were like him – you know, studious types, musical types. They do exist you know, everywhere, even in places like this. Gentle, thoughtful people who don't fit in and aren't bothered by it, and who find each other somehow, in the places only they seem to know. They grew their hair long and went to concerts, not just classical stuff. Pop or rock or whatever it's called. Those boys who dressed really smartly and had mopeds – Mods – he was part of that, so he wasn't some kind of oddball. He just did that and liked Mozart at the same time.'

She refills our tea, offers us more bright cakes from the packet.

'It's not like what the papers say, all that business about being a loner or a hermit. He wasn't at all. You want those explanations because he's different, but when people who are different find each other, they're less different. Like here, like the Salvation Army – out there we're strange and we look odd and people laugh, but when we're here we're the same.'

She stops for a moment and takes a mouthful of her fluorescently iced pink cake; reaches out for her tea, then puts it aside without tasting it.

'He wasn't bullied. A couple of teachers found him hard going because he probably knew more than they did. One in particular had a problem with him – used to stand him up in front of the class and invite everyone to say what they hated about him. Like some kind of tribunal. We complained to the school and something must have got done about it because we never heard about it again. Anyway, he was doing well there, stayed away from people who didn't like what he liked, and they stayed away from him. Most of the time. There's no mystery, nothing hidden down below.'

'Sex,' says Gary, louder and more abruptly than he intended. I'm not sure it's a question or a statement, but either way she isn't fazed. She isn't smiling, but there's satisfaction in her eyes, because we have become predictable.

'I was wondering when you'd come to that. I'm amazed that you held off so long ...' She has some of that superiority we saw in him, though it is softer, less sarcastic. She pours Gary another cup of tea, mostly to distract him from his own embarrassment. It's the first time I've seen Gary embarrassed by the word *sex*. 'The answer is, I don't know. Some, none, a lot, and who with ... I don't know. I'm not the sort of person one talks about that to, and he's not the sort to talk about it. He was a loved and loving boy, and he was happy. That may not be what you want to hear, but that is how it was.'

What is it that we want to hear? She doesn't know and nor, I realise, do we. We have come to slake our curiosity, and to make some kind of amends.

Amends for what? He may still be guilty.

'Out of interest, what was the name of the teacher who gave him a hard time?' I ask.

'*That* I can tell you — I remember the name very well. Mr Goodship. I recall Ida and I laughing at his funny name. To start with, that is — before we realised that the things he did were not in the slightest bit funny. He got a job somewhere else and that was the last we heard of him.'

Gary and I try hard not to look at each other. We are solving something, but it isn't the murder of Zalie Dyer.

'He was just himself. He didn't need protecting, no one hurt him or made him suffer. I don't think he was bullied by the other boys, because, though he wasn't very open and forthcoming about feelings, he didn't hide them either ... I'm not sure I can say it better: there wasn't much on show with him, but it didn't mean there was anything hidden either. He ... he just wasn't exactly like other people, but, then, who is?'

'Any toys?' asks Gary.

She looks at him, surprised. And then she is not at all surprised, and smiles. 'Well, as he probably told you, he wasn't much of a child even when he was a child. But there were toys, it's just that he didn't really use them for playing.'

Gary laughs. He probably wishes she was his aunt. I know I do. The stray thought comes in that I know nothing about Gary's family, except that he is single, his parents live in council housing to the west of the city, and he has a sister whose name he hasn't even told me. Then it occurs to me that he has told me and I've just forgotten. Not forgotten; I just wasn't listening.

'There are children like that.' She finishes her tea. 'I expect you'll be wanting to see his room now. It's what policemen do, isn't it?'

'That won't ...' I say

'Yes we'd ...' says Gary

' ... be necessary.'

' ... like to.'

Interview

'Okay, so you know me.' We are back in the interview room, and I am back on the case. 'But how much do you actually remember? I've always wanted to know what it was like for you—'

'Me?'

'Not you specifically — teachers: they get older but the kids stay the same age. Don't they all merge into one?'

'No!' he says, offended. I didn't mean to offend him, and I'm surprised by my own harshness. 'I remember a great deal, it's just that the order it happened in tends to change. It's the opposite of a novel in that way, isn't it?'

This isn't really a question, so I leave it. I don't want Gary coming in and finding us talking about nineteenth-century fiction.

'So, they've let you back in have they, Ander?' He uses my name for the first time and I feel both unmasked and somehow affirmed. 'Though it's Alexander now, your lanyard tells me.'

'Yes,' I say, fingering the managerial harness around my neck, 'for now, yes they have, but mainly because they can't decide what to do.'

'There's a statute of limitation for crimes, isn't there, so there must be one for investigating crimes, too,' he answers.

He no longer looks frightened. He sits up straight and holds his head just high enough to look a little downwards at you. Like he used to. They have returned his glasses to him, and he is reading some classical music magazine his solicitor has brought. He has been truculent, sarcastic, confused, bewildered, terrified, incredulous, broken and dignified. Now that it has happened, now that he has been charged, he seems more relieved than afraid.

Some people fall apart as soon as we charge them; some clam up. Mr Wolphram looks as if he's been released, which is the opposite of what he is supposed to feel. You charge people, especially people like him, against whom the evidence is circumstantial, so that they'll feel the walls close in, so they'll start telling the truth, or telling the kind of lies from which a truth can be deduced: *that it was an accident, that he never meant this, never planned that, that it was a mistake, that she fell, that he didn't intend to kill anyone ...*

For the umpteenth time, I figure that if he's guilty he's one of those criminals who will give no ground, confess nothing, surrender no information; someone who will go to prison and beyond without giving up his secrets. And for another umpteenth time I also think that, if he's innocent, he's rather more confident of his innocence, and of its being recognised by a jury, than he should be. There are still no other suspects, the press have judged him, the public, too, and whether he's in a remand centre, in a jail or out on bail and back in his flat, he is in more danger than he knows.

The worst thing for him now would be to be released.

His solicitor is not one of the usual on-call *this-wanker/that-wanker*s that Gary and I are familiar with. It is a young woman with dark bobbed hair in a black trouser suit. She introduces herself, but I don't catch her name the first time. There are people like that, and I'm one of them: who stop listening as soon as someone introduces themselves or gives them directions. It's as if a screen comes down and the white noise fills the ears. She reminds me of her client's rights, then tells me that they have been breached, and that she will take this up. Oh — I register that bit. Good. I hope she does. I'll be backing her all the way from the other side of the lawsuit. From inside the dock, if comes to it. Her card, which she offers me, tells me that she is a partner in one of the Dickensianly named upper-crust law firms near the school. *Cashman, Price and Strang*. Gary hasn't come up with a nickname for them because he doesn't have to: all he would want to say about them is already in the name. *CPS* – ironically, it's the same acronym as the Crown Prosecution Service they have so often foiled, outspent or driven to settle out of court.

Lucy Hall, her card says. I know the firm. They were long-established even when I was at school and walked past their offices every day: two floors of a big treacle-stoned Georgian mansion and a front garden with a fountain surrounded by black Mercs and Lexuses. The garden used to be lawned and landscaped, but now it's crunch-gravelled for the tyres of private-plated 4×4s. *CPS* are good: old-school polish and new school technocracy, plus the kind of legal menace only serious money can purchase. It's like everything Mr Wolphram buys: it's the best because he'll only buy it once.

What I don't know, though I'll know it soon — I'll piece it together a few hours after I've left the room — is that it's not Mr Wolphram paying Lucy Hall but her father, Neil. It's not *pro bono* but the effect is the same, because one lawyer who believes in what they're doing is worth a whole chambers doing it for the money.

This is for later, when suddenly things have an order and a logic they never had to begin with. In that respect Mr Wolphram was right: *It's not like a novel.* For now, Lucy Hall is just a solicitor, and, because Gary hasn't met her, she doesn't have a nickname. She just looks clever, thoughtful and kind. What I mean is: she became those things as I knew her better, because, when I first saw her, what I actually noticed was nothing. She was just a solicitor in a hot room with a man who might have strangled someone to death against a wall and then wrapped the body in Pound Shop binbags.

He would never have bought anything from a Pound Shop, I realise, but you can't rest a case on the argument that the defendant buys more expensive items than those used in the crime he is accused of.

'Could I ask your client some questions about his time as a teacher — questions that are nothing to do with the case?'

She looks at him — she is not surprised by this, which means he must have told her about me — and he nods.

'This is a strange request and I advise against it, but my client says it's fine so I agree to it. But nothing about the case is to be discussed, and I'll stay here nonetheless to ensure that,' she replies.

'Finally — some questions that won't incriminate me,' he smiles. It's a kind smile and one I don't deserve. His solicitor smiles, too, but it is for him and not me.

Mr Wolphram introduces me: 'Inspector Widdowson was a pupil of mine, some time ago, quite a good one as I recall, if a little muddle-headed. Vague.'

Ms Hall: 'We're asking for him to be released on bail.'

'Yes,' I say. 'I know, but I think asking for his release is a bad idea before he is cleared.'

'That isn't your call, I'm afraid − it's up to the client and their solicitor. We will be asking for bail, and since it will be impractical for Mr Wolphram to return home, we will be arranging some accommodation that you'll be made aware of in due course.'

'I *want* to return home,' says Mr Wolphram firmly. 'I'm innocent and my home is the only place I should be.'

'We'll discuss it,' says Lucy Hall, and looking at me to leave the room: 'between us.'

'You had a question for me?'

'Yes − my friend Danny McAlinden. You remember him?'

'Yes.'

'You drove him away. I saw him in your car. Then I never heard from him again.'

'That's a rather melodramatic way of putting it. I took him to the station. He went home, back to Newcastle, back to his father's. Initially it was just for the funeral. But he stayed on. A few days extra, a week, two weeks and then term ended and then ... well ... his mother's income held things together and his father needed him to work. He gave up his scholarship, became apprenticed to a silversmith for a while. It's possible that he had no choice, but I got the sense he decided himself.'

'And now?'

'I don't know − we stayed in touch for ... oh − a good ten years after that. His father retired and Danny was −

he used that word — *released*, and came back here for a while to work at the new Arts Centre in the docks. He took to it. I daresay if you'd gone to see more European films you'd have bumped into him at the box office, that's where I used to see him ...'

'Very amusing ... then what?'

'He worked part-time there and did a foundation course in music technology at the art college. Branched out into lighting and sound, acoustics for concerts and festivals. The last I heard he was setting up a studio for radio dramas and documentaries. That was about ten years ago.'

'How long was he here?'

'Five years, maybe six, seven. Long enough to do a degree and get some work experience. For all I know he's still here.'

Danny was here, so close all that time, never more than a mile or two from me, from where we are now. I thought I was the one who returned. But as Gary likes to remind me: *No, Prof, you never left, and that's not the same thing.*

'No, he isn't, but I thought you'd like to see this ... I know it doesn't exactly balance things, but it's out there ...'

I show him Danny's letter. He reads it — once fast, anxiously, afraid of another betrayal, and then a second time, slowly, for the pleasure and the reassurance. He smiles and is proud and moved, voiceless for a moment, then he whispers:

'Thank you' and takes off his glasses, rubs his eyes and closes them. 'Give me a few moments, please.'

Lucy Hall looks at me with — well, not exactly kindness, but certainly less contemptuous suspicion than before.

Danny. All that time I could have looked him up – Facebook, LinkedIn, Friends Online ... Everyone is findable. And my job is finding people. Other people's people at any rate. I looked up my old girlfriend, Claire Brett. She's still here, a few streets away, and though by the law of averages we should have bumped into each other a few times across the decades, I haven't seen her for twenty-four years. Same with Jonny Kebab. Though I know he lives in St Leonard's, he's always around town at openings, usually with a new wife, and always in the 'High Society' section of the *Evening Post*, the cut-price gossip column where Lynne Forester writes about Rotary Club balls and celeb weddings.

But distance and closeness do not work as we expect them to. In a big city you can see the same person three times in a week and wonder if some odd force is drawing you to the same places in the same slice of clock-time. Yet you can also live close by someone and never see them. Is there a science that explains it? An algorithm? Or is it more of a hauntology of encounters – like magnetism and counter-magnetism ... the way we are drawn to each other but also perhaps repelled. Is there some occult law makes us take the turning that avoids meeting X, or linger in the shop when we might two seconds earlier have met Y, or that makes our train late or prods us into not taking the entrance to the pub or the theatre where we would have bumped into Z? The same occult law that makes things happen stops them happening. The law that governs coincidence is also a law that prevents them; the law that governs no-incidence at all.

All this time, and we were close by.

We always think of it the wrong way round – how things happen, never how they don't; the things that could have happened and nearly did, still clamouring there, ghosts in the maybe, yearning for their lives in counterfact.

He was here for five years after school and I never saw him: he at the tech college on the other side of the bridge, I at the uni on the campus at the posh end of town. We were probably two or three streets away from each other a lot of the time. I probably walked into pubs he'd just left, shops he'd just paid at. We must have been constantly skirting each other, defying the law of averages which decrees that at some point, somewhere in our overlapping orbits, we'd meet. I probably handled a coin or a note that had passed through his hands, been in his pocket. He might have drunk from a glass I had used in the same pub a few days before. The city is the great ramifying map of our non-meetings, our flight paths crisscrossing over and over. But did I see him? Never.

'Why didn't he let me know?'

'I've no idea. I thought he would, but since he never mentioned it I supposed he and you had fallen out. No, not fallen *out* ... fallen *away*. The way children do. Chapelton was not a place, or indeed a place in his memory, he wanted to return to. Can you blame him? When he did come back, he looked different. Not surprising, I suppose: he was nineteen − he'd lived and worked away from books and classrooms, he'd been through things that most people go through much later, and when he came back here it was as if he was arriving for the first time. Slate cleaned. All wiped. Opposite end of town, different circles. Almost a different city. He didn't want to talk about people he'd known before − that goes for you, too, I'm afraid, beyond once asking, soon after he returned, if I knew how you were, and I didn't − and he'd changed physically as well: broader-shouldered, crew-cut hair, a harder, more angular face. Leather coat and boots ... he looked like a busker. Actually, I think he did busk, too, up on Cowbridge Road and down Park End Street and near the docks and the ferries. When the new Arts Centre was built there was money to be made.'

The thought that Danny might actually look different throws me. I'd probably not have noticed him even if I had been in the same room. I'd probably heard him busk, but no one looks at buskers and anyway ...

'What instrument did he play?' I ask, realising I knew of no instrument, no aptitude for music of any sort, with Danny.

'The usual,' says Mr Wolphram warmly, thinking back to a time before murders and murder charges, monsterings and interrogations, 'a dirty-looking guitar, surprisingly well-tuned from the little I heard. And it wasn't classical. There was no Villa-Lobos on the streets in those days.'

In my head Danny has always been as he was when I last saw him: slim and sad and desolate — and always going away. He had that air of someone made for leaving, so the thought that he was here provokes a sort of jealousy. Jealous at what? Not him, no, it's more a police-jealousy rather than an erotic or emotional one: jealousy that I went on without being in *full possession of the facts.*

'What about that last day?

'That was very simple and very sad. They'd given him a few days off, I think, maybe a week, but he knew he wasn't coming back. I certainly knew and he didn't need to tell me. I knew from the moment I came in on that ghastly trial. Boys didn't have many possessions in those days, did they? School uniform, weekend clothes for those who didn't get taken out by family, a couple of books, a family photo or two.'

'Nothing you'd come back for,' I say.

'Nothing, no.'

'And no one.'

'It's different with people, isn't it? They don't stay still or switch off or get tidied away when you're not with them. You got on with your own life, he with his, we with all of ours.'

'I suppose I'd have liked to hear from him, that's all. We were close—'

'Yes.'

'And inseparable.'

'No one is inseparable.'

'We went to see Evelyn in Hastings.'

'I thought you might. I expect she was making tea in vast teapots and organising hundreds of Christmas lunches. If you hadn't brought me here and accused me of things I'd never do or consider doing, I'd be helping her, instead of sitting here raking over the ashes of your schooldays.'

'You didn't tell your aunts you ended up in the same school as Goodship, did you?'

'No. Why would I? They'd only have worried. And I didn't know he was there when I applied. I only found out when I crossed him in the corridor. Even then he didn't recognise me until we were introduced in the staffroom. We left each other alone. A few years later he became headmaster. He took the management route. That was how it worked in the eighties.'

'Not before passing on his fondness for classroom justice to his protégé, though, by the looks of it.'

Wolphram looks down. 'Yes, well, these schools are all about passing things on – traditions, legacies ...' He looks up again: 'Isn't that what your parents pay for?'

Lucy Hall cuts in: 'Sorry to interrupt your trip down memory lane, but we need to discuss, my client and I, how to get him out of here, so I suggest you take all this up later, when he's been freed, when you've apologised, and when he's discussing what sort of compensation he's entitled to.'

'I didn't say I wanted compensation,' he tells her gently and with the air of someone who has been misjudged.

'You will when you've seen these.' She nods at the newspapers piled up in front of him.

'I know what's in them,' he tells her, reaching defensively for *Classical Music Today*.

'You don't,' I say. 'You really don't.'

*

Tonight Marieke is playing me a car parking on gravel. It's the gravel outside my neighbours' house. She tells me it sounds like the sea, and she is right — like the sea in shallow coves. She makes me listen to some sea-rinsed shingle she has found on the computer, some archipelagic reef in Cornwall as it gargles spume and pebbles. The two are almost indistinguishable.

Her other favourite: the sound of the cars on the ring road, recorded from the brownfield dogging half-place near the bridge. It sounds, she says, like a waterfall. She is right again — she loves things that sound similar but are completely different, so different they are almost opposites of each other, she says. This is where we found Zalie's body, this urban interzone and its nameless road where, if you close your eyes, you could imagine yourself in the Dales or in the Highlands.

That interests Marieke, too: how a road can have no name, and how it can stay nameless though surrounded by places that have been mapped, Apped and put on postcards. Places, she says, that have been *recorded*. The bridge or the viaduct or the zoo, seen by thousands of people every day, and then this weedy, muddy bankside, strewn with faded sweet wrappers and empty cans, consumer detritus and the going-going-gones of everyday life.

Marieke has a dozen memory sticks crammed with her recordings. She has labelled them and dated them: *record player, doorbell, watch, pylons humming, sinkhole gurgling, engine running, man coughing, keyboard tapping* ...

She pieces the world together like a detective.

Sigrid comes back alone from a Soulmates internet date. It was a short evening – so short she hasn't even eaten. 'That bad?' I ask, but she doesn't answer, just slings her bag on the sofa and pours herself a glass of whatever wine I have, and which I bought without paying attention to. Marieke is watching a documentary about Rock 'n' Roll, from which she is learning that the equipment contained in her pen-sized recording device used to be the size of a car. She is taking notes for her school project, which is a history of computers. 'Memory doesn't have a size, but the place you put it in has to have one' is how it begins. It's hard to argue with Marieke when she's on her special subject.

'Tell me about these sites,' I ask Sigrid as she prods my leftover chicken with a fork. She smells of hours-old perfume and beer-garden smoke. 'Another dud,' she says, and means the man and the occasion.

'I think you should go on one,' she tells me. 'Having someone to cook for, or at least learn to cook for, might change your life.'

It changed hers, I know that: from an easy-going, happy twenty-nine-year-old to a trembling, fearful indoor-wife with captivity-bred eyes, whose husband checked her whereabouts, decided on her clothes and locked her in when he went out with his mates. He even loaded an app onto her mobile that told him where she was all the time. Not that she was ever where she wasn't supposed to be, but that made no difference: it's hard to know what the controlling man wants — something to control, or nothing.

It happened slowly: small increments, some of them so small that even looking back, it was hard to pick them out. In the days when Sigrid and I still discussed it, I would date it to the moment he told her to shut her face and that she'd drunk too much — after only two glasses — at a wedding reception in front of everyone she knew; she dates it later, to the moment she found him throwing out all the books an ex-boyfriend had given her. I date it from the evening he called her a slut for dressing up to go out with her friends; she dates it from the day he called her a frump for not dressing up to stay in with him.

The point is, she tells me, that when you know it's time to go, it's already too late. The reason you know it's time is *because* it's too late.

'Yes, I'll get around to it,' I tell her. 'Actually, I was looking at one the other day ...'

She looks up, interested. It is certainly more interesting than what I've cooked.

Sigrid met her husband in the normal way: he was the friend of a friend. First meeting, they talked across a table to each other, two singles at a table of couples. *Didn't really hit it off* as Sigrid put it, *but then we didn't* not *hit it off either.* Then they met alone a few times. Cinema, drink, dinner in a restaurant, then dine in for two, or *DIF2* as it's called on Twitter. And then? The same, but a little less. Then a little less of everything: time, tenderness, conversation, sex. Different TV programmes, different bedtimes. And then? The usual: a year of living together, a wedding, a child, two jobs, two medium-sized salaries and a house, not exactly where they wanted to live but close enough. The whole marriage was like that: its motto was basically *but close enough.* To start with.

And eventually the less usual, but not so unusual after all: the jealousy, the threats, the work-dos she was forced to miss, the kicked doors and the smashed plates; the freezing-out of friends and relatives, the monitoring of post, the confiscation of phone … Separation, divorce, and then a short and on his part lackadaisical fight for access to Marieke. First it was weekends, then every month, and now he has dropped away almost completely. With people like Simon, apathy and indifference become qualities.

'You've been on a dating site?' she asks.

'Yes and no,' I tell her.

'That's your answer to far too many questions,' she says.

'It's for the case I'm working on—'

'The girl in the binbag and the weird teacher?' she replies, closing the door so Marieke can't eavesdrop. But since Marieke is probably recording us, it is a pointless precaution. 'I hope for your sake he's guilty — for his, too — ' she says, 'because what they've done to him in the press is horrific.'

'Yes — the girl, Zalie — she had a profile on Soulmates — like you. It's still up — I thought we could monitor it, check if anyone was watching it. There's bound to be the odd ghoul, but the picture isn't such a likeness that you'd make the connection. She's certainly still receiving the messages, the "likes" and the "chat requests" ... I read through her profile, checked the messages, looked for anyone who wrote and said odd things – nothing. You might have been looked at by the same men – you know, *local ogling*.'

Sigrid finds that plausible: 'Wouldn't surprise me – people look for people close by, if what they want is a relationship. People close by feel more real somehow, though they aren't any different from people far away—'

'The thought that they might see the same shops or walk past the same park ... sit on the same bus, turns them on, makes it feel more real,' I tell her. 'I'm assuming,' I add, 'there are ways in which normal sexual or attractional behaviour overlaps with perverted or stalking behaviour, aren't there? I mean, the way you hang around in places someone might be just so you can see them and accidentally deliberately bump into them. Think of all those Hollywood romances based on the tenacious guy who won't give up, stolidly waiting outside her house, her office, engineering the random bumping-into ... it's always guys, too, it's all based on treating refusal, the word *no*, as some kind of soft negotiating position, so—'

'Thanks for mansplaining men to me, Ander,' Sigrid says: 'Look ... Let's assume we're talking about normal people here: if all people want is sex, they might be willing to travel as a one-off. Anyway, they'd be on different sites for that nowadays. They'd be swiping them left or right, not poring over their profiles to see if they both like jazz or Cajun cooking or French philosophy.'

'So what did you do? The site told you you'd been looked at, and who by, right?'

'Right – you can see who's looked at you, and when they last checked you out. Even if they don't message you, you can tell you're being looked at. *Checked out.* I'd go through the people who looked at me, and most of the time I wasn't interested. Didn't even click on their profiles.'

'But if she'd wanted, she'd have been able to keep track of who looked at her even if they didn't leave messages.'

'Yes – so what?'

'I don't know, it might be important – she was looked at by hundreds of people, but hadn't opened half the messages she got – three-quarters of them.'

'Women get hundreds a week; men don't, that's why. It's a ratio thing: men outnumber women on dating sites by about five to one, so it's part of how they keep their customers interested, how they keep them paying – you're more likely to stay on and not cancel your direct debit if there's someone who's looked at your profile. Some of the sites have fake women, kind of like avatars, swooping down on the blokes no one looks at, just to keep them on another month, another year, topping them up with enough hope to keep that direct debit going. That's what I've read anyway. But as I said – it's different for women. I haven't looked at most of my messages, my likes and my hearts and my bunches of electronic flowers. I barely read past the first line most of the time.'

'Why not?' I feel there's something here, I'm not sure what and I can't explain it and I wish Gary was here because he'd turn it into something solid: that more people knew Zalie than she was aware of? Than *we* are aware of? I use the word *knew* in a cyber-sense, because we've only been looking at real people in physical proximity: neighbours, colleagues, friends, pub-mates and open-plan-office acquaintances. I even thought about someone who might have been one telescope away – a voyeur across the square or the playing fields. But no sign of that. What about the other kind of voyeur? I'll phone Gary and ask him to check her Twitter account, any online chatrooms or forums she was on … any virtual places she might have been seen and heard in ways we haven't yet clocked but which maybe she was conscious of.

Sigrid is still talking: '… you can usually tell immediately anyway: the guy's too old, too young, has a picture of his dick instead of his face … Or he can't spell, offers you a night of pleasure in the Travelodge, asks for hot three-way action or wants your mobile number straight away … Or slags off his wife, his ex, the child-support agency … That stuff tends to happen on the first date, not in the so-called chat. The *courtship* period as they call it on the over-fifties dating sites.'

'It's like getting a bad feeling about someone in real life, just online? The same signs … obsessive, nosy, threatening, insecure, bad history?' I ask.

'I guess so – but without the comeback. You can block them or ignore them, and, anyway, they send out reams of these messages, so they probably forget themselves who they've written to. Remember the ratio stuff: to have half a chance of even getting a reply, these guys have to send out dozens and dozens of messages. It's completely safe – no personal info, unless you're stupid enough to give an address or a workplace or a name – I don't even use my first name.'

'Well, Zalie didn't contact anyone. She'd got hundreds of messages and didn't even read most of them. Didn't answer a single one.'

'That's normal – she either found someone and forgot all about it, or took one look at them all rolling into her inbox and changed her mind. I did the same – joined up two years ago, then just couldn't face it. Made me feel a bit sick, actually – not the people, they were mostly okay, it was just all that need and loneliness, and all that hope, too. Mostly that, to be honest: the hope. My own included. Then I started again when I had a better sense of what I wanted.'

'Which was?'

'What I wanted from myself, I mean – what I expected from myself, rather than just expecting it from someone else, from some hypothetical other person who'd come in and make it all good.'

'And what was that? That you expected from yourself, I mean.'

'Company first, just that – I've got a decent job, a child … I own my own home, *some* of it anyway, live in a nice city and have lots of friends. That's already a life. I started from that. First time around, after Simon, I wanted … *thought* I wanted … another partner, husband, whatever. I couldn't imagine a life I didn't share with a man.'

'And that's changed?' I ask.

'Yes – I don't expect anyone else to do for me what I can't do for myself. That's the difference between me now and me after Simon and the shitty life he gave me. With that cleared up, I'm okay with dating sites: I've got half an eye open for someone I might fall for, but I'm also interested in just meeting people I don't work with.'

'So why was Zalie on the site in the first place?' I ask. 'What did she want from it?'

'You're assuming she was lonely or frustrated or couldn't find a real person in the normal world, aren't you?'

'I'm not assuming anything at all … Well, maybe a bit. I've always assumed that we start out wanting to be loved and by the end we'll settle for just being known. But maybe that's just me. We know she had a boyfriend – met him a few weeks after joining that site, actually – so she didn't even really use it except to look at once in a while. She looked at a couple of profiles, but sent no messages. Basically, she joined up, met someone in her real life, then never got around to cancelling. Or let the subscription run itself out.'

'*Real life* – thanks a lot ...' says Sigrid. She looks at her watch, drinks some more wine. 'Maybe she was curious.'

'About what?'

'All the other fish in the sea? The great online aquarium? Maybe she wanted to see if she knew anyone on there ... I've spotted a couple of people I know on these things ...'

'I don't get the sense she was curious. She had Tim, so there'd be no need to keep checking the site. I reckon she was happy and sorted and people who are happy and sorted – who love someone and are loved back – aren't exactly mysterious, are they?'

'Well, in that case you and I must be unfathomable enigmas ...'

'And yet we're not.'

'No.'

Dating

On Zalie's Soulmates account, they're still viewing the
corpse. Sure, she's dead, she'd probably be the first to
admit it, but onscreen she's looking good. Some might
say never better, because she's attracting fans from all
over the country. Most of them know she's a corpse,
and they'll be going to her Instagram page for the same
reason they're checking her swelling Facebook friend-
request list and the shoals of new Twitter followers she's
attracted since she died: for a hit of her mortality, to be
close to the story, part of the action. How do you follow a
dead person? Where do you follow them to?

They can't leave her alone. It's not the dead who haunt
the living, it's the living who haunt the dead.

If there are worms devouring corpses in the
cyberworld, these people are the worms. In the old poems
Mr Wolphram used to teach us, there'd always be some
poet threat-seducing his lady with flowery language
about how she'd be dead soon, so she'd better sleep with
him. Ideally right now – *as soon as this poem's over*, was
his gist, *but you can start taking your clothes off in the last
verse.* He'd paint word-pictures of the worms burrowing

into her white flesh, eating her eyes and blacking out their suns, chewing off her lips. It was the worms' job to represent all those abstract things – Time and decay and forgetting – that we were supposed to fight so valiantly as we *seized the day*. As we *squeezed* the day. 'The grave's a fine and private place', I remember learning, 'But none, I think, do there embrace'. What would that poet be writing now? Would he be Facebooking his *carpe diems*? Leaving them on dating sites like landmines for women to click on and trigger? *Seize the day*: it means what it always meant, even back then, when the sexual menace was at least creatively worded: seize *my* day, seize *me*.

Every form of life dies in its own way, calls forth its own decay. This is ours: a profile on a website, a face made of pixels, and a click-bait swarm of views as Zalie decomposes beneath a gravestone icon decked with emoji-wreaths.

Her being biologically dead (one day we'll actually have to say *biologically* to make it clear what sort of dead we mean – there'll be such a *range of options*) seems almost beside the point. Until you remember that her parents, her sister and brother, and her boyfriend, Tim, are in agony out there in the real world, what's left of it. They are in such pain it's as if they have no skin on their flesh and the world is made of salt. They've been flayed by the horror of it, and by the press, and by the statements and the briefings they have to give to prurient interviewers and politicians with made-to-measure sympathy-tweets.

Tim: who we suspected at first, according to convention, but who was across the Channel and is now broken and alone, ashamed among the flashbulbs and the headlines, helpless as his friends sell pictures of him to the papers: smiling at New Year in Edinburgh, backpacking in

Greece, cuddling Zalie on the suspension bridge. That's the one the newspapers like best. Whoever sold it must have made a packet of cash: Zalie is a head shorter than Tim, so her face is at the centre of the picture. The contrast between her big, rainwater-grey eyes that turn down a little at the edges, giving her a sadness she doesn't have but just wears lightly as a perfume, and her wide happy smile, is beautiful. I can't stop looking at it, it's so lovely and almost painful to see. She is completely *in* the picture: not looking outside or beyond the moment. She inhabits it totally. Tim does, too. No wonder he's beaming – his face is less complicated, has no contrasts like hers, but he is happy and whole because for that deep, bottomless instant everything they want is aligned with what they have, which is each other and which is endless, and which is *now*: the two of them, there and then on the bridge with the water spreading out below.

You want to reach into the picture and pull out whatever it is – some of the air they breathed, a handful of the light – and sprinkle it over your own life.

Tim knows each of the people who snapped the photographs and sold them to the shitty newspapers. He hates them, doesn't answer their calls, deletes their emails and messages. Maybe some of them feel genuinely bad, maybe some just want more access to him for more cash: 'a close friend reports ...', 'a member of Tim Marchant's inner circle said ...', 'childhood friend of murdered girl's boyfriend spoke exclusively to us ...'

They are three, four, five rings out. They want to be part of the story, they want to be the ripples from the dropped stone.

Tim is ashamed when he's with Zalie's parents, because he knows that he is young, and that he must move on, find someone else and leave this place; that his future days will look like a betrayal of the girl he loved. He already knows this; even in the thick of his sorrow, he knows — he and Zalie's parents are in it together, but only up to a point. They have no choice, they are on a train called grief and it won't stop. And why would they want it to? But he must. Somewhere up ahead he will tell them: 'This is my stop,' and he will get off.

He will dread it and want it, too, the falling away.

Gary is sieving the Soulmates messages. 'Sorting the chaff from the ... er ... chaff.' Anything obviously generic he puts aside. Anything that looks individual, or tailored to giving or receiving personal information, he reads through. In the three days since we last checked, there have already been another ninety-eight messages.

'I thought I was bad with words. Then I read these guys,' he says, 'compared with them I'm Noël Coward.'

There they all are: the needy, the seedy, the passive-aggressive; the cerebral and the dick-led, the lonely hearts and their collectors. And the normal — the ordinary people, like Zalie, like me, like Sigrid, Gary, Deskfish and Small-Screen, like Tim and like Zalie's parents, like Jack with his broken *herat* ...

Two hours later, nothing. 'If there's something there, Prof, I can't find it. I also checked out the blokes who'd just looked at her — you know, clicked on the profile, viewed it, then went off to leer at someone else or buy more tissues. I just scanned them — it'd take hours to look at them individually. Nothing.'

'What are we actually looking for though, Gary? That's what I'm losing sight of: if someone looked her up and took a homicidal fancy to her, they'd still be unable to find her. There's no information that'd help them even find the city she lived in, let alone where in that city she lived. They could guess obviously, but Kent's a big place. And why her rather than anyone else?'

Gary sits back and shakes his head. He runs the tip of the pocket clip of his pen lid across his teeth, then swabs off the white gunge on his fingertip and rolls it to nothing between finger and thumb. Sometimes he smells it first, and the smell seems to reassure him of something. By this time, everyone has turned green or left the room. I am inured to it, which sounds like an advantage until one considers what it reveals about me. Maybe it helps Gary to think, because he is fearsomely focused right now. 'We keep getting close and then walking past it, Prof. Let's go back, right back to when she joined the site.'

'That's a year before she was killed, Gary − we're talking thousands of these messages.'

'Okay, point taken. Let's go forward instead − if there's anything to be found, it'll be around the time she was looking up information about stalkers − voyeurs or whatever, the one-handed binocularists ... The moment she started to feel watched ... Check her activity on the dating site against that.'

'What am I looking for?' I ask. Gary's got the momentum again. I like the way he doesn't enjoy the inversion of the hierarchy, the way he's too engrossed in doing the job to play for power with me.

'Don't look for anything logical, Prof − look for the accidental, the oddity, the thing that could easily never have happened but did ...'

'Thanks − that narrows it down,' I reply, aiming for sarcasm and mis-hitting my tone. Instead, I sound grateful, which I should be, because what Gary tells me to do now changes everything. We are about to make what Gary calls a *monumentous breakthrough*.

The dates she looked for stalker advice were 25–29 November. If it's connected to something she saw online, that something will be close by. Surely. A few hours, a day, two days, but not much more than that.

We look through the week before, working backwards, from the morning of the 29th. She received twenty-six messages and eighty-three profile views across three days. She logged on nine times, too, which is more than she had done in the whole three months before. She had been with Tim for almost thirteen months – long enough to know she wasn't interested in other blokes. So what was she looking at? And why was she suddenly, after weeks not bothering with the site, checking it at such short, such breathless, nervy little intervals? One of the checks is at 1.38 a.m.; the other at 5.45 the same morning.

Gary is standing over me. 'Those aren't the habits of someone in a normal state of mind. Look—' he jabs the log-in times with his finger when I look up at him, baffled: 'Don't you get it? She can't sleep. She's worried. If she'd met some handsome wordsmith like me, then maybe, yes, she'd be checking for replies, hooked on the rush of contact and repartee. But she hasn't. She hasn't messaged anyone *ever*, let alone recently.'

'That leaves the other possibility – the only other one – that she's checking for someone she *doesn't* want to see.'

'That's right, Prof – she's scared, creeped out. She suddenly logs in nine times in three days – months of not going on the site, looks up information about stalkers in that same three-day window, then forgets about it. Or doesn't.'

'Then gets killed.'

'Yep, then gets killed. But not straight away. And in her own flat − not at the other end of town or some faraway edgeland or a dark alley or the ring road. *In her home*. What's the link? And if she was afraid of someone online, why didn't she tell people?'

'I suppose there's still a bit of a sense that internet dating is for the desperate, or those who can't meet people in the real world. You sure she told Tim that she'd joined a dating site?'

'She did! Look back over the notes: he said she told him soon after they met and that she'd leave the site. They didn't have secrets.'

This is stuff I should know, but I don't. I left all the computer checks to others and I was wrong to because now we're getting close and we should have got closer sooner.

'Okay, but she was still on the site, wasn't she?' I tell him.

'Yes, well, technically yeah: you pay by direct debit, and the longer you sign up for the cheaper it is. I know this, Prof, I've been there and done … well, not much. She went for a one-year package and then a six-month package, and had another twelve weeks of the second one to go. You can see the reminders here', Gary marks them out with his pen: they're from 'Admin' and the subject line is variously 'Get three months extra FREE if you buy now', 'Premier Service just got cheaper!' and 'Get Ready for Valentine's Day!'

I've got it now. I know what Gary means. 'She wasn't looking for a soulmate, or any sort of mate … she was checking to see who was checking on her?'

'Exactly. But why?'

'Because she knew him, or she'd seen him, or she knew he'd seen her somewhere other than a computer screen, that's why.'

'You got it, Prof.'

Of the men who have *checked her out*, sixty have sent messages and nearly two hundred have simply looked at her, read her profile, and moved on. There's no way of telling how they did it, or what went through their minds: you can't see their palms sweat or hear their breathing like you can in an interview room.

The messages are of no use. Generic, apart from a couple so clumsy they can only be sincere. I imagine Sigrid trawling through stuff like this, and wonder how she picks out people to 'chat' to and then *take it further*. She tells me that anyway it's the body that decides in the end. The head and the heart are hopeless against the body. You might like the way someone speaks or writes, but what happens when you meet them? The words don't matter: it's the other person's smell, the temperature of their skin, their open pores. It's all happening under the words you speak and the thoughts you think.

All those brains cells, all that language, all that education, just to get told what to do by your nose.

One of Sigrid's dates: 'He looked great, talked nicely, dressed like a gent, was kind and funny ... solvent ... just didn't have any ... smell. I couldn't ... how can I explain it? I couldn't steer my body towards him ... it kept veering away. I had to close my eyes to see if I could jump-start the erotics, but no ... nothing.'

Of the direct messages to Zalie, only five are what we'd call 'local' – the site triages people according to distance: 5 miles, 15, 30, 40, 60 and 70+. They're from Brighton, Southend, Folkestone, Dover, Romney, Deal. And London. Lots of London. Men leave much more information on the site than women: the guys look genuine, some of them look handsome and might even be the age they claim to be. Two of them even tell the site where they work. One of them tells us his favourite pub. Just in case someone might want to check him out *offsite*. A woman giving that information is putting herself in danger. A man doing the same is just trying his luck.

I look for the repeat viewings of Zalie – anyone who has clicked on her more than once … anything that looks obsessive or fixational. I then try to match them to Zalie's own browsing. That takes just a few minutes, because she only looked at a couple of dozen men in all the time she was signed up. And only six of them in the days and nights we're interested in. And of those six, four of them she looked at more than three times in the first week of joining the site. And of those four, there's one she looked at two, three, five, eight, fifteen times in all. Recently. A week before she died.

There he is.

Mister B. Age 32. Actuary. That's not as boring as it sounds (Okay, it is but I'm not!).

Height: 6.2.

Hair: Dark.

Style: Smart casual. Dressy when necessary.

Looking for: Casual/serious/fun/chat/friendship.

'Got all the bases covered, hasn't he?' says Gary.

Likes: Cooking, jazz, travel, Thai food, Scandinavian crime fiction, European cinema.

'Ah, our old friend *European cinema* …' says Gary, 'that's good enough for me: let's pick him up right now …'

Dislikes: Politics, cyclists, curry.

'It's a pretty basic profile, isn't it? He checked out Zalie twice, didn't message her at all. But she checked him out almost ten times. Didn't contact him, but looked at that profile over and over.'

'Did she recognise him?'

'Not from the photos – he didn't upload any face shots.'

'Did she recognise any other bit of him?'

'For Christ's sake, Gary, this isn't a *Carry On* film!'

'Okay, Prof. Sorry.' He puts on a mock-solemn face. Then a real thinking face. Then he's keen again, and then he's got it: 'Turn the question round: did *he* recognise *her*?'

'That's more like it. Well, if so, he doesn't give any indication of it – no messages, no chat requests, nothing . . .'

'Check how far away he is,' says Gary.

The site tells us: 0 miles. The next closest person who viewed her was 1.3 miles away.

'Oh Christ,' says Gary, 'To be 0 miles they need to have the same postcode – these sites use the Post Office zoning system that delivers your mail. We're talking a few houses away . . . literally the same street.'

We're almost there now. Gary enlarges the three shots of 'Mister B' that he has posted online: a pint of beer (denoting easeful blokeishness), an exotic snow-capped mountain (that's travel, plus money: broad mind/broad wallet), and a record by Miles Davis (jazz vibe: classy but not recondite). He's telling everyone: I'm homely, intrepid, educated. I like vinyl, craft beer, and I can afford to ski. There's no face, but we don't need the face now.

'Same street? It's the same bloody house! It's that guy from upstairs! Ben!' Gary yells to Small-Screen: 'Tell the Drone – we're bringing him in.'

'Don't do that, Gary – not right yet. Leave him to enjoy Mad Lynne's hospitality a little longer. Let him think he's safe. His flat's empty so we'll get warrants to search it, check his phoneline, his internet, his bank accounts . . . the whole lot. Same goes for the girlfriend.'

As we wait for Deskfish to arrange the paperwork, Gary and I turn to the station TV.

'It's Mr Lawnder!' I shout at the screen.

'Who?' asks Gary.

'Don Lawnder, young guy who taught English, had a kind of breakdown after two terms then went to work in the parks . . . Turn it up!'

The remote has been lost for so long that no one even remembers it, so Gary goes over and unmutes the TV:

' . . . a kind, supportive colleague and a generous teacher. The school has behaved despicably towards him . . . cut him adrift on the say-so of a lynch mob.'

'You believe he's innocent?' It's Ellie Nash again.

'He's innocent of the allegations made about him during his teaching days, yes – this is a witch-hunt culture . . .'

'What about murder?' asks Ellie who obviously owns the story now, even more than Mad Lynne does.

'That's for the justice system to determine, but the man I knew was gentle and thoughtful and highly intelligent – not the sort of person who would turn to violence.'

Where did they find Lawnder? Whenever I've thought of him, which is more than occasionally and less than often, I've imagined him moving slowly amid municipal greenery, making small changes to places we don't notice.

But I'm wrong. I'm stuck in time – I'm stuck where I left him. Don Lawnder isn't: he wears a blue canvas jacket and round glasses like the poets he liked so much. He looks strong and well. He's standing outside a stately home in Hampshire. I recognise it from school trips:

Shapley Hall. There's a bar at the bottom of the screen that calls him 'Dr' and tells us he's an 'Architectural historian'. His voice is as soft as ever, but hardier, and though he hasn't grown, he has bulked out and looks less like a battered sapling. His skin has the near-tan of someone who spends most of his life outdoors, and he looks a lot better on his — what would it be? — fifty-five? sixty? years than I look on my forty-seven. Lean, intelligent, fearless, he lays into Chapelton College:

'When the time comes, the school and its headmaster, the attention-seeking ex-pupils with their lies, will have to account for themselves and the way they've been complicit in the demonisation of an innocent man.'

Cut back to Ellie Nash, bright-faced in the arc lights and with her hair blown about by the wind.

'As more people come forward to speak for Michael Wolphram, to defend his reputation or just ask for him to be treated fairly, we have to pose the question: Did the police move too fast on this? Did they let the public's need for a suspect affect their judgement in those crucial early hours?'

'Yes!' shouts Gary, clapping delightedly, 'Yes, they did!'

*

To reach Ben's flat we've had to come in through the back, opening up a fence-panel in the garden of the house behind and crossing the lawn. This is because of the heave of TV vans and photographers on motorbikes on the pavement in front, spilling onto the road so that cars have to klaxon to be let through. The crowd is bulked out by members of the public, and the selfie sticks poke up like masts in a stormy marina. We have surfed from the fatberg to the monster on a wave of headlines. There's new graffiti, too — around the surrounding houses and walls, because the house itself is guarded twenty-four hours a day.

We have *KILLER, Peedo* [sic] *scum*, the mandatory *ROT IN HELL* (twice in different hands), and *HANG 'IM* in huge letters. The apostrophe is painted as a noose, the fat bit of the sliding knot carefully done to express the braiding of the rope. I wonder if there's a lynching emoji. If not, this should be it. Then the flowers and the tea lights, a field of them, spreading out along the street. Her parents' house is mobbed, too, their front gate covered in teddies, flowers and cards which the TV cameras scan like barcodes and broadcast as visual filler while their reporters confect packages about *outpourings of sympathy* and *shocked communities united in grief* …

The front of the house is a contradiction of tributes and memories, abuse and threats. There can't be many streets which housed the murderer, the victim and the falsely accused. And the murder itself. There's something for everyone here: the sad and respectful, the angry and blood-lustful, the nosy, the indignant and the outraged.

One of the channels has pulled together a documentary for the New Year TV sump. It includes the obligatory showbiz shrinks-for-hire, conspiracy theorists, ex-colleagues, tenuously remembered friends, neighbours-with-grudges and a few of those pupils currently *coming forward* and *breaking their silences*. It won't include: Danny, Don Lawnder, Neil Hall, or any of those who have spoken up for Wolphram. The programme is called *Schooled in Murder?*. They've asked someone from the investigation to appear and Deskfish has agreed.

Even the shop where she bought her last meal has a few bouquets and candles in front of it. As well as a sudden tripling of customer-flow. The office where she worked, her local pub and even her gym. They're hunting her down wherever she went. She's dead but they won't stop haunting her.

What strikes us immediately – Gary and I and six *frenzics* – is the soullessness of Phelps's flat. All chrome and leather, it's generic bloke-habitat: huge flat-screen TV, hi-fi, DVD and Blu-Ray players; framed photographs of mountains and sunsets; Xbox (just the one console, Gary notices), CD cases, titles facing outwards, slotted into CD towers. There's a low, grey, frosted-glass-topped coffee table with a pile of men's lifestyle magazines, edges flush with each other and aligned with the corner of the table. There are two thick slate coasters underlaid with green felt so they can slide noiselessly along. The sofa is big, rectangular, deep and made of black leather. The cushion on one side is so deeply imprinted by Ben that I could probably guess his weight. Three remote controls and the Xbox console are lined up in front of it.

The kitchen is as spotless as Wolphram's and laid out in the same way. The window overlooks the gardens of the houses behind. There are two of everything on the draining board. But no more than two: two knives, two forks, two spoons, two plates. Two wine glasses and one pewter pint tankard. A line of craft beers. A few bottles of New Zealand or Australian wine with names that sound like soap operas: *Blossom Hill, Hardy's Crest, Murray's Landing.*

Gary opens the cutlery drawers. Empty. In a cupboard by the fridge there are more plates and cutlery, but they're still in the box they came in. The Lansdale's receipt is

Sellotaped to the side. All unused. No guests. No one to get back to but each other.

'I'm getting a bad feeling here, Prof ...' says Gary. 'Emptiness. I don't mean empty drawers and stuff. I mean a hole somewhere where there shouldn't be a hole.'

I know what Gary means. For all the symmetry, the paired plates and glasses don't feel right. The cupboard under the sink contains only cleaning products: bleach in three different brands, antibacterial sprays, wire brushes, a bumper pack of sponges, oven cleaner, and carpet foam. Washing-up gloves — five pairs still in their unopened bags. I am about to move the bottles of cleaner and root my way to the back of the cupboard, but Gary stops me.

'Leave that to *frenzics*, Prof, what we're after is the gut feeling, we need to look at the stuff not move it about. Everywhere has its vibe, its *bouquet*, you'd call it. What are you getting?'

'Control.'

'It's those coasters, man, controlling people love coasters. I'm not getting a sense of a couple. Or even two people, to be honest.' Gary shakes his head: 'It's just him, isn't it? Nothing's hers. It's like she doesn't live here, just stays here.'

In the bathroom, Ben's grooming products occupy a whole shelf, and are neatly lined up. Hers are in a small bag in the mirrored cupboard above the sink. Minimal, too: lipstick, foundation, blusher and eyeliner. One of each, whereas he has two different shaving foams, four razors and two hipster moisturisers with fake-English names intended to summon up Jermyn Street panache: *Chatterton's Classic Grooming* and *Dashwood's Skin Care for Men.*

In their bedroom, it's the same: plush and impersonal as an expensive hotel room. *That's what it wants to be,* I think, *the whole place: a hotel suite.* On her bedside table she has a photograph of her parents and her sister with a baby. In the drawer, her contraceptive pills and a book with an art gallery bookmark with a tassel. It's the first time we've found anything that could be described as her space. His wardrobe is large but reiterative: three pairs of the same shoes for work, two of the same going-out shoes, two pairs of identical trainers, five of the same shirts ... all of them labels, brands, designer stuff with motifs.

There are no traces of her in the flat except here, and what little there is is either scrubbed clean or tucked away.

'She doesn't live here, Prof,' says Gary, 'she just moves her body around the rooms then puts it down in bed until it's time to go to work again.'

'I don't see anything suspicious though,' I tell him.

Gary is at the laundry basket, lifting the lid and peering in. 'Nothing there, Prof, nothing in the washing machine, nothing in the drier.'

'Must've done the washing before heading out to enjoy the newspaper's hospitality. But I still can't see anything odd.'

'Don't worry, Prof, *frenzics* will find something. Anyway, what we really need's his computer. It'll all be online with him. In the old films your cops would arrive, find nothing, then at the last moment, just as they're leaving feeling shitty, one of them notices the key to a lockup that's crammed with evidence. No need for lockups anymore. Today's lockup is the laptop, and he's taken his with him.'

I phone through an order to have Ben's computer seized. Chloe's, too. Mobile phones and tablets. We need to find out where Lynne Forester's newspaper is keeping him.

'I'll take care of it,' says Gary, and leaves me there in the hallway.

SOCOs are dismantling the washing machine, taking the clothes and shoes out in evidence bags. They're putting the wireless Wi-Fi hub into a bag. The forensic vacuum cleaner is aspirating the welcome mat and the rugs and the wall-to-wall carpeting. In the kitchen they're bagging up a pair of used rubber gloves, taking the sink out and swabbing the inside of the pipes. They've found masking tape, binbags, bubble wrap. You'd use them to put out the rubbish, wrap a present, carry something fragile. It's Christmas after all.

They're ordinary, quiet, cupboard-things, yes, but right now they look like instruments from hell.

*

As I wait for Gary back at the station, I decide to look some of them up.

For Mrs Pizzi there's an old funeral notice: *Elaine Pizzi, 1940–2008. Funeral at Bartlemas crem. No flowers. Donations to cancer research.*

Angela Mason, 78 Westway Rd. Chair of the French Society, and there she is on their Facebook page.

Lawnder, Donald, Dr: Professor of Architecture at King's College London. Beneath his name, a list of his books: one is *The Medway City Zoo: A Modernist Masterpiece.* 'Donald Lawnder was instrumental in the listing of one of south-east England's modern treasures

...' it says on his Wikipedia page. It links to the zoo's website, which promises a two-year Lottery-funded restoration project overseen by Lawnder and English Heritage.

I chase them down in a frenzy of Googling: Neil Hall, Rich Nicholson, George Cobbleson, Flynch, Bowden and Tristan; Bosworth, Vaughan, Lewis, McCloud, Goodship and Morbender. Some I can't find, while others, those with generic names, David Jones, Jonathan Smith, could be any of the similar sounding, similarly employed people in banks and SMEs, Chamber of Commerce types with what Gary calls 'painted-on suits'. A lot of them have Facebook pages with pictures of themselves in running vests with numbers on. It's a world of half-marathons and personal bests. Many of them send their kids to Chapelton.

I wonder how many of them blank it all out, the bad stuff, sieve it and refine it until all that's left are the good things, connected up by ... well, nothing: connected up by holes.

Morbender died in 1991. A cagey obituary says he was 'a little ready with punishment'. 'Old-school values and old-school methods.' Then, at the end: 'He leaves a wife, two children and three grandchildren.'

McCloud is still alive and runs an English-style boarding school in Hong Kong: *Modelled on the classic English public school, and staffed by teachers from the UK's finest universities, Chapel Down College teaches the British curriculum to prepare pupils for the world. The school lives by the ethos Mens sana in corpore sano: a healthy mind in a healthy body*. There's a photograph of McCloud looking well-preserved if a little freeze-dried, but it's hard to tell how recent it is.

It's not because I'm curious – I could have done this anytime in the last quarter-century – it's more to feel their names at the ends of my fingers, right down to the letters; to explore the traceability of them all. I leave Danny until last.

I'm about to type in Daniel Patrick McAlinden – I get to the small *c* in the *Mc* – but Gary pulls my hand away.

'Stop it, Prof. Leave them alone. Leave *him* alone. The past may be your local, but he doesn't drink there anymore. And from what you've told me he never did either. Just because you can find people doesn't mean you should. In real life, outside the films and the stories, the *long-lost friend* stays long lost, which is usually how he wants it. Anyway, *this* is what you should be checking out.'

He takes out a long roll of printed paper. Websites URLs, times, durations. There's a folder with images from homepages, and bank statements with direct debits and standing orders underlined in red. They've worked fast, because there's a pile of printouts of Phelps's browsing histories.

'Did she know about this?' I ask. 'Chloe, I mean?'

'There's no evidence she did, Prof. But, then, there's knowing and there's *knowing*, isn't there? Especially with the wives and the girlfriends of these people. He deletes his browsing history and has a password. Sometimes he uses her laptop for normal things like banking or booking train tickets, but not for this kind of stuff. He has the password to hers, she doesn't have his. Says it all.' Gary shows me a list of the sites he visits. They're violent, abusive, demented places. I can tell that just from the titles.

'Did you take a look at any of them?' I ask Gary.

'Prof — there's stuff on there I couldn't bear to watch even if it was a film and I knew it wasn't real.'

'I'm sorry.'

'It's okay, that's the job. But, yes, I did. A bit. Lifted the lid. Caught the stench. *Breathed the fumes*, as the poet would say. It won't hold up as evidence — we've been through this before, Prof: the looking versus doing stuff, thought versus deed. But in the context of other things, yes: it goes into a case.'

'Other things being DNA, witnesses and a confession, yes?'

'The first one'll do. That's why I've sent what your man would call a *lapidary* reminder to that private lab in Cheltenham asking where the hell their results are. I reckon they've read the papers, seen the telly and decided *they've got their man ... no hurry anymore.* They can get on with doing those paternity tests for the daytime TV circus or whatever they make their bread and butter money from.'

'And the dating site?' I ask.

'Not much there. He was writing to different women in different ways, a dozen or so on the go. In the old days you needed a magic potion and a lab to be Jekyll and Hyde, now you just need a smartphone. One or two replied, asked for pictures, chatted a bit, but then lost interest. No reason. Just decided against him. I'd like to think their instinct sniffed something amiss even in cyberspace — that would comfort me. A bit. A bad cyber-feeling. But he had no aliases, just different personalities and that one nickname for all sites: *Mister B.* One message he'd be all romantic and smooth, the next he'd be wanting no-strings one-nighters with strangulation games. "'Til our lips go purple!" he says. No dice on any front.'

'What I don't understand is why he never messaged Zalie. He'd have recognised her straight away as the woman in the downstairs flat.'

'You answered your question right there, Prof: he didn't need to, did he? She was right there all the time. Send her a message online? What's the point when he can talk to her in the hall or on the stairs or while she's putting her bins out?'

'Hiding in plain sight.'

'Not even hiding, Prof. If anyone was hiding, Zalie was.'

He must have met her, or approached her, or engineered some kind of encounter outside the house, on the way back from work, getting their bikes, picking up the post from the doormat. He could have watched her without arousing any suspicion – why would he? He was at home. The problem was: so was she.

Small-screen

Ben is on the bridge. He's looking down, but because of the meshed wire barriers he can't hang his head over. He can't even do the toying-with-the-possibility-of-jumping, suicidally-meditating-on-the-void routine. That's health and safety for you – you can't even choose your own dénouement.

But this is a symbolic action, contends Gary, not a serious suicide threat: 'Small-screen ending, Prof.' Ben knows that bridges are traditionally where things come to their climax. He's seen enough films and played enough Xboxes to know that bridges are good places to end things. Unfortunately, it's now much easier to jump from just under the buttresses, to scramble down and find a ledge, then make your leap. He must know that. But, then, no one would see him. You can't get the TV crews down there and you'd have no *scene*. There'd be nobody to film him with the blue-strobing police lights crossing his final-act face, no police negotiators trying to persuade him not to jump. He's seen it on telly and he wants the lot: loudhailers, helicopters, police negotiators.

Instead it's Gary hurling bathos at him: 'Should've brought a ladder, mate!'

This is Ben Phelps starring in the movie of his own capture. He's not going to get caught in a newspaper's rented flat while his girlfriend looks at him and sees a murderer and wonders whether he was always going to be that murderer. Or whether just one of the many versions of what he might become happened to get picked from the crowd of his possible selves. Whether he'd have murdered *her*. But she hates him, that's for sure. And now she's free.

He could tell from the phone call that we were onto him. He watched as Lynne Forester answered – in the middle of recording his *version of events*, the version where he didn't kill Zalie, where he was shocked, horrified, and where he pocketed ten grand – and saw her face alter, heard her voice shake as she listened to Gary. It was good to see her scared finally, that was something. He enjoyed the fear. A small victory. And he'll miss the money. The money would've been really handy. And would it have been so bad after all if that weirdo Wolphram got put away? 'The Wolf'. He always knew that guy wasn't right.

He wasn't going to wait for the police.

So Phelps is going to get caught on the bridge, for no reason other than the dramatic decor, which is an excellent reason in a world which to him is no more than a TV screen. He's going to hold out until the TV crews get here, until Lynne and Ellie Nash and all the country's news channels are here to film it.

The cars have stopped, and the commuters – ignoring the loudhailers telling them to stay where they are – are getting out and snapping him with their phones. The flashes seep like slow fireworks into the fog. It's muffled and Christmassy. Festive, even, like tinsel flaring in treelights. They'll be live-tweeting it. Hashtag Medway Bridge. Hashtag Jumper. Every thirty seconds, every ten seconds, every five, and there's another dozen, another twenty, another fifty pictures, tweets, updates …

Gary and I are walking slowly towards him. Each time Ben turns or looks down or back at the massing crowd, we step a little closer.

I wonder if they've announced that Wolphram's being released, that we have another suspect. If the people on the bridge have heard the news, whether the headlines have cut in across the 5 p.m. drivetime shows, the Christmas singles, the last-minute ads for last-minute presents. The ribbons of BREAKING NEWS under the quiz shows and the soaps. Gary is scrolling down traffic update sites, the bridge hashtag, Zalie's name, Xmas rush hour, Wolphram … and he's swearing: 'Why the fuck do I have to look at my phone to find out what's happening in my own life? In front of my fucking eyes?' All we can hear from the police cars is the switchboard asking for situation reports from all the cars in the area.

What's our report? *We're here and it's now.*

We start to walk towards Ben. He's less than a quarter of the way across the bridge, eighty metres or so along its span. He knows that the closer he is to us, the better it is for filming, because the TV vans don't have to go the long way around. Gary says Ben won't do it. I'm not sure. And not just because he hasn't got a ladder. It's because he's waiting; nothing's going to happen until the press get here.

He shouts at us and tells us to stay where we are. He grips the mesh and looks like he'll try to climb it. We stop. He lets go.

Never underestimate inconvenience as a deterrent for site-specific suicide: for some reason I remember verbatim a sentence from a report I read on bridges. When I was a young policeman the area force was consulted on measures for suicide-reduction here. We suggested what we suggest best: barriers. The experts agreed, and a sort of caging with finger-fine mesh that turns back inwards at the top was fastened to the barriers in the nineties. Same as they used in the zoo. There were objections by the City Conservation Society, who wrote letters to the newspapers strafed with the adjective *unsightly*. But the number of deaths halved after that. Did it mean that suicides just took their desperation or their resolve elsewhere?

You certainly don't see, as you once did, the hovering, fretful depressives who used to haunt the bridge and who sometimes jumped. Or the decisive ones, with their faces on automatic, walking purposefully to the exact spot they'd planned. The bridge stopped being a place to think about suicide in the way it used to be, a place to contemplate it, even if you'd never do it, or to mull over the physics of falling or gauge what it would take to make you want it. The way I used to go and hang my arms off and calculate just how much misery I'd need to tip me over. I imagined it as the kitchen scales at home when my grandmother baked: me on one side and on the other a black flour being slowly sifted until ... until it drops down and up I go and my weight in shadow takes my body's place.

If you saw someone standing there now, you could bet they were admiring the view or enjoying the cut of the wind, the smell of the estuary or the thrill of such pure height that the tonnes of iron and steel holding them up feel like a platform of air. They weren't in the hell of themselves and wanting to end.

For a while people used the buttresses. The buttresses are different; they're built into rock and concrete and rubbly grass, and have the incremental, graded fall where the body, having leapt from a place with no clear vantage point and far from any photogenic chasm, falls and breaks itself against a rugged slope, its bones crunching and chipping and dislocating in their sockets as it half bounces, half rolls, until, skin flayed, flesh ripped and twenty or thirty feet down, it finds a sheer edge and drops over. It's a lot to take in, even when you want to die, and it doesn't have the perfect end-note of a clean fall through the void.

If it's finality you're after, and ease of identification at the other end, you'd be shortlisting other locations.

The last thing the suicide-to-be wants is a demeaning struggle with the banalities of their chosen spot: with the undergrowth and the rocks, the bits of fencing, the dogshit and cans and used condoms. All to finish up broken on a B-road as the commuters jam on the brakes or near some fly-tipped oven wedged on the slope.

'He won't do it, Prof. He's only standing there because he's seen it in action films and video games ... those things always end with edges and ledges: cliff tops, railway tracks, windowsills, skyscraper roofs, you name it ... But this isn't an action film and this guy doesn't have the guts to jump. Or the time.'

'I don't want him jumping and I don't want him getting any famous last words in before he goes.'

'You and me both, Prof. You ready?'

'I'm ready!'

I realise I have no idea what I'm ready for, let alone if it's the same thing Gary is ready for.

We walk slowly towards the middle of the bridge's span. Gary stops occasionally to look at the view, though there is no view, there's just a cold, thin wind and darkness below. The headlamps and taillights of the cars, bumper to bumper, make it impossible for us not to be seen, but the bridge lights have been turned off, as we asked. That will make it harder for the rubberneckers to film on their smartphones.

Gary is walking deliberately slowly, dawdling like a tourist. As we get closer, Phelps calls out with threats to jump but Gary ignores him and wanders on. He's cooler than I am – I'm sure Phelps will jump. He keeps gripping the bar and the wire and trying to get a foothold on the mesh. We're about twenty metres away now.

Gary shows me his phone: 'Look, there's even an app – YourBridge, or you can scan the QR code on the signs and get a spoken-word tour in a choice of voices ...' Gary scrolls down and starts walking again. Phelps is still shouting that he'll jump, but there's less and less will to do it.

Ten metres. Phelps has taken out his phone and is trying to make a call. That buys us time. He's trying to get through. Someone answers. Phelps starts to speak. Pauses and listens, then turns his back to us to check if the TV crews are here. They're not. But Gary is and he cuffs him wordlessly and takes the phone out of his hand. He puts it to his ear.

'Ah, Lynne, Gary here ... I think you already know what's going on and where we are. But, anyway, great timing – saves us calling you later. You'll be at the station first thing tomorrow morning with all you've got on

Phelps. Tapes, transcripts, the lot. I hope you don't turn up so I can drive over myself with a warrant and a police car and pick you up at your place of so-called *work* ... '

He puts the phone in an evidence bag and hands it to one of the police officers who have suddenly materialised around us. He turns to me. 'Imagine being such a loser that your last words were going to be for Mad Lynne Forester.'

*

'Let me tell you a story about that bridge, Prof.'

Gary has calmed down but I'm still shaking. His phone is beside his drink and it vibrates with ignored calls, crossing the tabletop in spasms. We're in the Harcourt Arms. They haven't taken down the MISSING poster for Zalie that's behind the bar, except now there's a tea light under it, shining up at her chin. There are bouquets and candles outside the pub, while inside the drinkers look solemn as they tweet photos under the tables from the place Lynne Forester called *Zalie's favourite watering hole*.

'When we were teenagers, me and my mates used to hang around the bridge after school. There or the zoo. The animals had gone but for some reason all their shit was still there, bits of fur everywhere, and it was a great place for skateboarding and smoking until they locked it all up and put CCTV everywhere. We did what teenagers did, even you probably ... That corner shop Zalie shopped in − back then the owner sold cigarettes and booze to underage kids. We'd go and drink our cans and cough our way through Marlboro Reds at the top of the hill and check out the traffic and the ferries ... if there were lorries we'd look underneath them to see if there were migrants hiding there. The papers were full of that stuff, and we all dreamed of being the schoolkid hero who caught one of those poor sods from some Calais camp or the tunnel. But no luck, thank God, and all we saw was the posh kids in their Chapelton trackies coming back from games, and we made wanker signs and gave them the finger.'

'People like me, you mean?'

'People like you, Prof. It still goes on; always will – same finger, different hands. Anyway, often there was this girl – reddish-blonde hair, kind gentle face, must have been about eighteen or twenty or something. It felt like a huge age gap but it wasn't really. She'd be standing there in the middle of the bridge. It was a couple of years before they put those barriers up. When the Samaritans used their old number. Nineteen ninety-four or five.'

Gary checks his phone. Sees there's another message and doesn't read it.

'Sometimes, she'd talk to me. Never said anything big. Weather talk. Nice day. Less nice day. Crappy day. She seemed so adult to me, so grown up. She sighed a lot, had those faraway thoughts adults had. I used to wonder, *Will I ever think stuff like that?* Her hair was always in the sun ... it wasn't, of course, that's just how it felt to me, like one of those seventies easy-listening album covers.

I was spotty and chubby, had chafing legs in itchy trousers, a nylon shirt with yellow underarms and BO ranging from fresh-and-fierce to historically stale. She asked me my name. She was so beautiful and peaceful standing there with the wind in her hair that I felt I was spoiling things by saying 'Gary'. Why couldn't I be – I dunno – Oliver or Jacob or Gabriel? Alexander? But you know me, I can't lie, and say Gary I did, Prof. Gary

Maffett. Music to the ears. We chatted a bit — she said she was from St Leonard's and was studying at the art college. She had paint on her fingers, at the edge of her jumper, on her shoes. I know because I kept looking at everything but her eyes because I was too shy. I saw all these bits of detail, bitten nails, scuffed shoes, stuff like that. We said goodbye and I went off feeling stupid for not having anything interesting to say, and there was like a little pull at my back. I turned to say I'd like to see what she painted ... but she was gone. Finally, my big line, Gary's big chat-up gambit. But no one to hear it. I had to go to where she'd been standing just to make sure, I thought her smell would still be hanging there. And it was ... is how I remember it. I still smell it now, Prof, when I pass the spot. Then I looked over and there was nothing down there. In the water, in the mud, on the road. Nobody.'

'She jumped?'

'I guess so. There were other people on the bridge, one of them some kind of amateur photographer, and they hadn't seen her, let alone someone jumping. We looked down but no cars had stopped on the road and there was no one pointing and screaming down below. They told me I'd made it up, said I should be ashamed of myself.'

'You *sure* you didn't imagine it?'

'As sure as you didn't imagine all that stuff that happened in your school. I kept an eye on the *Evening Post* to see if they'd found a body or if anyone had gone missing. In those days we didn't have computers in every house so you couldn't look it up. Online news wasn't what it is now. For weeks afterwards I read the paper and I can't have missed more than a handful of news bulletins. Didn't find a thing: no bodies, no missing persons, no appeals.'

'You could probably find out now. We've got all we need at the station, all computerised, all linked up, going back forty years.'

'Don't you think I have, Prof? I've looked at every possible bit of archive, I started in Hastings and St Leonard's and there was nothing there, so either she was lying or no one missed her. That happens, too, you know. I checked coroners' reports, news sites, *MisPers* and unsolveds, from here up to London and then Dover, Folkestone, Ramsgate, all the way to Portsmouth, Brighton ... I checked the big ferry towns where people go in and out and no one cares. Then the resorts – Margate, Gravesend, Broadstairs, end-of-the-pier places ... Checked with river rescue, the psychiatric hospitals ... But no. She's the ghost in my head. I reckon she's perfectly preserved in that mud, like those ancient Irish warriors in the bogs. We did poems about them in school. Turns out some of them weren't so ancient after all. Probably not warriors either. Still, that's all water under the bridge, isn't it, Prof? We're all friends now, eh?'

'Maybe she just escaped ... *really* escaped: left no trace, no memories, no friends, no family, no body. Maybe that's what she wanted: one minus one equals zero. Maybe you should leave her alone.'

'That or she wanted me to see, so one person would know.'

'Or that.'

'Anyway, Prof, I didn't want that murdering bastard down there – not with her and all the others. They don't deserve that.'

Gary finishes his drink and waves for a repeat round.

'I'll tell you something else, Prof. Every now and then – nothing regular or anything, just when I remember and can be bothered — I leave a little bunch of flowers for her, tie them to the railings at the spot where we spoke. It's not a ritual, I don't get all solemn or anything ... I just do it because now it's part of me.'

*

The theory? We'll never know for sure, but here is the theory:

Phelps recognises Zalie from her profile on the site. He has no need to message her — he can see her anytime he likes. This bit's hazy, but goes something like this: he stopped her, chatted, tried it on, got told to piss off, mentioned he'd seen her on the site, freaked her out. He watched her, kept on at her and one day he just came in.

He says she let him in. He's lying, but we can't prove that. There's a scuff mark on the bottom of her front door that matches his shoe, and that will help us to argue that he forced his way in. It's consistent with having the door shut on you and wedging your foot in to stop it. The forensics matched it to him, found a print of his on the inside of the door, and traces of him in her hallway but nowhere else. Which makes it easy to disprove his claim that she invited him in and they had a drink. They found traces of her on the washing-up gloves, and the tear marks on the masking tape in his flat match those on the binbags he wrapped her in. There's even DNA from his saliva on the matching edges of the tape.

The detection is done.

We have enough to put him away for life, but it's as if his vanity won't allow him to admit that he forced himself in. He sticks by the story that she asked him in but somehow changed her mind at the last minute. That she 'didn't have the guts to go through with it'. That she 'changed her mind'. That she 'flipped' and attacked him first. He is vain to the end: she wanted it, to start with anyway, just 'bottled out'. He is computing how, despite being a murderer, he might still salvage some sexual *amour propre*. He says he didn't mean to kill her, just to pin her down and stop her screaming. He's holding out for manslaughter, thinks he might avoid a life sentence, wants to pitch this as a flirtational encounter gone wrong, and himself as the victim of a misunderstanding. He'll blame her because he can, and he can because she's dead. She will become his victim a second time. Why not? It's a genre after all, and it has worked for other men. There are already comments below the bar on Lynne's latest article condemning the 'mixed signals' women give off, and the news of his arrest has only been out a few minutes.

He knows, too, that introducing some ambiguity about Zalie's sexual motivation will hurt her parents even more. That gives him power. They'll never know why she answered the door or how. The randomness of it will ache in them, the catastrophe that needed so many variables to happen and could so easily not have. If she had stayed out until later, or gone to bed earlier; if he had gone out to his work Christmas party instead of skipping it or if his girlfriend had skipped hers instead of going … A shift of one or two degrees, a mouse click left or right, and there'd have been nothing: Zalie still here, with the life she was entitled to, but not this: a hole in her parents' lives the size of life itself.

We skip the celebratory drinks at the station. No one is up for it. There is an emergency cupboard of beer and supermarket Prosecco; there's even a fresh packet of plastic glasses, but no one is in the mood. Even Deskfish, who is about to become the nation's crime-solving hero, looks depressed. But why, when we've given the country the Christmas present it wants? It's more dramatic, more fraught with reversals than the two-part star-studded BBC Christmas special. But most of all we've given *the nation* justice, and it's all the more thrilling because of a dose of injustice.

But no one is clapping or cheering or pouring drinks.

*

The Chief Constable wants it announced immediately, so people can go back to their families *relaxed and reassured* he says, *ready to enjoy the festive season with their loved ones.* Turkeys in their tinfoil crematoria, corkscrews at the ready, fresh batteries in *the nation*'s remote controls.

New suspect, new story, we discover, because Lynne and the other reporters are already asking: *Police Blunder as Wrong Man Charged?*

'You'd better get used to headlines like these,' says Lucy Hall. She has come for Wolphram as we release him. 'You'll announce that Wolphram's been *released without charge* and *exonerated.* That's the wording I agreed with your chief. *Exonerated* – say it.'

'*Exonerated.* Yes. I've seen the statement. The CC will make a statement and Press Relations will send it out to the media straight away. I'll say the same thing when I do the press conference.'

She looks suspicious and only partly mollified. 'Also an apology – it's probably better if you make it now than after we've taken legal action. I'll be advising him to sue the newspapers, too. Whatever you're doing

317

to help him now changes nothing about what's going to happen when we take the police to court – you understand that?'

'Oh yes,' I say with enthusiasm, 'absolutely.'

She begins to turn and go, but there's one last thing. 'What's your first name?' she asks. I notice the tiny dent in her nostril where a nose-ring used to be, the hole now filled in with flesh but the delicate perforation-scar still visible.

'Alexander. Ander, as was. Is that your father asking?'

'Yes,' she replies. 'He wondered what had happened to you. Asked me to check if it's you he knew from school. What do I tell him?'

'Tell him ... tell him ...'

Gary has arrived in the car and opened the front passenger door. 'Get him in!' he shouts.

Wolphram comes out, escorted by Thicko and Small-Screen. They're trying to look like bodyguards from an action movie, scanning the rooftops and speaking into walkie-talkies, though there's no one here but us. Wolphram has had his hair cropped. He has shaved and changed clothes. You can tell he hates them because he half walks, half writhes in his outfit: jeans, trainers and a sweatshirt with a hood over which he wears a faux-leather jacket. The trainers are a special indignity for a man used to wearing leather shoes, even at weekends. Everything is one size too big for him. He looks like an emaciated rocker from a pub band. His disguise is completed by thick grey-lensed glasses that make his eyes look like celebrities hiding behind the smoked windows of a limousine.

Gary sounds the horn to hurry me up.

I turn back to Lucy: 'Tell him we managed to stop this one in time?'

Gary has asked for Wolphram's car to be released, but we have two hours to kill before it's ready. I've seen auto-forensics at work: it's like a machine autopsy, the parts splayed out on sterile sheets, weighed, photographed, sampled and slid under microscopes. I'm surprised they can put it back together in two hours.

'I'm behind on my Christmas shopping,' Wolphram says acidly when we ask where he wants to be taken. So we take him shopping and stay close to him. There's always the chance he will be recognised. Especially if he speaks.

We follow him with a trolley, looking like a reclusive mogul's bodyguards. We listen to him with his deep, expensive voice, walking his refined tastes from aisle to aisle. The supermarket jingles grate on him. The Christmas songs run on a loop. All he wants is to be back in his flat, in his listening chair, with a box set of Keith Jarrett and some George Eliot.

Instead, he's here, among the two-for-one offers and the bullet-hard frozen turkeys. There's hardly anything left to buy. The meat counters are so bare that all that's left is the blood collecting in the bottoms of the trays. He looks around and blinks.

Someone will recognise him – today, tomorrow, in three weeks. And for the rest of his life. But the later the better, so he has time to graft a new life onto the stump we've left him with. So he gets used to his prosthetic life, his new face, his bad clothes.

Gary is on the lookout for the surreptitious smartphone taking pictures, the whispering, the pointing. Someone phoning the newspapers on their *Binbag Murder Hotline*, which remains open to suck up the dregs of news and gossip. He has been lucky so far. Provided he doesn't speak too loudly, because he can't change that voice.

There's no guarantee that people have heard that he's free, that there's a new suspect, that he's innocent. *Exonerated.* Some of them won't care. 'And some of them will think it's a new form of execution,' Gary tells me: 'He was found guilty and immediately exonerated by lethal injection.'

Besides, all the stuff from school is still out there, all the allegations from ex-pupils and teachers. That won't go away because there's no exoneration from rumours. They have no body, and facts are not bullets. It is like shooting at smoke. It'll be the shadow in his peripheral vision, something always on the outskirts of his mind wherever he goes, whenever he almost forgets.

He's strong, I tell Gary, *he'll get through this.* But Gary says it's after the crisis, after the trial, after the extremes, that the survivor cracks. When life slackens and the flat time comes again. 'But he's resilient,' I say.

'That's what I mean, Prof: all that resilience might be the end of him.'

And now in the supermarket a few people notice him. Something about him snags on their attention and pulls them back for another look. They can't quite piece it together. Until one of them does: a young mum with a calm toddler in the trolley seat and a baby in a carrier on her front, gets it straight away. *Where have I seen him before?* She looks at him, he is right beside her where the good wine is. *Where have I seen him before? Everywhere.* He looks at her and he is scared again.

She is sure. She nods a little. *Yes, I'm sure now.* He raises his eyebrows and his expression asks her what she'll do about it.

'Would you mind reaching for three bottles of that one up there?' she asks. 'I can't quite get to it with the baby.'

Gary has come up close just in case, but now he hangs back and watches.

'Of course.' Wolphram gets up on tiptoe, hands the first one carefully to her and then places the next two into her trolley, flat on their side so they won't break as she pushes it. He does this slowly, in detail.

'Thank you,' she says, keeping her eyes on him, and then, quietly, 'I hope you have a good Christmas', and she is gone, back to her husband who is already at the till saving their place in the queue.

And that's it. The recognition scene, the first in many to come.

Wolphram is cheered by this because it's a stranger's kindness. His gaunt face has filled out with pride, not at himself, but at the fact that the good he still thinks of people is well placed.

I know that kind of double-accounting: we like to count kindness twice, three times, four ... in order to help it tally favourably against unkindness. Thus a stranger's one-off grace holds its own against a whole country's routine brutishness. Wolphram will count it over and over when he does the sums of what the world has done to him.

The people hunting him down to lynch him are now hunting him down to fête his innocence and make him perform it. But she helped him just by doing nothing.

That's what it has come to: kindness is being left alone.

'Has he even ever *been* into a supermarket, Prof? He walks around here like an astronaut,' whispers Gary, relieved.

It's true. He walks as if he's about to float away; he looks around, everything catches his attention. The man looks unhoused, uncountried, unplaneted. Away from his things, his books, his music and his friends, Wolphram looks like a millionaire stranded in a foreign land with the wrong money, rich in a currency he can't spend.

*

Gary and I drive Wolphram to White Cliffs Auto-Forensics. 'Let's hope they gave you a free service,' says Gary. Pike Road Trading Estate is where the bathroom showrooms and carpet wholesalers are, the MOT garages and the shops that sell railings and front doors, ballast and paving stones; where the fork-lifts rest at night and the local buses go to get repaired, stripped for parts or left to rust as husks, their last destinations still in their blinds: Cheriton, Golden Cross, Hythe Hill. There's a van festooned with Union Jacks that sells bacon and sausage baps from 6 a.m. to 6 p.m. *Benji's British Food.* People drive in and out of here all day, and to those of us who know how cities work, the industrial estates on the edges of towns, skirting the bypasses, the Park and Rides and the commuter rat runs, are where a whole other life takes place – far from the sourdough bread, the milf and the olive platters of the suburbs.

'You're unrecognisable,' the man at the desk tells Wolphram sourly. 'But I'll still need photo ID.' He's heard Wolphram is free and resents it; thinks of all the stories he might have been able to tell.

Wolphram looks up at the CCTV. Then around the empty courtyard. Everyone has gone home early. There's a light on in Barry's Bathrooms across the road, but that's to deter burglars. While Wolphram signs half a dozen forms, reading each one carefully, the car is brought through a secure automated gate by a man in a plastic oversuit. He too looks disappointed. These privatised forensic services and DNA labs like catching the big cases. It gives them something for their promotional material when they bid for government contracts.

There's no big final scene with Mr Wolphram. He would never make his exit on a bridge. He just wants to drive away and see his aunt, spend two days imagining that none of this happened, though it will be all over the news – even his innocence is news, which is a kind of guilt – and work out how to *get his life back*. Work out which parts of his life even still exist, after this.

'I'm not sure whether to thank you or not,' says Wolphram. He's smiling, or trying to. He's tired, traumatised, eviscerated by what has happened to the life he had. But he can't help himself: he's courteous and he won't let go of what keeps him civilised. Thirty years from when he taught me and four days from when we took him in, I realise it: he is someone who holds on in a big way to the little things – politeness, civility, consideration … the small change of civilised life. But there's enough for everyone in the small change of civilised life.

'You'll let my solicitor know when they're finished with my flat? I'd like to see in the New Year at home.'

Gary: 'You're not going back to that flat, those prod-nosed gossiping neighbours, are you? Not after what they've said about you! Go away for a bit, then come back and start suing people. Christ! You can probably sell your story to the papers at the same time as you're suing them – how's that? Postmodern or what?'

'I'm not going anywhere … *Gary*,' says Wolphram, speaking the name for the first time, slowly and emphatically and sounding as if he's learning how to pronounce it. 'I shall return to my home and drive my car and go back to my shops. Things will return to normal because *I* will return to normal. Also, I shan't be selling my story.'

*

Lynne is waiting for us with the transcripts of her interviews with Ben and Chloe. That, at least, was a victory for Gary – allowing them to be classed as evidence, banning her from using them until we had finished with them. They're on a memory stick, and she has even transcribed the first three hours. I skim through the pages. Phelps doesn't need to be translated into redtop cliché, he already speaks it. They're all about the 'suspicious Mr Wolphram', 'the nosy neighbour', how Zalie was 'so vibrant and neighbourly and always ready with a greeting'. About how he and Chloe 'sensed there was something not quite right with him' but forbore to say anything because, 'well, we didn't want to be accused of prejudice'. About how 'that could have been Chloe' in those binbags. 'I just wish I'd been able to stop it' is where Lynne stopped typing. Maybe it's when she answered our call; more likely it's when she decided she had her headline.

Lynne is wearing the same mohair pullover and sits in the same seat.

'Any of your tea/coffee/indistinguishable hot beverages for me today?'

We don't answer, but she makes herself at home anyway. Takes my coffee from in front of me and I let her.

'I must say, this story just gives and gives. How d'you like the sound of this: *Veteran reporters thought they'd seen it all, but even they were conned by savage killer's double life.* That's what's coming out for the New Year. All while he was enjoying our hospitality. I was there in front of him, yours truly could have been the next binbag murder victim. I'll probably do one of those personal witness life stories on it. Chloe is giving us a juicy serialised piece called *Living with a Killer*. This is pure gold. It's not just the papers sold off kiosks, it's the advertising feeding off the circulation hike. We've had to hire an extra ten salespeople over Christmas ...'

Gary: 'I once read a public health report about rat infestations in the takeaways on Golden Cross Road ... found out rats have such a fast metabolism that they shit out the same meal they're actually eating ... that's you that is. Aren't you ashamed?'

'No,' she says. 'Okay, sometimes I am. That's the short answer. You want the longer one?'

Gary says nothing.

'I'll take that as a *yes*. I don't make things happen,' says Mad Lynne, 'I'm just the way they happen. I'm the form they take. That's all. The online sewers full of angry bastards blood-sporting the latest wounded celeb or the latest broken nobody ... the click-bait, the Have Your Says, the online comments, the slanted headlines, the innuendo ... that's all there anyway, Gary, there's no more or less than there ever was, it's just now we can see it.'

Gary is red-faced, pulsing with anger, bloaty with rage, but also with recognition. I think he's going to kick the desk over, throw her tea in her face. A copy of her own newspaper is on the table, with her piece on the front page for the third day in a row. *FREE!* is the headline, nicely ambiguous: outrage at liberating a pervert, or relief at justice done at last. She has both bases covered, does Lynne.

Gary reaches for the paper and rolls it up tight and grips it.

I finish the gesture in my imagination: he leaps up, and as she gasps in surprise he drives the rolled-up *Evening Post* down her throat, hard and very fast, so it's already past her voice box and halfway to her collarbone by the time we realise what he's done, and it's drilling through gristle, tearing her tonsils, ripping through the tissue of her trachea, choking her on her own words. Her face swells, the white foundation cracks with grey, her eyes bloody up with airlessness, her lips go violet as the blue of asphyxiation mixes with the *Rectory Red* shaded lipstick … She is swallowing her own headlines, suffocating on her lies …

… but only in my wandering mind. Gary still holds the *Evening Post*, but in a slackening grip. I'm fiddling with a pen, to hide my shaking hands, and my head is giddy with what it has just screened.

'It's okay,' she says calmly (but later when I remember this, I also think that she is sad about it, too), 'I know what you think of me. I don't care. Anyway, it's all over, isn't it? Happily ever after. Scales of justice and all that: guilt in its proper place, innocence shining through in the end.'

Gary has nothing to say. I have had nothing to say for some time.

'I have to go – got a Skype meeting with my new editor in a minute,' she says. 'One of the nationals. I can't tell you which yet, but you'll know when you buy tomorrow's papers … He doesn't like being kept waiting. He's a man of few words, but his cheques are eloquent.'

Returnity

'I've got a job for you,' Vera says. She turns to Marieke and says: 'There's nothing, is there?'

Marieke shakes her head. She holds out the digital recorder. 'Listen.'

'I have. He's given up.'

She shows us upstairs. I've never been up there, though Marieke has recorded every room and played me the recordings. She swore she heard things once, just a few weeks ago, and played me back a series of hums and whispers and room-static. She even parsed them for me, assured me they were the sounds of presence. 'Coming closer, falling back, coming closer, falling back.' Not today. Not for a while.

In their bedroom, Vera's and Victor's, are three open suitcases filled with his clothes. His smart shoes are in their original boxes, but his underclothes and slippers are in a binbag.

'I think you know what I'd like you to do with these,' she says.

I nod. 'Will you want the suitcases back, Mrs Snow?'

'No.'

Victor's books, detective thrillers in large type, themselves bought from charity shops, are in a pile by his bedside table. I bag them up, too, putting a few aside for Gary.

As I load up the car, I notice that Vera has thrown Victor's last crossword out, too, and it lies on top of the recycling by the door. I check to see if it has been completed and it has. She knows what I'm thinking and says: 'It's all right. I finished it myself.'

The Cancer Research shop on Coles Hill is still there, where we used to go, Danny and Neil Hall and I, for vintage clothes before the vintage shops arrived and made them expensive. It's mostly pullovers now, rows of dead men's cardigans, mushroom-coloured trousers, polyester shirts and low-end high-street suits. Coats: endless racks of coats. A riot of beige.

Marieke browses the old cassette tapes and the records. Five for a pound. She chooses a few. She has no way of knowing this – no normal way – but I have bought her a record player for Christmas. As I carry the suitcases through the shop, I can see her drawing the records carefully out of their sleeves and checking for scratches. I watch her. She holds the edge of the rim against the flat of her hand, raises the record so the grooves catch the light. She has never played one or owned any, but already she handles them like an expert. Like Wolphram. Like the man used to in the old music shop. It's instinct, or foreknowledge, or the leftovers of a previous life that hasn't quite been wiped by a return to factory settings.

At the back of the shop there's a little sorting room where a couple of old ladies not far off Victor's age are pricing up their donations. I'm glad Vera isn't here for that – there's something so final about watching his clothes get swallowed up into the great sea of castoffs. The body goes back into the earth, the clothes back onto the market.

There are no ashes, but this is his scattering.

'Maybe I didn't believe enough to bring him back,' Vera told us: 'or maybe *he* didn't.'

*

It's when the parents say *and they lived happily ever after* that the child feels the anxiety. The child is right: what happens after the ever after? What happens in Returnity, after you've squeezed the day?

It's all over, but in the way things are never really over: they just die as events and start new lives as consequences.

I'll take Marieke back to mine and cook fish fingers under the grill and she will turn them after exactly five minutes of watching the clock. I'll slice tomatoes she won't eat and array them with futile precision around the plate. She'll sit on the sofa with her legs sticking out over the edge. She'll fall asleep around ten, and I'll fall asleep an hour later. Sometimes less. Tonight, almost certainly less. I'll doze. The night will take the day's bones and sweat them into dream-stock, and at midnight the tiny click of the boiler thermostat will wake me without my even knowing I heard it. It could be anything, I think, a fox screeching, a beer can dropped by a passing drinker, a car changing gear — and I'll scoop her up as she sleeps and take her to her bedroom. She is already in her pyjamas.

But first, while Sigrid is out with her office mates, we'll go to the bridge and record. We'll start at the buttresses where they've all started, and then edge out to its span where they've all stood: Danny and me and the poor kid they held over, Gary's lost woman with the sun in her hair, Ben waiting for the credits to roll on the film of his capture.

And all the strangers: the ones whose bodies were found and the ones they never recovered; those who waved or called out and those who slid away quietly; those who changed their minds just in time and those who changed them too late; those who knew something beautiful as they hurtled to their deaths and said goodbye to the pain and the mistakes. Those whose lives looked better backwards, who lived happily for a few seconds with the years on rewind. Those who hit the water or the road, and those who hit the estuary silt; whose outlines – arms splayed, legs out, curled or balled up – briefly shone like a footprint on the beach before the water gluts it and the sand fills it and everything goes flat and traceless again.

They've all been here, pushed by the pain at their backs or pulled by the peace up ahead; there's the lady with the big skirt who survived, and the ones no one knows, no one saw; there are the gulls and the ghosts, and there's me at twelve, fifteen, twenty, thirty and forty, all my ages in one, looking down from the bridge and rinsing an adult's eyes in the tears of a child.

This is what I'll tell them, because it's what I tell myself:

The estuary has everything I want and everything the ghosts want, because it is the opposite of Heraclitus and his river: it is water that hasn't yet flowed and sand that hasn't yet passed through the hourglass. Together they make a clay that hasn't yet been fired.

There's still time to change everything.